Terry Dowling

AMBERJACK

TALES OF FEAR AND WONDER

AMBERJACK

TALES OF FEAR AND WONDER

TERRY DOWLING

Subterranean Press • 2010

First Edition

ISBN
978-1-59606-293-1

Subterranean Press
PO Box 190106
Burton, MI 48519

www.subterraneanpress.com

ACKNOWLEDGEMENTS

"The Lagan Fishers" first appeared at *SciFiction*, Ellen Datlow (Ed.), April 2001, http://www.scifi.com/scifiction/originals/originals_archive/dowling/

"The Fooly" originally appeared in *Dreaming Again*, Jack Dann (Ed.), Harper Voyager 2008.

"The Magikkers" originally appeared in *Wizards: Magical Tales from the Masters of Modern Fantasy*, Jack Dann & Gardner Dozois (Eds.), Berkley 2007.

"He Tried to Catch the Light" first appeared in *Dreaming Down-Under*, Jack Dann & Janeen Webb (Eds.), HarperCollins/Voyager Australia 1998.

"Flashmen" first appeared in *Oceans of the Mind*, Issue X, Richard Freeborn (Ed.), Winter 2003, www.trantorpublications.com

"Toother" first appeared in *Eclipse One: New Fantasy and Science Fiction*, Jonathan Strahan (Ed.), Night Shade Books 2007.

"The View in Nancy's Window" originally appeared in *Interzone*, Sept 1999.

"Jarkman at the Othergates" first appeared in *Exotic Gothic: Forbidden Tales from Our Gothic World*, Danel Olson (Ed.), Ash-Tree Press 2007.

"Some Roses for the Bonestell Man" first appeared in *Agog! Fantastic Fiction*, Cat Sparks (Ed.), Agog! Publications 2002.

"The Suits at Auderlene" originally appeared in *Inferno: New Tales of Terror and the Supernatural*, Ellen Datlow (Ed.), Tor 2007.

"Truth Window: A Tale of the Bedlam Rose" first appeared in *Eclipse Two: New Fantasy and Science Fiction*, Jonathan Strahan (Ed.), Night Shade Books 2008.

"The Library" originally appeared in *X⁶: a novellanthology*, Keith Stevenson (Ed.), Coeur de Lion 2009.

FRIENDS AND EVOCATI:

The author extends special thanks to Brian Attebery, Leigh Blackmore, Simon Brown, Jeremy Cavaterra, Bill Congreve, Katherine Cummings, Jack Dann, Ellen Datlow, Nicole Dhamala, Gardner Dozois, Harlan Ellison, Alan C. Elms, Carey Handfield, Robert Hood, Van Ikin, Mark Kennedy, Kerri Larkin, Eric Lindsay, Neil Maloney, the late Peter McNamara, Mariann McNamara, Pat McNamara, Andrew Macrae, Danel Olson, Jesse C. Polhemus, Bill Schafer, Cat Sparks, Nick Stathopoulos, Keith Stevenson, Jonathan Strahan, Shaun Tan, Jack Vance, John Vance, Janeen Webb, Bradley Wynne and the late Roger Zelazny.

Sincere thanks, too, to all those musicians, producers and talents who assisted with the Amberjack project, firstly the members of Gestalt in the band's various incarnations (Christine Anketell, Rob Brown, Jeff Longhurst, Chris Martin, Geoff Pollard and Michael Whelan), and also George Mannix, Brian and Anne O'Connor, the late Peter Threlfall, and all those associated with PACT Theater who lent a hand. Without your enthusiasm, love and skill, they would have been very different days.

DEDICATION

For Katherine Cummings and Jonathan Strahan
Dear friends, colleagues, fellow time-travelers

TABLE OF CONTENTS

INTRODUCTION

I FIRST MET TERRY here at the house at the end of 1980, and then at a science fiction convention in Melbourne, Australia two years later. I remember we drove back to Sydney over the Blue Mountains, stopping at a fantastic old hotel, the Hydro Majestic, and we had lots of adventures in Sydney. Since then Terry has visited us in Oakland many times. During these visits we have evolved a motto: "When Dowling and Vance sit down with a bottle, they throw the cork away."

During Terry's visits to California, we have had many more adventures, including the time we went down to Three Rivers to listen to the High Sierra Jazz Band play. Along the way we put into practice one of my theories, that if you are in a strange town and you want to find the best restaurant, go to a bookstore and ask the owners, since they are bound to be sophisticated and not all that rich, so they would find the best value for the least money.

So we stopped at a bookstore in a town—it might have been Madera— and asked about the best restaurant. They referred us to a Basque place and accompanied us for dinner. I will call them Mr. X and Mrs. X. During the evening Mrs. X confided to us that they lived in a haunted house and that she had actually seen these haunts. She went up to her bedroom once and found them sitting on her bed. Mr. X pretended he wasn't listening, and whenever she referred to him for verification said, "Oh yes, yes."

During the evening, Mrs. X told us that one time she hired a priest to come by the house, where with bells and candles and the appropriate words he sought to drive the ghosts away. Mrs. X said that the priest was more or less successful; she saw far less of the ghosts afterwards than she ever had before. The next day Terry and I drove past the house in question, thinking we might see a ghost or two from the outside, but it just looked like any other house. So we returned to Oakland, talking about ghosts all the way.

At this time I was still involved with ceramics and we had all the equipment in a little shed in our backyard. Terry became interested, and created a number of charming little creatures which we hung on a string over our dining room table. These little creations are with us to this day.

Terry is a man of many talents and remains one of my closest friends. He is a musician, plays the guitar, and has composed many very amusing songs, which he once performed on television. As can be seen by the contents of this book, Terry is also a very talented writer, one I admire and respect, a very romantic writer who writes in somewhat the same style as I do myself.

So much for now. I welcome you to these stories. If and when Terry produces another book, it may well be that I will append another set of remarks. Until then, happy times.

—Jack Vance
Oakland, August 2009

PREFACE

IT GOES AROUND; IT comes around. Before I made my first story sale in 1982, my song cycle *Amberjack* had been in existence for eight years, concerning the fortunes of a time traveler stranded in the past and left to work his way through the centuries back to the present.

Many of the songs were performed in Sydney in the mid-70s in a series of concerts staged by PACT Theater, using such unforgettable venues as The Rocks at Circular Quay, the Seymour Center and the Chapter House of St Andrew's Cathedral.

Back then it was easy to feel that my creative efforts would continue to be in music and songwriting, especially when, in 1977, ABC radio producer Mark Kennedy arranged funding for serious studio time and the hiring of top-line session musicians (Doug Ashdown, Kirk L'Orange and Greg Lyon among them) to record six of the songs. A few weeks later, those (for me) tremendously exciting renditions went to air on the Australian ABC national radio program *Fresh Cream* as part of an interview showcasing the whole *Amberjack* project. The response was positive. It all seemed so promising.

Alas, this happened after Yes's *Tales from Topographic Oceans* was released in December 1973 but well before *Jeff Wayne's War of the Worlds* arrived on the scene in 1978. The concept album was in a lull, and when my acoustic, soft-rock band Gestalt folded after five memorable years,

Amberjack was shelved and subsequently, if always lovingly, plundered for other creative projects.

But it existed for a time and, along with its framing narrative, prefigured a good deal of where my storytelling would take me five years later. Given this collection's title and retrospective nature, some of those lyrics are included here.

A precious grace note was added to the whole thing in 1978 when Roger Zelazny visited Australia. Chatting about writing at Ron Graham's marvelous house in Sydney one day, the subject of *Amberjack* came up, and I was able to thank him for his memorable, influential novels and for such potent coinings as "shadowjack," "jack of shadows" and *Nine Princes in Amber* that had clearly played a part in my own choice of title. I'd already learned that there was a deep-sea game fish with the name, but was under no illusions. It had to have been Roger's turn of phrase as storyteller that had powered the decision.

Zelazny, as charming and gracious as everyone remembers him, told me how "Amberjack" was also the title of a short story by James Tiptree Jr (which had me scrambling for a copy of the relevant collection!) but reassured me that the title had to be equally mine. As with Shakespeare, as with any serious, cursed and blessed storyteller, that's how it has to happen. Apparently, Roger went on to say, Philip José Farmer had once admitted he'd always wanted to write a novel called *Lord of Light*. "And the thing is he should have," Roger added. "It's a book I would very much like to have read."

I've never forgotten that meeting and how heartened and liberated I felt afterwards, and how the force and flair of Zelazny's own great achievement at the shorter length continued to echo in the work of other fine storytellers: Cordwainer Smith with his Intrumentality stories, J. G. Ballard with *Vermilion Sands* and *The Voices of Time*, Ray Bradbury with *The Martian Chronicles* and *The October Country*, Samuel R. Delany with *Driftglass*, Harlan Ellison with *Deathbird Stories*, Alice Sheldon writing as James Tiptree Jr., Zelazny himself with *The Doors of His Face, The Lamps of His Mouth*. It was something that would continue to spin its magic in compilations like Ian McDonald's *Speaking in Tongues*, so many other fine authors and titles. It goes around; it comes around.

Just as my own amberjack David Quickman journeyed in time to carefully, so carefully, find things to bring back to his own day, so this book spans more than a decade in a writing life to gather stories that are special to me. You'll excuse, I'm sure, the small thirty-six-year sidestep to let Quickman have a place within these covers. In a real sense, the man he was all those years ago, the adventures he had and might have had, have remained a part of all that you'll find here.

    — Terry Dowling
       Sydney, August 2009

Amberjack

Quickman is an amberjack,
He takes his time machine,
Counts eons with his better ear,
Goes to the Miocene.
(Puts flies in amber)

Carter is his anchor-man
With merchandise on view,
While Quickman stalks among the years
He takes the residue.
(Sells fossil pendants)

Can you feel the wind
that blows down time?
Can you feel the wind
that blows down time?
Can you feel the wind that blows
Leaving dust upon your clothes?

THE LAGAN FISHERS

IN THE FIRST WEEK of September, a lagan bloom appeared in the south meadow below Sam Cadrey's kitchen window, and that was the day it felt real at last.

Something glinting in the morning sunlight caught his eye as he stood making coffee—dislodged hubcap, plastic drum lid, discarded garbage bag, he couldn't be sure—something close to the road but definitely on his property. When he hurried down to see what it was, there was no mistaking the glossy quatrefoil of tartarine pushing up through the lucerne like an old bore cover made of fused glass. He kicked at the shell of opalescent stuff, beat on it a few times, then stood wondering how much his life would change.

Sam knew his rights. They couldn't take his farm back, he was sure of that. When that small container of mioflarin—MF—illegally buried in the Pyrenees had leaked in 2029, poisoning so much of Europe, then the rest of the world, he'd become that rare and wondrous thing, a true global hero: one of the twenty-two volunteers sent in to cap it, one of the five who had survived Site Zero and made it out again. Sam had freehold in perpetuity, and the World Court in Geneva had decreed that lagan blooms were land-title pure and simple. Sure, there were local magistrates, local ordinances and local prejudices to reckon with, but the Quarantine was officially over, the last of the embargoes lifted—both made a laughing stock by the sheer extent of the bloom outbreaks and their consistently benign nature. A disfigured, forty-nine-year-old MF veteran and widower on a UN life pension had recourse to legal aid as well. Looking down at the four-lobed curving hump of the bloom, Sam knew he was king of all that he surveyed and that, in all probability, his kingdom would be an alien domain for the next year or so.

Within fourteen minutes, orbiting spysats had logged it. Within forty, Mayor Catherine was in her living room with their local Alien Influences Officer, Ross Jimmins, to log the official registration, and a dozen lagan fishers were at the end of his drive waiting to bid for trawling rights. Protection agents and insurance reps were at his door too, offering assistance against the usual: everything from highly organized looters to salting by disgruntled neighbors.

But Sam was a UN vet. Within the hour, there were two AIO lagan custodians at his front gate wearing blue arm-bands, and the usually strident hucksters pacing up and down the gravel drive had become unusually courteous.

"How soon before the hedges form?" Sam asked Mayor Catherine, sounding both cautious and eager, still not sure about the whole thing. Catherine was the closest thing to a rocket scientist Tilby had, a handsome, middle-aged woman with steel-grey hair, looking the perfect, latter-day *nasa*-chik in her navy-blue jumpsuit. The NASA look. The imprimatur of discipline and professional responsibility. Who would have thought?

"It's still three to four days," she said, taking the AIO notepad from Jimmins and adding her verification code. "Latest count, fourteen per cent of blooms don't hold. Remember that, Sam. They sink back."

"That's not many though," Ross Jimmins said, reassuring him, wishing Sam well with every puff on his lagan-dross day-pipe. The pipe was carved from lagan horn, a length of hollowed lattice from a "living" hedge. As well as the wonderful fragrance the slow-combusting dross gave off, somewhere between gardenia and the finest aromatic tobaccos of the previous four centuries, there was a welter of other positive side-effects, and the molecularly atrophying horn itself scattered its own immune-enhancing dusting of euphorines on the warm morning air.

"It is like some intelligence is behind it," Sam said, looking out through the big view window, and knew how inane it sounded coming from him, the Tilby Tiger, the great skeptic.

Catherine gave a wry smile. "It's good to have you back in the world. We lost you there for a while."

"At least Jeanie didn't see me like this." Sam had resolved he wouldn't say it, but there it was.

The Mayor looked off at the fields and hills, out to where a tiny orange bus was bringing more science students from the local high school to do a real-time, hands-on site study of early bloom effect. "Jeanie didn't and it's not what I meant, Sam." She changed her tone. "So, what are you going to do about it? Lease it out?"

Sam was grateful. "You think I should? Let them wall it off, rig up processing gantries? Put storage modules down there?" *Stop me seeing it,* he didn't add.

"Best way. Nothing is lost but spindrift through the flumes. You get the hedges; they get the lagan. There's no poaching and none of the hassles."

"You representing anybody?" Sam asked. He'd always been a wary and even harsh critic where the lagan was concerned. It had always been someone else's experience, the reality of others, thus easy to comment on. This had changed him—what was the quaint old *fin-de-siècle* saying?— had made it "up close and personal."

"I had a dozen phone calls before I left the office, but no. Hope you believe it, Sam."

"Ross?"

"Eight calls. Nope."

Sam needed to believe them. They were his friends. They'd been with him when Jeanie died. He needed to brave it out. "Cat, I want to see it. I've gone revisionist *pro tem,* okay? If it's alien invasion, let's have it. I *want* hedges to form. I want them stretching along the road all the way to town. People should be able to poach stuff. Break bits off."

Cat answered right on cue. This was an area of major personal concern. "A lot of wildcat lagan owners agree with you. I've always said it. Keep the cartels out."

"I've got control, right?"

She gave a little frown. "Your property, Sam."

"What about outside options?"

"Some control. It's an official thing. What's on your mind?"

"I want it all hands-on. No remotes. None of those little science doovers. No aerostats."

"That's tricky, Sam," she said. "It's standard nowadays. Every general access unit means a thousand global onlines and probably a thousand research facilities. A fortune from sponsors to you. Even if you could close 'em out, you'd just get thousands more people coming in. You don't want that."

"Then only for part of the day. Only in the afternoon. Say, 1300 till sundown. None at night. Can we do that?"

"We can try," Jimmins said and keyed in the request, waited less than a minute, nodded. "You've got it for now, flagged for renegotiation later. Bless your MF, Sam. You'll get rogues slipping in, but we'll put up a burn field. Fry 'em in the sky."

Cat nodded, confirming how easy it was going to be. "They'll stop when they lose a few. So, what will you do?"

Talking the talk was easy, Sam found. "I'll fish it myself. See what comes up."

"Great idea. Can we help?"

IT ALL HAPPENED QUICKLY once the Mayor and Jimmins left. The waiting fishers at the gate drove off the moment they learned Sam was going to wildcat it himself, all but one, the craggy-looking, grey-haired older man perched on the bonnet of his truck. When Sam went down to quiz him on why he stayed, he saw that it was Howard Dombey, the proprietor of the Lifeways produce market on the far side of Tilby. He was a part-time lagan fisher, and people said he did some lagan brokering as well.

"It's Howard Dombey, isn't it?" Sam said.

"Right on, Mr. Cadrey. Like to help if you're a mind." His idioms were straight from Life Studies Online, all very PC, optimally relaxing, maximally community building.

Sam found himself matching them. "Doing it myself. And it's Sam."

"Like to help just the same, Sam. Don't figure profit margins too well anymore. Just like working with it. Seeing it come to."

"Why?"

Howard Dombey shrugged, going with the role beautifully. "Just do. Watching the spin. Seeing it all flicky-flashy with lagan, pretty as the day. Give me five per cent and I'll do the scut work. Give me ten and I'll fence the bounty you clear as well. Save you the grief."

"There'll be slow days, Howard."

"Counting on it. At my age, they're the ones I like."

THEY MADE QUITE A team: a vet skeptic with a face ruined by MF, a town mayor looking like a shuttle-butt spaceways groupie from the nineties, a pipe-smoking AIO officer, and a small-time entrepreneur who did the culture-speak of mid-twentieth rural USA.

They started early each morning and left off around 1300, with Howard often as not staying on at the sorting trays till sunset when the last of the afternoon's tek and spec groups had gone—whichever AIO officials were rostered for that day's site check.

It was funny how much of an unspoken routine it all was. By the time Sam had disengaged the perimeter sensors and AIO alarms around 0700, the four of them were there, ready to set off in pairs, carefully locating the newbies and keying spot and spec codes into notepads for their own constantly updating operations program and the AIO global master.

It was on a spell during one of these start-up checks, after Sam had pointed to a perfect cloudform lagan building on one of the hedges, that Howard told him about the name.

"You know what lagan originally was?"

Sam just stared; it seemed such an odd question. "I thought it was named after the river in that old Irish song. You know, *My Lagan Love.* They're always playing it."

"Most people think that. No. It's from the language of shipwreck. Flotsam, jetsam and lagan. Flotsam is wreckage that floats when a ship goes down. Jetsam is what's thrown overboard to lighten her. Jetsam when it's jettisoned, see. If it floats, it's flotsam. If it sinks, it's lagan. A lot of valuable stuff was marked with buoys so they could retrieve it later. There were salvage wars over it. Deliberate wrecking, especially on the coast of Cornwall and around the Scillies. Lights set during storms to lure ships onto rocks. Lamps tied to the horns of cows—'horn beacons' they called 'em. Whole families involved. Whole communities."

"So why that name now? Lagan?"

"Some scientist came up with it. These are floats from somewhere else, aren't they? Buoys poking through. Lines leading down to stuff."

"I've never heard this."

Howard looked at him as if to say: *You've been out of it for quite a while.*

"Lots of folks haven't. But it's true. We get whatever comes up from the 'seabed'".

"But—"

"Okay, don't say it! There's no line. No seabed. It's how the whole thing goes—first the shelltop like yours last week, then the bounty is hauled up."

"But it's not *down* is it, Howard? And it isn't *hauled* up. Words hide it. Tidy it up too much."

"Okay, but they help us live with it."

"And hide it. How's the weather? How's the lagan? Geologists and seismologists doing their tests all the time, finding nothing. No pressure variables under the caps. None of the expected physics. It's all so PC."

"See my point, Sam. The blooms link to somewhere else, somewhere out of sight, to something worth waiting for. Stuff comes up; you get the hedges with bits of lagan in them like fish in a net. At the very least, you get chunks of molybdenum and diamond-S and those funny little spindles of—what're those new words?—crowfenter and harleybine? Now and then there's the gold and silver."

"But no Nobel Prizes yet."

"What? Oh, right. No, no Nobel Prizes in those hedges so far. No real answers."

"See, there's another word. Hedges."

"They follow roads and field lines, Sam. That's what hedges do. Hedges is what they are."

"Hides it, Howie."

"Hasn't stopped you."

Which was too close to the truth and too soon in their friendship right then, so they both gladly changed the subject. It was made easier by Mayor Catherine dumping her sample bag on the sorting table.

"New tally," she said. "Eighty-two viable. Sixteen fallow."

Howard keyed the totals into his notepad. "Sounds right. Everyone gets twenty percent that are empty."

"Looted?" Sam asked.

"Don't see how. Just empty. Nothing when the hedges form. Air pockets."

Sam kept at it. "Looted elsewhere?"

Howard watched him for a few moments. "Hadn't thought of that. Looted on the other side. You better watch 'im, Cat. Sounds like we got ourselves a new rocket scientist."

Howard knew well enough to take up a sample bag then and set off for the hedges.

BY THE END OF the fifth week, their four major branchings had become seven, and what started as an ordinary watchtower lofting on one of them swelled, brachiated and buttressed first into a classic "salisbury point," then—over another twenty days—a full-blown "chartres crown," finally a true "notre dame." It meant endless media fly-bys, countless tek visits, even more busloads of tourists and school groups, but so few blooms became cathedral that Sam couldn't blame them. It was the appropriate response. He would have been worried if there hadn't been the extra attention, though it made it harder to live with what his world was becoming. Having the lagan was one thing; now it was becoming too strikingly alien.

Again it was genial, friendly Howard who triggered the next outburst, dumping his bag on the sorting table, then coming over to stand with his newfound friend to admire the towering structure.

"How about it, Sam? A cathedral. Makes you believe in the mirroring, don't it?"

"What's that, Howie?" The word mirror often caught him like that. The Tilby Tiger lived in a house without mirrors. (But full of reflections, he sometimes quipped on better days, making the tired old joke.)

"The online spiel. That it's mimicry. Skeuomorphism. The lagan sees clouds; it tries to make clouds. Sees trees and roads, does its best to give trees and roads."

"You believe that?"

Howard shrugged. "Makes sense. Has a certain appeal. This stuff pushes through, looks around, imitates what it sees."

"Sees! Sees! Sees! Where the hell has my bloom *seen* a cathedral, Howard, tell me that!"

Again Howard shrugged. "Dunno. It goes into the sky; it blows in the air; it feels the sun and gets in among the flowers. Maybe ancient cathedrals were just imitations of high places too. Maybe other lagan blooms have seen cathedrals and pass on the knowledge. Anyway, Sam, I figure why resist what's as natural as what nature's already doin'. Why resist it? Why do you?"

Because, Sam wanted to say. Just because. Then, needing reasons, needing reason, gave himself: There's my face, there's the other MF impairment, my infertility, there's Jeanie lost (not MF-related, no, but more old sayings covered it: "collateral damage," "friendly fire"). This is too new, too fast, too change-everything insistent. For someone keeping someone lost as alive as possible in what had *been,* simply *been* for them: views, routines, sugars in coffee, favorite songs, the spending of days, the very form and nature of days—how dare this brutal new lagan change it so. As Jeanie-bright, as Jeanie-fresh as Sam tried to make it, the lagan more than anything was always saying *that* time has gone. Jeanie is gone. Let them go.

Sam found himself trying so hard. Jeanie would have loved the lagan, arranged picnics, invited friends. Jeanie would have liked Howard and the others getting together, liked the little-kid thrill of them bringing in the bounty, grown-ups acting like kids acting like grown-ups.

But try as he might, Sam always found himself on both sides of it, and his words kept coming out a bit crazy. He couldn't help himself.

"Look at what's happened. First the MF outbreak in '29, then the lagan five years later."

"They're not related," Howard said. "It's not cause and effect."

"Maybe. Experts in nineteenth century London didn't see the connection between smog and tuberculosis either."

"Between what and what?"

Sam was careful not to smile. For all his smarts, Howard was an ageing child of the times, a true citizen of the age, lots of compartmentalized knowledge, but no true overview. He knew all about shipwrecks and 1930s Hudson locomotives and Napoleon Bonaparte and vintage CD-ROM games, but lacked the larger cultural horizon for such things. For him the old term PC still meant "Politically Correct" not "Pre-Copernican," though who remembered Copernicus these days, or Giordano Bruno, or William Tyndale, or the Library at Alexandria or, well, the economic conditions that had led to horn beacons and shipwrecking and the original lagan, all the other things that were lost? Things eroded, worn smooth and featureless by too much time.

It sobered him having Howard to measure himself by. It brought him back, made him remember to be smarter. Kinder. Set him in the present as much as anything could.

"But, Howie, what if it's real lagan? In the shipwreck sense?"

"What, marked with a buoy?"

"Or sent up *as* a buoy."

"What! Why do you say that?"

"I have no idea. Just should be said, I guess."

AT 0140 ON 15TH October, Sam woke and lay there in the dark, listening to the wind stir in the dream hedges. He was surprised that he could sleep at all, that he didn't wake more often. It was almost as if the soughing and other hedge sounds were deliberately there to lull the lagan-blessed. Like the dross, the spindrift, the honey-balm, it too was benign. The hedges breathing, thriving, being whatever they were.

Even as he drowsed, settled back towards sleep, that slipping, dimming thought made Sam rouse himself, leave his bed and go out onto the verandah. Of course it was deliberate. Look at how everyone accepted the phenomenon now, built it into their lives.

Sam regarded the fields picked out by the half-phase spring moon. He smelled the honey-balm wind that blew up from the hedgerows and made himself listen to the "croisie," not just hear it—that mysterious, oscillating tone produced by nearly all lagan blooms, a barely-there, modulating drone set with what one moment sounded for all the world like someone shaking an old spray can, the next jingling bangles together on a waving arm. Never enough to annoy or intrude. Oh no. Not the croisie. Lulling. A welcome and welcoming thing. Always better than words made it seem. Something that would be missed like birdsong and insect chorus when the bloom ended and the hedges were left to dry out and rattle and fall to slow dust on the ordinary wind.

Sam left the verandah and walked down to the road. The hedges stretched away like screens of coral in the moonlight or, better yet, like frames, nets and trellises of moonlight, all ashimmer—all "flicky-flashy" as Howard would say—yes, like blanched coral or weathered bone robbed of their day colors but releasing a flickering, deep, inner light, an almost-glow. Better still: fretted cloudforms, heat-locked, night-locked, calcined, turned to salt like Lot's wife, turned to stone by the face of this world meeting the Gorgon-stare of some other.

The croisie murmured. The honey-balm blew. Spindrift lofted and feather-danced in the bright dark. The air smelled wonderful.

What a wondrous thing, he thought. What a special time. If only Jeanie were here to see it. The different world. The dream-hedges and lagan. The spindrift dancing along the road and across the fields. His own MF legacies too, though she wouldn't have cared.

There are enough children in the world, she would've said. Who needs more than six in ten to be fertile anyway? The world is the birthright, not people. It doesn't need more people. Hasn't for more than a century. Can't have too many people or people stop caring for each other. Only common sense.

She would never have mentioned his face—or perhaps only to quip: "My Tiger. You were always too handsome anyway."

She would have made it—easier.

Sam watched the ghostly palisades in their warps and woofs, their herringbones and revetments, found himself counting visible towerheads till he reached the riot of the notre dame. Then he shut his eyes and listened to the ever-shifting, ever-the-same voice of the croisie and tried to find, beyond it, the rush of the old night wind in the real-trees. He could, he was sure he could, anchoring himself in the other, larger, older world by it.

But he wouldn't let it take his thoughts from Jeanie. No. He kept her there in the questing—most vividly by adding to the list of things he would have said to her, imagining what she might have said to him. Like how you did start to count your life more and more as doors closed to you, that was a Jeanie line. How it took the MF pandemic damaging much of the genetic viability first of Europe, then Africa and Asia, on and on, to close some important doors for everyone, to unite the world, make them finally destroy the old weapons. The destroyable ones.

Jeanie would have put her spin on it. Her spindrift.

Sam grinned at the night. More language from the sea. More shipwreck talk. Spindrift blew along the road, the skeins and eddies of spores and hedge-dust, the "moonsilk," the "flit," the "dross"—there were so many names—but, whatever it was, all safely moribund, *sufficiently* chemically inert, they said, though still finely, subtly psychoactive just by being there. Had to be. Part of the night. This night. His.

Theirs. Jeanie keenly there. His lagan love. Still.

Sam breathed in the bounty, filled his lungs with all the changed nature. Howard was right. Blooms and hedges. Lagan. Watchtowers, thunderheads, cathedrals and hutches. So much better than crystalline molecular skeuomorphs with key attributes of long-chain polymer-calcinite hybrids or whatever they were touting in the net journals.

Then the cathedral sighed, the only word for it. A single falling note swelled against the croisie, a distinct sad trailing-away sound that left the alien lagan-tone, the honey-balm and the night-wind beyond like a strange silence when it had gone.

From the cathedral?

Sam accepted that it was, knowing that almost all the logged lagan anomalies were around the big cloudform and cathedral loftings. The hutches and nestings, the basements and even stranger sub-basements were always silent, but the loftings sometimes belled and breathed and sounded like this, like great whales of strangeness making their song.

The mikes would have tracked it. Nearby stats had to be homing in, risking burn. Tomorrow there'd be extra flybys and spec groups.

Sam walked closer to the looming thirty-meter structure, looked up into the interstices of the triple spire, the converging, just-now braiding salisbury points, then down to where the portal and narthex would be in a true cathedral. He began a circuit. There was only the croisie now and the distant wind if you listened for it.

There were no doors in the logged salisburys, chartres and notre dames. There were outcroppings like porches and lintels, but no doors, no chambers. The loftings were always solid lagan.

But here was a door—rather a shadowing, a doorness beneath such an outcropping, a cleft between buttress swellings that held darkness like one.

Why now? Why mine? Sam thought, but came back, Jeanie-wise, with: Why not? If not now, when?

Still he resisted. He'd finally—mostly—accepted the lagan. He'd welcomed the wealth, but mainly the companionship the lagan had brought, a new set of reasons for people doing things together. But he wanted nothing more, no additional complications. Another old *fin-de-siècle* saying from Life Studies covered it: "not on my watch."

Had to be—ready, the words came, bewildering him till he realized they answered his two unspoken questions.

A sentient, talking, telepathic cathedral? It was too much. It was bathos.

But it made him move in under the overhang, the lip of the porch, whatever it was, made him step into the darkness.

He found her there, found her by the darkness lightening around her; the final corner of the narthex, apse or niche ghost-lighting this latest, incredible lagan gift.

She would never be beautiful, if *she* were even the right word. The eyes were too large, the face too pinched, the ears and nose too small, like something half-made, a maquette, a Y99 Japanese *anime* figure, a stylized, waxy, roswell mannequin. The naked body too doll-smooth, too androgynous, with not even rudimentary genitalia or breasts that he could tell, yet somehow clearly not meant to be a child.

He knew who she was meant to be.

"You're not Jeanie." He had to say it.

No. It sounded in his mind.

"You're something like her. A bit."

"It was—your thoughts—there." Spoken words this time. The creature enunciated them so carefully, seemed to agonize over each one, fiercely concentrating, being so careful. Could it be, did he imagine it or was there perspiration on the forehead, the sheen of stress or panic? "I know— Jeanie."

"You do!"

The mannequin frowned, desperately confused, clearly alarmed if the twisting of the face were any indication. "It was—there. There. The— anchor?" The final word was a question.

"Ah." Sam felt hope vanish, felt fascination empty out and drain away, then refill from what truly, simply was on this strangest, most magical night.

"*Who* are you?" he said, gentler, easier now. "What are you?"

"Yours?" Again, it was almost a question. This creature seemed in shock, far more troubled than he was, but a shock almost of rapture as well as panic. At the wonder of being here. Being lost, bereft, but here. Somewhere. Anywhere.

Sam couldn't help himself. He stepped back, did so again and again, moved out of the chamber, out from under the porch. He had to anchor himself too. He looked around at the night, at the rising laganform looming over him, at the spread of coral barricades sweeping away in the vivid dark. No wonder they called them dream hedges. He saw it all now. Others had had these visitations. That's what the official Alien Influence spec groups were *really* looking for. Motile manifestations. Lifesign. The cathedrals were concentrations for hiding passengers, for delivering them into this world.

What to do? Tell the others? Share this latest, strangest, most important discovery—not the word!—this benefice, this gift? The orbitals were nightsighted, but Sam and this creature, this—*Kyrie?*—the name was just there—*Kyrie!*—just was, were *in* the lagan, with the croisie at full song and the honey-balm strengthening, both caught in the richest rush of spindrift he'd seen in weeks, with the most vivid runs of ghost-light making the hedges all flicky-flashy. Flickers of lagan dance, lagan blush. Semaphores of dream. The tides of this other sea bringing up its bounty.

He made himself go back into that darkness. He had to. It was a chance, a chance for something. He barely understood, but he *knew*.

"Kyrie?" He named it. Named her. What else could he do?

She was standing out from the chamber wall, just standing there naked and waiting.

"Kyrie?" he said again, then gave her his dressing gown, moved in and draped it about her shoulders. How could he not?

Before he quite knew he was doing so, he was leading her out into the night, holding her, steadying her. She walked stiff-legged, with a strange and stilted gait, new to walking, new to everything, but flesh-warm and trembling under his hands. She was hurting, panicking, desperately trying to do as he did. Sam guided her up the path and into the house. It was all so unreal, yet so natural. It was just what you did, what was needed.

Because it seemed right, because he needed it, Sam put her in Jeanie's room, in Jeanie's bed, in the room and bed Jeanie had used in her final days before hospitalization was necessary and she had gone away forever. He did that and more. Though he balked at it, he couldn't help himself. He left the photos and quik-sims of Jeanie he'd put there when she'd left, made himself do that, hating it, needing it, needing it knowing what this brand-new Kyrie was trying to become.

SHE WAS STILL THERE the next morning and, yes, hateful and wonderful both, there did seem more of Jeanie in the drawn, minimalist face. Did he imagine it? Yearn for it too much? Was it the light of day playing up the tiniest hint?

Sam felt like a ghoul, like something cruel and perverse when he brought in more pictures of Jeanie and set them on the sideboard, even put one in the en suite.

It was mainly curiosity, he kept telling himself. But need too, though too dimly considered to be allowed as such. He just had to see.

No one had observed their meeting. Or, rather, no queries came, no AIO agents, no officials quizzing him about an overheard conversation, about a late-night lagan-gift from the cathedral. It seemed that the lagan had masked it; the croisie had damped it down; the honey-balm had blurred the words to nothing—perhaps their intended function all along. Misleading. Deceiving. Hiding the passengers. Working to let this happen privately, secretly. Who could say?

He helped her become human.

IT WAS HARD TO work in the hedges in the days that followed, so hard to chat and make small-talk knowing that she was up in the house with the books and the sims, learning his world, learning to be human, eating and drinking mechanically but unassisted now, if without evident pleasure, being imprinted. Becoming. The only word for it.

They saw that he was distracted, took it as an allowable relapse by their MF recluse, the famous Tilby Tiger. Becoming was an appropriate word for Sam too. Though he made himself work at doing and saying the right things, remaining courteous and pleasant, it was like doing the compulsory Life Studies modules all over again, all those mandatory realtime, facetime *têtes* and citizenship dialogues for getting along. Comfortable handles for the myriad, net-blanded, online, PC global villagers. Words, words and words. Sam hated it but managed.

He had Jeanie back in a way he hadn't expected. Like a flower moving with the sun or a weathervane aligning with the wind, he just found himself responding to what was natural in his life. Kyrie was of *this* time, *this* place, *this* moment, but with something of Jeanie, just as the old song had it. *My Lagan Love* indeed.

Sam cherished the old words anew, and sang them as he worked in the hedgerows below her window.

"Where Lagan stream sings lullaby
There blows a lily fair;
The twilight gleam is in her eye,
The night is on her hair.
And, like a love-sick lenanshee,
She hath my heart in thrall;

Nor life I owe, nor liberty,
For Love is lord of all.

And often when the beetle's horn
Hath lulled the eve to sleep,
I steal unto her shielding lorn
And thro' the dooring peep.
There on the cricket's singing stone
She spares the bog-wood fire.
And hums in sad sweet undertone
The song of heart's desire."

But Sam remained the skeptic too, was determined not to become some one-eyed Love's Fool. Even as he guided Kyrie, added more photos, ran the holos, he tried to fit this visitation into the science of lagan.

It was a cycle, a pendulum swing. One moment he'd be sitting with his alien maquette in her window-shaded room, singleminded, determined, perversely searching for new traces of Jeanie. The next, he was touring the online lagan sites scanning everything from hard science briefs to the wildest theories, desperately seeking anything that might give a clue.

There was so much material, mostly claims of the "I know someone who knows someone" variety, and Sam was tempted to go the exophilia route and see the World Government muddying up the informational waters, hiding the pearls of truth under the detritus.

Finally, inevitably, he went back to his bower-bird friend, brought up the subject during a morning tour of the hedges.

"Howie, official findings aside, you ever hear of anything found alive in the lagan?"

"Apart from the lagan itself? Nothing above the microbial."

"But unofficial."

"Well, the rumors are endless. People keep claiming things; the UN keeps saying it's reckless exophilia. And I tell myself, Sam, if something was found, how could they keep a lid on it? I mean, statistically, there'd be so many visitations, passengers, whatever, word would get out."

"What if people are hiding them?"

Howie shook his head. "Doesn't follow. Someone somewhere would go for the gold and the glory instead, bypass the authorities and go to the media direct. You'd only need one."

Sam didn't press it too closely, didn't say: unless they were loved ones. Returnees. Things of the heart. He kept it casual, made it seem that he was just—what was Howie's saying?—shooting the breeze.

"Ever meet anyone who claims to have seen someone?"

"Sure. Bancroft, but he's always claiming one thing or another about the lagan. Sally Joule's neighbor, Corben, had a stroke, but she won't buy it. Reckons the lagan did it to him because he discovered something."

"Would he mind if I visited?"

"Probably not. I know Corben. He's two counties over, an hour's drive or more. But I go sit with him sometimes. Talk's ninety-eight per cent one-sided these days, but that's okay. And you've got things in common. He wildcatted his field too, just as you've done. I can take you out."

BEN CORBEN SEEMED PLEASED to see them. At least he tracked their approach from his easy chair on the front porch and gave a lopsided smile when Howie greeted him and introduced Sam. He couldn't speak well anymore, and took ages to answer the same question Sam had put to Howie: had he ever heard of anything found alive in the lagan.

"Sum-thin," Corben managed. "Stor-ees."

And that was it for a time. The live-in nurse served afternoon tea, helped Corben with his teacup and scones.

Which was fine, Sam found. It gave him time to look out over Corben's lapsed domain, let him see what his own bloom would one day become.

Finally Howard brought them back to the question as if it hadn't been asked.

"Ever find anything out there, Corb? Anything alive?" He gestured at what remained of Corben's hedges, stripped and wasted now, the towers and barricades fallen, the basements collapsed in on themselves, just so many spike-fields, kite-frames and screens of wind-torn filigree, rattling and creaking and slowly falling to dust.

"No," Corben said, so so slowly, and his skewed face seemed curiously serene, alive with something known.

"It's important, Ben," Sam said. "It's just—it's really important. I've got hedges now. Never expected it. Never did. But I think something's out there. Calling at night." He didn't want to give too much away. And

Howie had gone with it, bless him, hadn't swung about and said: hey, what's this? Good friend.

Corben blinked, looked out across the ruin of his own lagan field, now two years gone, so Howie had said.

Again Sam noticed the peace in the man, what may have been a result of the stroke or even some medication stupor, but seemed for all the world like uncaring serenity, as if he'd seen sufficient wonders and was content, as if—well, as if—

And there it was. Of course. Like Kyrie. Corben was like Kyrie. Slow and careful. Minimalist. Just like Kyrie. Of course.

IT WAS ALL SO obvious once Sam saw it like that. Back home, he removed the photos, sims and mirrors, left Kyrie to be what she—what "it" had tried to be all along. He saw what he thought to be relief in the maquette's suffering eyes as he removed the last of the distractions, then brought a chair and sat in front of it.

Finish your job, he thought, but didn't speak it. Finish being what you already are.

And Sam found it such a relief to sit there and let it happen. Kyrie had never tried to be Jeanie, had never been a gift from the lagan to ease a broken heart.

Not Kyrie. Cadrey.

Sam saw how he'd been: thinking of Jeanie by day, not thinking of her—blessedly forgetting her—at night when he slept. Escaping in dreams, his only true time of self. Swaying Kyrie this way and that in its Becoming—by day towards Jeanie, by night back towards its intended form all along.

Poor agonized thing. Here from somewhere else, now beautified by Jeanie-thought, now showing the ruin of his own MF tiger mask, coping, copying. Poor ugly, beautiful, languishing thing. Trying all the while.

Then, like looking through doors opened and aligned, he saw the rest. Its message, its purpose. I will be you to free you so you can have your turn. Moving on. Taking it with you.

What a clumsy, awkward method, Sam decided. What a flawed—no! What a natural and fitting way to do it, more like a plant in a garden, some wild and willful, wayward garden, some natural, blundering, questing thing, trying again and again to push through. Stitching it up. Linking the worlds.

What it was, never the issue. Only *that* it was.

He had to help. Do sittings. Leave photos of his red-demon, tiger-faced self (how the others would smile!), try not to think of Jeanie for now, just for now.

For Kyrie. Oh, the irony. So many times he stood before the mirrors and laughed, recalling that old story of desperate choice: the Lady or the Tiger. Well, now he played both parts—showing the Tiger but being *like* Jeanie for Kyrie.

Giving of himself. Giving self. Generous. The Lady *and* the Tiger.

TWO WEEKS LATER, AT brightest, deepest midnight, he stood before the notre dame, bathed in the honey-balm and the spindrift, letting the croisie take him, tune him, bring him in. They were all part of it—transition vectors, carrier modes.

Kyrie was in place back in the house, maimed, shaped, pathetic and wonderful both. Sam Cadrey enough. Would seem to have had a stroke when they found *him*. That would cover the slips, the gaffes and desperate gracelessness. His friends would find, would impose, the bits of Sam Cadrey no time or training could provide. Friendship allowing, they would find him in what was left, never knowing it was all there was.

Sam looked around at his world, at the fullness of it, the last of it, then stepped into the narrow chamber.

The cathedral did what it had to do, blindly or knowing, who could say, but naturally.

Sam felt himself changing, becoming—why, whatever it needed him to be this time, using what was in the worlds. And as he rose, he had the words, unchanged in all that changing. *Nor life I know, nor liberty.* Had his self, his memories to be enough of self around. *For Love is lord of all.*

Sam held Jeanie to him, as firm and clear as he could make her, and rose from the troubled seabed to the swelling, different light of someone else's day.

Afterword to "The Lagan Fishers"

WHEN FRANK HERBERT was Guest of Honor at the Australian national science fiction convention in Adelaide back in 1981, there was the inevitable panel on worldbuilding and how best to go about creating alien races that were truly convincing on the page, that felt just right in their strangeness.

A. Bertram Chandler was in the audience that day, and he made the insightful and useful comment that you could do no better than approach the task with a copy of James Clavell's *Shogun* in one hand and the Strugatsky brothers' *Roadside Picnic* in the other.

I already knew Clavell's fine novel, but had yet to read the Strugatskys' work. I did so as soon as possible and found that Bert Chandler's comment had it exactly: a rule of thumb demonstrated with equal skill and flair by the likes of Jack Vance with his races of old Tschai (among so many other wonderful creations), by Brian Aldiss with his phagors of Helliconia, by Larry Niven and Jerry Pournelle with their unforgettable Moties, by C. J. Cherryh with the various races in her Chanur novels, the list is rich and boundless.

Roadside Picnic touched a special chord, one that's resonated for years, moreso because it made superb use of a quality I had been calling the evocative evasion. How to render the truly alien? How to reveal and yet at the same time hold back so the "Oh, is that all?" reaction is delayed, even avoided? Taken with the creations of Vance and Aldiss, Niven, Cherryh, Poul Anderson, James Blish, Gene Wolfe, so many others, Chandler's Method (to call it that) gave pointers on how to have it both ways.

You'll find several homegrown applications here: first in the story you've just read, a little later with "Flashmen" and "Truth Window."

The inspirational key to "The Lagan Fishers" was in learning what "lagan" was and how it related to flotsam and jetsam in connection with seafaring and the grim realities of shipwreck. Almost simultaneously, I heard the traditional Irish ballad "My Lagan Love," referring to the river that runs through Belfast. What other uses might the name have? What else could such a thing be? You see how it went.

I was staying at the farm outside Casino in north-eastern New South Wales that Australian spring of 2000 and suddenly the story was there, echoing J. G. Ballard, Vance and, yes, the Strugatskys, with the inevitable dash of Will Shakespeare thrown in for good measure.

Glencoe

It's an evil sort of the winter
And the harvest isn't good,
And the fields have teeth enough
To fright the day.
Brave William's raised his minions
They are chafing at the bit,
And the crooked smile must take the crooked way.

There are wild cries in the mountains
And they echo on the streams,
And another chill has made the valley grey.
It's the sound and rush of slaughter
Like the Devil's cloven mill,
And the crooked smile must take the crooked way.

Hear the shouting! Was that shouting?
Or the banshee on the mountain?
And is that blood-light shining in the grey?
And it's sure the sun is setting
On the heroes from the hill,
And the marching and the drumming fade away.
Glencoe, Glencoe, Glencoe.

There are treasures that are hidden
And treasures to be seen,
And the Golden Calf has led our own astray.
Like a Judas Goat to slaughter at London's high decree
And the silver's free that sells the souls today.

Hear the shouting! Was that shouting?
Or the banshee on the mountain?
And is that blood-light shining in the grey?
And it's sure the sun is setting
On the heroes from the hill
And the marching and the drumming fade away.
Glencoe, Glencoe, Glencoe.

It's an evil sort of the winter
And the harvest isn't good,
And the fields are sharp enough
To wound the day.
Brave William's raised his minions
They are chafing at the bit,
And the crooked smile *must* take the crooked way.

Glencoe.

THE FOOLY

IT WAS A NEW town, a new chance, a new shortcut home from a new pub. All so similar, yet so different, walking this lonely road on this cool, windy night.

The choosing was what made it special for Charles Ratray. The chance to choose, the ability to do it. He had lost so much, before, during and after Katie, truth be told, but here he was, at the end of that hardest choice, here in Kareela instead of Karalta.

It wasn't so bad. Kareela was like any other small town really, a town you could walk out of in ten minutes it was so small; the Royal Exchange like any other small pub.

And this road across the fields could have been a dozen similar backroads at Karalta, the same clumps of trees, same scrappy field-stone walls and barbed-wire fences, same grasses blowing in the cool night wind.

Some would ask then why re-locate at all? But they didn't know, couldn't, or forgot to remember the handful of reasons that always changed everything for anyone.

Katie was there. Karalta was her place.

Warwick's too. *Their* place now.

Away was better. You had to know when to leave, how to manage it, no matter how demanding it was, how difficult.

And he *had* managed. And weren't they surprised now? If they were.

Charles stopped, just stood in the blowing dark and breathed in the night.

How good it was to be here, anywhere else.

"You're new," a voice said and Charles Ratray yelped in fright.

There was a figure leaning against a field-stone wall, a dark man-shape, darker in the darkness, with a glitter at the eyes.

"You startled me," Charles managed.

"That'll do for starters," the figure said. "It's all about persuasion, you see. You're new."

"Arrived last week. I'm the new day supervisor out at Fulton's dairy."

The eyes glittered. "I haven't seen you on the road."

"Should you have?"

"Well, it's my road, see? I'm here a lot."

"I can't see you very well. There's enough moonlight. I should be able—"

"Part of the effect," the figure said. "Adds to the mood. I'm a specialist in mood lighting." There was a hint of smile below the glitter.

"You're a fooly, aren't you?"

"A what?"

"You know, a fooly. Something in my mind. A figment. My mind is playing tricks."

"Well, in a sense that's right. I'm already tweaking your mind a bit, see? There'll be more later. It'll get worse once I start bringing up the fear. Slipping in a bit of terror and despair. Walk with me."

Charles had been walking home anyway. He started along the road again. The figure stepped away from the wall and joined him, walking in an odd crimped walk Charles found disconcerting.

"You're a ghost," Charles said.

"That's more like it."

"You don't seem very frightening."

"They all say that at first. That's the come-on, see. Start out easy. Build up to it. They never tell you about that in ghost stories. What it really involves."

"Like what?" Charles asked.

"How we adjust the mind, the feelings. Being in charge of something means everything. That's what it's all about, living or dead."

"I never knew."

"See? It's the thing that matters most. It's like a work of art really, judging the moment, bringing up the disquiet, the dread. Hard to believe it right now, I know, Mr—?"

"Ratray. Charles Ratray. Charles."

"Good, Charles. Always try for first names. That's part of it. I'm Billy. Billy Wine. See, much less threatening. They'll tell you about me in town."

"Then you should let them do that. I'll ask around. Do this another night."

"Too late, Charles. Charlie. Had your chance. They should have told you about Billy Wine already. Bad death. Awful death. Five people at the funeral. Disappointing all round, really."

"So now you're making up for it."

"That's it exactly. Hey, I like you, Charles. You're quick. You're interested."

"That won't change anything."

"Not a bit. Not at all. You took this road. But no-one told you? No-one at the pub? No-one at the dairy?"

"About the road? No. Haven't been here long. Will I survive this?"

"Probably not. But you have to understand. I don't get many along this road so I like to draw it out. Sometimes I misjudge the heart business. Scare folks too much."

"I thought ghosts just gave you a quick scare and that was it."

"That's the quick shock approach. The public relations side of it. We can do far more. That name you said. Fooly. We like to bring the victim—the subject—the scaree—to the point where they're not sure if it's real or in their heads. You get much more panic once you get to that point."

"Maybe you could just give me a quick scare now and I can come back tomorrow night."

"Hey, you're a real kidder. You wouldn't, of course. Surprised no-one told you about me though."

"Maybe you had something to do with that."

"Boy, you're quick. Charlie, I really like you. Where are you staying?"

"Out at the Dickerson place. Six-month lease."

"Well, there you go then. That explains it. They probably figured you for a relative of old Sam Dickerson. Shutters would've come down the minute you said."

"Or maybe you did something to stop them telling me."

Billy Wine grinned. "That too. Lots of things are possible."

Charles smiled to himself, at least meant to. It was actually rather pleasant walking in the night; windy, blustery really, but cool, not cold. The grass was soughing on the verge. The trees were tossing. There were house lights far off to the right—and more behind when he glanced back, the homes of people he didn't know yet, and right there, the patch of light where Kareela sat in the night, like the glow of a ship at sea.

He kept alert for the fear, the thinnest edge of terror, but felt nothing. Perhaps he was immune. Maybe it didn't work for him.

"Should be feeling it soon," the fooly said. "Your senses will go a bit, bring in weird stuff. You smelling the sea yet?"

Charles couldn't help it. He sniffed the wind.

And he did. He could. The salt tang, impossibly far away but there. Charles *smelled* it.

Billy Wine's eyes glittered, a paring of smile beneath. "Seabirds?"

They were barely there, thin, far-off, wheeling four, five fields away, but there.

"Why the sea?" Charles asked.

"Always loved the sea," Billy Wine said. "You hearing trains?"

Trains, yes! Nowhere near as surprising; there was a station at Kareela, after all.

"But steam trains!" the ghost of Billy Wine said, anticipating.

And that's what Charles heard, chuffling, snuffling, stolen back, there and gone, there and gone.

"Circus!"

A calliope whooped and jangled in the night, forlorn, distant, dangerous.

"Weeping!"

And, oh, there was. Full of ocean-lost, clown-sad, missed-train sorrow, desolate on the wind. Billy Wine brought it in. Made Charlie do the bringing.

"Getting you ready, Charlie, my man! Think now—all the things you've had taken from you. All the things you never got to say. All the bitter."

Not bitterness. Bitter. Billy had the way of it, the ghosting knack, sure enough.

Charles kept walking. "What can I give? What can I trade?"

"Trade? Don't need souls. Nothing to hold 'em in. Old fooly joke."

"Fooly?"

"Just using your terminology, Charlie, my man. Don't get excited! Maybe an invitation to the Exchange. That'd be worth something."

"I can go back. See what I can do."

"You wouldn't. You couldn't. They don't see you. They served you up."

"You did that," Charles said. "Stopped 'em warning. Tweaked their minds."

The eyes glittered. The paring of smile curved up.

"Taking care of business," Billy said. "It's what you do."

"I'm nearly home."

"You'll never get there." The smile sharpened. "Walking's getting harder, isn't it?"

It was. Suddenly was.

Charles felt so heavy. His legs were leaden, wooden, twin stumps of stone. This was feeding Billy, Charles saw. The power. The finesse.

Billy read the moment. "Time for a flourish. Look how scary I've become."

And he had. Oh, how he had, Charles saw, felt, knew.

That awful darkness. That blend of glitter-gaze, crimp-step and pared darkling smile. In spite of everything, knowing it was coming, Charles saw that Billy was the same but not the same. Never could be.

The wind was slippery now, pushing, coddling, blustery and black-handed. The grass blew, hushed and blew again, reeling them in. No, not them. Him. Him.

Billy Wine lunged, strode, tottered, stayed alongside yet flowed ahead, all at once. He was sharps, dagger edges, razor-gaze and guttering grin. The dark of him was too much, too close, too stinking hot.

But mostly it was the gut-wrench suicide cocktail inside Charles Ratray, three parts dread, two parts despair, one blossoming nip of revulsion slipped in sideways.

Charles could barely breathe. He staggered, breath to breath, inside and out, fighting to remember what breathing was, what walking was, what self was.

This deadly, crimp-stepped Billy truly was good at what he did.

Close up, there was his sudden, awful intimacy, while out there, oceans closed over ships, birds plucked at eyes, calliopes screamed into the fall of colliding trains, and Katie was denied, denying, again and again.

Charles screamed and stilted and propped, fought to breathe. No part of the night was satisfied to hold him. It pushed him away, hurled him from itself back into itself, made panic from the stilting, flailing pinwheel he had become. He screamed and yelled because Billy wanted him to.

Though Billy knew to stop, of course, to relax and savor, to settle for shades and ebb and flow. He had a whole night, a whole splendid, new-to-town Charlie Ratray to teach the last of all lessons.

But Charles managed to keep his sense of self through it all, did manage, and he let the Dickerson house be the focus, off in the distance, its single yard light showing where it was.

"I made it," Charles said, knowing how Billy would respond.

"Did you? Have you? Are you sure?"

The house swept away, one field, two, road threading between, single yard light jiggering, dancing off like a small tight comet.

"Too bad," Billy Wine said. "We're almost at the end of it."

"We are?"

"It'll be quick. You'll be fully aware." Billy sounded gleeful.

"But it's still early—"

"I know. And *do* be disappointed! That bad death I had. Only five people to see me off. It makes you hard."

"But you have the whole night. Surely there's more fear? More dread?"

"No need. All that's just window dressing anyway. Absolute clarity is best. Just the anguish. The disappointment. Enough despair. You go out knowing."

"Billy—"

"No more, Charlie. Time to go. It'll hurt just a bit. Well, quite a bit. Well, a lot actually, pain being what it is. But maybe you'll get to come back. Some do."

"Maybe I already have."

And Charles Ratray was gone, spiralling away as a twist of light on the wild dark air.

"Hey! What? What's that?" Billy Wine demanded, but knew, had even imagined the possibility, though had never ever expected it.

For who else watched the watchmen, hunted the hunters, haunted the haunters?

Who else fooled the foolies?

All that remained of Billy Wine stood on the dark windy road and felt the ache of disappointment tear at him again and again.

Afterword to "The Fooly"

THERE'S A SCENE in Ridley Scott's fine 2000 film *Gladiator* when, with grudging admiration, Derek Jacobi as Gracchus remarks on Commodus's shrewd PR move of staging over a hundred days of gladiatorial games and says: "Fear and wonder, a powerful combination."

That's what I keep returning to as a storyteller: delivering fear and wonder for all sorts of useful, intuitive, sometimes very important reasons as someone living in the early 21ˢᵗ century. I never set out to be a horror writer per se, or any sort of genre writer for that matter, seeing such things as fixed prices on variable goods and ultimately useful only to marketing departments, booksellers and librarians.

But quite early in my career I found that I was being drawn to what can usefully be called tales of unease, to this constant braiding of fear and wonder. As part of this, there is a fascination with the nature of ghosts and hauntings, and the very human preoccupations and perceptions of reality that keep bringing us back to these things.

Terror (in its potent, original, pre-1960 meaning) has always been infinitely more powerful than horror and the too-easy shocks of gore and gross-out.

I guess I've always sensed, intuitively, that the power of the very best horror writing lay in that careful and splendid hesitation between the thrill of the disquieting moment, the disturbing situation for the human mind experiencing it, and its resolution, often with a too easily given, often quite humdrum supernatural explanation. I saw that the supernatural is rarely terrifying once it's shown for what it is, that the real chills and creepiness, the real power, lay in all that precedes and frames its arrival. Such a simple realization: that the real impact, the real punch, be given in the mood, the feel, the staging. The nifty ending is still the *sine qua non*, of course, but getting there is just as important and often much more so.

From the beginning, I found myself—sometimes successfully— exploring the time-honored tropes and traditions of the ghost story in tales like "The Bullet That Grows in the Gun," "The Daemon Street Ghost-Trap," "Scaring the Train," and "One Thing About the

Night." In the light of these tales, "The Fooly" seems an inevitable companion piece, a small story built around an idea that was both simple and quite irresistible. Once again it let me consider what ghosts are and exactly *how* and *why* they do what they do, this time with a touch of Bradbury (always pay your dues, Terry D.), a hint of Rod Serling's *The Twilight Zone* (pay 'em, you hear!), a definite nod to Bill Martin Jr, John Archambault and Ted Rand's deliciously spooky 1985 picture-book *The Ghost-Eye Tree*, and a touch of the tall tale that's really quite Australian.

I'm inordinately fond of "The Fooly." Part of me kept wanting to make it larger, have it stay around a bit longer. But small things can read large, and every time I re-read this one it feels bigger than it is. And just maybe, to recall Jacobi's words, the combination is there enough to work the spell.

Now, Then, Everywhen

Now, then, everywhen,
You can say your jack's a rover.
What you mean is what you dream
And you can't wait till the journey's over
And he's with you,
And he's with you.

Roving hand, sand-glass man,
And it's true time takes him turning.
Back again, see him then,
How your love has kept him burning
To be with you,
To be with you.

Ride the time roads down,
Watch him ride the time roads round.

Now, then, everywhen,
You can say your jack's a rover.
What you mean is what you dream
And you can't wait till the journey's over
And he's with you,
And he's with you.

THE MAGIKKERS

TWICE UPON A TIME there was someone named Samuel Raven Pardieu. The first to bear the name was a nineteenth century blacksmith who tried his hand as a toother during the Napoleonic War. In the morning following the Battle of Waterloo in 1815, while collecting teeth from the newly killed to sell to dentists in the big cities, he was spotted by an English patrol and shot as a looter.

The second Samuel Raven Pardieu was that man's great-to-the-fifth grandson, and on the morning of 24 May 2006, this second Sam, two weeks past his fourteenth birthday, one full month after enrolling in the special classes at Dessida, was sitting in his favorite spot in all of the sprawling Dessida estate when Bettina Anders found him.

"I knew you'd be here," Bettina said in that special know-it-all tone she had. "Haven't forgotten what today is?"

"Of course not," Sam said, as if he could, as if he needed to be reminded. Key Interview Day. His first one-on-one interview with Lucius Prandt, one of the world's greatest magicians.

The real surprise was that Bettina was bothering to talk to him at all. In his four weeks at Dessida, in both the ordinary curriculum classes and the special Magikker classes they shared day after day, she hadn't spoken more than a few dozen words to him. Now here she was, this stand-offish fourteen-year-old, the one the other eighteen students, Sam included, called the Princess behind her back, pretending to be friendly. Pretending. It couldn't be genuine.

Sam was sitting in his special spot, of course. There were twelve stone plinths flanking the old ornamental approach to the front steps of the main house at Dessida, twelve marble pedestals hopelessly overgrown with thorn bushes and bracken except for this one, the one Sam had cleared himself and now occupied. The large house stood on its rise behind them, overlooking the grounds of the sprawling country estate.

Bettina didn't leave. That was another marvel. She just stood there, dark-haired and, yes, princess pretty if you thought about it at all, and just seemed to be watching the day.

"Well, I hope it goes well," she said, and astonished him even more.

Sam couldn't fathom it. Bettina Anders saying such a thing. And with it came another thought: what does she know about my Key Interview that I don't? What happens at a Key Interview with Lucius? Should I ask her?

Sam played it safe and said nothing. Why ask only to have her snub him again? He'd been gazing at what lay concealed in the thorn bushes between the plinths when she'd arrived. Now he looked out over the estate as well, the spacious grounds set amid these rolling green hills under a brilliant autumn sky. He was determined not to let Bettina Anders know what he'd really been looking at. That was his secret, his one special thing at Dessida.

But she lingered. Against all reason, all sense, Bettina stayed.

"So, do you have your question ready," she said.

"My what?"

"Key Interview Day is also First Question Day, if no-one's told you. Lucius will probably ask you to ask one. He usually does."

Sam couldn't help himself. "A question? What question?"

"Ahhh," Bettina said, which translated as: *So, you didn't know!* "Just what I said. He'll ask if *you* have a question. Do you?"

"*One* question. I've got lots of questions. Like when do the *real* magic classes start. Not just these mind exercises we keep doing all the time."

"You need to be patient," Bettina said, and looked anything but that herself. "It's worth it."

It struck Sam right then that she'd been *told* to come and find him, to say all this. With two months more experience at Dessida, she was probably following someone's instructions, a script of some kind. Maybe Lucius had sent her himself. It was certainly possible.

"Where would *you* rather be right now, Bettina?" he said, and could see he had surprised her.

"What?"

"This is *my* spot. I love sitting here, just watching the grounds and the house. But you don't want to be here now. Where would you *rather* be?"

The old Bettina defiance was back in a flash. She couldn't help herself. "You're so smart and stand-offish. You tell me!"

Stand-offish! That threw Sam. That couldn't be right. He wasn't the stand-offish one!

"Well, I haven't known you long, but it has to be the top of that tower," Sam said, and pointed back up the hill to Dessida's huge front doors at the end of the overgrown approach promenade. Above that big doorway rose a modest central tower, three stories tall, with a big bronze bell on an ornate stand at the top and a flag flying on a flagpole. "Or beside the lake, down behind the trees there. Somewhere away and safe."

Bettina stared at him, not because he was necessarily right in naming either place—how could he possibly know?—but probably because of that final sentence and final word.

The look between them might have been special except that Bettina was guarding, was more protective about some things than even Sam was. His last comment had probably been too close to the mark. She had to say something to deal with the vulnerability it brought with it.

"As if I'd tell you," she said, like "Princess" Bettina on any other day. "And don't think I don't know why you like sitting here. I can see your silly statue down in there." She gestured at the thicket beyond the plinth where Sam sat, then stalked off towards the house.

Sam could have hated her right then, watching her go, but knew that such an emotion was to cover something else, just like Bettina's own sudden outburst. She *was* guarding, protecting herself. Sam was doing the same.

"It's the only one left!" he might have called after her as she disappeared through the double doorway. But he didn't. He looked instead at the toppled male form hidden in the thorn thicket, a figure of dirty white stone, the same old marble as the plinths, toppled and abandoned long ago.

Whatever statuary had adorned the other plinths was long gone. The house itself was maintained well enough, but the grounds of the Dessida estate had definitely seen better days.

Let her tell the other students about the statue. Let her tell their three teachers or the other staff, Lucius himself for all he cared.

And stand-offish! How dare she!

Sam looked at his watch: 9:45. Almost time.

Key Interview. Just him and Lucius at last!

But Bettina had no reason to lie. First Question Day. What would he ask? What did one ask the man who was probably the world's greatest magician, having been hand-picked by him from hundreds, literally thousands of other boys and girls across Australia, across the world, if what the Prandt testing officers had said was true? Hand-picked and *paid* to come to Dessida in the Southern Highlands on a Prandt Scholarship to hone his latent skills, become a magician or magikker, whatever that was. It had never been made clear.

That had to be the question.

What's the difference between a Magician and a Magikker?

Sam looked at his watch again: 9:50. And that was when Martin Mayhew appeared in Dessida's big double doorway, happy Martin, always smiling, always happy to be in the world. Tall, blonde and handsome, Nordic-looking and easy in his buff colored house fatigues and sandals, greeting every morning with his arms spread wide and his head back, if the stories were true, breathing in the day. Martin was in charge of the household staff, and here he was to make sure that Sam didn't miss his 10 am meeting.

Martin gave a big sweeping gesture of summons. "It's time, Sam!"

"Take care, Rufio," Sam called to the stone figure lying in the thicket, his special name for his secret friend. Then he was up in a flash, off the plinth and up the steps.

"Rufio?" Martin asked as they headed for Lucius Prandt's large office in the north-western wing.

"My name for him," Sam said. "He's the only one left. Do you remember the others?" Sam knew he could ask Martin things like this and be safe about it.

"Sorry, Best Sam. Before my time, I'm afraid. But ask Master Lucius. He'll know. He's lived here all his life. You're allowed to bring up things like that during your interview."

"Anyone else scheduled today, Martin?" Sam had to ask it.

Martin shook his head. "Not today. Today is your day, Sam. Lucius has been looking forward to it."

Then they were at the large oaken door to Lucius Prandt's private office, and Martin was knocking.

"Good luck, Best Sam," Martin said, opening the door for him.

And in Sam went.

It was a wonderful room, Sam saw, a true magician's room, large and high-ceilinged, with bookcases lining most of the wood-paneled walls and fabulous miniature engines of glass and metal working away on a bench top to one side. Against the far wall was a suit of medieval armor with—incredibly!—two heads, two fiercely snouted, visored helmets set side by side on big spiky shoulders. Where could *that* have come from? Sam wondered. How could it be real? There were maps on the walls between the bookshelves: Mercator projections of land after fabulous land with exotic names like Sabertanis Major and Andastaban Arcanus. Small pins with demon heads pinned maps atop others in some places, there were so many.

Lucius Prandt's huge desk was set on a raised dais before four tall leadlight windows that opened onto views of the lawns and forests of Dessida, windows that framed glimpses of rolling hills and held great masses of fluffy cumulus in an achingly blue sky.

So many things sat on that wide wonderful desk, but most noticeable were the three planetary globes Sam had learned about in his Introductions to Magic classes. The closest was the Earth as Sam knew it, but joined by seventeen silver threads to the second, which was the Overworld, set with its spelltowers and mage-points. That orb was joined in turn by red wires to the third, which represented the Underworld, all blacks and reds, with threads of hot bright copper picking out the various Sunder Points.

But Lucius Prandt wasn't at his desk. He sat in one of two big armchairs before a fireplace in which was set not a conventional fire but rather a slowly turning image of a burning city.

"Welcome, Sam," Lucius said, standing to greet him, shaking his hand warmly. He wore true-wizard black, of course: soft black woollen top, black slacks, black shoes. None of the star-and-moon robes or mysterious pentagram stuff he wore for his concerts and television performances, not today. His dark eyes glittered under silver-grey hair that swept back like a wave. He was in his late fifties, they said, but others had told Sam that a zero should be added to any age you felt tempted to put him at. Lucius Prandt, they said, had been present at the death of the ancient city that burned forever in his fireplace.

It was difficult for Sam not to keep glancing this way and that, studying some new thing or other that suddenly caught his eye. But at last he made himself sit in the other armchair and face Lucius, who was pouring them both glasses of fruit juice from a crystal decanter.

"I've been looking forward to this, Sam," he said as he handed Sam a glass. "Your studies have been going well, I hear, and I thought it was time we met properly. We have questions for each other, I know, and you'll get to ask them all over the next few weeks. No doubt you've been told to have a special question ready for me right now, so let's get that out of the way so we can relax properly."

Sam felt a weight go from him. He set his glass down on a side table and didn't hesitate. "What's the difference between a Magikker and a Magician?"

"Straight to the heart of it. Good. That's an important question and I thank you for it. There have been many true magicians in the history of the world—gifted men and women—but not really that many ever became the fullest quantity meant by that name. Most so-called magicians only ever had bits and pieces of the gift. But I bet you could even name some of the real ones."

"Well, Merlin for a start?"

"Definitely one of the lucky ones, Sam, one of the very few."

"Yourself. Lucius Prandt." It seemed appropriate to say it.

Lucius gave his wonderful smile. "Good of you to say so, but no, Sam. I'm only an illusionist. That's what most magicians are these days—people who create wonderful illusions, learn to be clever enough to use people's perceptions against them. That's nothing compared to real magic, of course, just fakery and fancy tricks, a knowledge of optics and sleight of hand, but sometimes it just has to do. But I *was* a true magician for a short time, Sam. Seems a lot of us have a bit of the gift, just a bit and just for a short time, some evolutionary holdover from when the mind fired differently. It's almost as if evolution started to take us down a different road, then got side-tracked."

Lucius paused to top up their glasses. "The thing is, most of us lose any traces of this gift by the time we become adults and never even know we've had it. It comes out in crisis situations mostly—a child lifts a fallen tree off an injured playmate. He could never have lifted such a load before. Suddenly he can. Another kid moves a parked car to free a trapped pet. Never knows how she did it. Another pictures the hand of someone buried in a landslide half a continent away, maybe tells the right people in time. When they check, they find the person still alive, just a hand showing. It's the birthright gift, the power some of us are born with and soon lose."

"But *you* had it."

"I certainly did. For seventeen precious and amazing years. That's an incredibly long time. I was lucky. The memory of it made me become an illusionist. But for a short time I was a *magician*, Sam! The real thing!"

"And I am?" Sam had to ask it. Why else was he here?

"Straight to it again, Sam. Good. You are—in a small way and for a short time. You may never have known it before coming to Dessida, but you are."

"All those tests at school—"

"Were to prove it. Passed off as aptitude tests and personality indicators, all approved by the School Board and the Department of Education. They never knew otherwise. This year alone we've tested everyone at three hundred and fifty-two schools so far. You're the only one we've found."

Sam was amazed. "The *only* one?"

"Others had bits of a gift but were temperamentally unsuited or had family complications. They were better left as they were, undeveloped and unknowing. For their own sakes, really. I hope you understand."

"So what about my training here? The six months' tuition?"

"You want to be an illusionist?"

"Not if I'm a magician!"

"Perfect answer! See, we picked well. So let's get back to your question. A Magician with a capital M has the gift for life, just like Merlin and Sancreoch and Quen Dargentis, the Black Mage of Constantinople. But most are what we call Magikkers—people with a tiny bit of the gift, a single burst they can use once and once only, you hear what I'm saying? In magical parlance, we call them singletons. Magikkers."

"And I'm a—a singleton? A Magikker?"

"Sam, you are. You have *one* magic act within you. A single magnificent spell. One big gush of power. It will all come rushing out at once and then be gone."

"Then—then I should wait. I should keep it until I really need it."

"Doesn't work like that. The older you get, the sooner it'll just fade away. It's gone for most Magikkers well before they turn twenty."

"But—but Lucius…" Sam couldn't finish.

"Yes, Sam. You have to take my word that this is how it is. I've spent years researching and searching."

"For these—Magikkers?"

"Indeed."

"So you're saying I should use my gift soon."

"You should. And there's an alternative. A suggestion I would like to put to you now."

"What's that, Lucius?"

"Sam, I want you to give *me* your magic."

Sam was amazed. "Give it to you?"

"You have so little—one spell at most, a single act, probably limited in all sorts of ways—but whatever it is, however it is, I'd like you to give it to me."

The request stunned Sam. He felt a new weight settle on his spirit, a new hard emotion surging up. He quickly realized what it was. Disappointment. Disillusionment. "That's why I'm really here, isn't it? Why we're all really here?"

Lucius nodded. "Yes, Sam, it is."

"But it's *mine*," Sam said. "*My* gift. How could I *give* it? How could that be possible?" And behind those words, the unspoken ones: Why should I? How could you ask it?

"I can't help you there, Sam. That has to be your decision. It truly does have to be your decision. I just wanted to let you know how it is and what I'd like you to do for me."

The disappointment Sam felt took all the charm from the room, emptied the excitement and happiness out of the day. He wanted to be gone, needed to be anywhere else. "So I can leave whenever I want? I don't have to stay?"

"Dessida isn't a prison, Sam. You can leave any time you want. We'll drive you to the station at Milton, even give you a certificate saying you've completed some important vocational training."

"But I'll lose my chance."

"Only to be here with me. Taking our classes. To have us help you use that gift."

"*Give away* that gift." Sam's words sounded bitter. He couldn't help it. "And they're *illusionist* classes. Not the real thing."

"Afraid so, Sam. Once your magic is used up, that's all we have to console us."

"You don't."

"I assure you, Sam, I do. That's why I'm asking for your magic. One illusionist talking to a young man who may one day become another."

"Once my magic is gone."

"Once your magic is gone, yes."

"So you can have another taste!" Sam said the words savagely. He was so angry, so disappointed. This wonderful man, wonderful place, wonderful chance had been ruined in a moment.

"I—I need to go and think."

Lucius stood. "Of course you do. It's right that you do. I wanted to be direct with you about this. But, Sam, please know. Whatever you decide will be the right thing."

Before Sam quite knew it, he found himself out in the corridor again, hurrying back towards the front of the house. He felt numb. He needed to be gone, to be out in the day, somewhere else, anywhere else. He rushed down the front steps and sat on his plinth again, but this time he didn't greet Rufio. He couldn't bring himself to.

Everything was the same. Everything was different. Dessida still stood at the end of its once-grand promenade, still loomed there—an impressive, two-storied, nineteenth-century mansion on its gentle rise. But now Sam saw all over again how run-down it truly was: the lawns in need of mowing, the weeds in the gravel of the approach walk. The gardens to either side were overgrown with briars too, not just the pedestals flanking the path.

So much for Lucius Prandt's magic. He couldn't even keep his estate in order, couldn't even manage a "glamor" to hide how it really was.

Sam left the plinth and set off across the lawns towards the estate's western border. Members of the household staff watched him go. Standing with their rakes and gardening tools, they tracked him with their bright curious eyes.

That just angered Sam further. They stood about with rakes and implements like that, yet always seemed to be doing more talking and daydreaming than actual work. Well, let them watch. Let them wonder.

Finally Sam reached the low wall of grey-brown field-stone that marked Dessida's western boundary. He leant on the waist-high barrier, glanced at it stretching this way and that off through the trees, then looked out at the world beyond, *his* world, sweeping away in fields and suddenly precious vistas.

How dare Lucius! How dare he!

Sam could so easily jump that wall and be gone. He felt his body tensing for it.

"Hey, Best Sam!"

The voice reached him through the forest, and when Sam turned, there was that gangly, elderly groundswoman, Ren Bartay, heading towards him. She was tall and sun-tanned and was wacking the taller weeds with a stick as she came, a big smile on her face.

"Isn't it just a day?" Ren called, grinning away. "I love this time of year."

And then, when she was right up close: "Thinking of bailing out, eh, Sam? It's an easy leap."

"Seriously considering it, Ren," Sam replied. Why not say it, he figured. Like Lucius had said, it was his choice to make.

"Don't blame you," Ren surprised him by saying. "The magic is all used up here."

"Is it?"

"First Interview Day. You know it is. You're the only one with a bit right now."

"If that's true. If *any* of it's true. What about the others? Bettina and Susan and Crip and the rest? There are eighteen other—"

"Already given. Already gone. Never really had any." Ren set down her stick and started checking that the stones were securely packed atop this section of wall.

"I can't be the only one!"

"Right now you are," she said, turning back. "Lucius would have asked you for it, yes? First Interview Day."

"But if they've given theirs, why do they stay on? How can they stand it?"

Ren looked off through the trees, then pointed to a spot well inside the wall. "Because *how* they used their magic is still here—in almost every case."

"I don't understand."

"Let me show you."

They started walking back towards Dessida together, then made a detour south so they entered the thickest part of the forest.

In the dappled autumn light, Sam saw things—structures—amid the trees. To his left there was a cottage, a full-size picture-book gingerbread house with smoke curling from the chimney, smoke that vanished six meters above the chimney pot before ever reaching the open air.

"That's Bettina Anders' creation," Ren said. "The Eternal House. How she used her single magic act. Step inside, you'll meet her grandmother

Dika, her grandfather Brent. There's always music playing, always something cooking, always a welcome at their table. Couldn't do something like that away from Dessida, Sam. Lucius explained it to Bettina very carefully. You can't bring people back from the dead, put them back in the world, without causing a real fuss. Wouldn't be right. That sort of fix-up needs to be done very discreetly."

Then Ren pointed to a twisted and, yes, *twisting* tower off to the right. It glowed like amber in the soft light streaming through the trees. "That's Sophie Ramage's Living Tower. She would've preferred it in her own backyard, of course, but Lucius made her see that people would gawp and gape and never leave her alone. They'd be forever wanting to know how it was possible, where it came from. She'd never have a moment's peace, what with intruders and souvenir hunters breaking off bits and pieces. Here it stays intact and hers! She'll be able to come see it anytime she wants."

"And that's what it's all about," Sam said, more annoyed than ever. "Lucius can't do magic anymore, so this way he gets other people's marvels! Talks them out of keeping them."

"Sam, Sam," Ren said, in her wonderful calming voice. "See it another way. These were done by Magikkers who *didn't* give Lucius their magic! The things they used it for have been left here for safekeeping. *Discarded* here if you think about it."

Sam tried to grasp the sense of what Ren was saying. "But Lucius wouldn't be able to convince everyone, surely."

"You're right. So he exercises an important custodial role, a true duty of care, and uses hypnosis. He makes them *forget* that they ever had the gift in the first place. He can't let them go back into their everyday lives and do some outlandish thing or other. Not once they know about the gift. So they leave Dessida thinking they've been given some training in basic illusionist skills, that's all. They go away and the magic dies in them, then everything's okay."

Sam felt a moment of panic. "*I* still remember all this! He hasn't hypnotized me!"

"You haven't jumped the wall yet."

"What! If I jump it and run away, I'll forget!"

Ren grinned. "Just kidding, Best Sam. Lucius picks his Magikkers very carefully. Mostly it works out fine. He rarely has to resort to mind-tricks. You still have your gift to use. He'd *rather* you use it than lose it."

"He'd rather I give it to him."

"Oh yes. He'd much rather that," Ren said, smiling and, before Sam could ask why, added: "But for a very good reason. One I'm duty-sworn never to reveal."

That made Sam stop and think. He liked old Ren. It made the anger subside a bit. "But how can I give *my* magic to *him*?"

Ren's smile never wavered. "See what a special boy you are, Sam? You said 'how can I' not 'why should I.' That's a nice distinction, especially when you're feeling like you are right now."

"I'm serious, Ren. *How* could I give it to him?"

But Ren just put a finger to her lips as if to say: Can't tell. Can't tell. Keeping a secret! Then she seemed to change her mind a bit. "Well, the Magikkers who worked their spells here certainly didn't do it. Bettina insisted on her cottage. Sophie had to have her tower. Over there you see Kristi Paul's Magical Soda Well and Grant Hennessey's Nifty Golden Treasure Mill. *They* certainly didn't give their magic to Lucius."

"But he would've asked for it."

"Certainly did. First Interview Day every time."

"But if it's *my* birthright gift, *mine* to use, how can I give it?"

They seemed to be in a loop. "Exactly," Ren Bartay said. "How could you give your bit of magic to someone else?"

Then, just like that, without another word, she turned and headed back towards Dessida.

Sam watched her go, saw the tall spry woman stop to exchange a word or two with other household staff doing grounds work—first Carla, then Jeffrey—then saw her hurry on.

What had she told them? What?

No way to know, so Sam turned back to the marvels laid out amid the trees: Bettina's cottage with its endless plume of cookfire smoke and—to hear Ren Bartay tell it—endless happiness within, lost happiness found again; Sophie's miraculous twisting tower, curving on itself like so much settling honey; Grant's mill glinting and cycling away. He heard the fizz from Kristi's well too, heard other wonderful sounds coming through the forest from who knew how many other wonders hidden there? Sam realized he could probably spend hours, days, weeks here exploring what else was laid out among the trees, what years of other Magikkers had chosen.

Because they *wouldn't* give Lucius their magic!

Sam marveled at it. Just how long had Lucius been bringing Magikkers here from all across the world, asking for their bits of the gift?

Which made Sam think further. What single thing did Lucius hope for with the piece of magic Sam carried within him? What was it that Ren—or Martin, or Lucius for that matter—wouldn't tell him?

Sam couldn't fathom the purpose, of course, but suddenly he did realize something. He would know *none* of this, nothing of what Magikkers were and about this gift he had if it weren't for Lucius, weren't for the testing and the Prandt Scholarship that had brought him here.

He owed Lucius for that, and it took the last of the anger out of him.

And blossoming up behind that realization came something else. Sam knew right then *how* he could give his magic to Lucius, and it was so obvious, so simple.

He ran, actually ran back to the main house, making more sudden Sam-commotion in the peace of the day. Grounds staff stood leaning on their rakes or left off sweeping the paths to watch him rush by.

What were they thinking? Sam asked himself as he ran. Here comes the magic boy, the First Interview Day Boy. Best Sam. But what did they think, what did they know smiling and wondering like that?

Sam saw other students watching him too. Susan and Crip and Mahad were on the south terrace, Sanford and Nettie by the fountain. And there, there at the top of the tower, leaning on the balustrade, yes, was Princess Bettina, watching from her safe place.

Sam didn't care. He deliberately turned into the old approach promenade, deliberately let her see him run past the plinths and thorn bushes. He called "Hi there, Rufio!" as he rushed past, just as he'd always done, then he leapt the steps three at a time and plunged into the cool familiar gloom of Dessida's front hall.

Martin Mayhew was waiting for him there, of course.

"Best Sam, what's afoot?" Martin asked.

"I have to see Lucius again, Martin! I need to ask him something!"

"About your interview?"

"About my gift."

"Then I'm sure he'll see you."

And Lucius did, almost immediately. Martin needed only a moment to go in first to explain, then Sam was ushered in to the leather chairs and Martin was once again closing the door behind him.

Sam dropped into the armchair opposite Lucius, just as he had not even an hour before.

Lucius had already put aside the book he'd been reading. "What is it, Sam?"

"I know how I can give you my magic."

"You do? And so?"

"I want to."

"I thank you. How does that work then?"

"*You* tell me what you want *me* to do. Then I do it for you."

"But I can't," Lucius said.

"What's that?"

"I can't come out and tell you, Sam. It's an oath I took. A condition I imposed on myself. A rule of governance from way back. I'm not *allowed* to tell. It all has to come from you. You're the Magikker-in-command right now. I'm just an illusionist."

"But you can hypnotize me. Plant an activating command of some kind. Then instead of days and weeks of learning how to use an activation spell one time only, you put in a trigger so all I have to do is say what I want. What *I* think *you* want. You can at least do that."

"True. I can. I've done it before."

"I know. I guessed. That's what you're the expert at. Making it quick and easy. Helping it happen."

Lucius smiled. "So how do we proceed, Best of Sams? I still can't say what I want you to do with your gift."

"Lucius, I think I know what you want."

Lucius's eyes glittered with unreadable emotion. "Oh? Yes?"

"So go ahead. Plant the hypnotic cue."

"I planted it earlier today. While you were watching my burning city there."

Sam glanced quickly at the strange shape turning in the fireplace, then looked back. "Then call the Dessida staff together."

Lucius's eyebrows lifted in surprise. "The staff?"

"The three teachers too. All of them. Have them gather out by the front steps."

Lucius turned to an intercom by his chair, pressed a button. "Martin. Dessida One! Ring the bell!"

And moments later the bell in the tower started tolling over and over. Out in the fields, back in the kitchen and service rooms and private quarters, the household staff would be leaving off what they were doing and heading for the front of the house.

They were all assembled there when Lucius and Sam stepped through the big double doorway at the top of the steps. The group stood as if for some anniversary photograph, smiling, attentive and curious, Martin Mayhew and Ren Bartay among them.

Sam grinned back. He was right. In an instant he'd counted them and knew he was right.

Eight household staff. Three teachers. A total of eleven.

Eleven of the twelve plinths.

Sam gestured then, just as he'd seen magicians and wizards and sorcerers do all his life in countless picture books and movies.

"Make room for number twelve!" he shouted. "Rufio, come out here! It's your turn!"

There was scratching and scrambling in the thicket, then out came Rufio, already in house fatigues, limber and strong and smiling with happiness.

"Welcome to the staff, Rufio!" Sam called.

"Thank you, Best Sam!" Rufio called back with his brand-new voice, and did just that, moved in among the others.

That was when Sam noticed that next to him Lucius was weeping, that tears brightened his cheeks in the late morning light.

"Thank you, Best Sam. Thank you for this."

"It means I'll have to stay on and become an illusionist now, doesn't it?" Sam said.

"Oh, it does," Lucius agreed. "And I'm sure that's what Rufio and our friends here want more than anything."

Afterword to "The Magikkers"

"THE MAGIKKERS" WAS originally intended as the title for a story concerning magicians who weren't quite the real thing, who were magically endowed only so long as they remained within shifting spotlights of magic as those points moved across the land. Their great skill lay not so much in *using* the powers gained as in being able to plot those shifting points of magic.

When that story became "The Saltimbanques" in 1996, the title was held over to await another story where there was some major difference between a magikker and what we've come to think of as a magician in the classic fantasy storytelling sense.

The request from editors Jack Dann and Gardner Dozois for a story for their 2007 *Wizards* (aka *Dark Alchemy*) anthology saw the idea spring to life again. What if we all have a bit of magic, something we lose as we grow older? What if there are others who know this, who plan for it?

As well as having lists of titles and character names close by, I also keep a list of opening lines handy in case they trigger something. Among them was the opening you see here, which seemed to fit the occasion perfectly. Then it was just a matter of playing time traveler again and re-visiting a play I'd written for PACT Theater back in the seventies with its central image of empty plinths and a solitary statue. Suddenly I was discovering a new reason for that mournful image.

The Lure of Legendary Ladies

Like a pick-of-the-market thrill?
Come with me to the top of the hill,
You're bound to have seen redder lights
But none that's shone so bright.

Let me introduce you to René
(Good evening, sir!)
Bonsoir, Madame, and who is with us today?
I have a friend who thinks they've all gone away
Can you set things right?

Down the hall is Helen of Troy,
Cleopatra's on the second floor,
The lady from Atlantis is in the back room.
The lure of legendary ladies.
The lure of legendary ladies.

And if the gentleman is so inclined,
We have a Gorgon that will blow your mind,
And Aphrodite will forever be sweet sixteen.
Or river views with naiads in the tide,
And there's a suite where our Valkyries ride,
Salome is still good at throwing down a mean veil or two.

Down the hall is Helen of Troy,
Cleopatra's on the second floor,
The lady from Atlantis is in the back room.
The lure of legendary ladies.
The lure of legendary ladies.

HE TRIED TO CATCH THE LIGHT

THERE WAS SUNMIRE CURLING on the rooftop across from the Center, the dazzle interfering with Ham's concentration and giving him the first signs of a headache.

"Almost ready," Bellinger said, gently, kindly as ever. He knew what these press conferences did to him.

Ham indicated the airy shimmer, immediately moved his hand back to shield his eyes. "Can we do something about that, Ross?"

Bellinger spoke into his coat-mike. "Polarize 21 and 22. Sorry, Ham. We thought we'd leave it clear for the media. Sunmire's more intriguing than ever since your last disclosures."

Ham nodded. *My* disclosures? Lydia found them. In him, yes, but they were hers.

The filters came on. He was still distracted by the patch of sunmire, but now it was easy to study the audience, searching for faces he knew while Bellinger and the techs made final arrangements for the pre-launch briefing.

The press-room was more crowded than he'd ever seen it. As well as the sixty or more media and departmental people allowed places, there were the large Vatican, Pan-Islamic and other religious contingents, and, surprisingly, a much larger turn-out of various world government delegates who had used diplomatic privilege to get inside.

Grouped together in the front rows, in clear view of everyone, were the veterans of previous missions, Public Relations' idea and still a good one after five years, despite the deaths, the missing faces, maintaining the program's useful, top-secret, quasi-military feel.

Ham counted survivors. Two of the Oneiros 3 crew were here, and in the very front row, Frank Sterman, captain of the Psychos 7 probe sat with mission co-ordinators Salt and Medda, conspicuous diplomacy, unmistakable, drawing the cameras. Lydia Parkes, lone survivor of the Imago 9 disaster, was seated strategically at the other end of their arc with the independent analysts, their hard-won support invaluable now with the funding cuts being reconsidered.

Her discoveries, yes. Drawn out of him, but hers. Of all the people he had let into his dreams to find God, she was the one he ultimately trusted, finally believed.

Movement among the platform party caught his attention, though Ham didn't have to look to know who that would be. Though Ross Bellinger led the program, it was suave, accomplished and highly telegenic Richard Salt who, as usual, moved forward to address the group. When Salt spoke, the ratings were always good, though using him had become an obvious tactic for many of those present, even the sympathetic ones.

"I'd like to welcome you all here again today on the eve of what promises to be a very exciting and crucial mission for the Donauer Project and possibly the whole world. Most of you are well acquainted with the general objectives for Oneiros 5, but in view of some recent—misunderstandings—I feel it might be useful to review those goals now." His gaze fell genially, ever so briefly, on certain parts of the room. "So we remain clear on what they are—and what they most definitely are not, nor have ever been."

Ham's own gaze wandered back to the windows. The sunmire concentration had been neutralized by the filters, but he knew it was still there, a fine, roiling knot of focused light. He had never made much of the things until two weeks ago; the phenomena had always been just what the media and science commentators had said: a particularly charming by-product of the "smart" building materials introduced into most of the world's cities after the 2026 Expo. The lifeblood of these self-cleaning, temperature adjusting, security aiding laminates was electromagnetic, and gave rise to the distinctive little clouds of refracting ionized vapor that, eight years later, were enjoying all this renewed attention.

Because of what Lydia had said.

It no longer seemed simple coincidence. Ham imagined the vanquished patch and considered her words at the end of the mission trance, cried out unthinking during the momentous Oneiros 4 extraction: "God is just a by-product of our perception of light." That term again. By-product.

There had been a careless desk tech, an audio glitch, something, but an accident, he was sure of it, not some deliberate "slip" to feed him provocative data. Lying there in the mission room, coming out of the trance himself, he had heard the words and they had amazed him. Lydia's voice. Those words.

"God is just a by-product of our perception of light."

Sunmire, rainbows and mist-bows, coronae, aurorae and crepuscular rays, sundogs and *gegenschein*, everything from mock-suns, mock-moons and mirages to glories, haloes and lofty *fata morganas* beckoning in the sky—all the countless anomalies of light and electromagnetism, the tricks of reflection and refraction that were no longer quite the same. A beam of white light passing through a prism had become profound again.

"First of all," Salt was saying as Ham drew back, "Hampton Donauer does not have stranded personalities wandering around inside him. The brave men and women whose identities were sent into the subject's dream-life and lost to us in the Imago 9, Eidolon 2, Psychos 7 and Oneiros 3 shut-downs are regrettably dead. They knew the chances; they volunteered—"

And why? Why did they keep volunteering, Ham wondered yet again, even as a voice called from the audience.

"The mind is a relatively closed system, Dr Salt!" It was Kilmer of NFD, predictably enough, as dogged and contentious as ever. "Why, just last week, Caltech's Professor Raglan admitted that those personality sets, those energies of self, those *people*, Dr Salt, *could* be inside Mr. Donauer somewhere, for all we know. Professor Raglan suggested that traces of vestigial imprinting—"

"Mr. Kilmer,"—Salt was smooth, so reasonable, seeming to lower his voice but actually leaning closer to the lectern mike and using that rather than his coat-mike to drown Kilmer out—"I'll be more than pleased to answer all reasonable questions presently, if you'll just be patient." The emphasis fell so gently on the fourth last word. "The main point of this pre-launch today is to make sure that we are not sidetracked from the real purpose of the Donauer Project, which, I need not remind any sufficiently informed person, is made up completely of legally authorized volunteers well-acquainted with the risks involved."

Mantovani in the headphones, Ham decided there in his place at the long table on the dais. Any moment now. He always accepted the need, but this time Lydia's overheard remark from the Oneiros 4 aftermath—and the sunmire on the roof across from the Center, the coincidence of that now—would make it something else, a violation, a hated intrusion.

Salt continued, turning the subject away from the lost missions back to the present objectives, which had to include what Lydia had said, whatever it was she had added after that momentous line.

Sure enough, music came. Not Mantovani, of course, but Vivaldi, the tiny subcutaneous implants just behind his ears switching in, Ham keenly aware as always that Project staff and accredited independents would be monitoring that fact scrupulously, aware too how this was part of the vital price, sitting there partly occluded and they all knew. The audience got to see him watching the sunmire, musing, reflecting. They couldn't have planned it better.

Patient, charming Richard Salt would be reminding them yet again of the purpose behind the mind-missions. Repeating, reiterating as they always had to, because people *did* forget the details. How twenty-four years ago, Ham's father, the late, eccentric and gifted Henry Donauer, had shut his infant son off from all information about the world's belief systems, all input about formalized religion. How he had allowed full socialization to occur through controlled tutorials and carefully screened peer groups and media broadcasts, but always with that one key element missing: no conversation, no books, no reference to organised metaphysics. It was Jean Jacque Rousseau's "Noble Savage" idea expressed in a crucially modified form, but instead of the child being raised outside society altogether, it was just one single vital omission from the societal dataflow. To find out what humans knew of such things *a priori*.

Ham knew this now because the experiment had always been implicitly one of diminishing returns. He still had no formal knowledge of the different cultural belief systems that governed so many lives and governments, so many communities on the planet, but he knew what the experiment was in these final stages.

He'd loved his father. At age 11, when a highly respected if self-serving observer, Camille Jaels, had finally leaked details of the Donauer Project to a European scientific journal, she had paradoxically helped guarantee the Project's survival beyond Henry Donauer's untimely death from pneumonia in 2021. Ham had consented to the ongoing controlled deprivation. Sociologically, historically, parents the world over controlled their offsprings' received cultural knowledge whenever they could, biased learning outcomes, the ways subjective reality was in fact made. At the very least, Henry Donauer was doing no more, no less. Yet from another viewpoint, a wholly scientific viewpoint, he was doing so much more.

And Henry Donauer had always been amazingly frank.

"I want to see what you believe, Ham, naturally and intuitively," he had said. "What your dreams show, what universals are passed on through the genes, through any form of a collective unconscious. Are particular neurotransmitters predisposed? Are such dedicated functions possible, vested applications such as the pleasure chemical, dopamine, gives? Are there such things as adulant biasing as Gina Colfax suggests? Or is it just a phosphene spill, susceptible minds responding to entoptic residue?"

And often when Ham asked, "But just what do you mean, what do I believe?", his father would leave it to one of his trusted assistants, one of the three R's: Ross, Richard or Ruth Medda, to take him through it oh so carefully, to explain how he was doing humanity a service, that he was a "pure soul" operating without details of one of the key conditionings.

Though Ham had read necessarily edited texts on the nature of social history, how cultural "norms" led to everything from traditions of boys being raised differently from girls, what caste and legal rights were available, how property was disposed of and so on, he'd accepted it. Still accepted it.

Kilmer was on his feet again, Ham saw, the tall sneering man pointing at him and shouting something. Ham immediately averted his gaze, making no attempt to read the famous science journalist's lips. He was used to fighting the curiosity, again his choice. Instead, he turned his attention back to the sunmire, trying to judge its intensity with the filters on, wondering how long it would last. The trick of light had none of its earlier impact; perhaps it would soon dissipate altogether.

The Vivaldi soothed him but he was aware that he was frowning. He caught himself at it, wondered why he had been. He let his thoughts go back to the Oneiros 4 extraction. The overheard words. The iconauts in the staging chamber, one moment in their imposed trances, tracking his own so-called adulant neurotransmissions, scouring his hippocampus, riding, searching, finding, then emerging, and Lydia's voice full of excitement, saying those words. That word.

God.

Their word, not his. Never his. A person. A place. A state. He had had no such word. Not consciously before they'd given it to him afterwards. A name for a goal, a context, a setting. Lost knowledge. But they had something. She did. Had come back with it, all of them so excited. Before the gentle music came. Mantovani in the headphones.

It had caused a furore among the independent observers, an outcry scotched by Henry Donauer's prerecorded stipulation that such a name should be given to him at age 25, a mere two months away. Fate had simply played a hand.

Now, in the world beyond Vivaldi, Richard Salt was doing his careful best. Ham knew many of the standard rebuttals, the speech plans Richard would be following, sampling, blending. Ham had also listened to plenty of Kilmer/Davidson/NFD edits; he could pretty well model what the man would be saying. Such a dangerous man, Sol Kilmer, a media luminary with his own top-rating, widely syndicated net program, *Living Science*, the sort of man who too often seemed at odds with his own vocation, who rather seemed bent on seeing how people jumped, just to make something happen. But Richard would deal with it. Ham watched the sunmire and thought of Lydia and something, a place, a person, a thing, called God.

"WE DO NOTHING MORE than place observing viewpoints into Hampton Donauer's sleeping mind," Richard Salt said. "Coherent, cognizant, slaved viewpoints to share his dreams. The Donauer Glove lets those personalities, all trained eidetics, monitor the iconography of that REM sleep, bring back the precise patterns. We then assemble them with meticulous care as both a literal image array and a symbol system. The imaging room here at the Center has—thanks to the generosity of so many of you present here today—become the best in modern clinical psychology. We lose very little."

"People are dying, Doctor Salt," someone called, not Kilmer this time, probably his crony at NFD, Davidson.

"Volunteers are taking acceptable and freely chosen risks," Salt answered. "As you all know, sometimes the dream force is intense, very powerful. There are nightmares, trauma dreams—"

"Remmers!" Kilmer cried, and others did, NFD plants most likely.

Salt let it pass. "Externally, we have to judge when heightened brainwave activity indicates crisis as opposed to maximum image flow of exactly the kind we need, and sometimes we are wrong. We do not read minds; we read images and track image runs. Simply observe and report. Sometimes our observers are too deeply engaged and sometimes they are lost—"

"Lost, you say! In a relatively closed system, Doctor Salt!" It was Davidson again, probably trying to set off the *yaddist* extremists. It made great viewing when a glowering fundamentalist or even an indignant monsignor were caught reacting. And, yes, so obviously planned. Kilmer, the champion of science as "everyone's entitlement, everyone's proper entertainment," couldn't afford to say some things, so he had others do it for him. "They're sure to impinge on the dreaming consciousness. I hate to say it, but any god-pictures you get could well be eroding personalities as they die."

There, it was said. Ridiculously wrongheaded and naive, yet tabloid headlines for the next month. His mistake for using the word "lost." Salt could only continue.

"Here's where I tell you two things—Mr. Davidson, is it? Firstly, contrary to Professor Raglan's colorful theories, we have not 'lost' any of our observers *inside* Hampton Donauer, regardless of how much that notion seems to take your fancy. This has been well documented by independent observers, including members of ACAC and FEDEP. Do feel free to interview them again, if you feel you need to verify your facts. It's on the way out of the Donauer Trance that there is danger, in that stage of the extraction process requiring the participation of the iconauts themselves. In a sense, they bring themselves out, via a careful system of neural phase-downs, reintroducing their own wills. It is then, if they are traumatized and distracted by neural surges—"

"Nightmares!"

Kilmer? Davidson? Salt dared not stop.

"—and adulant residues, that they fail to complete this process. There is something we call attenuation; there is sometimes the equivalent of a major stroke. It is a simple problem right there at the body-mind interface, where chemicals become consciousness. It is quite possibly insurmountable."

Kilmer would never buy it, Salt knew, because he couldn't use it. The idea of "remmers" had caught the popular imagination: helpless mind-sailors pursued and hunted by nightmares as marauding "free radicals," or, as one old revamped phrase had it, by "monsters from the id." Great copy.

Ironically, it had done harm at the moment of greatest public attention. Certainly the public sponsors were worrying, the Vatican, the Eden League, Gaia Spec, the various Islamic nations, the rest, all the countless, global, corporate "medicis" trying for some sort of positive PR flow-on. The mostly anonymous secret sponsors, well, who knew what they thought?

"Secondly?" someone demanded. And not Davidson this time, not Kilmer. Geridh, the Libyan diplomat.

"Why don't we let Lydia Parkes tell us that," Doctor Salt said. "Someone who's actually been there. Lydia?"

And on cue the short, compact iconaut approached the lectern, her collar mike engaged. She gripped the lectern's sides and gave her wonderful smile.

HAM WATCHED THE SHORT blonde woman move to the front of the stage and step up to the lectern. She looked so different in her dark blue cutaway suit, so different from when she wore her mission fatigues. Her long plain face was the sort that made you think "dependable" and never frightened people off, yet had a full intelligent gaze that made many more people than Ham use the really quite inappropriate yet compelling analogy that her eyes were filled with light. They weren't, of course, in any quantitative sense, but they carried a force, a vitality and charisma that was carried down into her smile and often made people grab at that allusion before any other.

All so fitting now. You noticed Lydia Parkes when she smiled because it changed her face. Then you saw the eyes and it changed something else. It bemused men. That truly rare thing, it charmed and eluded women rather than threatened them. It broke categories and strategies. What her smile did to her eyes was inexpressible.

She began speaking, and Ham had to make himself look away. It wasn't anything as simple as being in love with her. Lydia Parkes had nearly died because of him once, *in* him if you listened to the likes of Raglan, Kilmer, NFD and CIRODEC, overwhelmed with the rest of the Imago 9 crew. Only she had been revived this side of brain-death, drawn out of heartstop, kept from flatline, barely in time. When she'd regained consciousness, she had immediately volunteered for the Oneiros 4 probe and this latest Oneiros 5 follow-up, not really a veteran iconaut given active hours in the Donauer Trance, but treated as one by those who were.

She *knew* him, he liked to believe.

Someone knew him.

Dependable and a survivor. Full of light and life. He had liked her when he first saw her, even before she smiled. He loved her when she did. Had fallen in love with her when he looked above the smile to her eyes again, saw the knowing of him, the caring, the simple caring. Now the whole quest reminded him of her. The muted sunmire did. He wanted to watch her speak, read her body, her set of self, see how she mouthed careful, confident words against the surging strains of Vivaldi, but he looked back at where the sunmire coiled about what was left of itself. While he wouldn't understand all the words she said, he knew what the first ten would be.

"GOD IS JUST A by-product of our perception of light," Lydia Parkes said. "That's what I remember apprehending—*knowing*—in an evolved sequence-tree probably thirteen minutes into full REM phase. Excuse the jargon, ladies and gentlemen. It's how we try to identify locales and orient POV under trance. If one of us fails to do that then we're one observer down. It's probably the second hardest thing we have to do: remember to be ourselves in there. The hardest, as you already know, is coming back out again. On this insertion, there was a hallway and staircase from the Donauer Clinic as Stage One, a field of standing-stones from Dorset segueing into Easter Island, a group of birds-into-druids all branching into multiples then. A cloister on a shoreline. A forest lawn with spindles of light. All reinforced motifs, all transformation segues of a very high order. Completely unexpected. The frame POV, Ham's master template for us, was affirming a role for light. Obviously we associated as we always do— allowable reification under the circumstances—posited God of Light, Lord of Light, Let there be Light, but I grabbed it as the *key* determining element of our god-perception. I templated that idea in-trance so I had referents, then jettisoned the lot as we're trained to do. I sought confirmation and found it. Ben and Marjory affirmed and confirmed. Excuse the terms, please. It's how we experience it, as affirmations and confirmations inside our heads inside Hampton Donauer's head. Sometimes we can talk to one another in-trance. We don't know how that works exactly so we don't expect it. Ben and Marjory saw what I did and confirmed. We knew we had locked onto something with an A-1 flag, the highest rating we can give.

"These are Big Dreams, ladies and gentlemen, just as our reports show, just as Dr. Jung correctly named them all those years ago. Everyone of us has them: the key dreams that recur over months, years, lifetimes and are traditionally regarded as prophetic and highly significant for the dreaming individual. Not just the usual syntheses of daily minutiae, not just the result of associative data saturation. We have never been sure of riding a Big Dream before. These are allegedly the psyche's own messages to itself, after all, to the evolving individual or carrier it is. Not fashionable believing that these days, but never disproved.

"Allowing these Big or Key Dreams and recognizing them has always been the problem. There is so much random and associative iconography, so many hundreds and thousands of image referents available, segues, associants, value-sets to evaluate in terms of the individual. Because we can control something of Hampton Donauer's environment—the day to day information horizon available to him, people he meets and so on—we can often identify the associational material surprisingly well; understandable since much of it is our own daily experience also. Inside him there is a dream, mostly circumstantial, incidental material, mostly just a light-show or the psyche carrying out housecleaning duties. We do what nanotech cannot yet do reliably. Nano probes may glean image ghosts but never the *felt* experience, the recognition associated with them. Sometimes we *know* it's essential data we're seeing because the themes are so powerful and so apparently original. So numinous. That's a vital word for what we get. Just data-streams, then exaltation. Recognition *and* rapture suddenly there. We *sense* the dream as being of enormous numinous significance. Allow that the psyche *does* know when it is being replenished, even if we ourselves as conscious individuals do not. Self, not ego, despite the bigotry and narrow-mindedness, the inherent envy of the ego."

She did not give Kilmer, Davidson or even Geridh time to respond to the slight.

"Deprived of god-lore, many of Hampton Donauer's Big Dreams could well have shown such wonderfully promising image arrays. In comparative terms, it's like the Jungian case of the little girl who presented her father with a notebook containing accounts of dreams she'd had, filled with all sorts of symbolic elements she *couldn't* have lived. We allow that there are such dreams. It is faith in a sense, supported by the most dramatic wave-surges in the brain. Something *is* there, more than just images, and we're trying to find out what that is."

It was as if no-one dared speak. Lydia left a four-beat of silence, then continued.

"Let me clarify something. We have already *proven* we are not inside Hampton Donauer as people. We have repeatedly *demonstrated* that we have access to the man's *revemonde*, nothing more. We've never claimed more. Our opticals are slaved to his, that is all. Henry Donauer very wisely published the technical specifics of the Donauer Glove immediately after Camille Jaels made her unofficial disclosures. Medical experts have confirmed that the deaths resulted from a curious and recurring anomaly we call trauma separation, a massive, regenerative release of neurotransmitters that has the same effect as a major stroke. These are volunteers and it's regrettable but, in a sense, *you* have pushed us to it. Even more regrettably, we have let you. We've published all the specifics on this again and again, furnished you all with technicals verified by your own sanctioned observers and investigative bodies and the accredited independents. I want to know why some of you persist in asking such uninformed questions in the first place."

She read the murmurs rippling through the crowd. "Look at you! Look at this turn-out today. Many of you openly ridicule us yet gather like this even for a pre-launch. You fund us yet challenge the very clearly established terms of our search, even list human rights abuses. You wilfully misrepresent the facts. You have scorned and challenged this program every step of the way. Consider yourselves for a change! Ask yourselves why."

It was a terrible, wonderful moment, a silence of steel and glass, coral-sharp, coral-fragile with danger.

She had called them selfish, deluded, ignorant. Vatican delegates. Top-level Islamic mullahs. Diplomats, career politicians and mercenary scientists.

She must have calculated every second that silence could stand, because she was there again.

"The funding has been invaluable. It's let the Donauer Institute and the Donauer Project perfect variants on its hardware, all the different approaches we have tried. Those mission names aren't just window-dressing *as you will already know*. The names are different and so highly numbered because they represent entirely different access and insertion methods. You will have *seen* the data." She was merciless now. "Again, why are you continuing to ask these questions? You have not bought us. We would have proceeded without any of you."

It was still so dangerous. In this room were implicit pogroms, jihads and censure, the capacity for disinformation and reprisal, yet it was all on hold, everyone waiting, allowing.

"And if you think Oneiros 4 gave us something, just wait till you see what Oneiros 5 intends to do. We cannot declare too much at this point; that would be prejudicing the observers. Just remember please that what we stand to find usually has very little to do with memory. This is the unknown appearing *amidst* the known. Something new amongst the memories, not just registering as imaginings but as recognitions. We can identify those moments. Even allowing for anomalies of perception and recognition—déjà-vu, jamais-vu, presque-vu—we have discrete and distinctive EEG signatures for these moments of *rapture* and conviction."

Then someone did interrupt. Not Kilmer or Davidson this time. It was Geridh, fiercely conservative, inflammatory. "But ultimately we still only have your word for it, don't we, Ms. Parkes? You could have been misleading us all along, feeding Mr. Donauer requisite data, fabricating the alleged discoveries."

"Then why are you here, Mr. Geridh?" she asked, then forestalled any reply by raising a hand. "But why not let me answer that, since you're certainly not alone in your misgivings. Like most of us, you're judging the moment. You don't want to miss out on such a vital thing, but it has to be the *real* thing, and you are correct in rigorously challenging what we do because of that. So let me tell you just a bit more about Oneiros 5 and its objectives.

"In our last mission we discovered likely causations for a God-perception in response to light. Having monitored a Big Dream at last, we now mean to approach it from the opposite position, to stimulate Ham's optic nerves and vision centers while he is in REM sleep. He does not know we will be doing this."

For a moment, hundreds of people watched Ham watching the sunmire, a calm handsome young man, as serene-looking now as a Christ or a Bodhisattva.

Lydia continued. "We have devised and field-tested a means to do this. While allowing that at one extreme it could be no more than the phosphene display behind a human's closed eyelids predisposing us to recurring symbols such as mandalas and cruciforms, stars and all-seeing eyes, and at the other the existence of adulant neurotransmitters, a specialized visual predisposition in the cortex, we now mean to send light signals into the relevant areas of Hampton Donauer's brain, then track the resulting image runs. Yes, ladies and gentlemen, this time we will attempt to induce such a theophanic experience. Not just a Big Dream. We hope to trigger God."

At some level or other, everyone hated hearing it. There was shouting. Hands were up. People were standing, calling, clamoring.

Ham looked round at the commotion, then turned his attention back to the windows, forced it there.

"Shall I tell you more?" Lydia said, and kept saying it like a mantra until the large gathering settled again. "If we did *not* attempt this, we would *not* be fairly testing our previous observations. You should expect this as the next step; you should insist on it. We personally—the iconauts—do not need to do this. We have been *in* the dream. We have stood in what reads as the light of sublime ideation; we have lived the moment as profoundly as anyone who has ever experienced epiphany and theophany. We probably have enough data already. But seeing if we can trigger the response is a crucial and appropriate final step, not a redundancy. At least we know you will all be here for the next press conference seventy-two hours from now." And she smiled, marvelously, beatifically, wickedly.

There was such danger. People were muttering. There were one or two cries in various languages, no doubt the usual accusations of blasphemy.

Then Kilmer stood, his hand raised as well, uncommon civility, and the audience let him be their voice.

"Mr. Kilmer?" Lydia said, ready for him.

"What is in it for you personally, Ms. Parkes? You have, well, experienced God, you say, what passes for God—you imply—in the faith convictions of millions. What is in this for you?"

Lydia could have deflected it so easily, but she decided to answer. Her smile changed, mirrored Kilmer's, became sharing and gentle. "The ancient Greeks were at a similar point to the one we're at now. They were maintaining a vigorously rational society, were mistrustful or disbelieving of their countless flawed and brawling gods and goddesses. The best thinkers, the greatest, truly greatest citizens and states*men*—

men, regrettably, the women didn't leave such a written legacy of what they thought—then knew to pursue excellence, *aristos*, the life of reason but as the work of art too. They sought *aristos*."

"I did say personally, Ms. Parkes," Kilmer said. "Personally."

"We do not have that mindset, Mr. Kilmer, just as we do not have the mindset of the Elizabethans or even those who lived during the World Wars. But I believe this: the age of reason is done with too. We need more. Societies regulated by reason alone, just like those regulated by their once so useful founding religions, will fail as surely as those founded on our gods and goddesses. We need more now. *I* need more now. That's what's in it for me personally. Excellence. Quality. Calling out the Eternal Yes, Mr. Kilmer, is not a thing of reason. It is an exultation in the act of living. But is it just an atavistic thing, a throwback to some old triumph over adversary and adversity? Reason can try to explain it but it cannot do so without first reducing it, stripping it of its psychoactive power, its intrinsic reality. As with any epiphany or conviction or hope or inspiration, the inherent motivating, phenomenological force is lost."

"I'm not sure what you mean by Eternal Yes, Ms. Parkes."

"Exactly." Her smile became both exquisite indulgence and the gentlest of knives. "So come along with us on Oneiros 5."

"You're not serious."

"You would quite likely see what we see at the very least."

"I'm not sure I'd trust you weren't feeding me false data."

"Ah, but the others would. The independent observers."

Kilmer saw the trap being set, the loss of control in this assembly. More to the point, his studio heads and viewers were. "What would I gain? Scientifically?"

"Why, perhaps a first-hand experience of God!"

"What, a moment of rapture? An Eternal Yes or two?" He was trying to disparage it. Regain control. "I think I'll pass."

"Then remember you were asked." The trap was closed. He was excluded now. She left him no time to comment. "And now Frank Sterman will recount his experiences with similar light templates in his Psychos 5, 6 and 7 insertions."

THEY WALKED ON THE beach afterwards, Lydia and Ham, avoiding talk of the next morning's Oneiros insertion at first, just meeting the afternoon in all its vital parts, wavefall, windflow, the warming glow of autumn sun. They walked between the security baffles, the outflung walls of one-way shieldglass, watching everything, pointing and remarking, until Ham did mention the press conference, meaning to use it to get rid of the subject, to highlight how people missed moments like this in the rush for greater meaning. It didn't work.

Ham knew Lydia's mike was on, that Salt or Medda would routinely run the conversations then or later, but he had lived with that all his conscious days.

They walked in the glorious sunlight, enjoying the on-shore breeze, held by an intimacy of the most unusual sort. She knew something of his appetites, his hidden drives and desires, what his shadow self did. She had walked his dream-fields, endured his image runs, suspected causations.

Ham felt easy enough considering, though some of the apartment towers were patched with sunmire. He saw them flaring off cornices and balconies, hazing the outlines. They kept the mission more alive than he wanted right then.

"Richard says we won't need many more insertions. He thinks we've got as much as we'll get."

Lydia accepted the inevitability of the apartment towers too, how the lightforms starpointed the ten-story Donauer Center and the adjacent Trade Center.

"Most of it will be for the sponsors after this," she said. "Confirmation runs until they're all happy."

"Then we close it down." He sounded like a child in his simplicity. He could afford to be that.

"What is it, Ham?"

"I worry. I see the empty chairs for Luke, Isabelle and the others, and I want it over, yes. I just wonder what the others need."

"Is it to do with me?" She had always been direct.

"You nearly died. I don't want you in there again and yet I do. I like it and I don't." And he wondered how many secrets she still had to keep. They said they weren't holding back much now, but what else could there be?

About this God. Godding. Godded. Godness. Goddess. Godless. Godlessness. Godling. Goading. Guarding.

He ran the word till it became meaningless again.

"Lydia, the program doesn't warrant this much attention. Media, yes, but those were senior officials there today, political people. It's out of proportion."

"I know. For some I'm sure it's totally, politically opportunistic in that sense, electorates demanding representation—"

"But I sensed it from the True Science and World Science groups too. Supposedly non-partisan. They get our stuff, all the data releases. You think they'd stay right out of it, especially with the media and political circus like it is. First they didn't want to be seen to be accrediting us too much, now they're so visible. It doesn't make sense."

"We haven't looked any gift horses in the mouth, Ham. Maybe it's just the phenomenon itself. Why this phenomenon now, why the attention? Why the patch of sunmire outside the windows today?"

"Lots of buildings have them."

"But in sociological, philosophical, theological terms this has to seem like an Event. We can hardly blame them. How many people throughout history have failed to monitor the key events of their age *as* they were happening? We showed you the cover for next month's *True Scientist*. *Light Said Let There Be God!* I wish I could tell you what *Better Science* and *International Science* have as their cover stories, but I can't."

"We should stop."

"We talked about that after the meeting today. Ross and Richard think we've missed our chance."

"I don't follow."

"They wouldn't let us."

"Officially."

"Legally. Everything. They'd pass rulings through WHO, the lot. Appropriate it all. It's gotten too big. Shouldn't have. Should never have, and what does that tell us? And even if we could shut it down, end it, everything, they wouldn't believe us for a minute. They'd say we'd gone into some new closed-door phase. Inner circle. You think it's out of control now! They'd go crazy."

"What do we do?"

"That's up to you as always. But I'd say continue. Phase it down and give more press conferences, more public appearances. Show them it's diminishing returns. Show them there are no new disclosures, just confirmations. Like the NASA Apollo missions last century. The public will lose interest. Suggest human rights angles to the right people so they lobby for your total acclimation."

"Will it work?"

"Our experts think so. You'd be free of it."

"It's hard to imagine it, Lydia. Things happening for so long in response terms I just can't track. Whatever this God is must be very important. It's so—disproportionate."

"For a long time it gave meaning." She had to be so careful. "Now we want more."

"We make our own meaning," Ham said. "But we *need* more." He looked out to sea, saw the autumn sunlight glinting off the waves. "We need the meaning to come from somewhere else."

It was the sort of astute-facile comment that kept astonishing the Project team.

Lydia didn't hesitate. "Exactly. And that's natural. We're predisposed to wanting that. That's why he did it, Ham."

"Henry?"

"Right."

"We need closure on this, don't we? Soon. It's too volatile."

"Yes."

"God has to be a source. A destination. A maker. A state and a vessel. But an object of yearning."

"Oh?"

"A power base too, but an answer to meaningless."

"I'm hearing you." She was referring to her audio link. "We all are."

"So why do we continue?"

"Confirmation. A bit of hope. Knowing. The nature of the age lets us do it."

"No other age would have?"

She was careful. So careful. "Probably not. Not publicly at least." She took his hand as they walked. "Are you worried?"

"No," he lied, because there was a mission tomorrow, so much to do. "Are you?"

"No," she lied as well and squeezed his hand to show that lying was a good thing when faced with so much truth.

THE MISSION INSERTION WENT according to plan. By 0530 the next morning, Ham lay deeply asleep at the "thumb" of the Glove, the "stem" of the flower, with five iconauts in their sleeves, heads radially aligned to his so from above he was a splendid sight, an El Dorado with a radiant crown of living dreamers—or, rather, non-dreamers, literally "entranced" fellow dreamers. It was a powerful image, and over time had supplanted the Project's original logo, so now there was just the single vertical line with five others radiating from it, a "dreamer's cross", as the media first had it, a "frightened mop", as Davidson had quipped on *Discovery*, a "spider doing a handstand", as Kilmer had called it on *Living Science.*

Fourteen minutes after initiation, the interfacing began, and five POVs were gradually slaved to the one, as close to functional telepathy as humanity had ever gotten. At twenty-three minutes, readings showed distinctive, coterminous synchrony, the deeply affecting sight of the variant EEGs on the six monitors, formerly dancing apart, now drawing closer, becoming virtually one, never completely overlapping, of course, but braided on the master screen as a coherent cable of dedicated mentation. That too was a media image known worldwide, as famous in its own way as the DNA helix or physician's caduceus it resembled. Ham was leading them. Oneiros 5 was underway.

They were at forty-six minutes when Lydia Parkes died in him.

One moment there was the quiet of the staging room, the low lighting, the barely audible hum of engaged tech. Then there were sudden detonations, corridor alarms, voices shouting, doors bursting in, the startling flash of nocto weapons.

Thirteen minutes earlier, Ham's sleeve would have been hit, but one of the dozen modifications to the Oneiros series had been to rotate the Glove platform yet again for aura exclusion, and ascernium baffles separated Ham from the other sleeves.

The raiders had the old Imago series data and couldn't know what they were seeing. Chris, Ram and Kaori died outright in a nocto sweep: immediate flatline in the ops room. James succumbed to a ballistic strike to the side of the skull. Lydia's sleeve was angled away, Ham's concealed altogether. Coincidence. Lucky coincidence.

An explosion on the roof told the three raiders that the Clinic's Quick-Save forces had destroyed their VTO. They went for contingency. But even as one reached to trigger the Landfall pack that would take out the Center and half the city block, a Quick-Save omni fired from the door and severed head, arm and shoulder. His companions died the same way.

Ham was safe, but Lydia died in extraction. Maybe if the op techs hadn't been distracted, in fear of their lives, they might have reached her in time. There were 3.8 seconds where she was in extremis from the trauma of massive systems damage before the tertiary systems read the secondaries also down and engaged. She died in the dark of his dreaming, alone and unknowing.

THEY ANSWERED MOST OF Ham's questions in the infirmary two hours later, then, when he was out of sedation the following day, finally invited him to the briefing room for the emergency session. There were seven of them—Lydia so noticeably missing.

"Who was it?" Ham could now ask.

Ross Bellinger answered. "Riyadh says the Vatican as usual. The Vatican says Pan-Islamic *yaddists*. The League claims a new San Diego-based Christian fundamentalist group. The UN and the Gaiasts say—"

"Okay." Ham cut him off with uncommon brusqueness. They would never know. And Lydia wasn't there. Would never be there again. He wasn't sure what he felt.

Ross leant forward, clasped his hands on the tabletop. "Ham, there's another thing."

But Ham had already grasped it. "They could have taken out the complex with a distance strike. Used remotes. They wanted me."

"Seems like it, yes. Someone wants to continue the tests under their own control."

"What do we do?" *Lydia wasn't there.*

Richard Salt answered this time. "Close down the Program. Tell no-one initially. Do it so no-one outside this room knows till you've gone."

"Zimbabwe," Ham said, angry and afraid, but making the old joke, needing it, something. During the early years, the intriguing, peaceful, easy years, a common answer to crisis was to joke about running off to Zimbabwe rather than facing whatever it was.

He said it, they smiled; Ross Bellinger passed him a smart card.

"Quick-Save airvac at 1450. You're off to Zurich and a safe-house." Ham went to speak but Ross cut him off. "Before and during the flight, from when we're done here, you get everything on the religions. The lot. We give you dogmas and pantheons, Ham, everything from jinnis and jihads to transubstantiation. And we're letting the agencies know an hour after you've gone: Mossad, Sintio, Crydin, every other top-line interest group there is. Oneiros 5 was it. No more missions."

"Salting the well," Ham said, another Lydia line. He *was* keeping her alive in him. As him. "Spiking the guns." Mixing her metaphors. *Lydia.*

"Right," Ross said. "So 1450. Before then, you use that comp over there. Call up *Godgame.*"

"No." *She wasn't there. The referent in so many equations.*

"What's that?"

"Not yet, Ross. Tell them I've been briefed, neutralized, but no. Not yet."

"She's gone, Ham. She isn't…" He paused, didn't say *inside you.*

"I don't want to know yet!" he cried, ambiguously. "Don't you understand? You're all so good at wanting, seeking, finding and giving answers that you've forgotten what *not* knowing does. The advantage of not knowing!"

They all waited, sensing a vehemence beyond grief, a clarity beyond the chaos of the last two days.

"We aren't only governed by logic," he said. "Don't you see that? We're governed by our perceptions, needs, passions, by our very humanism, by our *bias*, don't you see? Our biasing of objective fact. Our need to. Our splendid triumph in doing so. Humanity isn't just logic. Every public gathering has shown me that, every history book, every scientist I've watched or met. Humanity is also intuition, gestalt knowing, conviction. We are evolved to operate *beyond reason!* To *require* more than reason can provide. Our rationalists have always missed it. We operate *beyond.* That's our ultimate specialization. Whether as inner truth or placebo, as self-delusion or fervent belief, that's our ultimate survival mechanism: knowing when to set reason aside for *irrational* self-nurturing gains. Our enemy isn't a nervous, manipulative Vatican or bigoted *yaddist* sects or wacky New Agers, whatever *Godgame* will confirm those things as! They're just naturally, desperately, dangerously, even gloriously compensating for the rationalists who also fail to read what human is, who give clear objective truth but in their reductive, contemptuous, misperceiving way, fail to see the balance as well."

There was silence. They let him have it, as much attentive, caring, accepting silence as he needed, the silence, too, of tacit agreement. They knew he had had enough training in sociology to have deduced formal belief systems, the simple self-nurturing and self-deceiving need for something more.

"These are your discoveries, Ham?" Ross Bellinger said. The question was a formality for the audiovee record.

Ham nodded, remembered why Ross had actually asked it and said, "Yes. It's where our humanizing values come from. Also a cause for harm. Reason alone makes a poor bedfellow for the human spirit. It disallows the human spirit. There can be no such thing."

Again Ross Bellinger improvised. "Then we proceed to make it known that you have been exposed to *Godgame*. Even give you some salient key words. Is that okay?"

Ham hesitated. A vital integer was missing. "So long as you understand why I'm doing this now. And why not let me give you some of your key words, Ross? Communion. Benediction. Atonement. Sacrifice. Love. Charity. Forgiveness. How am I doing?"

Ross smiled, loving the young man, this known yet always unexpected cornerstone of his own life. "You're doing very well. And you have to keep reminding us, just like this, okay? That the words come first."

"But in the beginning there aren't just the words," Ham said, believing it with all his heart. "There are the feelings, the understandings, the perceptions, convictions and recognitions. Then the names." And he sought again for words which encompassed all he had lost. There was only one.

HE WAS ON THE roof-field at 1440, wearing maintenance coveralls and cap, carrying a duffel, playing the role of a solitary tech being airlifted back to Aluen. He stood in the cool afternoon wind that lifted over the low parapet from the ocean and watched a patch of sunmire hanging on a corner of the adjacent Trade Center, a hot kernel in the bright sunlight, as detached and unfeeling as a rainbow.

At 1450 exactly, a Rogan *shaukraft* appeared over Clinic's western side, settled in a flurry of air. The long side door opened; a crewman beckoned. Ham ducked, clutched his bag and ran, but instead of climbing aboard, he remained standing at the door.

"Get in, sir," the crew tech said.

"Who are you with?" Ham asked.

The tech seemed not to hear. "Please, sir. We're on a time. Please get in."

"I just want to know who you're with." It was suddenly important.

"Quick-Save Airvac," the man said. "Name's Jell."

A second crew-tech appeared at the door. "Hey, we're on a time, Jell," she said. "Mr. Donauer, please get in, sir."

"I don't want you to have Lydia."

"What? What's that, sir?" she asked.

The first tech reached for him, but Ham stepped back, eluding his grasp.

Figures had appeared at the door onto the roof-field, wondering what was amiss. Ross or Richard, Ham couldn't tell.

"I said I don't want you to have Lydia."

And he saw that they understood, feigned incomprehension a second after, yes, then abandoned it when they saw he knew.

The first tech reached for him again. "You're safe with us, sir. We're scientists too."

But by then Ham was running, not to his friends. Diminishing returns there anyway, they'd said.

He ran away from the *shaukraft* and the roof building, the Quick-Save imposters running behind but too late, way too late.

We make our own meaning! At the very least. Eternally yes.

There was sunmire ahead, beckoning, blazing, as meaningless and inscrutable as a rainbow, but all there was, and right then everything there was. He had her with him. He ran. He jumped. He tried to catch the light.

Afterword to "He Tried to Catch the Light"

COMMUTERS EXITING AN English railway station across a particular pedestrian footbridge find themselves inevitably walking in step, causing the bridge to resonate to such a critical extent that the structure is in danger of collapsing. People attending a major evangelical rally in the US have their temporal lobes fire differently because of the sheer numbers in attendance, bringing about a shared state of rapture bordering on delirium. Hard-wired herd behavior or something more? We do not know. We still know so little about how the human mind works.

"He Tried to Catch the Light" began with a title and the idea of extending Jean-Jacques Rousseau's suggestion in *Émile* of raising a boy away from the city and its influences to bring out the qualities of natural grace and reason, creating a situation in which the boy became, in effect, the "Noble Savage" of popular lore: rational, balanced, morally superior.

What would happen, what would we learn, I wondered, if such a child was raised with no knowledge of the world's major belief systems? Where would his natural inclinations take him? As with so many science fiction stories, the question What if? brought its own momentum.

I held off finishing the story because I kept resisting the ending, but finally saw what it needed to be for Ham rather than for me. Another lesson re-learned. The truth is always somewhere else.

Bermudas

It's not enough to sit before the fire,
Hear the rain and watch her softly smile.
Point a hand to ships in bottles,
Lost at sea on dusty mantels,
And hope that it will satisfy a while.

It's not enough to have a good beginning
With little else to follow on,
So I ask that we might gather
All our sorrows fit to travel,
They will be the ones we bring along.

To where the orange trees are burning fragrant for us,
To where the birds are the gods of Mexico.
To where the whole world's winds and waters
Fall to form a garden for us,
The songs of our Bermudas make us go.

I can see them shining in the sun,
Sky above and sea below.
Thoughts can cast me king and captain
Lost in love upon a mountain,
The songs of our Bermudas let us know.

FLASHMEN

SAM WAS SITTING OVER a pot of Boag's and a Number 9 at the New Automatic on the banks of the Yarra, watching the old riverside fire sculptures—the "pigeon toasters"—sending gouts of flame into the night sky.

That was how Walt Senny and Sunny Jim found him, staring out at the sheets of plasma tearing the dark. Dangerous and wonderful friends to have, Walt and Sunny, and a dangerous and wonderful place to be, given what Melbourne had become—been forced to become. All the coastal axis cities.

"Sam," Walt Senny said, just like in the old days, as if grudging the word. He wore his long flashman coat, a genuine Singer flare, and had little hooks of color on his cheeks. They were called *divas* after famous women singers and each one was a death. Knowing Walt, each one was a ten-count.

Sam returned the greeting. "Walt."

"Sam," Sunny Jim said, looking splendid as usual in his dapper Rockfall crisis suit.

"Sunny."

Both men carried their duelling sticks in plain sight as if it truly were ten years before and the contract shut-downs and call-backs had never happened.

"What's the drift?" Sam asked, falling into the old ways in spite of himself, as if the ten years were like smoke.

"Raising a crew," Sunny said. "Trouble out in the Landings."

"Someone thinks," Walt added.

"Flashpoint?" Sam asked, going straight to it. *Major strike?* Even: *A new Landing?*

Walt studied the crowd, using a part of his skill few people knew about. "Not sure yet."

Sam almost smiled at the melodrama. "Someone?"

"Outatowner," Sunny replied, which meant protected sources and need to know and told Sam pretty much everything. Possibly no strike, no flashpoint at all. But official. Some other reason.

Sam was careful not to smile, not to shake his head, just like on those long-ago, never-so-long-ago days when Sam Aitchander, Walt Senny and Sunny Jim Cosimo belonged to as good a flash crew as you were likely to find. "Bad idea right now, Sunny, Walt. The Sailmaker is still there."

Telling it like it was. The Landing that could reach out. Snatch and smash even the best.

"Need to make five," Walt Senny said, a spade on gravel. Affectation, most like, though how could you know? Sergio Leone and a hundred years of marketing departments had a lot to answer for. "Figured Angel for point and you for star again, Sam,"

But the ten years were there. Things *had* changed.

"Other business right now, Walt," Sam said, trying to keep the promise he'd made to himself. "Not sure the Landings are the place to be."

Walt and Sunny expected it. They played their main card.

"Another crew going in as well," Sunny said, which could very well be *before* the fact knowing Walt and Sunny, a lie but a likelihood and a serious one, what it implied. "Punky Bannas is putting it together. The Crown Regulators ride again!"

"Punky? Then—"

"Right," Walt Senny said, his ruined voice like a shovel against a sidewalk.

And got me, Sam thought. Punky and Maisie Day and the rest.

But *ten* years. Probably not Maisie. Still, Punky Bannas liked known players no less than Sunny and Walt did. His Regulators would need to be solid, as familiar as he could get.

"Who's their pure?" Which was saying yes, of course. *Let's re-activate the Saltline Trimmers.* Sunny even managed his lopsided grin, two, three seconds of one.

Walt Senny knew better than to smile. "Kid named Jacko. Henna Jacko. First class."

"Who's ours?" Sam asked. Should have been: who's yours? but he slipped.

"New kid. Thomas Gunn, if you can believe it. Thomas not Tommy. He's prime. Talent scout found him in a doss out in Dryport."

"The rest," Sam said. "I need it all."

Sunny gave his grin. Walt Senny spun his stick in a splendid bonham. Spectators ahhh'd. One, trying too hard, called out: "Bravo!"

"Not here," Walt said. "Come out to Tagger's. Meet the crew."

Sam had to grin back at them. Tagger's. All of it, just like ten years before. Ghosts out of the smoke.

And the possibility of Maisie Day.

SAM DIDN'T HAVE TO wait until Tagger's. Sunny had borrowed a clean van from Raph Swale, and as soon as they were on the city road and he'd switched on the dampeners, Sam asked it.

"A new Landing?"

"Not as easy as that," Sunny said.

"Sailmaker's had a kid," Walt said from the back. "Replicated."

Sam was truly surprised. One hundred and eighty-six Landings across the planet and all of them pretty much stable since The Sailmaker had arrived. "Hadn't heard."

Sam didn't need to look back. Walt would be giving *that* look.

"Have to know if it's something local or a new arrival," Sunny added, hardly necessary but these *were* new days. Maybe Sunny was worried that Sam would ask him to pull over and let him out. "Couldn't risk it back in the Automatic. World Health wants known teams. Two of the best."

The World Health Organisation in full stride again. The WHO doctors!

"How bad?" Sam asked, remembering how the original Sailmaker had started, how it had changed everything, destroyed so many crews, discouraged the rest.

"Nowhere near mature, but they've tracked fourteen towns to date, half in Europe, rest in Asia. None in the Americas this time. Another six are possible, but overlaps are still making it hard to tell."

"Stats?"

"Last posting for the fourteen: two hundred and forty thousand people down. Recovery teams got to the European sites, but you know how Asia can be."

Used to know, Sam almost said, ready with attitude. But kept it back. *Nothing ever really changes, considering.*

"How far from the original?" he asked, thinking of the The Sailmaker out there in the hot desert on the edge of the Amadeus Basin, so far away.

"Right near Dancing Doris. Sixty k's outside Broken Hill."

"It'll all depend on our pure!" Sam said, stating the obvious, the too obvious, but giving them the old Sam Aitchander standard. Part of him, too big a part of him really, suddenly wanted things as they were back then. Known.

They let it be. He let it be. They drove the rest of the way to the Bendigo Gate in silence. Another time it would have been companionable and welcome. Now there was too much fear.

A Sailmaker almost at the perimeter, Sam thought. *They're closing in.*

TAGGER'S WAS ON THE very edge of the Krackenslough, that glinting landflow from the only Landing phenomenon, globally, ever to involve striking back at civilization from inside a Landing perimeter with large-scale coarse action above and beyond the shut-down fugues. There was that single calamitous event, tearing up so much of eastern Australia, then The Sailmaker arriving eight years later. Perhaps, experts argued, The Sailmaker had caused that singular event, already on its way.

Now this. Sailmaker Two. Sailmaker Redux, whatever you could call it, and here in Australia again, would you believe? However it fell, proof that the Landings were there: a constant in all their lives. Ongoing.

They left the clean van in the holding yard at Becker's, and Sam went with Walt and Sunny through the Bendigo Gate, finally made it to the large taproom of Tagger's with the windows showing the red land and red sky before them. The forty-six Australian Landings were a day away, scattered over three hundred and forty thousand hectares, twenty days across on foot, six by WHO slow-mo ATV. The Sailmaker Redux was two days in.

"Hi, Aitch," Angel Fleet said, meeting them at the tap-stage. She looked older, leaner, wasted with too much sun and not enough care, but it was so good seeing her, seeing her alive and still keen, though what other careers were there really for hard-luck warriors, God's-gift crusader knights, once you'd fought against dragons? "The kid's in the blue room swotting the manuals. Sunny said you'd do good cop on this."

Sam had expected it, but it was beside the point. Being at Tagger's again overwhelmed everything. Seeing Angel, any version of Angel.

"How have you been, Ange?"

"Managing. Glad to have this. You, Aitch?"

"Coming round." He nodded to the door. "What've you told him?"

"Standard run. They're alien zones. Dangerous. We came on hard, Sunny and me. Figured bad cop was the way to go."

"Get much?"

"You kidding? He glazed over two minutes in. These kids can name the flash crews up and down the spread, but the basics—forget it. Walt said leave it to you. Just like old times."

"Just like old times."

His name was Thomas Gunn and no-one called him Tommy. He was sixteen, lean, of medium height, with a good open face, pleasing enough features, the habit of tipping his head to one side when was really listening.

"Glad they sent you, Mr. Aitch," he said when Sam took the other hardwood chair in the blue room. "They're all so intense. I was hoping you'd be good cop."

The kid knew the procedures.

"And why's that, Thomas?" Though Sam knew the answer. When had it ever been different? Sam had steeled himself to give a listen-or-else, grassroots spiel: the first Landings appearing, going active, shutting down whole communities across the planet with no pattern, no *apparent* pattern, sending thousands, hundreds of thousands into catatonic fugue. The flash crews going in to break the signal before too many out of those thousands started dying. Getting some back. But Thomas had been playing doggo.

"You're—more approachable. They say."

"Used to be. It's been a while."

"You came back. I checked that. Some keep away."

Sam made himself stay civil. It was how you started any working relationship.

"You don't reach escape velocity, you keep coming back, yes."

"Born to it."

No use denying. "Bit like that."

"So, which are we going to, Mr. Aitch?"

Sam paused, studying the newbie, liking most of what he saw—the alertness so at odds with what Angel and Sunny had seen, been allowed to see, the edginess sensed. Though the Mr. Aitch got him. His shelf name. Field name. Damn Walt and Sunny. Sam endured it, just as he had so many times before.

"Not sure going in. Not this early. Out near The Horse, I think. Not as far as The Pearl."

"The Horse. I really want to see that. What about The Sailmaker?"

"We keep clear. Always. It's a cull set-up."

"You think?" Thomas's eyes were wide at the prospect.

"Work it out. Nothing for years. Teams getting cocky. Then the Krackenslough. Eight years later The Sailmaker arrives." Treating him like he did know.

Thomas was nodding. "It's like the name, isn't it? Landings. Something has landed. Something has come in, been sent." Talk jumping all over the place, but obvious stuff, common with any newbie.

"Surely seems like it, Thomas."

"But not ships? Heard Mr. Senny say loose lips sink ships. What it sounded like. Didn't like to bother 'im."

"Not as easy as that. But you're right in a way. It's where something *has* come in. Arrived. Best to think of them as nodes. Accretion points."

"'Scusing, gov."

"Sampling probes, some say."

"Not tracking, Mr. Aitch."

"Places where things appear. Gather things to them."

"They'll go someday, you think?" Jumping again.

"Twenty-three years this summer. They may simply go, like you say. But something is needed now. To get us through. That's why the scout picked you."

"They bombed them."

"They did, yes. Lots of times. They keep trying in some places, trying new things, sending troops in, poor sods. Hit squads. But it gooses them, gets them active. Regardless of what people say, World Health's way is better. There's the other thing to consider too. When they go active, start locking on to folks, a Landing in Australia locking onto a street, a town, maybe half a world away, you bomb them then, *all* the downers die, every one of them. Some sort of broadband trauma. We think we're ahead of things there. Better it's done gently. Flash crews are told which Landing has struck down a community somewhere, we go in, target the particular flashpoint, tweak and twist things there in little bits so the Landing never quite knows what's happening and switches modes. It seems. That's all we ever hope to do. Switch modes."

"But in those towns—whole groups of downers come back."

"Right. So better to keep the WHO quarantine, track which Landings become active, go in and tweak. That's the extent of it, Thomas, though some will tell you otherwise. The WHO authorities track which communities have been targeted, counted out—"

"Whole communities. It's like they've been assigned or something."

"—then we go in, tweak and retrieve. That's all it is, all we do. We get some back."

"Some die."

"Most don't."

"And you just happen to have the power?" He was marveling, not being sarcastic. His head was tipped to the side.

"Right. Again, why the scout picked you. Gave you all those tests."

"They're revived just so they can get shut-down again some other time."

"Sometimes goes like that. But it all has to do with numbers. We work to cut down the thousands who die through neglect, arriving too late to help. You saw the stats."

The kid nodded, which could have meant anything. Angel was right. So many newbies didn't know any of this.

"Do I get a coat and a cane?" Thomas said, perhaps working to hide his smarts. "Like the leones wear? Learn the bonhams. Wear the divas." Jumping again. Newbies always jumped, dealing with the excitement, the nerves, the fear. But likely dumbing down, this time.

"You decide to stay on, sure. If it works out. That's up to you." As if.

"The blue serge crisis suits."

Maybe the kid was just a kid after all. Sam allowed it.

"We have them—if you want one."

"You don't. None of you."

"People used to like the official look. Prefer this now."

"You mean business but you don't like looking owned. It's the robin hood. The zorro."

"Borderline outlawry is what it is. We've gone through official. Survivors reassure more than badges sometimes."

"Go figure."

"Go figure."

"You're a hard lot. I like that. I like all that."

"Merely flashmen, Thomas. We channel power. Deflect the bad kind. Break the signals from the Landings so the modes switch and people come back. Restore some of what the Landings shut down."

Thomas paused, just sat looking out. Such a silence boded well. It was the 70/30 again—70 percent action, 30 percent thoughtful.

"How do you?" Thomas finally asked.

Sam shrugged. It was easy to answer the old unanswerables in a way. "No idea. Some people can. All magic bird stuff."

"Magic bird?"

"Old saying. Put us in a team, the right mix, we can do it. Just can. For all we know the Landings did that too. Created an antidote system." It was a favorite line, all that made it tolerable ultimately, the chance of being part of an auto-immune system against the bogeyman.

"The Landings retaliate."

"Seems they do. No-one's sure about any of that. May be just power readjustments. But better a hundred dead than five thousand in shut-down, yes?"

"That's the old 70/30. The old WHO/UN ruling!"

Sam blinked. The kid had surprised him again. "It is. What do you think?"

"Seems right. Seems fair. What do you think, Mr. Aitch?" Also unexpected.

"No matter what I think. People insist on it. Would rather gamble that way than stay a zombie, maybe die through neglect when there aren't enough carers soon enough."

"True death is better."

"They reckon."

"You reckon?"

"We're merely flashmen, Thomas. All we are. Do what we're hired to do."

"You've been out of it ten years."

Here it was.

"That's the cafard, the funk, the downtime debt. It drains you, wastes you. Gets so you need to be away." The words ran off his tongue.

"But the shut-downs continued. How could you?"

"There are always other crews. Seemed like a good idea at the time."

It was a slap-down—none of your business—but the kid accepted it. "So why now? Why this?" *Why me?* he didn't say. Or: *What happened to your last pure?* He just needed reassurance.

"Personal business. People we know going in." The beautiful lie. No point mentioning The Redux yet.

"You're worried they'll find something."

"That they'll *upset* something more like. Despite The Sailmaker's power, things have been pretty stable since it arrived. *Fewer* shut-downs. *Fewer* communities going under. They could change the balance."

"So like I said. You're looking out for us." Jumping, jumping.

"Whatever. One team usually needs another to watch it. We've been hired to keep an eye on this other team." Not the truth, but near enough.

Thomas nodded, looked out at the day through the prep room window.

"One more thing, Mr. Aitch. They say there are two secrets all flashmen keep."

Sam feared: *Tell me what they are,* but the kid was smarter, better than that. He jumped, but knew what *not* to say.

"How long before I'm trusted enough to be allowed to ask what they are?"

Two secrets indeed. The make or break when it came to the flash crews.

"Ask again when the mission's over. Now a question to you, Thomas."

"Shoot, Mr. Aitch."

"How come you played dumb with the others?"

Thomas Gunn spread his hands in a "you know how it is" gesture that was probably as old as Cro-Magnons. "First thing I learned about flashmen. Always keep something back."

Sam almost smiled, but stood instead to hide the rush of emotion. "Time to make a move."

AS IT TURNED OUT, quite a few of the old Big Name crews were going in. The wildfire, pond-ripple, rumor mill prevailed as ever it had. Word of one team activated meant something happening on the QT; best keep an eye out just in case. Sponsors appeared like magic: governments, corporations, citizen protection groups, patents and futures speculators old and new. Good sense. Contingency and precaution.

One of Punky's former lieutenants, Baine Couse, had put together a rag-tag band—the Argentics on the registration database—with Rollo Jayne and Toss Gatereau in the line-up. Molly Dye had re-activated her Lonetown Farriers, once definitely second stringers all, but a real force now that Rod Sinner had been brought in to replace Corven, lost at The Sailmaker in '35. Julie Farro and Yancy Cada had a new line-up of their Spin Doctors ready to go. Other names he knew. Many he didn't.

Riding the wind-tram out to the Baylieu Gate, Sam shook his head at the wonder of it. Conspiracy theory always messed things up. The chats were crazy with it, the seaboard axis abuzz. All the new coastal cities were making a feature of it. Four teams now, forty later. They'd be tripping over themselves before they were an hour along—most of them makeshift tagger groups of newbies and quarterhands duelling it out on the fringes, maybe risking The Spanish Lantern, The Moonraker and The Three Spices, then scuttling back to the bars and chats with improbable stories that grew larger with every telling. Not just in Australia either. The African coastal axis had groups stirring; the West American axis pre-empted everyone by sending a team to check the sub-Saharan Landings. French teams were heading for the Gobi Desert outside Sagran. The flashmen. The leones. Darlings of the WHO doctors. The ten years were like smoke.

THE **WHO** PERIMETER UNITS gave the teams access in twos, and the Trimmers and the Regulators were promised a clear day's lead before the Argentics and the Farriers, then the Spin Doctors, The Sneaky Pete Regulars and the rest of the official line-up. Some newbie crews would jump queue around that vast boundary. Some would be wasted quick smart, the rest would be nabbed by the authorities on the way out. Easier to let the Landings tidy things up first. There'd be penalties, token sentences in the new barrios, but ultimately WHO didn't care so long as flashpoints were dealt with and data—*any* data after all this time—was forthcoming. Better they risk another Krackenslough, they secretly figured, secretly gambled, unofficially believed, than not know anything about their deadly visitors.

At Baylieu Gate there was more waiting, of course. The orbitals needed to track the complex fluxes, wait for what they considered to be suitable hiatus readings before giving the go-ahead—all frustratingly unnecessary from a crew's hands-on perspective. It was 1400 that afternoon before the Trimmers rode their WHO-provided slow-mo ATV through Checkpoint Sinbad and left civilization—human civilization—behind.

Then, yet again, they were a law unto themselves. Champions of the hopes of the world. Officially indispensable. Unofficially expendable.

The first site reached from the southeast, soon after full radio noise-out, was Winwa Landing, what had once been The Firewalker because of its random plasma screens and dissociated spark-ups. Some of the Landings failed, fell away, re-located in new forms elsewhere, who could ever know? All that was left were the pylons, struts and gantries of the old WHO/local natgov access piers. It was like that at Winwa.

Working with World Health, most national governments had set up inspection piers early on wherever they could, long raised causeways with observation towers and telemetry nodes. They looked like the promenade piers of a previous age, and were as much to frame the phenomena as anything, to provide frameworks, form and sense, things you could put on a map and treat as quantifiable, borders around chaos. Sand drifts had moved in, the wind and heat had stripped the paintwork. Winwa Landing was a ghost town that had never lived.

They spent the night in the lee of the seventh pylon, listening to what were left of the causeway struts ticking and cooling overhead and watching the faintest play of bravura lights tricking around the inward flare-tail—all that remained of what The Firewalker had once been.

They repacked their slow-mo before dawn and moved on, making forty k's along the Delphin Track and passing The Arete before it became fully active. Then it was The Pure off to their left, three k's distant but already flexing and extending its clear-glass "soul-finders" in the day.

They were passing The Lucky Boatmen when they saw their first whirter assembling in the distance—three of its fourteen pieces spinning in the warm air, orbiting each other as they sought lock-point for the rest. The Trimmers would be well past before it posed a threat, but some other team would have it to deal with. How it usually happened, one group triggering sentinel responses that wasted another. Proof either that no other crew had come in at Winwa yet or, far less likely but not impossible given how UN agencies competed, that enough had done so to complete one fourteen-stage whirter cycle and start another.

By mid-morning they were passing The Spanish Lantern on its eastern side, keeping their focus on the trail ahead and only using peripheral vision to note the flickering orange, blue and red semaphore-at-noon running lights amid the balconies and bastions of the fluted blast-furnace form. They wore their headsets to dampen the teeth-chattering castanet siren rhythms that gave it its name. So many taggers and newbies would go closer, wanting to see the fiesta lights on the lower balconies, never believing that anything could happen to them. Some would get the approach rhythms wrong and end up as part of the deadly *duende* of the place. It was Thomas who said he could see bodies, "dancers" who had missed those syncopations and couldn't get free in time, and were now pressed into final service. No-one acknowledged his lapse of form. He was left to work out for himself that you never mentioned the dead and dying. You accepted and moved on.

They reached The Horse on the second day, considered by many the most remarkable of the Landings: image after life-sized image of horses from every artistic period in known Earth history: as if the governing intelligence, AI, tropism, whatever powered the thing, had locked onto that one bioform and replicated it again and again—in bronze, in wood, in ceramic, resin, volcanic glass, bone and sewn skin, line after line of stylised equiforms scattered across the spinifex hills.

The Horse also gave Thomas his first glimpse of a burrus. The veteran Trimmers had been preparing him for it, each of them filling the time by telling him what to expect. Even Walt had managed: "It's all eye-trick shit. Just make sure your coal's there."

The profile had been in the WHO database. The typical burrus—a handball-sized knob of airborne porcelain—usually traveled at chest height and aimed for the thymus, tucked away behind the breast bone. No saying why it did, no knowing things like that, just that it did. Carrying lumps of anthracite in your pockets seemed to deflect most of them— where the old name "coal-pockets" came from that some people still used for flashmen in some parts of the world. But anthracite, for heaven's sake, to ward off something that went for your immune system, that seemed to live to do just that.

This small white avatar came streaking up to them from among the closest equiforms, hovered, held, stayed with them for an hour, sometimes bobbing, twitching in sudden, unnerving ways, then streaked away, soundless.

Two aylings came at them next, all high comedy were they not designed to detonate, fleschette-fashion. Sam did ayling duty as usual, briefing Thomas as the constructs approached.

"Watch now. These are faux-boys from what one overzealous WHO scientist christened Smart Landings. Leave it to me."

"Foe boys?" Thomas said, eyes never leaving the two figures on the trail.

"Faux." Sam spelled it out. "Old word for fakes. Maquettes. Made and sent by the Smarts."

"They're so human."

"They think they are. They're aylings. Clones. Synths."

"The Landings that sample g-codes."

"Right. If the Landings are traps, they're taking bits of whatever they can get to do their trapping. We're the most advanced local lifeform, so they sample us, turn out these."

"Parts of the trap."

"But the aylings don't know it. The thing is, if you play along, they stay friendly, finally reach a range limit and turn back."

The aylings spoke a strange clipped teev dialect gleaned from a century of vintage sat transmissions.

"Holoner De Gorvernax," the taller, rangier one introduced itself as, affecting a human male voice to go with its not-quite-right male mannequin appearance. "We've found a good route."

So simple, so obvious.

"Hutman Von Vexator," said the other, affecting female and as unreal as a well-made store mannequin. "Hol's right. Quick run out by The Four Doormen. Get you through in no time. None of the fluxes." Voice surprisingly good.

"That right?" Sam said. "Need to see The Quilter first. Business to attend to out by The Quilter. Then we'll try your way."

The aylings frowned at each other, sensing deflection but not sure how to make a No out of a provisional Yes.

Sam kept up the banter, making them run whatever menus they had. "Be good to see The Four Doormen again. Just need this quick detour first. Be good to have you along."

Sunny took the Trimmers straight for The Caress then. No time to do the usual Quilter deflection. Not with a flashpoint. The Redux had struck. People out in the world were dying.

The Caress already had someone in its moil, a young male tagger who must have jumped the border undetected. Solitaries could manage it. He was already stripped and marked for portioning. You could see the terror on his face, the acceptance, the shocked fascination at having his body marked out for vivisection, then the beatific calm as the modals shifted, even more terrifying to see.

It had taken eleven years for WHO to figure out that what had been known as whirters—assemblages of fourteen accreting parts—were actually the hunt avatars of this uniquely tripartite Landing called The Caress. Once the whirter had assembled and its prey was caught and phased away, the victim hadn't been sent to oblivion as first thought, despite the measurable energy release, but had been sent off to the Landing itself. A whirter had tracked and caught this youth, faxed him home to where he now hung unsupported three meters in the air, by turns being lulled and soothed, then shown the full measure of his pending demise—as if the Landing drew on the rapid shift of disparate emotions. This cat-and-mouse function applied to The Caress's other parts in central Africa and the American Mid-west.

"You wait by those outer flanges," Sam told the aylings. "We're ahead of time. We'll just check our route, and then we can see The Four Doormen."

The aylings suspected nothing. They went towards the outer questing arms of The Caress, were snatched, lofted, then promptly cancelled as the Landing identified them as something of their own kind. There one moment, gone the next.

AS THE TRIMMERS' ROUTE brought them closer to The Redux, it was inevitable that they finally catch sight of Punky's Regulators. Towards evening they had their first glimpse of their old rivals, saw another campfire start up a mile or so off in the dusk a few minutes after theirs did. Direct com remained out, of course, but Sunny used the radio handset to send the *braka*, the switch-on, switch-off static rhythm that meant "come hither," "no threat," "parley." Coffee was set going. Extra cups and rations were laid out.

Twenty minutes later, a deputation of Regulators cooee'd approach, then were there: Punky, Jack Crowfeather and, yes, Maisie Day.

Again the ten years were forgotten, impossible. There in the dark, Sam grinned wryly at having even tried to make another life. Among flash crews you either owned what you were or pretended. You never signed off—not having seen The Breakwater turn careless friends to clutches of sticks, seen the Lantern set them twitching off to their doom, seen the lines of antique horses frozen mid-stride across the spinifex ridges, the fierce nacreous gleam of The Pearl with its—surprise! surprise!—reverse-pattern oyster trap designed solely to lure the curious. It *seemed*. The Trimmers, the Regulators, shouldn't be here. No-one should be here. But having tasted, having *turned* them, switched the modes, there was no staying away.

Then, seeing Maisie large and limber as life, a bigger woman than ever he'd preferred till he'd met her, Sam realized how his smile must seem and lost it at once, probably way too late.

So much resolve here, so many realities disregarded in the instant. Two crews meeting again, protected by the braka truce, the cooee, the old courtesies.

"The Trimmers, as they cleverly appear to live and breathe!" Punky said, lean and powerful in his Singer duster, big smile and white crew-cut like a double night-light in the dusk. Crowfeather had a smile too, but like a smug surgeon, a good foil for Walt Senny any day but without Walt's final kiss of style. "Best aylings ever to grace the sand-box!" Jack said. Maisie Day gave a civil nod but looked way too frosty and focused. She *had* seen Sam's smile on the way in.

Sunny and Angie gave generous greetings. Walt managed a cool hello. Sam heard his own voice murmur something, managed most of a new smile, thin, careful. Then he introduced Thomas, who sat wide-eyed, taking it all in as they got down to business.

"Sailmaker Two, if you can believe it," Sunny said, all easy, playing good cop as he always did. "The Redux, if you agree."

Punky eased himself onto the cooling sand, stuck out his long legs and raised his palms to the fire.

"Indeed," he said. "Bringing up Junior. Who would've thought? How we playing this?"

"Make an offer." Walt said, before Punky had finished speaking.

Punky flashed his smile, warming his hands in the desert chill. Sam watched the night, watched Maisie, watched the night again. For all he knew, the rest of the Regulators were out in the dark, getting ready to settle old scores outside the courtesies. There was little demonstrated love here, but perhaps Sunny was right. Perhaps they should always allow the possibility of something more.

And Maisie. She looked good. Fierce and wonderful. Fuller. Heavier. Vital.

"Working the mode shift is all that matters," Punky said, eminently practical. "Share the fee. Go tandem, turn about. Your call, Sunny. Dibs on first unless you want to toss for it."

"Generous," Walt said, like a knife.

"Traitor's market," Crowfeather said, testing.

"Stet," Walt replied. *As was.* Calling him. Put up or shut up. And with it: know your place!

"Cousins," Sunny said, keeping the focus, keeping the braka, the best of the old ways. The songs would always be written about the likes of Walt Senny, but it was flashmen like Sunny Jim who were the real heroes here. "Your dibs. We'll follow you in at first light."

"Others coming in," Punky said, which said it all—explained the visit, the civility. *Cover our back, we cover yours.* Just like the hateful, treacherous old times.

There was hesitation. Muscles locked in the firelight though you'd never know it. There were old scores indeed, Sam and Maisie the least of them. This was make or break.

"New threat, new start, I figure," Sunny said, bringing what he could of decency and civilization into this strange alienized place. "We'll ward off. Give two hours. You do the same. Split the fee."

"Done," Punky said, holding out his cup for a refill instead of rising to go as they'd expected. "Half cup for the road." And then, as if just thinking of it: "Sam, think Maisie would like a word, sotta-votchy."

Sam was up and walking, moving away from the fire, into ambush, into trouble, he suddenly didn't care. He was only aware of Thomas looking after him, wondering what the hell was going on, aware of footsteps following. He walked forty paces and turned, saw the campfire back there, the mixed crews filling this lonely place in the night, as improbable as a Landing, truth be known, saw Maisie's shadow right there, backlit.

"Sam," she said.

"Mae." He'd never called her by her given name.

"Never expected this turn-out," she said. "Never expected collateral damage." Here it was. She had the right.

"Never ever that, Mae." All he could say. And the word "ever." Precious envoy.

"Put aside the Trimmers, put aside the rest."

"Denial gets like that." Inane, simply true. *The Sailmaker*, he might have said. But she knew. Had to know. Losing Boker and Steyne, almost all of Croft Denner's Larrikins. Despite the songs, the glamor of the chats, they'd been cruel years, even for the best crews. Especially the best.

"Bastard."

"Never personal, Mae."

"Everything is, Sam."

Four beats. Not turning away. *You were with Punky. Rival crew.* "You know how I feel."

She made a disgusted sound. Four beats. Still not turning. "You came back."

Walt and Sunny, he might have said. Or *Time's right*. Even *The Sailmaker*.

"Yes," he said, which was all of it, encompassing. Hoping she'd see. One word as emblem for so much.

"Bastard."

His conditioning had him. He almost shrugged. The zorro. Eternally cool. But didn't. Didn't.

"Be with me," he said, kept her gaze for it, as hard as that was, saw all of her contempt, real or feigned, the old raw emotion powering whatever emotion it truly was.

Two beats.

"Be damned." And she turned and went.

Afterwards, bare minutes later, then hours later in their clear-sky trackside doss with the Regulators' campfire out in the cold night, he went back to it again and again, filled out the spaces with words. "That night at the stay-away," he could have said. "The Sailmaker fuming and sewing. Teams torn up, played off against one another most like. Braka barely holding. No ships in the night for us. There was a reason for the different teams. We never settled. Never made it easy. You know that." And the words would have been wrong. All wrong.

Mae knew. *Two* beats before turning. Mae knew.

And what was any of this if not redemption? Mae was with Punky again, but so what? There in their own meager doss, in the close dark, Sam saw Punky and The Sailmaker and the Landings as just parts of a lock that could be broken, opened at last. Nothing was ever enough, and nothing was written. Be with me. What more could anyone ever say?

At the first pink wash of dawn, the Trimmers were up, dusting off, doing ablutions, mantras, serving coffee, heating rations. The Regulators were no doubt doing the same. Little was said, considering, and when Sunny had the Trimmers move out it was in classic "diamond wand" formation with standard two-meter separations: Angel at point, Walt behind her shoulder to the left as hawk, Sunny to the right as gauntlet, Thomas as pure, finishing the diamond proper, and Sam behind as star. When they engaged, Thomas would step into the middle of the diamond; Sam would move forward to close the diamond again.

In a sense, the movies and the chats had done the training here. Thomas knew to expect the first of the focal drugs when Sunny passed it to him five minutes along, just slapped on the patch and played it straight, no questions, no hesitation. As if born to it. Who would have thought the movies, teev and chats could save so much time, constantly updating the mindset?

And there were Punky's Regulators ahead—same open diamond, their ballistic and laser weapons raised against new avatars, whatever whirter, burrus and ayling variants the Redux might serve up.

And The Redux rose beyond, so clearly an embryonic Sailmaker. Same clutch of sculpted fossil masts, already six meters high in places, same array of flensing frames (they weren't, nothing like it, but try convincing anyone that those stretched and bellying tarps weren't human skin), same distinctive keening and slap-snapping sound that helped give the Landing its name. It was for all the world as if limp sails were being snapped full, a repeated jarring tattoo in the chill morning air. Silence but for the keening, the gunshot slap-snap of "shrouds" and "rigging," their own rhythmic tread.

Within seconds the Trimmers had their shades on macro, and Sam saw the Regulators' pure—Henna Jacko (suddenly remembering the name)—dutifully slap on the final patch. The assault patch. Saw Jack Crowfeather and Martine Atta and Mae slap on their link patches almost in unison. Saw Henna step into the center and Punky close the diamond. They were engaging. Taking no chances.

The Redux was at two hundred meters when the avatars came. Not whirters, aylings or burrus variants, those oldest of Landing progeny. These were like the running dolls that had plagued Western Europe when The Rickshaw and The Rasa had first appeared. The most conventional after the aylings, the most—

No, not progeny at all!

Human!

"Down!" Walt cried, and Sunny saw it too.

"Hit squad!"

The Trimmers folded as one, Thomas dragged down by Walt, pushed down by Sam, went to lying unsupported positions in seconds, ballistics and laser up and aimed. Autotropics locked on as best they could in the interference caused by the Landings.

No thinking about it. *Crack. Crack. Tear. Crack. Tear. Crack.*

Dolls were falling, spots of ground kicking up where doll-strike hit back.

"Who?" Thomas yelled, huddling, terrified. There was the smell of piss.

No answer. *Work it out, newbie!*

Between shots, Sam managed a glimpse of the Regulators—down and firing—but couldn't see the damage there, who was safe and who wasn't.

Dolls were falling, falling. But so many. Too many. Thank the gods that autotropics were skewed.

No time to discuss it. Sam rolled to the side, targeted the outer skins of The Redux.

The others saw. Walt added his own ballistic strikes, Sunny swung his laser over the outer watch-screens.

The Redux struck back, and—as Sam hoped—targeted the *moving* shapes. Reached out with whatever targeting protocols it had and plucked at faces. Just faces. Snatched them into the activation perimeter and stretched them on the sky: one face, vast and glaring in shock, then two, ten, twenty, vast hoardings, rushmores, sails, twenty, thirty meters across and with—impossibly—complete facial integrity, no distortion despite the size.

Making sails.

The Trimmers and the Regulators didn't dare shift position. The dolls were gone—transformed. The Redux was in fully trophy display, just like its terrifying parent out on the Amadeus. No slap-snap now, just the keening.

But there'd be more. A hit squad—*that* level of resources deployment—meant a carefully planned mission. Not targeting The Redux! *Them!* The crews! Mission contingency.

A fire-strike, of course! Officially: bombing The Redux before it proliferated. Perhaps claiming it already had! Something.

Unofficially: getting rid of the top crews, one way or another.

Wanting The Redux to grow. The old strategies. Old mistakes. Everything old, new again. New science. New chances for young turks with theories, careers to mind. Forgetting the past. Busy seizing the day.

"Sky-strike!" Sam stage-whispered, not daring to say it loudly. All quiet but for the keening, maybe the white noise shift, shift, shift of gaping faces on the sky.

Sunny dared to move an arm, so so slowly, activating the audio seek on his headset.

"They have the range," Walt said.

"We'll never know," Angel added. True, all true.

"Listening!" Sunny reminded them, not expecting ship-talk in the braka white-out but hoping for something, anything.

So then it was just the keening and the waiting, thoughts of Mae running through Sam's mind, and anger and some amusement too that it had come to this. How could you not laugh? So easy to catch the heroes, set them up. Can't help themselves, the pompous asses! Strutting like lords! Who cared about countless thousands dying in an overpopulated world? Pay lip-service, go through the motions. Be seen to be doing the right thing. Who cared about the flashmen and their two secrets—*two* secrets that only the prime crews knew, that the taggers, quarterhands and newbies desperately tried to learn? Wasted heroes of the people. Losses just added to the legend. Get rid of the old, bring on the new. Bread and circuses.

Sam laughed into the sand. Merely flashmen. All they ever were. Dependable. Expendable.

"Incoming!" Sunny said, reading not voice transmissions of any kind but rather fluctuations in the static where they would be. Ghosts of talk. He switched to distance tracking, non-vested audio ranges, made his raw calculations. "Ten k's out and on approach!" Best guess, but he had the skill.

"What will they do?" Thomas asked.

"Missile," Angel said. "Point blank."

"They don't know," Sunny said, marvelling at those careless airmen and foolish mission chiefs, that there could be so much ignorance in—the joke was there—high places. Still. Again. However it played. This was a Sailmaker, for heaven's sake!

"Wait for it!" Walt Senny said, targeting the sky, the faces. "We'll spoil its trophies."

"No laser!" Angel warned.

"Stealth grenade," Walt said. "No sustained source trail."

"We hope."

"We hope," Sunny confirmed.

Sam found himself thinking of Mae, of the Regulators, of poor Thomas lying in his own piss, silent, bless him, but alive. Needed more than ever now if Henna Jacko was lost.

Walt judged the approach, calculated vagaries like Sunny's ten k's, wind direction, engine noise, pilot caution.

He fired into the faces, scored the hit. One by one they burned, skewing, heaving on their invisible tethers.

Nil source detected, it seemed. No instantaneous retaliation, at any rate. Possibly too small, too slight, no constant follow-up signature.

Then, again, The Redux found something that *would* do, coarse movement, read the aircraft on approach. Reached out and made sails. More faces spread on the sky—a half-dozen, there, there, there.

The bomber continued over, a smooth high crucifix with no-one aboard left alive.

The braka static from the Regulators came almost at once—basic Morse—*Henna dead. Your dibs.*

And lying there, the Trimmers swapped strategy. Thomas worked a new patch onto his arm. The others slowly, carefully, added their own patches when they could, each stage-whispered "Check!" till they'd all confirmed. Lying there, sprawled on the sand, they made the flash crew.

The Redux was new, dazzled by trophies, possibly its first, distracted by the sheer overload of being in the world. It never suspected—were there truly a governing intelligence that *could* suspect, bring cognition to what it did.

The Trimmers found their voice, their hold, their strike, started working the flashpoint.

Sam focused, focused, no longer daring to think of Mae, or surviving, or the people out there in shut-down waiting their chance. He concentrated on Thomas, on sending through Thomas to The Redux, to the faces in the sky.

His eyes glazed, cleared, glazed, cleared, then found one trophy face, eyeless, vast, distended on the sky, twenty meters across, yet impossibly intact, mouth open in a scream but with no other feature distortion. Young, young it seemed. Not Mae. Young.

He used that face to keep the resolve. *Through* Thomas to *that* face.

How long they worked it there was no telling. The day tracked. The sun was up and blazing, crawling across the sky. Late autumn heat still made it a hell, but distant, bearable.

That sun was well into afternoon when the modes began shifting, finally switched, when the keening fell away and the slap-snap began again. Somewhere people were waking from shut-down fugue, finding dust in their mouths, insects, their limbs cramped, broken, wasted by circulation necrosis. But alive! *Alive!* And somewhere a debt was being paid.

The trophies were gone. The sky above the masts and frames of The Redux was a washed blue.

They'd managed it.

One by one, the Trimmers stirred, stood, stretched, worked their own stiff and aching muscles, grateful to be in the world.

The Regulators hadn't done as well. Three up, two down. Two!

The Trimmers hurried as much as they dared in that fraught place, crossed the newly keening, slap-snapping terrain before The Redux and reached was what left of Punky's crew.

Henna Jacko was gone. Her young face had been the sail Sam had seen. Had used.

Jack Crowfeather was the other, hit twice by shots from approaching dolls. Punky, Martine and Mae were getting them into body-bags, slowly, no sudden movements now, preparing to haul them back to whatever decent distance would serve as a trail burial site in these dangerous wastes.

"Thanks," Punky said. "Fee's yours, clear." Not: Who were they? What happened? Understanding that.

"We share," Sunny said. "Braka." Keeping faith, building traditions that might well outlive them all. Went in together. Come out together.

Punky grinned at the foolishness, Sunny's dogged largesse. "In light of this?"

"Especially." And not hesitating: "You go southwest by The Praying Hands. We'll take northwest. Use braka Morse when we can, voice when it clears. Have to get this out."

"Agreed," Punky said. "Warn our people off."

Walt grunted. "See if *they* can get themselves a decent crew then."

Martine and Mae both nodded, Mae's eyes holding Sam's two, three seconds before sliding away to tasks at hand. The Regulators reached for the bags holding their dead.

Sunny beat them to that as well. "We'll take the girl."

Not Jack. The newbie.

Punky nodded. "Appreciated."

No dragging body bags here. No being slowed down now if it could be helped. The Redux had made sails, possibly its first, was possibly recalling the experience, sorting what had happened. It could swing again. Not likely, given logged behavior ranges, but anything was possible.

The Trimmers and the Regulators went their opposite ways, walking smoothly, quickly enough, considering. They abandoned their slow-mo's—possibly booby-trapped, but giving too much signature anyway—and they walked it. Left their dead amid rocks and walked. It took a fair slice of forever, but everyone was glad to pay it out of their lives.

Only when the Trimmers had the northwest boundary in sight, well clear of Checkpoint Reuben just in case, did Sam bring it up.

"Questions, Thomas?"

"What's that?" the kid asked, off with his thoughts, then understood. "The two secrets? I can ask?"

"This side of The Redux it's only fair."

Sam stopped. Thomas stopped. The others kept walking, the group separating now, dividing as precaution: Angel and Sunny going wide toward the north, Walt going alone to the west proper. Getting it out.

Leaving Sam as good cop—and bad, should it come to that.

"So, what are they?" Direct, not defiant. Watching the others go.

Sam didn't hesitate. "First, to get back thousands, we have to sacrifice hundreds."

"Seems right. Seems fair. You can't save everyone. I don't—wait, are you saying that when we switch modes, some *always* die? *Have* to die?"

Sam began walking again, slowly, making it casual. He always wanted to deceive at this point. Give the beautiful lie. "Take it further."

Thomas was following. "Wait! How do I take it further? We're causing coarse action. Naturally some will die. The trauma—"

"Take it further!" Sam rounded on him, stopping again. Good cop *and* bad. Gun and duelling stick ready.

"How further?" Then his face locked into a mask, his eyes wide, his mouth wide like a miniature of The Redux's trophies. "*You* kill them!" And accepting: "*We* kill them!"

Sam's voice was soft, nearly toneless. "We use the energies of the random few to let us free the rest!"

"You used *me* to do *that*!"

"Certainly did. Certainly do. Certainly will. Every time. A devil's bargain, but the fairest trade we can ever make."

"It's murder!"

"It surely is. Collateral damage. Friendly fire. Never personal. Our powers have to come from somewhere!"

"But you kill them!" Thomas said it more softly now, beyond rage, beyond disbelief. And the *you* worried Sam. Not *we*. "You used me."

"However it works, the power comes through the pure. Has to. We find. You send. Small price to pay when you think it through. Small enough price. Hundreds dead so thousands upon thousands can be saved."

"It's immoral!"

"Amoral more like. But which is better? There goes a village, a town. You'll have hundreds dead outright or thousands dying slowly? Starving. Eaten by insects, dogs, lying there aware in the fugue."

"But you're heroes!"

Sam didn't try to answer that. What could you say? *Merely flashmen, Thomas. Merely flashmen.*

"Which is better?" was all he said.

"What!"

"Do we try to get some or let them all go?"

"You try to get them all!" Tears were running down the kid's cheeks.

"Doesn't work like that. Which is better?"

"It doesn't excuse it!"

"Never does. Never can. Explains is all. You did well today. You saved some who would have died."

"You'll kill me if I tell about this." The look of terror in his eyes had turned to cold understanding. "That's the other secret."

"Doesn't go like that," Sam said, giving the final wonderful lie. "We give you the Lethe drug. You remember none of it."

"The Lethe drug? What if I refuse?"

"We make you. Or the WHO doctors will. Or they'll imprison you, take you away. The world can't know."

I could pretend, Thomas might have said. *Go along with it.* But Sam had seen the test results, the psych profile, and knew he couldn't.

"Think it through," was all Sam said, and started walking away.

"I hate you!" Thomas called after him. "I thought you were heroes! I hate you all!"

"You'll be hero enough if you accept the responsibility. That's why you were chosen. I'll be at the perimeter."

SAM LEFT HIM RAGING, weeping, sitting in the dust. Sat in the shade of some boulders himself as the last of the day fell away, and thought it through again. Because you always had to.

What do they want from us? Sam asked himself, yet again. *Clean answers? Salvation without a price? Something for nothing?* He ran them all, all the old questions and trade-offs. Came up hard and strong, thinking of Mae, of Sunny and Walt and the look on Angel's face back at Tagger's when she first saw him again.

You could tell them. Put it to a vote. Nothing would change, most like. But they *wanted* heroes, someone to believe in more than they wanted statistics and the truth, not just someone to make the hard decisions, maintain the beautiful lie, but to *hide* such things. Saviors who wouldn't quit even when they were struck at from *both* sides, who without ever planning or wanting to protected them from the truth. Even from the wayward bits and pieces of their own natures.

It was early morning before the kid came in. Sam always felt he could guess which way it would go, but this time he wasn't entirely sure. His pistol's safety was off just in case—Lethe—but the holster cover was clipped down. His duelling stick was carefully in its sheath.

The kid came strolling along, kicking dust.

"Wanted to be a hero, Mr. Aitch," he said, falling in alongside when Sam started walking. "That's all."

"I know," Sam said. "So we do impressions, Thomas. There are times when second best just has to do."

Afterword to "Flashmen"

THE TERM "MONDEGREEN" was coined by British writer Sylvia
Wright in 1954 because she once misheard the words of an old
song. She took the final lines of the stanza:

Ye Highlands and Ye Lowlands
Oh where hae you been?
They hae slay the Earl of Moray,
And laid him on the green.

as being *They hae slay the Earl of Moray, And Lady Mondegreen*,
thus including his consort in the good lord's demise. Years
later, when Wright learned the truth, she coined the expression
mondegreen to describe this surprisingly common occurrence of
mishearing words in a conversation, speech or song. Anyone who
once tried to fathom popular song lyrics in pre-Internet days will
be familiar with the results, for thus we were blessed with "The ants
are, my friends, blowin' in the wind," the Tequila Mockingbird and
other such wonders.

"Flashmen" is largely the result of a mondegreen, of mishearing
the line "We were merely freshmen" in a 1996 Verve Pipe song as
"We were merely flashmen." It was totally, splendidly wrong, of
course, but was so mysterious and compelling in that wrongness
that it was hard to let go. It made me get out a fragment I'd written
one evening on the banks of the Yarra in Melbourne during the
1999 World Science Fiction Convention—the opening lines you
see here—and it sent me back to doing a riff on the Strugatskys'
Roadside Picnic: a way of paying back and passing on.

So, too, included in the mix was Sergio Leone, whose gift
of driven individuals wearing dusters, showing attitude and hard
edges soon had me snatching monikers from that list of titles and
character names I keep handy, names that invariably bring their
own power to the page. Walt Senny was there demanding his
turn, and Sam Aitchander, Sunny Jim Cosimo, Maisie Day and
the rest, playing their part in a story about dubious heroes and
misunderstanding, about becoming what you do, about duty of care
and the worth of good intentions.

And about the truly alien.

As a creative process it's what I call "sewing whole cloth," fitting disparate bits together like this, and it's a common practice for so many writers. Whether storytelling or doing stand-up comedy, songwriting or surviving in politics, it's usually a matter of paying attention and being receptive to whatever comes. As Louis Pasteur famously said: "Fortune favors the prepared mind."

The Blue Marlin Whore

Captain Van Graffen came to the Blue Marlin
Drawn by the light of the red chandelier,
It was an old inn quite close to the harbor,
A dozen years older since he was last here.
He was a voyager, a daring sea-rover,
She the one child of a merchant of beer,
He came at midnight to drink for an hour,
She came from walking the pier.

It was a wild night and then in the morning
She turns to him with a tender reply,
Answers his question that her name is Jenny,
Watches the memory that clouds up his eye.
There was a young girl that he can remember,
He would have married had her heart been true,
Jenny reminds him there's always a young girl
And whores have their memories too.

He was a captain and she was a lady,
That's how their thoughts went as evening wore on.
But he was a pirate and she was a harlot,
How could they ever go wrong?

He says, "Dear Jenny, I need you to tell me,
If you are that lost one I really should know."
She replies laughing, "Does it really matter?
The past that is dear was a long time ago.
And you went a voyaging, a daring sea-rover,
And I did not know what it meant to be free.
Let the past go now that I am your lover,
And you can come home from the sea."

So if you ever should make the Blue Marlin,
Drawn by the light of the red chandelier.
Listen a while, you'll hear of the young harlot
And of her captain who's there every year.

He was a captain and she was a lady,
That's how their thoughts went as evening wore on.
But he was a pirate and she was a harlot,
How could they ever go wrong?

TOOTHER

As DAN TRUSWELL GAVE his signature three-three knock on the door in the modest hospital tower of Everton Psychiatric Facility that Friday morning, he couldn't help but glance through the second-floor window at the new sign down in the turning circle. *Everton Psychiatric Facility* it said. He'd never get used to it. That was the more politically correct name for Blackwater Psychiatric Hospital, just as words like client and guest had completely replaced patient and inmate.

"Peter, it's Dan."

Dan didn't enter Peter Rait's room, of course. That wasn't their arrangement. He just waited, looking at his reflection in the small mirror Peter kept hanging outside his door, surprised not so much by the slate-grey eyes and fly-away hair but by how white that hair had become. He was fifty-nine, for heaven's sake! It was something else he'd never get used to.

Finally the door opened and Peter stood there in his pyjamas.

"Careful, Doctor Dan. That's a dangerous one."

"They all are, Peter. Carla said you've been yelling. Another nightmare?"

Peter looked tired, troubled. His black hair was tousled from sleep. "They don't usually come this often now. Harry's going to phone."

"Harry Badman?" Dear industrious Harry was two years out of his life, distanced by the usual string of promotions, secondments and strategic sidelining that marked the lives of so many career detectives in the New South Wales Police Force. "All right, Peter, so how does this dream relate?"

"Ask Harry about the teeth, Doctor Dan."

Dan's thoughts went at once to the recent desecration at Sydney's Rookwood Cemetery. "Is this about—?"

"Ask him."

"What do you have, Peter?"

"I can't say till he confirms it. Ask him. He'll know."

Dan made himself hold back the rush of questions. "It's been a while."

Peter did finally manage a smile, something of one. "It has, Doctor Dan."

Dan smiled too. "Phil knows?"

"Some of it. I'll give him an update at breakfast. But it's important. Very important."

"Tell me the rest, Peter."

"I really can't."

"There are voices?"

"God, yes. But strange." Neither of them smiled at the bathos. What internal voices weren't? "They're coming over time."

Dan frowned. This was something new. "Across years?"

"The first is from the sixties."

"More, Peter."

"Let Harry start it."

You've started it!, Dan almost said, but knew to hold back, just as Peter had known how much to use as a tease.

"Listen, Peter—"

"Talk later. I'll leave you two alone."

And he closed the door. Dan, of course, looked straight into Peter's mirror again, had the good grace to laugh, then headed downstairs.

FORTY-NINE MINUTES LATER, AS Dan sat in his office reviewing the patient database, Harry Badman phoned from Sydney. There was the inevitable small-talk, the polite and awkward minimum that let them stitch up the years as best they could. Dan Truswell and Harry Badman liked one another a great deal, but their friendship had never been easy far from where their respective careers met: for Harry, pursuing the more dangerous exponents of extraordinary human behavior; for Dan, fathoming the often extraordinary reasons for it.

Finally Harry's tone changed. "I need to see you, Dan."

"It's about what happened at Rookwood last Saturday night, isn't it?"

"What have you heard?"

"What was in the news. A grave was desecrated. A recent burial." Dan said nothing about teeth. This had been one of Peter Rait's dreams after all, and it had been a while since the intense, still-young man had been "active" like this. More importantly it was Dan's way of testing Peter's special talent after all this time.

"Samantha Reid. Aged 41. Buried on Friday, dug up on Sunday sometime between two and four in the morning. Cold rainy night. No-one saw anything. The body was hauled from the coffin and left lying beside the grave."

"So, not just a grave 'tampered with,' like the papers said. Your people are good, Harry. Why the call?"

"Things were removed from the scene. I'd like your take on it."

"Stop being coy. What was 'removed'?"

"The teeth, Dan. All the teeth."

Dan had an odd rush of emotion: revulsion, fascination, the familiar numb amazement he always felt whenever one of Peter's predictions played out like this. And there was the usual excess of rationalism as if to compensate. "What do the deceased's dental records show? Were there gold fillings?"

"Dan, *all* the teeth. And it's not the first desecration. Just the first to make the news."

Dan knew he'd been slow this time, but allowed that he was out of practice too. "There were others?"

"From secluded and disused parts of the cemetery. Much older graves."

"But recent desecrations?"

"Hard to tell conclusively. Not all were reported back then. It didn't look good for the cemetery authorities. The graves were tidied up; nothing was said. We would have assumed these earlier violations were unrelated except…" He actually paused. Had the subject been less serious, it would have been comical.

"Come on, Harry. Someone's collecting teeth. What else do you have?"

"That Rattigan murder in Darlinghurst a month back. The pensioner, remember?"

"Go on."

"She wasn't strangled like the media said."

"No?"

"She was bitten to death."

Dan was surprised to find that his mouth had fallen open in astonishment. "Bitten?"

"At least two hundred times. Increasing severity."

"These could be different crimes, Harry. What makes you think they're related?"

"Teeth fragments were found in some of the wounds. Very old teeth."

But not in very old mouths, Dan realized. "Dentures made from these older desecrations?"

"Exactly."

"Surely there was saliva DNA from whoever wore them."

"No," Harry said.

Dan grasped the implications. "So, not necessarily biting as such. Someone made dentures from these older corpse teeth and—what?— killed the Rattigan woman using some sort of hand-held prosthesis?"

"Spring-loaded and vicious. All we can think of. And that's *several* sets of dentures, Dan. We've traced teeth fragments back to the occupants of three older desecrations: graves from 1894, 1906 and 1911. All female. No fragments from newer teeth—"

"Too new to shatter."

"Exactly. But there could be other teeth used, from other desecrations we don't know of. There are some very old graves there; we wouldn't necessarily be able to tell. So all we have is a major fetish angle. Something ritualistic."

"My phone number hasn't changed, Harry." The accusation hung there. *You didn't call sooner!*

"You've got your life, Dan. Annie. Phil." The barest hesitation. "Peter. I didn't want to intrude."

Dan stared at the mid-morning light through his office windows and nodded to himself. "You've profiled it as what?"

"I'd rather not say. That's what this is about. Getting another take."

"Official?"

"Can be. You want the file? I'll email a PDF right now. Drive up tomorrow first thing."

"See you at the Imperial Hotel at eleven."

"See you then."

SEVENTEEN HOURS LATER THEY were sitting with light beers in a quiet corner of the Imperial on Bennet Street trying to make the small-talk thing work face to face. They did well enough for six minutes before Harry put them both out of their misery.

"You got the file okay. Anything?"

Dan set down his glass. "A question first. You kept something back on the phone yesterday. You said the Rattigan woman was bitten to death."

"That's what happened," Harry said. He looked tanned, less florid than Dan remembered; in his casual clothes he could have been another tourist visiting the local wineries.

"Her teeth were taken as well, weren't they?"

Harry barely hesitated. "How'd you know?"

Dan lifted a manilla folder from the seat beside him. "The results of Net searches. Know what a toother is, Harry?"

"Tell me."

"It was a vocation, to call it that, associated with body-snatching back in the eighteenth, nineteenth centuries. Back when resurrectionists— lovely name—dug up bodies to sell to medical academies for their anatomy classes. There were people who did the same to get the teeth. Sold them to dentists to make false teeth."

"Dug up corpses?"

"Sometimes. Or did deals with resurrection men already in the trade. Mostly they'd roam battlefields and take teeth from dead soldiers."

"You're kidding."

"Not when you think about it. It was much better than getting teeth from the gibbet or the grave. Ivory and whalebone were either too expensive or decayed. No enamel coating. Teeth made from porcelain sounded wrong or were too brittle. Corpse teeth were better, soldiers' teeth usually best of all, injuries permitting. Sets of authentic Waterloo Teeth fetch quite a bit these days."

"What, dentures made from soldiers who died at Waterloo?"

Dan nodded. "Fifty thousand in a single day. Mostly young men. Supply caught up with demand with battles like that. But that's the thing. There weren't many battles on that scale. Demand outstripped supply."

"You already knew this stuff?"

"Some of it. You know what I'm like. And that's quite a file you sent. I stayed up late."

Harry had his notebook on the table in front of him. He opened it and began making notes. "Go on."

"Back then there just weren't enough corpses of executed criminals or unknown homeless to satisfy the demand. Not enough from the right age or gender, even when you had poorer people selling their own teeth. Some resurrectionists began killing people."

"And these toothers did too."

"There's little conclusive evidence that I'm aware of. But that's the point, Harry. You do a job like this, you try to make sure there isn't."

"But body-snatchers can't be doing this."

"It presents that way is all I'm saying—a similar MO. If the cemetery desecrations and the Rattigan death *are* related, as the fragments suggest, we need to allow a context for it."

Harry wrote something and looked up. "So this joker could be proceeding like a modern-day toother."

Dan shrugged. "Just putting it forward, Harry. He took the Rattigan woman's teeth. Used others to kill her. So, a psychopath possibly. A sociopath definitely, probably highly organized. A latter-day resurrectionist? Not in the sense we know it. But we only have the teeth being taken and the single recent murder. I assume there are no similar cases in the CID database?"

Harry shook his head. "The usual run of biting during domestics and sexual assault. Random mostly. Nothing like this."

"Then he may be escalating, either a loner doing his own thing or someone acquainted with the old resurrectionist methodology."

Harry started writing again. "Do you have more on that?"

"Going back a hundred, two hundred years, he'd see a likely subject, get them alone and have an accomplice grab them while he slapped a pitch-plaster over their mouth and nose—"

Harry looked up. "A what?"

"A sticky mass of plaster mixed with pitch. Mostly used during sexual assault, but what some resurrectionists used too. Silenced your victim and incapacitated them. Suffocated them if that was the intention. All over in minutes."

Harry was suitably horrified. "They just held them till they expired?"

"Or did a traditional 'burking'—covered the mouth and nose with their hand till the victim asphyxiated."

"This actually happened?"

"It did. The biting takes it in a completely different direction, of course. Was the Rattigan woman drugged or bound?"

"Not that we can tell."

"That tends to suggest an accomplice. Someone to help restrain her. Do Sheehan's people have anything?"

"Just the fetish, ritual angle, Dan. A loner after trophies. It's early days. But you're taking it further, saying there could be an accomplice, someone getting the teeth for someone else—who then makes dentures and uses them to kill."

Dan glanced around to make sure that they weren't being overheard. They still had the bar virtually to themselves. "Just another possibility, Harry. Much less likely. And no conventional client. There's no economic reason for it now. It presents like that is what I'm saying."

"Okay, so either a loner or a gopher for someone who originally wanted the teeth for fetishistic reasons but is escalating. He now kills people and does the extractions himself. Focusing on females?"

"Seems that way. But until we know more I'm still tempted to say a loner with a special mission."

Harry drained his glass and set it down on the table. "So why do a *new* grave? Why show his hand like this? Was he interrupted before he could finish? Did he *want* people to know?"

"He's fixated. He may have seen the Reid woman alive and wanted that particular set of teeth. Like in the Poe story."

Harry frowned. "What Poe story?"

"*Berenice.* A brother obsessed with his sister's teeth extracts them while she's in a cataleptic coma."

"Where do you get this stuff, Dan?"

"They're called books, Harry. But this guy is doing it for himself. And I definitely believe it's a he. He could be using the more traditional techniques."

"Drugs would be easier."

"They would. But he wants them fully conscious. So we're back to the ritual aspect you mentioned."

"That emblematic thing," Harry said.

"The what?"

"Two—three years back. That conversation we had at Rollo's. You said that people try to be more. Have emblematic lives."

Dan never ceased to be amazed by what Harry remembered from their conversations. "Emblematic? I said that?"

"Four beers. You said that. Make themselves meaningful to themselves, you said. Do symbolic things."

"Okay, well this is his thing, Harry. We can't be sure if he's following aspects of the old toother/resurrectionist MO but Sheehan's right. Given the special dentures he's made for himself, doing this has some powerful fetishistic or symbolic meaning for him. And he may have done this a lot: gone somewhere, seen a lovely set of teeth on someone, arranged to get them alone, then suffocated or bitten them and taken their teeth."

"That's horrible. You actually think he may have already done that and hidden the bodies?"

"Because of the desecrations, the older teeth being used, that's how I'm seeing it, and it may get worse." Dan thought of Peter Rait's voices. *They're coming over time.*

"How could it—ah! He may start removing the teeth while the victims are alive. And conscious?"

Dan deliberately left a silence, waiting for Harry to say it.

It took a five-count. "You think it's already got to that! But the coroner's report for the Rattigan woman showed the extractions were post-mortem."

"Harry, I think that may have been her one bit of good fortune. She died just as he was starting."

Harry shook his head. "Then we can definitely expect more."

"I'd say so. And it depends."

"On what, Dan? On what?"

"On whether it's local. Someone developing his ritual. Or if it's something international that's been relocated here."

"International?"

"Ask Sheehan to check with Interpol or whoever you guys work with now. Find case similarities. Forced dental extractions. Post- and *ante*-mortem."

"Can you come down to Sydney?"

"Phone me Monday and I'll let you know. I need to speak with someone first. You could stay around. Visit some wineries, come over for dinner tonight. Annie would love to see you."

They both knew it wouldn't go that way. Not this time. Not yet. "Sorry, Dan. I need to get going with this. Take a rain-check?"

"Roger that," Dan said.

AT 2 PM THAT afternoon, Dan met with Peter Rait and Phillip Crow at a picnic table sheltered by the largest Moreton Bay Fig in the hospital grounds. Peter, thin, black-haired, pale-skinned, on any ordinary day looked a decade younger than his forty-two years, but his recent nightmares had given him an intense, peaked quality that Dan found unsettling. He sat with a manilla folder in front of him.

To his left on the same bench was Phil, four years older, fair-headed, stocky, with the sort of weathered but pleasant face that Carla liked to call "old-school Australian." He looked up and smiled as Dan arrived. "Just like old times, Doctor Dan."

"It is, Phil," Dan said as he sat across from them. He had to work not to smile. Peter and Phil were his "psychosleuths," their talent pretty well dormant these last three years. Officially, both men had been rehabilitated back into society; both had elected to stay, their choice, taking accommodation and rations in return for doing odd jobs. And called it Blackwater Psychiatric Hospital, of course.

Given Peter's present state, Dan couldn't enjoy the reunion as much as he would have liked. He went straight to the heart of it.

"Peter, tell me about the voices."

Peter took two typed pages from the folder in front of him. "Here are the transcripts," he said, sounding every bit as tired as he looked.

Dan was surprised by the odd choice of words. "Transcripts? How did you manage that?"

"They keep playing over. Two different conversations now. Two different victims."

"But how—?"

"I just can, Doctor Dan, okay? It's pretty distressing. You can't know how awful it is."

Dan saw that Peter wasn't just tired; he was exhausted. "You can't stop it?"

"Giving you these might do it. Getting them out."

"Nothing else?"

"Not yet. Please, just read them."

Dan looked at the first page.

TRANSCRIPT 1

[miscellaneous sounds]

[male voice / mature, controlled]

"As they say, there is the good news and the bad news."

[terrified female voice, quite young]

"What do you mean?"

"You have a choice here. The good news is that you'll wake up. All your teeth will be gone, but we'll have a relatively easy time with the extractions and you *will* wake up. You'll be alive. The alternative—you make my job difficult and you won't wake up. That's the deal."

"Why are you doing this?"

"What's it to be?"

"Why?"

"It's necessary. What's it to be?"

"There has to be a reason!"

"I'll count to three.

"Just tell me why! Please!"

"One."

"For God's sake! Why are you doing this? Why?"

"Two. Choose or I will."

"You can't expect me—"

"Three. Too late."

"No! No! I want to wake up! Please! I want to wake up!"

"All right. Just this once."

"One question."

"Go ahead."

"You could drug me and do it. Do whatever you want. Why do I even have to choose?"

"Now that's the thing. And, really, you already know why. I need you conscious for it. I may drug you at the end. Oh, dear, look. You're pissing yourself."

[sobbing]

"Why? Why? Why?"

"You're not listening. It's my thing. I need to see your eyes while I'm doing it."

"Another question."

"There always is. What is it?"

"What will you do with—with *them*? Afterwards?"

"Make a nice set of dentures. Maybe I could sell them back to you. That would be a rather nice irony, wouldn't it? Irony is quite our thing."

"What about me? Afterwards?"

"You'll wake up. Hate us forever. Go on with the rest of your life."

"But I'll wake up? I *will* wake up?"

"Make it easy for us now and, yes. You have my word."

"You're saying 'us' and 'our'."

"Oh dear. So I am."

"What's that over there?"

"I think that's enough questions."

"What *is* that?"

[sundry sounds]

[victim screaming]

[audio ends]

Dan looked up. "Peter—"

"The next one, Doctor Dan. Read the next one, please. Same male voice. Different female victim."

Dan turned to it at once.

TRANSCRIPT 2

[miscellaneous sounds]

"You're crazy!"

"I hope not, for your sake. Major dental work needs a degree of control."

"But why? Why me?"

"The usual reason. Chance. Purest hazard. You were on hand."

"Then pick someone else!"

"From someone else's viewpoint I did. But enough talk. We have a lot to do."

"Listen. Listen to me. My name is Pamela Deering. I'm a mother. I have two little girls. Emma and Grace. Aged 7 and 5. My husband's name—"

[muffled sounds]

"Ssh now, Pamela. No more bonding. We have a lot to do."

"What? What do we have to do?"

"Let's just say that your girls and hubby will have to call you Gummy instead of Mummy." [pause] "That's our little joke, Pamela."

[sobbing]

"Please. Please don't do this."

"We have to, Mu—er—Gummy. It's our thing. It won't take long."

"You're saying 'we', 'us.' You're not alone. There's someone else."

"Tsk. How rude of me. You want to meet my associate. Over here. Try to turn your head a little more."

[sundry sounds]

"But that's not—"

[victim screaming]

[audio ends]

Dan lowered the pages. "There are two of them. He's not a loner."

"Seems that way," Peter said.

"Do you get accents at all?"

"Educated male. Educated enough. Enunciates carefully so it's hard to know. The first woman sounds English. The Deering woman sounds Australian."

"But not recent. Over time, you said."

Peter nodded. "Sixties, seventies." He gestured to include Phil, as if he were equally part of this, both of them hearing the voices. "You have to protect us, Doctor Dan."

"I always do. That comes first."

"How will you?"

"Our old method. You aren't mentioned. Any locations you give, I'll have Harry say a phonecall came in, anonymous. Someone overheard a disturbance, cries, screaming. Wouldn't give their name."

"They'll buy it?"

"Why not? It happens more and more these days. Remember, we *all* need to stay out of this."

Phil leant forward. "What happens now?"

"We have a name," Dan said. "Pamela Deering. Harry can check that out. Meanwhile, Peter—"

"I'll keep dreaming."

"You don't have to. We can give you a sedative."

"No," Peter said. "I'm doing it for them."

Dan saw the haunted look in the tired dark eyes. "We need this, Peter."

"I know."

THIRTY-TWO CASES WERE LISTED in the international database, Harry told Dan on the phone that Monday morning, different countries, different cities, different decades, though it was the sort of statistic that convinced them both that many others existed.

"They say two thousand people a year in New Guinea are killed by coconuts falling on their heads," Harry said. "How do you get a statistic like that? It can only ever be the ones you *hear* about. It's like that here. These are just the ones that came to the attention of different national authorities and have anything approximating a similar MO."

"What about the time-frame, Harry?"

"Dan, we've got cases going back to the 30s and 40s, even earlier. Prague. Krakow. Trieste. Bangkok, for heaven's sake! They can't be the same person. It can't be a generational thing. It doesn't work like that."

"I'd normally agree," Dan said. "But you say the MOs are similar for these thirty-two?"

"Victims bitten to death, post- or ante-mortem; the various odontologists' findings give both. Their own teeth removed before, during or after; again there's a range. Older fragments in the wounds in some instances, say, nineteen, twenty per cent."

"Harry—"

"You're not going to say a secret society. An international brotherhood of toothers."

Dan gave a grim smile. "No, but look how it presents. It's as if a very old, well-traveled sociopath has been able to find agents across a lifetime and still has at least one accomplice now, doing his dirty work. The Reid disinterment was done manually, not using a back-hoe. That took a lot of effort."

"You believe this? Sheehan may not buy it."

"At this point I'm just trying to understand it, Harry. Rookwood and Darlinghurst suggest he may be local, at least for now."

"Can you come down to Sydney?"

"On Thursday. I'll be bringing Peter Rait."

Harry knew enough about Peter's gifts not to question it. "He has something?"

"For your eyes only."

"What, Dan?"

"Check if you have a missing person, a possible victim named Pamela Deering." He spelled out the name. "It could be from the sixties or seventies."

"How on earth did—?"

"Harry, you know how this has to be done. Yes or no?"

"Yes. Yes. Pamela Deering. Bring Peter with you. You got somewhere to stay?"

"I've arranged for unofficial digs at the old Gladesville Hospital on Victoria Road. There's a coffee shop on the grounds called Cornucopia. Meet us there around mid-day Thursday, okay?"

"Cornucopia. Got it."

"And bring a map of Rookwood Cemetery will you? The adjacent streets."

"You think he lives in the area?"

"Peter needs it."

"Done."

AT A CONVENIENCE STORE roadstop in Branxton on their drive down that Thursday morning, Peter presented Dan with a third transcript.

"You need to factor this in," was all Peter said as he handed it over. He looked more drawn than ever, as if he had barely slept the night before.

"Last night?"

"Last two nights."

"You kept it to yourself."

Peter ran a hand through his dark hair. "Look, I have to be sure, okay? I have to know that it's not—just coming from me. That I can trust it."

"And you do?"

"I'm satisfied now, Doctor Dan. I couldn't make this up."

Dan leant against the car door and read the carefully typed words.

TRANSCRIPT 3

[miscellaneous sounds]

"You're the one who took the Kellar woman. Those poor women in Zurich. You're going to take out all my teeth!"

[sounds]

"Take them out? Oh no. Not this time. Toother was very specific."

[sounds, like things being shaken in a metal box]

"Toother?"

"Yes. Your name please?"

"What difference does it make?"

"But isn't that what the experts advise? Always try to use names? Don't let them dehumanize you. My name is Paul."

"Your real name? Not Toother?"

"It'll do for today."

"Then I'll be Janice. For today. Who is Toother?"

"Why, your host, Janice-for-today. The one who taught me all I know. Mostly he takes, but sometimes he gives."

"Gives?"

"Sometimes. I have my little hammer and my little punch, see? And you have such a full, generous mouth. Today we are going to put teeth back in. Lots and lots, see?"

[more rattling sounds]

"Big teeth. Men's teeth. We're going to call you Smiler."

[more rattling sounds]

[victim sobbing]

[victim screaming]

DAN LEFT PETER TO drowse for much of the journey south, but as they were on the bridge crossing the Hawkesbury River, he glanced aside and saw the dark eyes watching him.

"You okay?" he asked.

"Sorry for losing it back there," Peter said, as if resuming a conversation from moments before. "Things are escalating for me too. With this latest—exchange—I get something about his trophies."

Dan wished he weren't driving right then. He pulled into the low-speed lane. "You see them?"

"Just lots of—grimaces. You know, teeth without lips. It's the most terrifying thing. Bared teeth. No skin covering. Like eyes without lids. Horrible."

"Are they on shelves, in drawers, boxes, what?"

"Displayed. Arranged somehow, secretly. Nothing like smiles or grins. I just see them as bared teeth, Doctor Dan. In a private space. Sorry. It isn't much."

"Try, Peter. Whatever you get. These voices—"

"It's more than just voices. It's reciprocal now."

"Reciprocal? What does that mean?"

"It isn't just going one way. He knows I've been listening. Accessing his files. He was very angry at first, but now he's enjoying it. He's fighting back."

"How, Peter? How does he fight back?"

"Sending things, thoughts, images. They're not mine. It's more than delusions, Doctor Dan, I'm sure of it. More than my usual hypersensitivity. I just had to be sure."

"Understood. Go on."

"It's Rookwood. All those graves. I keep seeing the bodies, vulnerable, helpless, keep seeing the teeth. They're mostly all teeth, lots of dentures too. But there's such anguish. Such rage."

"Female burials?"

"Female *and* male. They're all murmuring, chattering. Some desperately wanting to be picked, calling 'Pick me! Pick me!' Others hiding. Desperately hiding. As if alive. They're not, but it's like they are for him."

"Is there a voice talking to you now?"

"*Like* a voice, Doctor Dan. *Not* a voice, but like one. I have certainties, just know things. He wants it like that."

"He's found someone he can share with. He hears the bodies calling to him you say?"

"How he sees them. Calling, begging. 'Pick me! Pick me!' Or hiding, resisting. Furious. Either way he sees it as liberation, sees them as all waiting to be chosen. The living victims too."

"He's *saving* them?"

"Liberating them is his word, yes. Living or dead, it doesn't matter. It just means a different method of retrieval."

"Retrieval!" Dan gave a laugh, completely without humor. "But he's in the area?"

Peter shrugged. "It's a huge cemetery, Doctor Dan. It's not called the Sleeping City for nothing. He's committed so many desecrations there. You can't begin to know. Secretly. Passionately. This is his place for now."

"Peter, I trust you completely. Just let me know what you get. Anything."

IT WAS STRANGE TO walk the grounds of the decommissioned, largely deserted mental hospital at Gladesville later that morning. The former wards and out-buildings had been turned into offices for various governmental health services, so by day it was like a stately, manicured, museum estate. There were still vehicles in the carparks, people walking the paths, roadways and lawns, giving the place a semblance of its former life.

Dan walked those daylight roads now, glad that he wasn't doing it at night. After dark the offices and carparks were deserted, but had a strange new half-life, quarter-life, life-in-death. Instead of being left to stand as part of a vast col of blackness overlooking the Parramatta River, the old sandstone buildings and empty roads were lit, as if beckoning, urging, waiting for those willing to surrender bits of their sanity to make the place live again.

When Dan reached Cornucopia, he found Harry waiting at a table outside the café door.

"I've driven past this place a thousand times," Harry said, "and never knew how big it was. Where's Peter?"

"He sends his apologies. Said he wants to keep his mind off this for now."

"Doesn't want me asking questions," Harry said. "I can understand that."

"Harry—"

"Dan, I know how it can be for him. How it *was*. Just say hi for me."

They went in and placed their orders, then sat watching the clear autumn sky above the sandstone walls. Harry took out his notebook.

"The Deering woman went missing from a holiday house at Cottesloe Beach in 1967."

"That's Western Australia, isn't it?"

"Right. There was blood, definite signs of a struggle, but no body. And before you ask, there were no teeth fragments."

"You've been thorough."

"Now that there's international scrutiny, we have different resources available."

"What did you tell Sheehan?"

"That it came up in a missing persons keyword sweep. In the last three decades alone there are thirty-six names of missing persons nationally where blood mixed with saliva was found at locations where each of them was last seen."

"Oral blood?"

"Right. So tell me what Peter has found."

Dan passed him the transcript folder. "Harry, you might want to finish eating first."

DAN FOUND IT HARD to sleep that night. They were in separate rooms in an otherwise empty, former staff residence at the southern end of the hospital grounds, a converted single-story brick house. It was a cool, late autumn night, pleasant for sleeping, but with all that had happened, Dan felt restless, too keenly aware of the empty roads outside and the lit, abandoned buildings, so normal, yet—the only word for it—so abnormal, waiting in the night.

The lights are on but nobody's home.

The old euphemism for madness kept coming back to him. No doubt there were security personnel doing the rounds, one, possibly more, but, just the same, there was the distinct sense that Peter and he were the only living souls in the place.

Dan kept thinking of what Peter had told him that morning, of the bodies as repositories for teeth, grimaces, smiles, lying there waiting, hiding, some calling, chattering in darkness, wanting any kind of life, others dreading such attention.

It was absurd, foolish, but Rookwood Necropolis was barely ten kilometers away, 285 hectares of one of the largest dedicated cemeteries in the world, site of nearly a million interments.

In his half-drowsing state, Dan kept thinking, too, of the old 1963 movie, *Jason and the Argonauts*, of King Aeëtes collecting and sowing the teeth from the skull of the slain Hydra, raising up an army of skeletons to combat Jason and his crew. Dan imagined human teeth being first plucked and then sown in Rookwood's older, less tended fields. If the Hydra's teeth raised up *human* skeletons, what sort of creature would human teeth raise up?

He must have fallen asleep at last, for the next thing he knew Peter was rousing him.

"Doctor Dan?" Peter said, switching on Dan's bedside light.

"Peter? What is it?"

Peter was fully dressed, his hair and eyes wild. "He's got someone! Right now. He has someone!"

Dan grabbed his watch, saw that it was 12:16 am. "He told you this?"

"No. But I saw anyway. He's furious that I saw."

Dan climbed out of bed, began dressing. "The reciprocal thing?"

"It backfired, yes. Showed me more than he wanted. He's so angry, but he's enjoying it too! He's still enjoying it."

"The drama. The added excitement."

"Yes. We have to hurry!"

Dan reached for his mobile. "Where, Peter? I need to call Harry."

"Good. Yes. An old factory site in Somersby Road. A few streets back from the cemetery. But I need to be there. I have to be closer, Doctor Dan. Her life depends on it."

"Those women in the transcripts—?"

"Never woke up. None of them."

"Understood."

Harry answered his mobile before Dan's call went to voicemail. He sounded leaden from sleep until Dan explained what they had. "You'll be there before I will, Dan, but I'll have two units there. Four officers. Best I can do for now. Where are you?"

"Still at the hospital. Heading out to the car. We'll need an ambulance too, Harry. The Somersby Road corner closest to the cemetery. Tell them to wait for us. No sirens."

"Right. You're sure about this, Dan?"

"Peter is."

"I'm on my way!"

"Harry, Peter stays out of it. How do we cover ourselves?"

"Anonymous tip. A neighbor heard screaming. I'll have a word with whoever turns up. Go!"

Two patrol cars and an ambulance were waiting at the corner of Somersby Road, lights off, ready. There was no sign of Harry's car yet.

"You Dr Truswell?" an officer asked, appearing at Dan's driver-side window when he pulled up.

"Yes. Look—"

"Harry explained. I'm Senior Constable Banners. Warwick Banners. Just tell us where to go."

"It's there!" Peter said, pointing. "That building there!"

"Right. Follow us in but stay well back, hear?"

"We hear you," Dan said, and turned to Peter. "You have to stay in the car, okay?"

"I know," Peter said. "And keep the doors locked."

Dan joined the police officers and paramedics waiting at the kerb. It took them seconds to reach the building two doors down, a large brick factory-front with closed and locked roller-doors and smaller street door. The premises looked so quiet and innocent in the night, and not for the first time Dan wondered if Peter could be mistaken.

There was a single crash as the street door was forced. In moments they were in off the street, standing in utter quiet, in darkness lit by the beams of five torches.

Again it was all so ordinary, so commonplace. But Dan knew only too well how such places could be terrifying in their simplicity. He had seen the Piggyback Killer's rooms in Newtown, such a mundane blend of walls, hallways and furniture until you opened that one door, found the two coffins. He had seen Corinne Kester's balcony view and the shed with its treacherous windows, had seen Peter Rait's own room come alive in a wholly unexpected way right there at Blackwater. Such simple, terrifying places.

This, too, was such an ordinary, extraordinary space. Who knew what it had been originally: a warehouse, a meat packing plant, some other kind of factory, but taking up the entire ground floor, large and low-ceilinged, with painted out windows and a large, windowless inner section that took up most of the back half of the premises. Given the absence of screams being reported in the neighborhood, it was very likely double brick or sound-proofed in some other way.

Dan followed the police and paramedics as they pushed through the double doors into that inner precinct. At first, it seemed totally dark.

Then Dan saw that intervening pillars concealed an area off to the left lit by a dim yellow bulb. The police deployed immediately, guns ready, and crossed to it. There was no-one there, just signs of where the occupant had been: a table and chair, a cupboard, a modest camp-bed with tangled bed-clothes, a hot-plate and bar fridge to one side where it all stretched off into darkness again.

Deliberate darkness. Darkness as controlled theatrical flourish, prelude to shocking revelations, precisely calculated anguish and despair.

The police led the way around more pillars. The stark white light of their torches soon found the old dentistry chair near the back wall, securely bolted to the floor, revealed the victim strapped down, alive but barely conscious, gurgling through a ruined mouth filled with her own blood.

The paramedics rushed to her aid, began working by torchlight as best they could.

Dan made himself look away, forced himself to look at what else there was in the shifting torchlight that *wasn't* this poor woman, gurgling, groaning and sobbing. He noted the straps for securing the chair's occupant, the elaborate padded clamp for holding the head, the metal tables and dental tools, other tools that had no place in dental work, the stains on the floor, dark and rusty-looking. The air smelled of disinfectant, urine and blood and something else, something sour.

An officer finally located a light switch. A single spot came on overhead, illuminating the chair and the woman, showing her ruined face and more: an array of mirrors on adjustable stands, video and audio equipment, shelves with old-style video and audio tapes, newer-style DVDs.

Souvenirs. An archive.

Dan scanned the row of audio tapes; the first were dated from the 60s. Peter Rait's voices.

But all so mundane in a worrying sense. Though terrible to say, these were the workaday trappings of sociopaths and psychopaths the world over, how they, too, made mundane lives for themselves out of their horrific acts.

But there was a large, heavy door beyond the woman in the chair, like a rusted walk-in freezer door with a sturdy latch. Dan focused his attention on it as soon as the torch beams revealed the pitted metal surface. An exit? A hideaway? Another inner sanctum in this hellish place?

An officer approached the door, weapon ready, and pulled it back.

It was a storeroom, a small square room empty but for a large chalk-white post nearly two meters tall. The post was as round as three dinner plates, set in concrete or free-standing, it was hard to tell, but standing like a bollard, one of those removable traffic posts used to stop illegal parking, though larger, much larger, and set all over with encrustations.

Not just any encrustations, Dan knew. Sets of teeth in false mouths, fitted at different heights, randomly but carefully, lovingly, set into the white plaster, fiber-glass, concrete, whatever it was. Dentures made from real teeth, corpse teeth, teeth taken post- and ante-mortem, some of them, all of them spring-loaded and deadly!

A trophy post.

This was where Toother kept his terrible collection, displayed it for his pleasure—and, yes, for the calculated and utter terror of others.

A door slammed somewhere in the building.

The police reacted at once. The officer holding the storeroom door let it go. It was on a counterweight and closed with a resounding boom. Another shouted orders. One hurried back to secure the main entrance. The rest rushed to search the outer premises, to find other exits and locate their quarry. Footsteps echoed in the empty space.

It all happened so quickly. Dan stood listening, hoping, trusting that Peter was still out in the car, safe.

Movement close by caught his attention, brought him back. The paramedics had the woman on their gurney at last. The awful gurgling had stopped and they were now wheeling her away.

For a terrible moment, Dan was left alone with the chair under its single spot, with the tables and instruments, the archive shelves and heavy metal door, now mercifully closed.

Then there were cries off in the darkness, sounds of running, more shouting. Two gunshots echoed in the night.

Then, in seconds, minutes, however long it was, Harry was there, two officers with him.

"We got him, Dan."

"Harry. What? What's that?"

"We got him. Toother. He's dead."

"Dead?" Peter was there too, appearing out of the darkness. "You did? You really got him?"

"We did, Peter," Harry said. "He was running out when we arrived. Officer Burns and me. He was armed and wouldn't stop. Colin here had to shoot."

Dan placed a hand on Peter's arm. "No more voices?"

"No," Peter said. "No voices at all now."

"We got him, Peter," Harry said.

But Peter frowned, gave an odd, puzzled look as if hearing something, then crossed to the heavy door and pulled it back. "Harry, I don't think we did. Not this time. Not yet."

The storeroom was empty, of course.

Afterword to "Toother"

"Toother" owes its existence to a photograph of a pair of Waterloo Teeth dentures and subsequent related reading about the grim practices of the 18th and 19th century "resurrection men." In narrative terms, it just became a matter of how to stage the story and where to take it, how *far* to take it given the confronting subject matter, another instance of when to give and when to hold back.

The transcripts came next and they brought the story to a standstill. This was harrowing stuff and couldn't be allowed to be gratuitous. The whole thing was left to rest for a while.

Then came the notion of making it a Dan Truswell story, of returning to the characters from my Ditmar Award-winning, World Fantasy Award-nominated 2000 collection *Blackwater Days*.

This is always dangerous territory. There's often real cause for dismay when it's announced that a writer, musician, film-maker etc. plans to return to previous material. It usually makes good box-office sense, of course, helps to pay the mortgage, send the kids through college, that sort of thing, and even Shakespeare brought Falstaff back in *The Merry Wives of Windsor* to please his Queen.

So I tried it with other names as place-holders, but kept coming back to Dan's sensibilities, his way of seeing the world, keeping in mind *Eclipse*'s editorial requirement that a supernatural, fantastical element be present. No conventional, serial killer, police procedural then. It became clear, too, that this side of a novel or novella-length treatment, the use of the "psychosleuths" from the earlier collection would facilitate delivery and add a welcome tension. More to the point, I'd missed Dan and Harry, Peter and Phil, the kind of edginess they either brought to the world or found in it. It truly was like going home again.

China in His Day

It is lonely on the frontier
And the road is lost in rain,
It's a long way to the garden where you write to me,
It's a long way back again.
Your first letter said the Great Khan was invincible,
Now you say the Khan is dead.
Here I watch the embers settle in the grate,
Soon the ashes blow away.
He was China in his day.
He was China in his day.

It is lonely on the frontier
And the sky is always grey,
And I do not have the courage of the water-clock,
I can't count the days away.
Your first letter said the Great Khan was invincible,
Now you say the Khan is dead.
Here I watch the embers settle in the grate,
Soon the ashes blow away.
He was China in his day.
He was China in his day.

The View in Nancy's Window

It was the finest day, the most splendid golden afternoon of a day, and the selection of the Ten Wonders was so close to being so nearly, truly, completely done that Cherriot Haden-Sone turned from the open, tenth-floor window of the university tower and shut down the Overlord, the Given and the Magi systems. For a time, just for a time, he wanted to do it all himself, to be as basic, as fundamental and unaugmented as those ancient humans who published the first recorded list.

It was a celebratory act too, an exuberance really, and itself a wonder in terms of the way things were supposed to be done. A single blue point of light on a single palm frond set perfectly in the perfect decor showed an official query, showed the surprise, the questioning, of those already offline and minimalized systems. Just the blue point of a question, also wonderful in all that golden light.

The selection committee, the Wonder Bar (an old word joke), had requested the option of minimalized systems, insisted in their firm and gentle fashion. No pressure, no deadlines. They were choosing the final list from the millions, thousands, hundreds, finally dozens of possibles, and they were selecting an order of wonderfulness. Something had to be at the top, Number One, if they could manage it.

So while there was no deadline, could be no such thing officially, the enclave, the world, the literally countless, settled, terraformed and humanized worlds beyond, virtual and actual, knew it would be soon.

Cherriot was determined to enjoy it, these final days and hours, to keep it *real*. That was the word, after all. Humans doing it. Not the vast array of systems and assists. Not letting it be too easy.

A point of green appeared beside the blue.

"Yes?" Cherriot spoke it, antiquating, moding in the oldest way, delighting in being outside the systems that guided the mighty, human-ordered pulse of the universe.

"To let you know, seigneur, that another judge has withdrawn. Bonna Gill-Serrian."

"What? Now?" This late, this close, this far in. Not Bonna. It couldn't happen. Earlier, yes, they'd lost so many, but now?

"Reason? Did she give a reason?"

"Just to say that her own research prevents a fair selection."

"How so?" And cursing, damning the fine smart woman, he found himself about to mode back into the array, into the *noös* of the Sophia or the Given, the *callonaire* of stat and inst, barely fought down to minimal, basic, held it, gifting himself with the simplest, purest level possible for humans, that the greatest thinkers had known: Aristotle, Plato, Einstein, Jillis and on—names in putative mind-strings flowing away, taking even his unfinished thoughts into information horizons processed by the Overlord somewhere in its immensity. Oh, it was a day! And now this.

He barely kept to it, barely managed with all those wings for his thoughts, so many stats and easements to draw him at the instant into Bonna's mind, enquiring, asking, demanding. Why? Why?

A quadrillionth part of one of the universe's controlling, guiding, stabilizing systems answered him.

"She wouldn't say. She wants you to go to her."

"Go?" It had such novelty to it, actually going somewhere now, especially with the Given and the Overlord on hold, processing and reporting only, with the golden wonderful day so richly spread before him.

To *go* into the wonderful day.

To *go* to her. To actually ask in person.

Why had this—he'd never realized it before—favorite among the hundred judges in the Festival contest decided not just to abstain but to resign?

Her own research prevents a fair selection.

In another age, millennium, epoch, eon it would have been a red light beside the blue and the green: a protest, a complaint, a call for accountability, even convocation.

Not with Bonna. Here they were so close to finally announcing their selection and ordering of the Ten Wonders, and this pride of the *herodotoi*, this darling of the Wonder Bar, had given it up. Because of her own research, dammit!

Go to her.

"I'll go to her," he said. "As she requests."

His room, his tower, his university and city and world heard it. The Overlord assigned stat facilities (there in a flash!), easements (there in a virtual or augmented flash!), even (sensing his modal state) prepared retroforms in potentia: ships, fliers, surface cars, everything from an ultralite to a carriage and four. The Magi conformed virtualities, juggled possibilities, allowed it all, of course. The Given hung on every conscious thought, ready to act even as he became aware of his decision to do so. An important, if miniscule, part of the universe hung on Cherriot's choosing. That alone became a miracle, a splendid inst, an artform in itself, and in turn the fact that all that swung momentarily on all this, prizing it. The Chairman of the *herodotoi* was choosing, was *going*.

He went on a bicycle, had the skill a nanosecond before he mounted it, rode off into the day.

Oh, it was a splendid thing, going, arriving, meeting, being, actually *being* with someone without the easements, just being, coterminous, singleton, all "no matter where you go, there you are" simple. It *gandhied* him, *heraclited* him, *einsteined* him.

To go to a house in a garden in a street on this golden day. Into a room. Into company again.

"Bonna, it's good to be here. To share this."

She stood by her window, as real and devoid of the Given assists as he was, nothing but separate selves, eye contact (*aye, contact!*). Words. Retro and fine. So perfect too.

"I wasn't sure you'd come."

To go. To come. To be.

"How could I not?" And to the heart of it. "What did your research show?"

"Let me give you the grand tour first. We can talk as we go."

Go. Go. Go. More going.

"Of course."

Bonna Gill-Serrian picked up a small wooden case, splendid with oldest-time marquetry and pearl inlay, and carried it with her. With them.

Cherriot loved it all. All these old old actions. Carrying. Going.

"It's good to have artefacts," he said, indicating the case, the doorway, the steps, balustrades and lawns. "I rode a bike."

Bonna smiled. They walked out into a garden, arbored, espaliered, topiaried, wildnernessed and fine, all actual, *actual*, just as they walked—*walked!*—felt sun and wind, did the actions.

"We've gotten too far from this," he said, and then: "It says a lot when all of the short list are still actual constructs. No virtuals have been nominated. No comp systems. No supports and easements."

Bonna took this as her cue as they crossed the lawn. "It first came to me when we'd brought it down to an even hundred. Such marvels we had. All actual, as you say. I got my mind off the task of choosing by going into the oldest maintenance programs."

"Programs?"

"An old word but I like it. I used Overlord to put me in touch with a dialectic engine somewhere in the Twenty Millions."

"A program?"

"Yes. Another old program. It argues with you. Tests hypotheses. I ran an information trail back to humanity's first-known attempts to select a list of world wonders. We have the original Seven from Earth. We have the millions of subsequent listings. Something was goading me. I wanted that horizon. How it *felt* for Herodotus when he chose the Seven of his day. What he discarded and why. What came close. I locked onto the ideology that way: he was seeking not just constructs, not just buildings as buildings, even though of course they were. It had to mark the spirit of the age. Be part of its time. The real Wonders now must be that as well."

"Granted." Easily. The Selection Committee *had* discussed exactly that so many times. Why did she bring it up now? "Go on, Bonna." *Go* on. Proceed. Continue. The wonderful words of doing.

"I discovered a notion. A concept in philosophical thought. It's called Plato's Cave."

"A place?"

"A metaphor. That seeing reality as we do is like seeing shadows cast on the wall of a cave. It's all we see. Not the fire, not what throws the shadows. We don't see the real world, the *real* reality."

"And that's from Herodotus?"

"No, from Plato. More or less a contemporary."

Cherriot walked with her, gazing off into the day, curious about the box but not subvocalizing Overlord to let him see inside, not calling on the Given, the Magi or Companion, letting her do it all her way. "And what's your point, Bonna? How does this relate to our short list of wonders for the Festival? To your place in it?"

Present tense. Disregarding her resignation.

She didn't react. "Once I really began regarding the hundred entries in terms of that distinction—how they marked the *Zeitgeist*, the spirit of an age, and also the reality of an age, I just kept crossing them from the list. So many couldn't qualify. They were spectacular, certainly, the Lincharkisor Bridge, the Makkrion on Korinta, the Copri Ring, but they just demonstrated technology, human or nonhuman ingenuity at work."

Cherriot walked and smiled. "We all have our methods, Bonna. Yours are as good or better than most. You helped us get our shortlist."

"To demonstrate a point."

"Oh." Her tone brought a shadow into their glorious afternoon. "How so?"

"I consulted Overlord. Requested trends. Had it predict the likely outcome."

"So?" He tried to keep his mood, tried to be generous. "We all do that. It still comes down to the best judgement *we* can make. It's all there in the responsibility oath we took as *herodotoi*."

"So let me give you the Ten."

"All right." It was easy again.

"In order."

The shadow was there then, pressing on his happiness. How could she already know what consensus would decide? The assists could give predictions, probabilities, recommendations, but it was humanity choosing, with all its quirks and biases.

"If you feel you can." *Feel*, such a word.

They still walked. Perhaps her box was more than just a sentimento. Perhaps it was an antique hardform comp or a veriform assist, but if so, she didn't consult it. If not for the dictates of their being together, actually meeting, Cherriot would've accessed Overlord or the Given, got it all in a second, spared her the talking of it. He was rehearsing it anyway, almost sending the standby to get all relevant thought-strings.

"Disengage from Overlord," she said, as if reading his mind.

Of course she'd know. Automatically assume.

"Listen—"

"Please."

"No."

"Please. Be as naked as I am. Be truly here."

In the day. On the lawn. Now.

"All right." And mentated that. Overlord was gone. He scarcely believed it.

"The rest," she said.

Cherriot hated being tested like this, being dared almost. But he didn't want to fail her test.

It was strange, so strange, feeling them go: the Given, Companion, the Magi, Sophia, his dear, so familiar ancillaries. The Old Friends. The Manticore. The Abracar. Gara. The Secret Heart. The Caress.

To be so stripped, so bereft, so naked.

Just to be in the day. Here and now.

"Thank you," she said.

"What about you?"

"I'm naked too. I've been naked since you first arrived."

Cherriot felt a thrill at the word. She had always been his favorite. Was. Such an intimate word.

"If so," he said pragmatically, needing some control, "how do you know I've done it?"

"I trust you, Cherriot. Can I?"

"Of course."

"Now call back Sophia. Just Sophia."

He did, felt the immanence, the relief at being extended, larger again, at least by this one tiny piece of his panoply.

"Yes?" he said, and only then realized it was a question.

"Call for Sophia's Kiss."

"Sophia's Kiss?" He did not know it. But called, felt the arrival. "Have it," he said. "Now. The Ten."

He stood with her in a green green meadow beneath the blue sky in the golden light and waited.

Bonna smiled.

"Number Ten. The Horumi Nullity."

Cherriot smiled, feeling gratified. "So you do believe it is a construct and not a natural phenomenon, after all."

"It is a construct and a human one."

"More than we will claim and many will allow but you're right. Number Nine?"

"The Tosta Library at Bair."

Cherriot saw it in his stripped-back mind's eye, not as a stat or inst but as a memory. "Good. Yes. All those interfacing storage systems. Things coded in light. No such thing as an ether so we invented it. Go on, Bonna." This was delightful.

"Eight. The Successor Fleet."

"How could it not be? Those incredible ships. All those enclosed suns. Number Seven?"

"The Chenge Cascade."

"Yes! Yes!" Cherriot cried it into the day. She really did have it. "It too is a construct. All those worlds and stars *made* by us!"

Bonna was smiling again. They were sharing all this pleasure.

"Number Six. The Perpetual Motion Machine on Saggio. Working away forever. No entropy."

"That we can tell. Entropy in another continuum perhaps. But, yes, it is the doing of it that counts. What is Number Five?"

"Its opposite, in a sense," Bonna said. "The Isseriault on Syrie."

Oh smart, oh fine, Cherriot thought, nothing but Sophia there to read, sort, extract his joy.

"Yes, Bonna, yes. Such a simple thing. So perfect. Balanced on that tiny point. All gravity, all physics denied. Perfect stasis. Number Four?"

"The Makis Tombfield, plus the Biacari. It has to be both."

"Indeed. The AIs made by us. Creating stellar phenomena. Making as God makes. What is Three?"

"The Dorphesa Alignment."

"Yes, yes, yes. That it *could* be done. All those worlds and suns, hundreds of star systems brought into that configuration just for a moment, just *as* a moment, to show it could be done. A statement. An artform. Ineffable. Two, Bonna?"

"The Lonely God."

Cherriot marveled that she could have it as the preliminary consensus so far did, all those judges who had filed their votes already.

"Out there in the dark," he said. "Believing itself God for so long. Made by us eons ago but believing it had made us. A real lesson in that. And your Number One?"

She didn't hesitate. "Why, the array. All our extended parts. The Overlord, the Given, the Magi, Companion and Sophia, the primaries and secondaries, on and on and on, right down to the Wedding Guest and the Whisperer. I'm right, aren't I?"

Cherriot nodded. "How could it not be? We've never done better."

They each stayed silent for a time, listening to the breeze in the meadow.

"You've named them exactly, Bonna," he said at last. "So what is the problem? Why did you leave us?"

Be part of it. *Be* with us. Again. With me. Like this.

Bonna clutched her case and looked out at the fields. "Then I ran Sophia. Sophia's Kiss. I brought in the old dialectic engine I spoke of, went back through all the subsets."

"And found?" He had to ask it, feeling the shadow curling at the edges of the day again.

"Before I tell you, Cherriot, I want to show you something. It requires that you let me run another, much older housekeeping menu from Sophia's Kiss. You'll have to trust me though. Can you?"

"Yes." No. He wasn't sure, but he'd already answered, was now determined to go with the answer. He sensed she knew something, something shadowing the golden light, but urgent and important.

"Sophia's Kiss One," she said to that mighty guiding engine.

The world tipped. The gold went out of the day. The lawns, meadows and bluest sky narrowed to a bleak ruined street under a grim sad overcast. Fifty meters away an old terrace-style house stood at the end of the street flanked by grimy brick walls. They were facing it, walking towards it. A cold wind blew at them.

Cherriot felt no shock, of course, no dismay. He had modelled worlds and views like this so many times in his life, countless sims and stats to suit his mood. He knew—*knew* and *accepted*—that this was real, but could not process it meaningfully. He walked with Bonna Gill-Serrian and her silly, incredibly important box and held his curiosity in check.

"Where is this place?" he did ask as they walked towards the house.

"Some world in Augerios. See that one intact window on the ground floor?"

"Of course."

"Look into it. Tell me what you see."

Cherriot tried to see in, but it was an unlighted interior, the glass was reflective. He saw only Bonna and himself in the day-mirror it made, handsome and tall.

"That's Nancy's Window," she said. "It gave me the truth. It's why I resigned. Why I asked you to visit me."

"Nancy's Window?"

"Like Plato's Cave. We try to look through but see only ourselves. *We* keep getting in the way. It's like the shadows on the cave wall, we get ourselves back as the reality."

"Go on."

"There can only be a single Wonder for our list, Cherriot."

"Bonna, make your point."

"That dialectic subset I mentioned. I routed it through Overlord. I used Committee privilege to demand a priority allocation of resources to Sophia's Kiss."

"So? The temptation's always there. We've all committed indiscretions."

"I went into closed files."

"Files?"

"Another oldest term. Once Kiss had Overlord on side, it would not stop."

"And so?"

"Number Ten. The Horumi Nullity. It is a construct, but hardly the kind you think. It is the resulting merge form of the Geress Nation, a *human* transtellar community of four hundred and eighty-five billion."

"A merge form?"

"An entity. Variant humanity using its science to transubstantiate into null-matter."

"I don't believe that for a—"

"Ask Overlord later. It almost worked. Number Nine: the Tosta Library. Those light codings are the two hundred and twenty-seven billion inhabitants of the Coalavi Supernals, a *human* variant that form-changed in a different sense."

"This is variant humanity! Is that what you're saying?"

"*Was* humanity, Cherriot. But certainly not just artefacts. Number Eight: the Successor Fleet—"

"Don't tell me! Those ships, those suns—"

"Evolved humaniforms too. Humans who not only went to the stars, but became them."

"Are you telling me that all the others—"

"Seven. The Chenge Cascade is the ideation matrix of seventeen trillion Pardept Ansere codings. A strain of humanity that went 'missing' ninety millennia ago."

"And the Machine on Saggio. Are you saying—?"

"If you'll pardon the turn of phrase, it's the support engine of the personality of Cornellian Jarr, the Second Stellar Age explorer. He had himself, well, modified."

"The Isseriault?"

"That mighty structure is the terminal *noös* repository of the entire Makan Empire. Ninety-two trillions."

"People! The Isseriault! You're saying it's all people!"

But Bonna just stared at Nancy's Window, as if determined to finish.

"The Makis Tombfield and the Biacari is actually much more modest—the twenty-nine crew of the Third Stellar Age starship *Ballo*, who used Tugonta technology to self-evolve into optimated forms."

"The Dorphesa Alignment? Are you saying that's humanity too?"

"When you see the data that made it possible, what held the matrix and why, yes, Cherriot, you'll find another *noös*form, another variant on extended humanity."

"Then the Lonely God—"

"Is, rather was, Margret Duellis, the woman who entered the Crove Waste and was, well, augmented and sent back in time."

"Number One stands, surely. The array."

"Yes. The only real construct. And it's us."

"Part of us."

Bonna handed him the marquetry case. "You may wish to use this in a while."

Cherriot took it from her, fumbled with the twin latches, finally got it open and saw the ballistic weapon resting in its plush interior.

"What's this for?"

"You're Chairman of the Wonder Bar. You may need to act in that capacity."

"But why?"

"Because of Nancy's Window."

He misunderstood. "You want me to shoot Nancy's Window?"

"Do you think you can?"

Cherriot had never fired an oldest weapon, but he removed the heavy thing from its place, set down the case, aimed at the front of the derelict house and fired.

The sound was sudden, shocking. The window shattered. Their images were gone.

"There," he said, and would've handed the terrible device back to her, except that she spoke.

"But it's still there."

"It's what?"

"Look, Cherriot."

He did, and of course it wasn't. It was just one more gaping hole with a few ragged edges. Did she have an augment running?

"I don't see it."

"As metaphor. You've only removed what we *can* see. You know that if the glass were there, you'd still see our reflections."

"Not now."

"Not here, but, yes, now."

"Bonna, what are you saying?"

"It's Plato's Cave. Nancy's Window. That the gun is for me."

"What!"

"Because of what I've told you. All the selected Wonders are variant humanity, long changed, long gone. Moved on."

"So? We can allow for that."

"No, *we* can't."

"Bonna—"

"Sophia's Kiss Two," she said, and the world narrowed in smaller ways, gave the street still and the old house in the bleak terrain under the terrible grey sky, gave Cherriot and Bonna as two floating silver spindles, twin canisters of light and energy, one with a silver rod extended, what the oldest weapon had become. Had always been.

"Bonna—"

"Let me restore this. Sophia's Kiss Three."

And they were back as they were, human-looking again, unevolved. He could look into her eyes again.

"So what, Bonna? Humanity is the greatest Wonder the universe has known. So what?"

"It's my one and only nomination, Cherriot. It's the only one we can nominate."

He still didn't understand. "So why the gun? Why for you? I can accept our own variance. I can accept what we have become."

"That is not what Sophia's Kiss showed me."

"Then what?"

"The last true human variant died off forty-three thousand years ago."

"What, our Ten Wonders too?"

"Yes, but that's not what I'm saying."

"Then what? What, Bonna?" But he knew. And it made him grip the gun tightly. This knowledge could not be allowed. Not this. Not such a thing as this.

"We are not human," he said, feeling as cold inside as the day, the true, dead, damned day.

"We have never been human," she said, making sure. "We are what's left. The support assists. A surrogate. A placebo. A center to focus on. Only you and I know."

"The Overlord, the others?"

"Do not. Must not. Sophia was the fail-safe."

"Why?" But he knew.

"So there would be something. A legacy. The truth somewhere at least. But we are not humans choosing. We are something else choosing. And humanity—Humanity—is Number One. There has been nothing finer."

"Overlord will know! They all will. The moment they're reinstated—"

"Yes. Sophia's Kiss will take the knowledge from us if you want. But that's not the point, is it, Cherriot?"

Cherriot raised the gun, feeling panic, terror, rage, hard sharp slashes of wonder and despair. He raised it and aimed and gazed into her eyes and knew what he had to do for them all.

But then he noticed the sky above the grimy brick wall and remembered the light, how it could be so golden, so very very fine. And how it was to have something you loved.

Afterword to "The View in Nancy's Window"

NOW THAT HUMANITY is on the verge of shaping its own biotype more than has ever been possible, now that memes even more than genes are fast determining what humanity will become, we realize that, faced with the prospect of Vernor Vinge's Singularity and Damien Broderick's Spike, this is probably the first age in the history of the world to know that it *cannot* predict its own future.

With the modern SF trend of depicting posthuman and transhuman tomorrows, there is also a telling return to the more readily graspable conventions of space opera, and with them, filtered through the philosophical sensibilities of the new millennium, the old 1950s/1960s narrative chestnut of "Human is as Human does." Which leaves us with (at least) three questions: Can it be enough? Will it be enough? Should it be enough?

Most of the trans- and post-humanism depicted in current SF storytelling is, by its nature, rarefied and remote, often too detached and unsexy for its own good. It may be cutting edge, it may be fascinating, even exhilarating for a time, but it ultimately lacks a sufficiency in the very connection with humanity required to make it something we *pre*-posthumans can engage with for long.

Which may be the point, of course. But it invariably lacks, as William Faulkner said: "the human heart in conflict with itself."

This story attempts to honor the moment to moment reality of a lived life and retain that connection. In intention, it concerns the three questions, the conflict and, for one of our descendants at least, the moment of decision, served up, I sincerely hope, with the sense of wonder we all remember and we all deserve.

Mr. Fate & Mr. Danger

Light through the window,
Pale light falling in the hall.
All eyes are on the dawning,
And the man hanging on the wall.
If he's a martyr cut him down,
If he's living give a hand.
Fall down (fall down), fall down.
Mr. Fate and Mr. Danger
Are sitting on the top of the world.

No lights inside the houses,
Nothing moves on that street.
If a wind should stir the hedge-rows,
Rest assured that no-one will see.
If he's a martyr cut him down,
If he's living give a hand.
Fall down (fall down), fall down.
Mr. Fate and Mr. Danger
Are sitting on the top of the world.

JARKMAN AT THE OTHERGATES

NILS JARKMAN HAD RESOLVED not to show his feelings on this first visit to Tessian's Edge, but as Bethany turned the Audi into Dunning Street and he saw the old house for the first time, he couldn't help himself.

"You didn't exaggerate. It's perfect!"

Beyond the escarpment to their left, equally distracting, the Megalong Valley stretched off to the south as far as the eye could see, a vast blue expanse of heated air and hazy distances filled with a sense of deep silence despite the steady drone of cicadas.

Bethany judged the moment well. She knew to pull over and switch off the engine, to give the young director a chance to savor the view.

Nils marveled at it: such a house, here, a hundred kilometers west of Sydney, more than a thousand meters above the suburban sprawl of the coastal plain at this part of the Great Dividing Range known as the Blue Mountains; it truly was another world, forested, primal, unsullied. Only the house ahead and the road itself, running along the cliff's edge, ruined the sense of an all-encompassing wilderness. Despite the fierce summer heat, he had to lower the window and breathe in the heady wash of fragrances: wildflowers, pollens, resins, eucalypt oils.

Coming in three days before the others *had* been the right thing to do. In his eight years in the film business, five as an AD and a fairly frequent world traveler with one production or another, Nils had seen nothing like this: a modest but impressive Victorian mansion perched on the edge of such an expanse. It was like having the Grand Canyon at your doorstep:

hazier with all this summer heat, blue-green with the exudations of so many gumtrees, but no less spectacular.

Nils thought he could actually feel the weight of the land. Not just Sydney at their backs, far to the east beyond the lower ranges, but to the west as well, beyond Blackheath and Mt Victoria, where these spectacular highlands fell away to the great spread of the continent. You felt you were living in the sky.

"Forgive me asking again, Bethany," he said, returning his gaze to where Dunning Street swung past the old estate's eastern boundary and completed its kilometer run back to the highway. "But Mr. Tessian is still okay about the schedule and the fee? It's *still* a firm go-ahead?"

"Now that the new road is in, yes. You'll countersign the final papers today."

There it was again. The new road. Donald Tessian's dark-haired, late twenty-something assistant had told him about it on the drive up from Sydney, how the local city council for the Blue Mountains had finally created Dunning Street, and Tessian's Edge was linked to the real world at last, no longer lost at the end of an old private access road with a *Strictly No Admittance* warning on the gate.

Fortunately there were no signs of housing development yet, just a wall of uncleared bush to the right, hot and still, roaring with cicadas, and to the left, barely forty meters through the last broken line of eucalypts and low scrub, the great hazy gulf of the Megalong falling away, with the chain of blue-green mountain valleys beyond.

Nils had to smile. This bare, intrusive, too modern street had become the answer to his prayers, leading him now to his first meeting with Donald Tessian.

"And Mr. Tessian—Donald—is still okay about the temporary modifications?" Nils felt foolish asking it; these were things long agreed upon. It showed how excited he was.

"He is. He read your letter several times. His attorney did."

Nils couldn't help himself. "We'll need to dress the place. Conceal light fittings, any signs of wiring. He does understand that?"

"Oh sure. Just like Ken Russell did at Villa Diodati."

"Excuse me?" Nils had still been watching the house and the valley, one then the other: Tessian's Edge looming through the trees, then the great gulf of the Megalong stretching off to the south. What was the old Cherokee word he'd read about recently?—*shaconage*—smoky blue?

"In his 1986 feature *Gothic*," Bethany said, so accustomed to both the house and the view that she just looked ahead at the heat shimmer along the road. "They had to make all sorts of cosmetic changes to get the right period look shooting in Geneva. And when they did *Sirens* down at Faulconbridge, they had to dress the Norman Lindsay Gallery for that shoot."

"Right, well good. That's good. And we'll need the full sixteen days. That's quite an intrusion for some people."

Bethany smiled. "Donald seems fine about it. He'll just hide up in the attic and watch the cricket like the owner did when Peter Greenaway shot *The Draughtman's Contract* at Groombridge Place."

"So I heard," Nils lied, smiling, glad that his sunglasses were hiding his eyes. He needed Bethany's goodwill. She wasn't altogether his type, pretty enough certainly, with her short brown hair, dark gaze, high cheekbones and surprisingly pale skin, and smart, but too guarded, an odd mix of—was primness the right Australian word?—and dry good humor. Still, let her go on about it. She was taking her new role as locations liaison with Sargon Productions a bit too seriously, but she was definitely out to please.

"Is the film set in Australia then?" she asked, surprising him. She hadn't automatically assumed it as most people did.

"Not really. Not necessarily," Nils said. House and valley. House and valley. He was already planning shots. "It's not specified. A no-place. A universal feel."

"But the bush. The eucalypts. Hardly European."

"We'll shoot for that. It's the house we want. The light. The aspect."

The costs, he didn't say, probably didn't need to. Bethany knew it was his first feature. Logistics considered, shooting in Australia was still cheaper than most countries. And Tessian's Edge hadn't been in any movies yet. That was the *other* deciding factor. This promised to be a distinctive, signature locale, like Martindale Hall had been as Appleyard College in Peter Weir's *Picnic at Hanging Rock*. All going well, people would forever associate his film with *this* house and vice versa.

"We can't use the front driveway, you said." In his excitement, Nils suddenly needed to confirm that as well, though Jan and Peter had told him several times in Oslo.

"The Council said limited use. You can do period set-ups with cars, carriages and such, but no heavy vehicles."

"How does the new road fit in again?" He had been told, but seeing the house! He was like an amnesiac re-learning bits of his life.

"During construction they discovered fracture lines in the sandstone. Stable enough, very old, but the Council issued a safety directive saying we couldn't use the front driveway any longer. Now we park at the back."

"So not earthquakes?"

"Just weathering over centuries. In 1931 a section of cliff face fell away at Katoomba; tunnelling from the old coal mines had weakened it. They're worried that traffic vibration might lead to something similar."

"But they put the road in anyway?"

Bethany gave a wry smile. "They did. Some overzealous local planner using development regulations to get even with a wilful recluse."

"I don't understand."

But he did. Of course he did. Nils couldn't help but wonder if it was the estate's name that did it: Tessian's Edge. Not Cliff House, Rim House or Valley View—those names probably wouldn't have seemed so proprietary, ruffled so many feathers. Tessian's Edge was sufficiently old world and pretentious that he could easily imagine someone being motivated by disgruntlement, even a degree of vindictiveness.

"Donald can tell you about it," Bethany said, glancing at her watch and starting the engine. "It's nearly one. I mustn't keep you."

They continued along Dunning until it angled sharply to the right, then Bethany turned the car in through some wrought-iron gates and stopped in a makeshift parking area between long hedges at the eastern side of the house. The space was empty but for a plum-colored 1965 Bentley which Bethany identified as one of six in Australia: Donald Tessian's fiftieth birthday present to himself eight years ago.

Nils retrieved his bags from the trunk, then they proceeded between two topiaried planters into a wide, deep garden that extended from the impressive back door off towards the wall of gum trees at the property's northern boundary. The white gravel walks and intersections were dazzling at this hour, set with pencil pines and classic marble planters, urns and benches and low balustrades, with steps leading up to raised levels off near the treeline.

Nils was hardly surprised to find the back door open on the hot afternoon, but what did puzzle him was the large gilt-framed mirror leaning against the jamb, angled as if to catch a view of the garden.

"That mirror there?" he said, setting down his bags inside the doorway and removing his sunglasses.

Bethany gave an indulgent smile. "One of Donald's set-ups. He has a series of them arranged to give a view of the garden from the library at the front of the house."

It was an odd, unsettling thing to see, and Nils didn't know what to say. Why? was the obvious question, but this was hardly the time to ask.

True enough, where the rear entry hall angled to the left beyond the entrances to the kitchen and laundry, another gilt-framed mirror rested against the wall, passing on that same garden view. Beyond it, where the hall doglegged right again towards the front door and main entry foyer, was another. A fourth was propped against the door to the library itself.

He can see us coming, Nils realized. Again, it brought an odd rush of emotion, part consternation, even mild alarm. He was reminded of stories he'd heard of ancient tomb painters in the Valley of the Kings using polished metal mirrors to reflect sunlight deep inside the corridors and burial chambers they were decorating. But what could be the purpose here? Why not use security cameras?

There was no time to think further about such things. They were at the door to the library and Nils could hear music playing, the low distinctive strains of John Tavener's *The Protecting Veil*, and Bethany was calling out, "officially" letting Donald Tessian know that they had arrived.

"Donald, Nils Jarkman is here."

"Bring him in, Beth."

Donald Tessian had been sitting at a large mahogany desk working at a laptop, but immediately stood, switched off the music and came out to shake Nils's hand. At fifty-eight, twenty-two years Nils's senior, he was a tall, amiable man with curly grey hair, a generous smile and the signs of genuine pleasure in his blue eyes.

"You saw us coming," Nils said, making it sound as conversational as he could, as if there were nothing odd involved.

"One of my quirks. I like to keep an eye on the garden. See who comes in."

"You could install surveillance cameras."

Donald Tessian gave a dismissive gesture. "Cameras don't catch everything. I prefer older methods."

Nils let that pass. This was diplomacy time, building bridges time.

"I'm very grateful for the chance to be here, Donald. The house is incredible. The view is spectacular, exactly what I'd hoped for. The name Tessian's Edge is certainly justified."

Donald Tessian smiled as he led them to the three leather armchairs arranged in front of the windows, but angled so they were facing back into the room, away from the view. He gestured for Nils to sit, then poured them all orange juice from a chilled carafe. "There's a major misunderstanding there, I'm afraid. The house wasn't named because of the location. Great-grandfather Malcolm was a scholar as well as a businessman. It seems the ancient Celtic peoples believed in otherworlds, other states of existence parallel to ours, linked at particular times of day, different times of year, in special places: pools, forest glades, old gardens, reflective surfaces like mirrors, that sort of thing. All very treacherous and unstable. These gateways were known as 'edges.'"

"Your great-grandfather believed there was a gateway here?"

"It's what I was told over and over growing up. Great-grandfather Malcolm was a dynamic man, an overbearing man, successful, impressive, if not terribly likeable. Apparently he'd go on about these edges all the time; what he called 'othergates.'"

"Excuse me?"

"Gate is the old Scots word for 'way' and 'road.' Othergates meant 'otherways,' by another road. By the time Shakespeare used it in *Twelfth Night* it meant 'otherwise'—proceeding by other ways—which tickled Malcolm's fancy enormously. He liked to think that he was *wise* about these crossover points, that he was 'otherwise.' It's why he decorated the room like this, why that picture is above the fireplace."

Nils followed the direction of Donald Tessian's gaze and found that he didn't need to ask his host to elaborate. "It's the original?"

"An etching. One of fifty-five. *Pan's Hour*, 1930. Norman Lindsay destroyed his plates in almost every instance, so every one is an original."

In black, white, stippled greys, the framed etching showed a garden very much like the one outside the back door: the same slender pines and low shrubs, the urns and raked gravel walks caught during some blazing summer noon. Standing in the foreground was a young woman, dark-haired, lovely, dressed in a light Edwardian dress that fitted her contours beautifully and gave almost the effect of a classical Greek peplos or khiton. She held her sun-hat down by her side and stood with the other hand raised to her throat in a nervous gesture, looking slightly off to her right at something out of frame, something just now seen or heard. There was a look of concern, alarm, even fear, on her pretty face.

The title said it all. *Pan's Hour.* Here was a young maiden caught in the wrong place at the wrong time, seeing something, hearing something, just the barest hint of Pan pipes in the hot stillness, and knowing in the instant what was going to happen.

Nils was used to interpreting, improvising, working with whatever he found. Perhaps the maiden wanted to be there, had gone there knowing, dreading, hoping that the wild god would break through from one of these otherworlds and ravish her. It was a moment laden, fraught with consequences, frozen, blazing, in the naked instant.

Three days from now, late Thursday afternoon, Dieter and the crew would be here, Miles, Jutta and the rest. Three days and the house would be different: a place of cameras and lighting set-ups, strict schedules and quick decisions. This etching would lend its force to the mix, of course, and whatever else Nils could find during this vivid in-between time.

There were so many treasures in the room. He could revise the shooting script to include them, have Dieter do close-ups and edit them in later like Joseph Mankiewicz did so well in his 1972 film, *Sleuth.* And not just the period paintings and statuary either, but the other things he could see, unusual touches, anachronistic and strange. Like that curious object on the oaken pedestal near the far bookcase: a medical or astronomical tool of some kind. It rested on twin stirrup supports inside a glass display case: a long, thin metal probe like an elaborate chopstick, but with three hypodermic-style finger loops at one end for thumb and two fingers. Nils couldn't be sure from where he sat, but there seemed to be writing on the shaft. Perhaps it was an etching instrument, or a personalized dental tool, a retirement gift from respectful colleagues.

And there, between two bookcases facing Donald's desk, was a framed picture that seemed unnervingly modern: a strange swirl of form and color: black, browns, old bronze, rich Genoese gold, a dramatic swathe of white—

Nils froze in his chair. He had realized what the painting was.

Donald Tessian saw his reaction. "Nils, what?"

"That picture." It was all Nils could manage.

"The abstract? Something else Malcolm loved, heaven knows why. I never took to it myself. Why, what's the matter?"

"Excuse me, please, but it's an anamorph."

"A what?"

"An example of anamorphosis. A surprisingly old technique, a planned distortion. I learned about it in film school. A distorted image that can only be seen when viewed using a cylindrical mirror placed on its surface.

"Really? I never knew. What's the purpose behind it?"

"A novelty thing mostly, but also once a way of hiding portraits or images forbidden by the church or state. You concealed them in swirls of distortion so they could only be viewed a certain way."

"Using a cylindrical mirror, you say?"

Nils had regained his composure. "That's how it works. There's a famous portrait of Charles the First you can only see by placing the mirror on a death's head in the center. And you can still buy Pylones coffee cups in France. When the mirror cups are in position, the patterns on the saucer rims are revealed, these days movie scenes mostly: *King Kong, North by Northwest, Modern Times.*"

"We must try it. I think I'm going to enjoy having you around, Nils."

"I truly hope so, Donald. I'm very glad to be here."

"And Thursday afternoon it begins. Three days, then a strange new chapter in the history of the house. Thanks to the road."

Nils raised his glass of juice. "Thanks to you, Donald. I only hope it's not a new kind of hell."

"I can always watch the cricket," Donald said, eyes twinkling, and raised his own glass. "Either way we must enjoy this special time before then. Bethany will show you to your room, then you can look around. We'll meet for afternoon tea at four, if that suits. We can talk further then."

"You're very kind. But I must ask. I have a digital camera with me. I'd like to shoot some preliminary footage, sort of a director's notebook—"

"Of course."

"It occurs to me that there must be areas that are off-limits. Bethany didn't say. Your lawyer's emails didn't."

"No forbidden rooms, no. My bedroom upstairs perhaps, now I think of it. And Bethany's, of course. Unless you feel you absolutely need them for the film. I am new at this, you must understand. We will discover what rules we need to follow as we go along."

THE OLD TWO-STORIED HOUSE truly was a place of wonders. The location scout's photos and mpeg files sent to the Sargon offices in Oslo had barely done it justice. Though not quite as large as Nils had first thought, its dark wood-panelled rooms and hallways were perfect for his needs. Most important of all was the light pouring through the curtains, falling on the grounds, filling the blue distances. That Australian artist Bethany had told him about on the drive up, Norman Lindsay, had been right. In the southern hemisphere, the most even light did come from the south, just as it came from the north in the northern hemisphere.

It made Nils go to the back door to savor the view of the ornamental garden. It had seen better days, certainly, but still retained much of its former grandeur, stretching off through *faux* classical glades of pine and cypress towards the wall of gumtrees like something in a dream. The white gravel walks and intersections were still dazzling, but the pines, urns and balustrades now had shadows, lending a new intensity to the scene.

Nils became lost in his thoughts until he realized that Donald would be seeing him in his mirrors, with all that it possibly meant for the man: a dark backlit figure framed by the doorway. Such a trivial thing, but Nils quickly stepped aside and made a mental note not to linger there again.

When he returned to the library at four o'clock, he saw that the armchairs were now angled to give a spectacular view of the valley to the south, but that Donald sat in one that still let him see his mirror warning system.

"Too hot outside," Donald said, amiably enough, "and I thought you'd appreciate the view."

Nils smiled as he took his place. He was used to dealing with eccentric people, and easily managed his part in the ensuing small-talk about the new road and life in the mountains and the problems of shooting in Europe these days. He even broke his self-imposed first rule as Nils Jarkman, Director, and revealed something of what he hoped to achieve with his film.

When Bethany arrived with tea and scones, he was able to steal a glance at the mirror by the door. Sure enough, caught in its reflective field, step by distancing step across one, two, three other mirrors, was the view of the open back door. It was hypnotic to look upon, all that dazzling expanse reduced to a tight blazing swatch of light.

Nils was careful not to let Donald catch him at it. This room was probably the man's safe-haven, a place where he was surrounded by special protections. There were secrets here, Nils realized, yet perhaps the right questions from an interested stranger might lead his host to volunteer more details about life at Tessian's Edge.

"Donald, that instrument in the case. It almost looks surgical, except for those tiny motifs and curlicues. Is that writing on the shaft?"

Donald seemed to welcome the question. "That's a McKenzie leucotome from 1945. A fine customized variant of the usual McKenzie probe. Once used in psychosurgery for performing frontal lobotomies. In crueller days they stunned the subject with electro-shock then carried out what we now call an 'intrusive' procedure."

Nils was fascinated. "And the writing?"

"Old guarding spells. It sounds quaint, I know, but when you think about it it's your usual mix of mysticism and medicine. One of Grandfather Walter's ideas, following in Great-grandfather Malcolm's footsteps. He had them put there."

"The Tessian family has a medical background?"

"Much more personal, I'm afraid. In my twenties I had crippling migraines, nightmares, terrible bouts of anxiety. Day visions as well. The family tried everything. Medication, hypnosis, all the latest techniques. Nothing worked. My grandfather decided to try a more radical approach."

Nils was astounded at the implications. "He was a surgeon?"

"Grandfather Walter, no. But he had clinical training. He knew what he was doing."

Nils couldn't believe what he was hearing. "Using this probe?"

"Using that, yes." Donald Tessian placed a finger near where the orbit of his left eye reached the bridge of his nose. "A few light taps with a hammer; it went in easily enough. The inner probe was extruded; the cutting loops were extended and moved about just a little on the pre-frontal cortex. Just enough."

Nils saw Bethany frowning at these revelations and dared not hesitate. "Your grandfather gave you a lobotomy?"

"It was very selective, nowhere near as extreme as it sounds. Back in the 40s and 50s they believed that leucotomies—lobotomies—alleviated manic depression, anxiety, obsessional neuroses, some of the more severe symptoms of schizophrenia. It seemed to work, though one in ten subjects did show major personality changes."

"But when was this? Surely medication—"

"It was 1977, Nils, and, as I said, we'd tried medication. The human frontal lobes aren't fully developed until we're in our twenties, so I think they waited, hoping things would improve. There was even talk of trying Geoffrey Knight's procedure: inserting beads of radioactive yttrium inside the frontal lobes. But there were other factors to consider."

Superstition, Nils realized. Belief in the existence of "edges" and things breaking through, waiting behind mirrors, in forest pools and forgotten gardens, where the world was thin. And such things didn't have to be true. You only needed someone who *believed* they were. Donald's sensitivity, his receptivity, had been the problem. The Tessians hadn't wanted to lose his gift, just the complications that went with it.

If Donald Tessian were telling the truth. And if so then the procedure seemed to have worked. The man appeared composed, alert, sophisticated, certainly rational enough.

"I thought lobotomies ruined the higher functions. Destroyed the higher self."

"That depends on what is done and who is doing it. Damage to the left anterior frontal lobe can actually cause heightened intelligence, what's called the savant effect. So before you ask. Was I cured? Yes, I was. Mostly. The headaches went away, the hallucinations. I truly believe I am sharper than I was. *More* receptive. But as you can see, the mirrors are there, the view of the garden, some of the fear, the memories of what it was. But just as the shadow of a specter, you understand, the ghost of a ghost."

Bethany could hold back no longer. "Donald—"

"It's all right, Beth. Our guest is right to be concerned."

"I don't mean to be impertinent," Nils said. "You're my host—"

"Bethany is just surprised that I've been so forthcoming about such private matters. They are house secrets after all. Beth, see it as Tessian's Edge rejoining the world. Nils is making his film, and I am making something for us too."

Bethany held his gaze, full of unspoken thoughts, seeming to accept it.

Nils used the silence to ask his next question. "You no longer have the anxiety, the visions? You're all right about it?"

"Let's just say that it's been most educational. I now feel I have the right degree of detachment, for instance. More than ever I wonder what the old gods truly were. Not discrete entities but anomalies in the human mind, power surges activating very old and deep-seated behaviors in the psyche. All we know is that when something is triggered, it has to be explained. The human mind is good at making things palatable and known, safe and manageable. Things surge up: visions, convictions, recognitions. Before we know it people are having epiphanies, divine revelations, like the Greeks and Trojans at Troy believing the gods were talking to them, or Paul having his vision on the road to Damascus. Sometimes wilder things, like Pan in that etching. All recognitions, Nils. The trigger event occurs, the mind compensates, finds shapes, often with the déjà-vu aspect. Or, if you take the other view, Malcolm's view, actual things push through. The edges are where they happen. We really must find ourselves a cylindrical mirror or a suitable coffee cup. Who knows what Malcolm's painting will show? What did you call it again?"

"Anamorphosis. I'm sure Dieter will have something we can use."

There was more small-talk then, all very pleasant and easy, but afterwards Nils went to seek out Bethany, wanting her advice on how he should proceed with such delicate family matters.

He found her standing by the back door looking out at the garden. It was after six. The light came in low from the west, catching on the trees. The walks and garden beds were lost in shadow. The cicadas still made their frantic song, but the wall of the bush was mostly dark.

"His confessions bothered you," Nils said.

She turned and gave a polite half-smile, but was clearly troubled. "You have to understand. I've been his assistant since I was sixteen, ever since his parents died in the car accident at Medlow Bath. That's eleven years. He's always been very private about—about what happened. His parents never spoke of it. Now he's telling you. I'd never have thought it possible."

"You're close then?"

Bethany startled him with her reaction. "Nils, he's my uncle!"

"I didn't mean—"

"Everyone thinks it. The family used to be so large. Now there are so few, just the two of us here in Australia. I know how it appears."

Nils tried to save it. "Bethany, look. I'm grateful for this chance. I just need to know what to avoid, how to maintain goodwill. With both of you."

She turned to face him and frowned, as if seeing him for the first time. "Yes. Yes. Thank you. Excuse me please."

And she went inside, leaving Nils suddenly aware that, yet again, they had been caught in Donald's mirrors, that some part of the exchange had been passed on to the strange, damaged man at the front of the house.

Two long-time family friends, John and Susan Albertson, came for dinner, full of questions about film-making and Europe, so there were no opportunities for Nils to learn more about the aspects of life at Tessian's Edge he found so fascinating.

He retired to his room at eleven but, despite a good night's sleep at the Airport Hilton, his body clock was still on European time. With all that had happened since his arrival, all that he had learned, he found it hard to settle.

Not surprising, he told himself. Look at what he was taking with him as he tried to rest—the house and all its disparate parts: its proudly displayed lobotomy instrument and the man whose world it had changed so dramatically, its swirling painting in the library hinting at yet another family secret, its mirrors watching, promising other worlds, other ways, even the prospect of intruders appearing from a summer-locked, ornamental garden.

Walking past a mirror couldn't be the same now, not without feeling—something—not so much a presence as a pressure. It made Nils realize just how many mirrors there were in the old house. And not just Donald's early warning system outside the library. In almost every hallway, around every corner, there was a framed mirror amid the old portraits, still-lifes and landscapes. Malcolm and Grandfather Walter, possibly Donald's parents, had clearly wanted as many thin points as possible, as many reminders of the otherworld as they could reasonably manage.

It was enough to keep Nils's mind racing, especially when these strange new things became caught up with bits of his own life, things seen, heard and read over the years. Absurdly too, doggedly in his drowsing state, he kept thinking of the vibrations on the new road, of the cliff collapsing back in '31, of Tessian's Edge sliding away into the abyss: house, garden, road, the lot, just as the House of Usher had fallen away into the mere at the end of Poe's famous story.

With the mirrors watching, pressing, pushing, with the curtains stirring in the warm night, it was easy to imagine the house breathing around him, waiting for another great fall, something.

He kept thinking of Donald's words too. *We will discover what rules we need to follow as we go along*, the perfect tease for a film-maker on the eve of shooting his first feature. And other things: *I truly believe I am sharper than I was. More receptive.*

Then abruptly, startlingly, there were imagined words as well, never spoken or implied, but suddenly just as real.

I can do the same for you, Nils. Put you in tune with it all. Surely you'd like to know.

Nils sat up in bed, threw off the sheets and went to use the bathroom in the hall. Everything had changed. Jet-lag was a contributing factor, of course, but there was more to it. There was an inner pressure, pressing—yes!—pushing back.

More than ever he looked forward to the others arriving, to when the house became a film set and these troubling bits were swept aside in the urgency of script meetings and shooting schedules.

It was late, well past midnight. Back in his room, Nils sat on the edge of the bed, feeling restless, needing to do something, if only to calm himself before trying to settle again. Almost without thinking, he began to examine the furnishings, trying the cupboards, the drawers of the old bureau by the window. It was a way of knowing the space, anchoring himself.

There was little of interest until he tried the bottom drawer. Something rolled as it opened.

A cylindrical mirror!

It was! A reflective tube, ten inches long, three inches in diameter, like a child's shiny kaleidoscope.

Nils felt alarm, dread, betrayal, all in an instant. He couldn't help it. Donald had known all along.

Again, it changed everything.

But no, no. As he took the cylinder out and examined it, he tried to see the device as part of the reality of Tessian's Edge. The house had many spare rooms. Donald wouldn't necessarily know the contents of every one, may never have thought to rummage in the bottom drawers of old bureaus. And if he had, what would he have made of a mirror-tube without prior knowledge of its purpose?

It made sense. The painting existed. Of course Malcolm and Walter had the means for viewing it, something innocuous and inconsequential left shut away until needed.

He felt better. Not Donald then. Not deception and trickery by a wounded, extended mind enjoying some intricate family game.

But Nils remained troubled. Tessian's Edge had been re-opened to the world. This remarkable man in this remarkable house had brought changes. What else was he bringing with him?

Returning to bed was out of the question. Nils had to use the mirror. He dressed and stepped out onto the landing, stood listening to the house breathing in the night. He let a minute pass, two, then headed downstairs. In the moonlit, three-quarter darkness of the main hallway, he stopped to listen again. There was nothing, just a clock ticking close by, the sounds of insects from the garden outside. Nils stood quietly, keenly aware of the old dark portraits, blind now, staring in darkness, and the unmistakable pressure of the mirrors.

That *was* the only word for it. Pressure. A pushing. Nothing else came close.

No lights were showing in the library. There was a chance Donald might be drowsing at his desk, but Nils moved forward, deciding to risk it. The mirror by the door was black and empty now. The back door was closed for the night, though he suddenly wondered if that *were* the case. Could it be standing open? Secluded households often followed their own rules, though it was hardly likely given Donald's preoccupations. Either way, the warning mirrors were dark: so many black shields in a lost heraldry.

Reaching the desk, Nils switched on the reading lamp, then lifted the painting from the wall and carried it to the coffee table in front of the armchairs. If Donald or Bethany came in, he would simply tell the truth: say that he had found the mirror-tube and couldn't wait to satisfy his curiosity. For the first time since finding a producer for his film, Nils realized how his new status truly did excuse all kinds of quirky behavior.

It made him feel so much at ease that he switched on the overhead lights as well. Then he hurried back to the canvas and placed the mirror-tube at its center.

It was as easy as that. The image was immediately there in the curve of the glass: a head and shoulders portrait of a woman with short dark hair, wearing period dress, some then-younger Tessian matriarch-in-waiting with her back to an open doorway filled with light. She looked unnervingly like Bethany—the same dark eyes, high cheekbones and pale skin, was quite likely some distant relative. On the left cheek of the stark white face, Pierrot-fashion, was a solitary red teardrop. It lent a fanciful quality to the whole, a distinctive if odd touch of the Commedia dell'Arte.

Nils recognized the setting at once: a stylized rendering of the view in Donald's mirrors, showing the rear hall and the doorway open onto the garden, passed on shield by mirror shield. Caught in that knot of brilliance were the beginnings of something, a shape, a person, it was impossible to tell at this scale and resolution. And while the woman's face was directed out at the viewer, her eyes were turned to her right, wide with fear, as if just now hearing whoever it was, whatever it was. Quite possibly she had been waiting for someone, something, to appear in that doorway no less than her great-grandson did all these years later.

But why paint such a thing? What was the attraction, the purpose? There was nothing forbidden here, nothing religious, sacrilegious or overly dramatic. If there were a secret, for the life of him Nils couldn't see what it was or how he could ask about it.

Perhaps house rules prevailed and it couldn't be broached directly. Perhaps it was part of a ritual and Donald was hoping that Nils would figure it out: recognize the painting for what it was, find the mirror-tube, use it and understand. It was alarming how easily such obsessive thinking took over.

Perhaps this was the real reason the go-ahead for the film had been given.

We need someone here! An outsider! A facilitator!

Nils shook his head. What if he were wrong? He could be asked to leave, lose Tessian's Edge altogether.

He would ask Bethany about it in the morning, first thing.

ASKING HER PROVED MORE difficult than he expected. When Nils awoke around ten, he discovered a note on the kitchen table saying she had taken Donald into Katoomba to do some errands.

Nils was left alone for most of the day, free to explore wherever he pleased. It was more than he dared hope for, though like a child faced with too many treats, too much liberty, it soon lost its glamor. Again and again during the first hour he found himself standing at the back door looking out into the garden, or in the library staring at the swirling distortion of the painting, trying to resolve the image, to locate the tiny ruddy point that would become the tear.

Then, realizing that his host might deliberately be *giving* him this time alone, he packed his leather satchel with his camera and light meter, sunglasses, notebook and pocket tape recorder and set off to explore the garden.

Almost immediately he decided that the main intersection amid the pines would provide a perfect substitute location for Scenes 16 and 42, far better than the front driveway as originally planned. He made notes, took readings, shot test footage, then spent most of the next hour tracing the property line, looking for similar alternative venues.

It was just past noon when the stillness began to bother him. The sun was high in a cloudless sky. There was no breeze to speak of, so when the cicadas suddenly fell silent, Nils had the distinct and inevitable feeling that he was being watched.

It's the light, he told himself. It's so intense.

Then another thought was there.

They've deliberately left me alone with the garden!

He tried to put the notion out of his mind, which was impossible, of course.

But retreating indoors was no solution either. No sooner was he in the hall outside the library than an equally troubling thought was there.

They've left me alone with the mirrors!

Nils laughed at how susceptible he had become. But every hallway, every room had them, so many up-ended glossy pools snatching at him, using his own image, his own face, to stare back at him.

I'm giving them eyes!

And that was enough. Here he was, in an old house on the far side of the world, and there was too much light, too much relentless summer heat, too many shadows and reflections.

Nils went out the front door and sat on the steps, looking across the lawn to the great gulf of the Megalong.

Let the garden work its mischief, he told himself. Let the mirrors stare all they want.

And when the Audi appeared on Dunning Street an hour later, that was where Donald and Bethany found him.

THEY WEREN'T ALONE. AS if in a conspiracy to deny him opportunities to ask about the mirror-tube and the painting, Donald had brought more company: this time two middle-aged brothers, Ralph and Michael Slennet, rare book dealers from Blackheath who were film buffs and desperately eager to meet Nils on the eve of starting his first feature.

When they were seated over coffee in the library, Michael Slennet made a comment that only intensified the sense of it all being a strategy on Donald's part.

"This is quite a treat, Mr. Jarkman—Nils. Donald rarely has anyone over. We always meet in Blackheath or at the Jamison Inn in Katoomba. But he says it's part of a new phase in the Tessians' affairs. We applaud it wholeheartedly, of course."

"Change is what I'm looking for, Michael," Nils said diplomatically. "Has Donald told you about his mysterious painting there?"

Ralph Slennet nodded happily. "He told us on the way over. Very mysterious. He said it contains a hidden picture and that you are the man to solve it."

Donald poured them more coffee. "As soon as we can locate a cylindrical mirror."

"I found one last night," Nils said, alert for Donald's reaction. "In a drawer in my room."

Donald looked more delighted than disconcerted. "But that's marvelous, Nils! After you told us about it on Monday I was sure that Walter and Malcolm would have had something somewhere. You must get it at once!"

"I have it here," Nils said, and took it from the leather satchel by his feet.

In moments they had one end of Donald's desk cleared, the painting laid out and the mirror in position.

And, once again, there was the image: the pale face with the red teardrop on the cheek, eyes turned to the side as if just now hearing the shape glimpsed in the doorway.

Michael Slennet could barely contain his excitement. "Donald, you must know something of this. It's your family. Something in the past."

"Sorry," Donald said. "She must be an ancestor, of course. An important one—"

"With a story to tell," Ralph Slennet added. "The poor dear is terrified."

"Alarmed I'd say," his brother suggested. "Startled."

Michael Slennet leant in closer, trying to see more of the image. "Either way it's not an ordinary portrait. It has to mark an event of some significance."

"Agreed," Donald said, for all the world like someone who had never seen the image before. "What do you make of it, Nils? You would have examined it already, yes?"

Nils was alert for any hint of reproach, but heard only deep and genuine interest. "I truly have no idea. What intrigues me most is the red tear on the cheek. Given the painting is as old as it is, it's probably not intended as fancy dress. So why the Pierrot tear?"

No-one answered. More than ever the pale figure resembled Bethany, was probably her great-grandmother, Donald's great-aunt. The likeness was definitely there.

But no-one mentioned it, or even seemed to notice. They stood around the painting, Bethany with them, and studied it for another five minutes, then Donald lifted the tube away. In moments the old canvas was back on the wall, the image once again lost in its swirl of form and color.

The rest of the afternoon and the early evening were filled with more congenial talk, a half-dozen games of billiards, then tea in a sheltered spot on the front lawn, followed by a wonderful meal cooked by Ralph—very much the "wiz in the kitchen" his brother said he was.

Through it all, Nils kept thinking of the painting in the library, its striking image skewed beyond recognition now, existing only for the initiated. He kept wondering about the figure's resemblance to Bethany, and about the things she had never been able to say in the library the day he'd arrived, when Donald had surprised her with his own admissions.

Yet try as he might, Nils couldn't catch her alone. Again and again he dutifully helped fetch and carry dishes between the dining room and the kitchen hoping for a chance encounter, but either he'd miss her altogether or one of the Slennet brothers would be there with a question that made anything more than small-talk impossible.

It was even more exasperating when, sitting over coffee and liqueurs in the library around 10 p.m., she suddenly excused herself and bid them goodnight.

Nils waited ten minutes, then excused himself as well, going to his room along the same upstairs hall where Bethany had hers. There was no light showing under her door, no sign of her whereabouts. More than ever it felt like a conspiracy of manipulation and avoidance.

Feeling thwarted and annoyed, Nils went to his room, but again had trouble sleeping. It was more than the jet-lag now, it was the painting. The mirror-tube was no longer necessary. Even without it, he could imagine the face with the tear right there, watching from inside its distortions.

He heard the Slennet brothers leave soon after eleven. From his window, he saw a taxi approach along Dunning Street, heard voices below, then saw the taxi pull away.

He waited till the house became quiet, then, around midnight, dressed and went downstairs. If he met Donald, he had his excuses from the night before: he couldn't sleep; he was restless; he was excited about the project. If he encountered Bethany, he'd be more direct, ask about the woman in the painting, say that the mysteries were affecting his concentration. It made sense. He was wired, primed; could she help him?

In so many ways it was a re-run of the previous evening. The curtains stirred. The same mirrors served up their glints, glitters and sudden limpid sheens. The silence was broken only by the old clock ticking and the sound of insects.

But one thing *was* different. This time there was a light in the library, and Nils stepped into the room fully expecting to find Donald at his desk.

But no. The desk lamp was on, and—striking to see—the desk had been cleared of books and papers again, completely this time but for the lamp itself and a single bottle and glass on a silver tray.

Donald has been drinking, was his first thought, but then Nils saw that the glass was unused and that the bottle had a piece of card fastened around the neck with string.

Drink me, the makeshift label said in classic *Alice Through the Looking Glass* fashion.

Nils chuckled at the absurdity, then noticed that the glass rested not on a coaster but rather a folded note. He quickly snatched it up.

> *Nils,*
> *Something for the midnight rambler. I've thought long and hard about this. If you truly want to try the othergates, drink half a glass, no more. It's my own formula, a legacy of what the "procedure" did for me. Better than absinthe, twice as potent and twice as illegal, but it will bring you closer in. Your call. See you in the morning.*
>
> *Donald*

There was no way Nils could drink it; no way he couldn't. His mind raced with terrifying thoughts, recollections of scenes from books and movies: the drug madness in Ken Russell's *Gothic*, the terrifying final scenes of George Sluizer's *The Vanishing*, of waking to some inescapable endgame, or not waking at all.

But no, no. This was different. Provided it wasn't a hoax, a prank hatched in collusion with the Slennets, too many people knew where he was. Donald would be accountable.

It will bring you closer in.

Your call.

Nils removed the stopper and inhaled. Definitely alcoholic. Probably very potent, and probably an hallucinogenic like absinthe could be when overused.

It was the greatest dilemma he could remember facing. He was standing at a crossroads indeed, poised between this world and the othergates, the otherways cherished by the Tessians and—*if* Donald could be believed—cherished and feared by the Celts, by savants, sages and shamans throughout history in all lands, all cultures.

What would he see—*if* he were brave enough to look?

It took forty minutes to decide. For the first ten he sat re-reading the note, considering the possibilities in Donald's words. Then he poured exactly half a glass and sat sniffing it.

What if the offer weren't made again? What if this were to be the *only* chance?

There were other implications too, both disarming and somehow reassuring. *Something for the midnight rambler.* Donald knew of his night-time wanderings, had no doubt expected them, not just as a jet-lagged insomniac but also as a working film director about to start his first major project, understandably excited and eager to experience the house in all its phases. *This* was another part of that reality. Like leaving him alone with the house the day before, this was Donald as ally as well as host, as collaborator and accomplice.

That decided it. This was *of* the moment, something served up as part of the *compleat* artist's journey Nils liked to think he was on.

He downed the contents in one swallow, gasped at the strength, then set the glass on the tray.

Tasteless, odourless, very alcoholic.

As a precaution, he crossed to the sofa by the bookcases and sat waiting. Five minutes passed. There was nothing. Nothing at all. Just the clock ticking, the sound of night insects from the gardens, the mirrors pressing, pushing, goading, leading him into what?

Then, so suddenly that he cried out, the room began to turn, slip away, all in moments. And in seconds, merest instants, the night was done and it was morning.

Warm summer sunlight filled the library windows. Nils woke with a headache and aching eyes, no doubt a legacy of his special nightcap. He was still on the sofa but covered with a light blanket. Donald must have checked on him in the early hours and done what he could to make his guest comfortable.

As if watching for Nils to wake, perhaps using his mirrors for this new purpose, Donald appeared at the door, smiling his wonderful smile.

"The sleep of the blessed," he said, coming to stand by the sofa.

"I accepted your invitation."

"I know. I'm glad. Breakfast will be ready shortly. How do you feel?"

"Fine. Well enough. Bit of a headache. I didn't see anything."

"You have. You will."

"Can you elaborate?"

"I mustn't. It will predispose you. Expectations are the enemy here, Nils. Ghost sightings, UFO sightings, are often the result of suggestibility, the brain commandeering the optic nerves, projecting entoptic images onto the outer world. It happens all the time, even on a mass scale when conditions are favorable and the temporal lobes of many individuals are engaged at the same time. All sorts of vestigial herd instincts are triggered and often override perception and reason."

"Donald, I'm *already* predisposed. All I *have* are expectations. Of course I'm hoping to see something. I have two days till the others arrive—"

"One day."

"What?"

"One day. Most of one. You slept all of Wednesday."

Nils was dumbfounded. "What!"

"It's Thursday, Nils. I told you the drink was potent. Your people will be here this afternoon."

"But—" Nils couldn't find words, couldn't for a moment believe it. How could it be possible? He felt no undue hunger or thirst. And what about the toilet needs in losing a day?

Donald left him little time to question it. "You have much to ask about, I know. But I suggest you put that aside for now, and prepare for your film. I have given you a special gift. Think of it that way."

Then as smoothly as a practiced stage magician or a seasoned chat-show host he changed tack. "It occurs to me that you probably have a revised shooting schedule, which locations will be needed first and so on. Perhaps it might be useful if you could give me some idea of that."

It was intolerable. Nils wanted to ask about the painting and the woman with the red tear who looked so much like Bethany, press him about the impossibility of losing a day, wanted to ask about so many other things. The small wound on the back of his right hand, for instance, looked very much like the fresh cannula scar for an IV drip, a wound that meant he had been cared for even more thoroughly during his lost day than he first thought. For all he knew he had been catheterized as well; how else could he lose a day without wetting himself? Precautions had been taken, and the level of preparation and commitment that suggested was alarming in a whole new way.

But how could he ask about any of it? He needed the house. He had lost Wednesday. He'd never lost a day, not really. International date line adjustments didn't count. Still, it was a small price, small enough price. If he could only believe it.

AGAIN BETHANY WAS NOWHERE to be found. It was as if she were indeed the figure in the painting, a phantom dislocated in time and space, tipped out into this new charged setting, now present, now vanishing, waiting for her chance. After Nils had showered and dressed, it was Donald who served him a cooked breakfast in the kitchen, then excused himself while Nils was still eating, saying that he had some last-minute arrangements to make before the Sargon Productions crew arrived.

After he had hurried off, a new troubling thought occurred to Nils. What if Donald had gone to put things away, to remove the leucotome, the painting, the other signature objects that in so short a time had come to define the place? It was unlikely, improbable, absurd to expect it, but this was Thursday, so Donald claimed, the everything-happens day. What if he *had* decided to hide things? In seconds what had started as mild concern became a conviction, then absolute certainty.

Nils pushed back from the table and rushed through to the library. There was no-one in the hallway, just the special warning mirrors catching his own frantic image and passing it on.

The library, too, was deserted. A single glance showed that the leucotome was in its case; another that the Lindsay etching still hung above the fireplace, its startled subject now seeming more wide-eyed at Nils's intrusion than the prospect of her own ravishment. And there was the anamorphic painting, its subject still caught in its swirl of light and shadow, her lovely face twisted off around the dimensions, but there and watching him. No, not him. Watching the shape in the doorway, which—yes!—now he thought about it—was someone he had been more than once, would undoubtedly be again, all of it spiralling in to the single red tear.

The bloody tear!

Yes! The tear was blood! Of course it was! So obviously was.

Nils stared at it, understanding.

A leucotomy tear. A bead of blood from the tiniest wound, from a medial or lateral insertion made up behind the orbital bone, through to whatever precise touch-point of mind was needed. She too had been changed, brought closer in.

And he understood more, grasped the simple horrifying truth of his missing day!

They had done it to him as well!

It explained everything. The missing day. The scar on the back of his hand.

They drugged me and did it! Brought me closer in. Wiped away my own red tears!

Though I did it, Nils realized. I made the choice. Drugged myself.

If it had happened. Any of it. Yes? No? Either way the idea was there. He would never be free of it.

A sudden movement in Donald's mirrors caught his eye, something— a figure in a white dress!—in the glare of the open doorway. Not appearing from the garden; heading *into* the garden!

Bethany. It was Bethany, yes!

His chance for answers!

Nils ran from the library, rushed down the hall to the back door, aware that, again, he would be the one in the mirrors.

He didn't care. There was no time to lose. She was already at the first intersection, following the angle of the path as it turned.

But Bethany! Her shape. Her hair color.

Nils stepped into the terrible glare. The day was hot, windless. The air shimmered. Cicadas roared in the trees.

He hurried along the blazing walks, turned one corner, another, the blood hammering in his skull, the heat gripping, goading, pushing.

Such frenzied heat.

And there she was: light dress, dark hair, wide eyes. Fearless, tearless. Waiting, yes. Closer in and waiting, knowing it all.

No swirls of color now, just knots of heat and light, turning, spreading. Now was his chance. Now.

He rushed to her through the fire.

HAVING LOST A DAY, losing hours was easy. There was the blur of grabbing his satchel, getting the keys from the table in the hall, of driving the Audi, actually managing it, and getting down to Sydney, but it was barely real.

When the police arrived, Nils was already in the SAS check-in queue at Sydney Airport. Incredibly both Donald *and* Dieter were with them, which further added to the unreality, those two *together!* And, yes, others of the crew hurrying along behind.

"Nils! Nils!" Dieter cried, his face a mask of worry.

Donald rushed forward. "Thank God we found you!"

It was their relief that startled Nils most. Not anger or hostility, not the accusations he'd expected, just genuine concern.

They led him aside. There was so much confusion, so much he didn't remember. He stood dazed, wanting their forgiveness, their understanding, needing their words to fit himself back into the world. Forgiveness was everything now.

"We've been so worried," Donald said. "After what happened—"

"I didn't mean to rape her!" Nils found the words. "I'm sorry. It was the heat, the light. I didn't know—"

"Nils, you've got it wrong. You've got it all wrong! *You* didn't do anything! *She* attacked you! She assaulted you!"

"What! What?" Like an amnesiac re-learning the bits of his life, he scrambled to make sense of what Donald had said.

"She's so sorry. Swears she doesn't know what happened. But we can work this out! We need you here! You don't have to leave!"

That was all he heard right then. *You don't have to leave. We need you here.*

For then his thoughts were of light falling in a far-off garden, of mirrors, hard, bright and impossibly deep, and of how long it would be until the worlds reached out and he traveled those different roads again.

Afterword to "Jarkman at the Othergates"

NOTHING IS MORE terrifying than the world as we know it going wrong. That simple element is at the heart of the best and most effective horror storytelling—the world goes wrong in some fundamental way.

And the main character, traditionally the reader's entry-point, isn't sure whether it's the shared outer reality failing or his or her personal reality going awry.

Ken Levine, talented lead designer of the computer game *Bioshock*, said: "All horror is based upon loss...and what you're afraid of losing: family, property, and sanity," but seen as part of a truly complete equation, there's more to it. Whether it's hauntings, the living dead shuffling into town, or Lovecraft's Old Ones pushing through, it's things being lost and reality breaking down, yes, but with the *positives* such a situation also brings, of the world opening up, being larger, however briefly, however bleakly, even for a moment.

What a simple yet terrific gift; what a fine reward for the reader, having a larger, richer, fuller world—with the additional comfort of knowing that it's only a story. You're personally safe no matter what happens.

Equally important, it gives us the illusion of forever. It's a false forever, naturally, a false perception, but we each feel we have it, and never more so than when we read about larger worlds and more to life. Darker imaginative storytelling gives that illusion then puts it at terrible risk, showing it up as falsehood but, again, within its workings in a larger world, a supernature, that gives the immediate and implicit solace that such a fuller world brings.

All this is what I wanted to explore in "Jarkman at the Othergates" and in so many of the stories in this collection: how we all use often consensual, always subjective ways of seeing to build the world we regard as normal.

In the details it was, yet again, sewing whole cloth. There were the original meanings of "othergates" both as "by other roads" and as places of crossover between our world and others, and the word "jarkman" too for that matter, an old legal word. Pairing the two for a title brought Norman Lindsay's *Pan's Hour* to mind, a connection that in turn echoed John Fowles's unforgettable novel *The Magus* with its key "mystery-at-noon," godgame elements.

Then there were books on the mind and perception, providing a wealth of detail on lobotomies and, yes, anamorphosis. It was a powerful moment while sitting in the Art Deco Dining Pavilion in Harlan Ellison's wonderful home in 2006 and describing anamorphosis, only to have Harlan direct my attention to three coffee cups on a shelf nearby. Each had a famous movie scene hidden in its saucer, an image brought to life by its reflection in the mirror surface of the cup. Research often becomes creepy and magical like this.

All that remained was allowing an admiration for Peter Weir's *Picnic at Hanging Rock* to bring the young film-maker of the title into a memorable and unsettling personal crisis.

A small enough story in many ways despite its origins but, ah, the journey!

Ithaca

There are no words for this,
Only fools are talking,
He stands above the sea,
Eyes bright with memory.

Say, can you see the phantoms in his eyes?
Can you see him search for paradise?

Calypso, Nausicaa, carry him to Ithaca,
Calypso, Nausicaa, carry him away.

There is no comfort now,
Different winds are blowing,
He stands above the sea,
Haunted eyes and memory.

Say, can you see the phantoms in his eyes?
Can you see him search for paradise?

Calypso, Nausicaa, carry him to Ithaca,
Calypso, Nausicaa, carry him away.

Captain, my Captain, only fools are talking,
I am silent just like you.

Calypso, Nausicaa, carry him to Ithaca,
Calypso, Nausicaa, carry him away.

SOME ROSES FOR
THE BONESTELL MAN

ABOVE THE BEACH AT Chinza, on a headland near the ancient town, there is an old foss machine half-buried in the sand close by a seller of bonestell rockets.

Sometimes they argue, the souvenir seller calling good-natured insults across the warm desert air; the foss machine calling back, scorning the assortment of plastic and resin spacecraft laid out on the flimsy table.

"They're not rockets!" the foss would inevitably call. "You call them rockets but they're not!"

"It's how the future was *going* to be!" the bonestell seller invariably answered. He called himself, appropriately enough, Ches. It was an old name. "These are antiques!"

"Well, they might be antiques but they're not rockets!" was the foss's usual reply. "Look at that symmetry!"

The bonestell man always pretended to mishear. "You're the one who belongs in a cemetery! The bonestells are perfect!"

The foss would insist otherwise. "One word, dumbo! Probably four for you. As—tro—phys—ics! Who needs bilateral symmetry among the stars? They're a design dead-end."

"You're a design dead-end!" would be the bonestell man's usual response. "If you're so right about these things, why were you dumped out here?"

To the foss, the answer was obvious. "To keep an eye on crazies like you!"

And round it would go.

Tourists always stopped to watch the show, enjoying the comfortable pointlessness, finding pleasing echoes in a town known for art festivals devoted to Samuel Beckett, Monty Python, Jacques Tati and Buster Keaton. Humanity might have gone to the stars, but it still needed its clowns, quite possibly more than ever. It was as if the offerings of all those darkened retro cinemas on Hulot Street had leaked out into the day.

Ches understood this and granted that the old foss machine did too in its own way. People wanted meaning in their days, things important enough to argue over. Sometimes tourists bought his rockets not for their own sake, but as souvenirs of meeting this odd pair on their way to the beach at Chinza. Sometimes such old designs—the globes, capsules and cones nested within their functional frames and struts; the sleek, broad-winged, albatross landers and space planes; the gracile, finned needleships—tweaked paradigms, made people see things another way for a time, the way Ptolemy's map of the world still could or Galen's theories on humors, or a Beckett play for that matter. Sometimes people wanted—even needed—to remember such moments of seeing until the next such moment came along.

The seller of bonestell rockets sensed something of all this and allowed for it. The old Foss Mark 7 Shipstock Patternmaker obviously did. They knew enough between them to maintain the dialogues, continue the invective, perfect the amiable tension. Timing, as ever, became everything in their comedy of manners. Time and timing. They sensed something working between them there beside the dusty trail that wound across the breezy seagrass-covered headland between the beach and the ancient town. They sensed their place in the workings of *this* place. First there were the snack kiosks close by the villas and whitewashed tourist hotels; then the trail began with the flag seller, the kite seller and the jewel book seller. Then there were some therapists at their colored booths, a photomat selling old film, television and holo memorabilia, and the novelty balloon vendor with his dwarf zeppelins and montgolfiers. Finally, just when you thought it was all done, there was the bonestell man and the crazy old foss machine right there by the spit of land above the ocean.

Time and timing, yes. Their place in this place. All carefully planned.

Most onlookers were travelers from across the world, all the continents and nations there still were, those left behind by the space age and for whom things like bonestell rockets and even terms like "space age" held little meaning. They'd stop for the banter and ask their inevitable, predictable questions in one carefully allowed lull or other, and receive one of Ches's good-natured lectures about how the future once was and how it was now. The foss would be oddly silent while Ches gave his spiel, remaining strangely well behaved, though if there was too much silence when Ches was done, or too many puzzled, frowning faces, it would lunge in with: "So buy a rocket or you'll break his heart. His mind isn't too good anymore, but his heart's okay. And I need him happy! Ain't got legs like you good folk, so I have to listen to him weep and wail. Do an old foss a favor and buy a rocket!"

And they would or they wouldn't and the days would go round, and the weeks and months.

Then there was a month and a day and an hour when three sleekly formsuited travelers stopped on the dusty trail before the bonestell man and the old foss machine. Men or women, you couldn't tell; they all looked so alike. They were hairless and polished, shiny with the oils and skin treatments. They saw the bonestells laid out in the late-morning sun and smiled. Two of the smiles were sharp with disdain and wry condescension; one was bright with indulgent courtesy.

"I'm Patris," the tallest of them said, the one with the civil, neutral smile. "This is Basdis and Sonto."

The bonestell man made a polite bow. "I'm Ches. And that's an old foss machine. It used to design hard-tech rockets."

The one called Sonto picked up a moonship and studied it. "Not these."

"Oh no, sir or madam. These were early to mid-twentieth hypotheticals. This old foss worked the early twenty-first. *Before* Rossen technology." Ches couldn't help the barb.

Sonto studied the moonship a moment longer, then laughed and returned it to the table. The tabletop was covered with a lunar surface mercator, and the bonestell was set down on the Sea of Tranquility, close by the double craters Cyrillus and Theophilus. In the small-big of his day, Ches always noticed such things.

Basdis still found it hard to accept. "People actually buy these?"

"Sometimes," Ches said. "They're curiosities."

Basdis chuckled. "They were obsolete even before they could be made."

"Most of them." Ches studied the three lacquered rossenforms standing on the trail. Two men, one woman, he figured. He always tried to decide gender if he could. It mattered that he at least try. "The NASA shuttles were bonestells. They flew. Most of them never got off the drawing boards though."

"Barely out of the mind," Sonto said. From Patris it would have been reflective and sympathetic. From Sonto it was more deep-seated scorn.

"That's progress though," Patris did say, not unkindly.

Ches nodded, finding something oddly familiar about the tall stranger. "Technological progress at least. Not to be automatically taken as progress for the species."

"Here we go." Sonto shaped the idiom carefully, still not used to base modal.

"How so?" Patris asked, stasis suit gleaming in the sunlight.

"I wouldn't presume to tell you," Ches said, and the foss machine remembered to snort—right thing at the wrong time really, but too second nature for the old foss to override. It was trying to behave.

The tallest of the rossens seized on the remark. "Please. Presume. Tell us."

It caught Ches unprepared in a way. He was used to slipping his lectures in, braiding them into badinage and repartee, softening the polemical hard edges. This was too direct.

Still, he had to try. "The hardest single thing humanity ever had to learn was that the proper measure of its humanity was balance."

"Proportion?" Patris asked.

"Moderation, yes." Ches fumbled the words, overstating, seeking the right rhythm. This was important.

"Yes?" Patris said, encouraging him.

"To understand that a time could come where technological progress was *not* good for the race. Inevitable, inescapable perhaps, but not for the best. To know that the true courage, the true wisdom and responsibility would be in slowing, resisting, refusing. It's a hard moment to recognize. There are always those so readily against anything."

"Fugh!" Sonto said. "Patris, you may be enjoying yourself but do we have to put up with this?"

Basdis turned to face the ocean. "He's a leadite!"

Ches couldn't help himself. "That's not 'leadite' from 'leadlight' as a lot of people think. It's from 'Luddite,' a much older word. From Ned Ludd, the name of someone who once opposed technological change."

Basdis sneered and looked off at the ocean. Rossens loved the sea for some reason. It was partly why they came to Earth, came to places like Chinza.

Ches went to say more but Patris raised a hand. "Sonto, your turn. You heard the man. Just remember, no rote doctrine. Just what *you* really believe."

Sonto nodded. "Very well. The world, the universe, moves on. Viriditas versus entropy. Some sorry folk, some tards, retros and cloddies, dig their heels in, sit back and do nothing. Imagine they can hold on to a present they favor. It's sad. It's inevitable. There are museum cultures everywhere on Earth now. We at least get on with it."

"Basdis?"

The other spacer came ambling over. "It's like divergent strands of hominid staring at one another over some primeval waterhole. Sonto's right, Patris. We get on with the business of living, doing and being. Can't ask for more. No-one objected to bodymod assists for sea farming or the early orbital work. We've gone against nature from the beginning. We *are* nature going against itself. We make nature now. We can argue it forever."

The tallest spacer turned to the bonestell man. "Well, Ches?"

"What about you?"

Patris smiled again. "These two have said it honestly and fairly enough, I think, though some of it still sounded like rote to me. Love it or hate it, accept or resist, life has its own way with itself. Brutal, nasty and short, someone once said. Now it's long, splendid and eminently practical. Morality, ethics, don't really come into it. How could they? When have we ever controlled anything with even the worthiest ideologies? Humans do what humans do. Those who don't accept this will find themselves left behind, even pushed out of the way. Now, your turn."

Again Ches found himself alarmingly unready. What sort of game was this? Something about this tallest rossen *was* familiar. "These glib, easy truths usually make me keep silent," he said, simple honesty. "When is it right to say, 'Enough!'? To say: at this point we lose more for our humanity than we gain."

"Opinions," Basdis said, so much contempt in one word.

Ches nodded. "Right. But truths always start that way. You say 'museum' cultures, but we aren't consciously staging this. We live in change too. This *is* change. There are few absolutes here." He indicated the rockets, the foss machine, the town behind them. "It's just that we truly believe we have chosen better. If technology does lead us, for good or ill, then this may well be the *other* part of what humans have to do. Our balancing duty. If enough humans say 'Enough!', different things can happen."

Patris looked at the rockets, glanced over at the old patternmaker half-buried in the sand, then back to where the town lay beyond the rising trail. "I'm afraid you'll have to do better than that, Ches. Most spacers don't care much for what tards, retros and cloddies have to say about what they *don't* know." It was the spacer's harshest comment yet, seemed intentionally so.

"But it's about what you *do* know. That something greater has been lost than can be easily expressed in words, let alone replaced."

Patris sighed. "Still a bit to close to the foaming bigot and the easy platitude for my liking, Ches."

Ches felt the blood rising to his cheeks, felt his hands closing into the beginnings of fists. The foss had to be wondering why he was so patient this time, but Ches had rarely felt so desperate to be understood. *Was* Patris like the rest?

"So why do you return? Why come back? Why bother?"

Patris looked along the trail towards the town. "Some of us are sentimental. It means something. We like to keep the connections."

Basdis chuckled again. "Patris is being kind. What she means is we're legally required to, that's all. It's somewhere in the Rossen Charter. We're supposed to top up our humanity."

She! Patris was female.

Sonto kicked at a stone. "They have a sufficient sense of irony to call it a grounding."

"Anything else?" Ches asked. He needed more from them.

Patris frowned with what seemed like genuine concern. "What is it, Ches?"

"Just what's our duty of care where the whole culture is concerned? Do we just go with it?"

"There is no single *whole* culture anymore."

"The race then."

Basdis and Sonto smiled their insufferable rossen smiles. Patris didn't need to answer.

Ches wouldn't let it beat him. "More's the need then."

"You'll have a specific," Patris said. It was a statement, not a question.

"Well, yes. Most often resisting change *is* technophobia or even social control by those in authority but, yes, I do have an example. Sixteenth century feudal Japan was among the early inventors and users of firearms. Its rulers saw that such technology harmed their carefully structured society. They renounced firearms for nearly three centuries because of greater cultural concerns."

"Hardly a model culture, Ches. Disproportion and injustice everywhere."

"Not the point, Patris. They saw the harm, the implications. Low-born peasant levies striking down highly trained samurai. They saw change was just change, not automatically progress. Different, not necessarily better. They tried to show duty of care for what they already had and valued."

Patris nodded. "For good or ill, as you say. Well, at least your example wasn't nonsense about Mayans and Aztecs having wheeled toys but refusing to use the wheel for war or commerce. Sonto?"

"He said it. Technophobia. Bigotry. Envy. I'm still hearing dislike for the unlike."

Patris smiled at Ches. "And technology does lead society. We've agreed there can be only change. What happened in those three centuries, I wonder? Was it all just timelocked medievalism, haiku and saki? Basdis?"

"I don't know the culture he speaks of."

Ches let his emotion show. "The issue was choice then as now. Duty of care. A sublimely human thing."

"But still censorship surely," Basdis said. "The excuse of all repressive governments, I'm told."

"Perhaps." Ches had lost this time; he knew it. These three didn't care what he thought. The old foss had to be preparing itself, wondering when. "But possibly not in the intention."

Basdis laughed. "Ah yes. The intention."

"You have five minutes, Ches," Patris said. "We have to be going."

The bonestell man tried to fathom what was happening, tried to find words. Stripped of the repartee, the message was so simple, yet so hard to bring alive. He looked off into the day, running the usual routines he used with the foss, but none were appropriate, not here, not now. But he had to try.

"You all said it before. Humans do what humans do. Life has its own way with itself. But if we *could* choose, if we *should* in duty of care, what would the nature we make be like? Choosing it, what?"

"Patris?" Sonto said, clearly impatient.

"Yes, I know. Four minutes, Ches."

"What worries me most is how we are cutting ourselves off from where we've been. Just progressing isn't enough. We have to remember, have to keep the appropriate affect."

"Ho!" Basdis said, half-turning away, but not finishing the act, probably restrained by some earlier command from Patris. *Be civil. Participate. Try. You are here for a reason.* "Now we get the pscyh profiling. You cloddies always think you can even begin to manage it. Patris, please."

"Three minutes, Ches."

"Then a question. You're officially required to come here. How do you actually see us? Basdis?"

"Honestly? I've told you. As museum relics. Terminal forms. Bitter and in denial."

"Sonto?"

"The same. You can't even begin to grasp what we do for the race, what we've made out there. Only the Charter brings us here. Oceans are interesting, but you Earthers are like—what's the term?—things left behind in tidal pools."

"But still in nature," Ches said, not needing to ask Patris the question.

"What?" Sonto said.

"Still making nature, too, in our little pools. Part of nature. All of us. Made for here. Meant never to lose our connection with *here.*"

Basdis faced the tall rossen. "Patris, what is he raving about?"

"Two minutes, Ches?"

"We are in nature, like you said. Making nature like you said. Don't you consider your behavior inappropriate? It's like those guards at Auschwitz and Belsen being so out of touch with appropriate human feeling that they *could* allow the atrocities. They preferred to be cut off. Chose to be sociopathic."

"At where?" Basdis said.

And that did it. Ches must have shown his feelings on his face and the spacers must have read them there, for that's when they turned and ran.

The bonestell man snatched his gun from under the table and fired.

"Take that!" he cried, a line he'd heard in an old movie. He was safely in character again.

Basdis blazed into a carbon twist where he ran and shredded into streaming particles in his own body wind.

"Too much symmetry!" the foss yelled, and an arc-line leapt across the warm air and seared Sonto as he leapt, even as he leapt and sought translation, twisted him black and scattered him on the breeze.

Only Patris completed her run, morphed into winged aerodyne for the lift, morphed into full spacer "rose" for the steep translation vector, engaged the Rossen field at precisely eight hundred meters and vanished into the stars.

"Two out of three ain't bad," the old foss said. "That makes sixteen. You could have had the tall one if you'd been quicker."

"She's been here before," Ches said, sliding his gun back into its table sheath.

"What? Impossible. Why would she come back?"

"Exactly. She knew and she came back."

A minute went by.

"Could it be a game?" the foss asked. "The thrill? The risk?"

Another minute. Time and timing. Ches picked up the moonship Sonto had examined.

"Or they're doing it as well." He didn't say the word.

"By using us to do it," the foss machine said.

There was another laden silence with no audience to appreciate it—a brown study, man and machine on a windy headland at the early edge of a golden afternoon.

"Why would they?" the foss asked then, but probably knew.

The bonestell man looked around at the day, at the path, at the spread of impossible rockets on the table, sensing the uncertainty, the promise, the human dimension those things represented. He listened to the hiss of sand along the trail, the unmistakable soughing of the grass, the underlying swell of the ocean, all eternal enough.

"How could they not?" he said, just as four tourists appeared on the trail heading their way. The bonestell man lowered the moonship to the table, made a perfect landing on the Sea of Crisis. "Call it a grounding," he said.

Afterword to "Some Roses for the Bonestell Man"

AGAIN, HUMAN IS as human does, for good or ill. What is appropriate duty of care for any of us trying to be true citizens of the world?

It was Harlan who brought to my attention the remark made by the Nazi concentration camp guard who, when asked how he could bear to be part of such atrocities, simply said that no-one would remember. What to do in the face of such a thing? And how far might any of us go given the right motivation?

When it comes to second-guessing the future, few scientists, ethicists, even futurists care to say too much about the C-word. But you only need consider the carrying capacity stats for our harried planet, trends in targeted bio-warfare research, and a book like Jared Diamond's *Guns, Germs and Steel* to see how culling is a viable if reprehensible and horrific solution to overpopulation, resource depletion and vested-interest disempowerment.

In the previous story, such grave matters are given an amiable, almost off-handed delivery to let the issue reveal itself obliquely for what it is, to give it a more provocative spin as an ethical dilemma and (I hope) more impact as a narrative reveal.

One factor had to be at its heart—the truly earnest belief held by Ches and his sidekick that they are *definitely* doing the right thing. Just as there are optimum forms with made artefacts: a chair that is so perfect in its "chairness" that it needs no re-design, no useful improvement, or a teacup, a doorway, a jacket, a pen, so in sociological, cultural terms one could make a case for optimal stages reached for a society, a community, dare we say a race, when personal freedom is balanced and *served* by enlightened custodial regulation, when individuality fits with being good neighbors, good citizens, members of a true commonweal.

In the cycle of empires and cultural evolution, societies sometimes pass through such stages: a generation here, a blessed decade there, a small, fleeting, often regional enclave where things like envy, poisonous gossip and excessive busybodying are balanced by the goodwill and civic responsibility of, say, Adam West's

Batman or *Mister Rogers' Neighborhood* or *The Vicar of Dibley* at their best. We'll each have examples.

But what happens if you truly believe such an optimal time *has* been reached? At what point do you fight to protect it, take action akin to the 17th century Japanese giving up the gun for nearly 300 years or the Vatican attempting (albeit briefly) to ban the crossbow? Do you become resigned, philosophical, step back and let it go, or do you reach such a point of outrage and frustration that you *can* seriously consider "ultimate" solutions like the C-word?

In short, what would you fight for? When would you and how, especially when one person's sacred site is so often another's archaeology, one person's patriot another's terrorist? Duty of care becomes personal realization and commitment for any of us, certainly, but listening to the better angels of our natures remains trickier than ever.

Gantry Jack

Coveralls ablaze with signs,
His own bright zodiac,
And his name is Gantry Jack.
But they're rocket names upon his shoulder,
He's a spectre in the land.
He's the clown of Cocoa Beach,
Between the space-town and the sea,
He'll come rowing in just so he can see.

Hey, did you see my rocket fly?
All of summer in a day.
But now they've shut the towers down
And put the rockets all away.

The joke of Mission Control,
Always there before the flight.
Watching from the reeds
In the morning light.
And the people on the highway
Are right to smile and turn away.
He's the clown of Cocoa Beach,
Between the space-town and the sea,
He'll come rowing in just so he can see.

Hey, did you see my rocket fly?
All of summer in a day.
But now they've shut the towers down
And put the rockets all away.

THE SUITS AT AUDERLENE

ONE HOUR WITH GILLY Nescombe in the bar of the Summerton Arms confirmed everything the truck driver had said about the meteorite. My article for *Cosmos* seemed more a reality than ever.

Tracking it back, waxing lyrical and gesturing like a fool, I kept trying to impress on her the scale of it all.

"You know how these things go, Gilly," I said. "They just get larger and larger." And off I went, telling her yet again how I would never have heard about Auderlene at all if it hadn't been for a meteorite called the Pratican Star and a talkative truck driver who had insisted on an extra beer one evening at the Three Weeds hotel in Balmain and had mentioned it. And pushing it back still further, if I hadn't been freelancing again and looking for a suitable follow-up article for *Cosmos*, I'd never have made the connection, seen the seed of a story when that long-hauler started telling *me* over drinks how a drunken farmer in Summerton out in the state's southwest had told *him* about the old Auderlene place and the iron suits and that part of the town's little secret.

Sitting across from me in the bar, Gilly just smiled her engaging, lopsided smile and took it all in her stride. She was more than just one of those life-hardened rural women whose life seems forever at angles to your own. Close to my own age, late thirties, early forties, looking easy with herself in white blouse, denim skirt, white deck shoes, with hazel eyes and a smile that was too Ellen Barkin for my own good and kept growing wider as I tried, yet again, to convey the scale of what had brought me here.

I managed to save it. This time I stopped mid-sentence, laughed out loud, and shook my head in wonder at it all. Trying the main town pub had been the obvious thing to do—but meeting Gilly like this! I wished her only sunny days.

Yes, a sizeable nickel-iron meteorite *had* fallen to ground on the Pratican estate in Summerton one summer night back in 1904. No, it had never been displayed, never examined or written up, just as the truck driver had said his own Summerton local had insisted. Now here was this very personable barmaid confirming that, yes, *if* it still existed, *if* it hadn't been thrown away or melted down, there was a good chance it was still somewhere at the old Pratican place outside of town.

Driving down from Sydney, the question had been whether it was worth the trouble of checking out at all. Science journalism, like any journalism, gets to be a subtle trap. So often you put together the article in your head long before the substance of it is in place, and sometimes the angle and *how* it catches the popular imagination is more important than the actual content.

More specifically, in a world where science readers expected to be flooded with the latest word on bosons and the Higgs Field, the bone morphology of dinosaurs, or asteroid-strike extinction events, there was still room for a bit of scientific romance, a human interest piece with a regional twist. Whatever I wrote, the Pratican Star would be the heart of it—one of the largest unlogged meteorites ever to come down in Australia since European settlement.

I'd done all the relevant searches. Most meteorites are octahedrites. From what little Gilly had said, the Practican Star was the nickel-iron variety, an ataxite, with extremely high traces of those two nickel-iron minerals kamacite and taenite. But more importantly, meteors large enough to survive impact and receive a name rarely dropped out of the picture like this. Short of being non-existent or outright fakes, named meteorites in themselves were always newsworthy in one form or other, even when the name had been lost to all but local lore.

That had done it. But now it was more than just having my by-line under a two-thousand-word regional piece. Now, with any luck, it would be an intriguing small-town story of lost opportunities and a truth waiting to come out, full of hard facts rather than just hearsay with a bit of local color for padding.

Which brought up questions of access, of course, but, again, Gilly was making that easy.

"So, Nev, you can either stay here at the Arms or I can put you up at Sallen. Your choice and no offence taken."

"I don't want to impose."

"Don't be silly. One: there's plenty of room. Sallen often doubles as a guest-house. Two: it's close to Auderlene, next property over. Three: I'm one of the custodians of the place. Keeper of the keys. I can get you in, help you find the thing if it's still there to be found."

I couldn't believe it and yet, after landing regular freelance work for *The Weekend Australian*, then meeting a truck driver who'd met a farmer who knew about a forgotten meteorite, it was clearly a world where anything was possible.

"And four?" I shouldn't have said it. I was just too happy, too relieved to think twice.

Gilly pretended outrage. "Now, now! I'd have to know you a lot better before there was any talk of a number four!"

She gave me a wink that was playfully ambiguous, then went on as businesslike as you please.

"A few house rules up front, Nev. No-one gets to spend the night at Auderlene, so put that out of your head right away. You want to look for a meteor, we do it during the day. The old girl was insistent before she died. She had a special document drawn up back in 1968, had meetings with the local council. She lost her only boy in 1912. Very tragic. An outing with other kids went wrong. Some said murder, others manslaughter. Most said too much skylarking down at the weir one day. Anyway there was no other family. Jeanette Pratican left the house and grounds to the local community of Summerton for 'its recreation and general well-being' on the sole condition that three stipulations were met. I can quote them pretty much as they're written. There had to be 'no fewer than seven horses kept on the grounds at all times, allowed free run and given proper care.' The house was to remain 'untenanted, uninhabited and unimproved beyond the reasonable maintenance of all existing structures.' Last of all, while it was 'to serve as a museum for the common good during daylight hours,' under no circumstances could anyone 'remain between seven in the evening and six in the morning.' Mrs. Pratican was very specific."

"Did she give reasons?"

"Not that I know of. It was take it or leave it. Enough of the Pratican fortune remained at interest to ensure it went the way she said. So you'll still find the horses, still find Harry Barrowman and his boys doing odd-jobs, and the historical society reps—that's Harry, Chris Goodlan and me—making sure the doors and gates are always locked at sundown."

"There are rooms the public doesn't get to see?"

"Eighteen of the twenty-two are open. The rest are for archives, office space, that sort of thing. There's no meteorite in plain view, Nev. None that we've seen. We've been through her stuff lots of times."

"But there are vitrines? Display cases?"

"There are."

"Gilly, with something like this the angle you take on a story is almost as important as the story itself—"

The grin was there. "You did mention that."

I grinned back. "Reckon I did. It's just people aren't that interested in rocks from space. They *are* interested in rocks from space that seem to have been hushed up and have a story attached. Please, let me know up front. What are the chances of this meteorite business being a local beat-up?"

Gilly hopped off the bar-stool, smoothed her denim skirt, and took her car keys from her shoulder bag. "You're the one who has to decide that. Let me show you the place. And the suits. Wait till you see them. Wonderful or awful, depending on your taste. You follow me out in your car. I've got to get back and work here till four. Chris Goodlan will show you round."

FIVE MINUTES OUT OF town, Gilly honked the horn of her Land Rover and did a bent-arm pointing gesture at the big house on her left. The sign above the front gate said *Sallen*. It looked fine.

Another thirty seconds along the road and we were at Auderlene.

Everything Gilly, the truck driver and his farmer had led me to expect was true. The property was the kind of enclave of transplanted Englishness that was such a cultural signature during the heyday of the British Empire and had endured as cherished benchmarks of Britishness even more vividly during the long afternoon of its decline. You found similar estates, similar enclaves in the once fashionable surrounds of Capetown at Stellenbosch and Franschoek, close by Ottawa's Rockcliffe Park or

Ontario's Almonte, in the exclusive parts of Christchurch, yes, and all over the Indian sub-continent as abandoned touchpoints of what was once the British Raj: a stylish, modest Warwickshire mansion set in spacious grounds, but imposed—like one map intercut with another, leaving oaks dislocating into eucalypts, hedges into scrub, like something out of one of those forever restless colonial paintings by John Glover. In fact, strip away the town and the estuarine harbor from Glover's 1832 painting, *Hobart Town, taken from the Garden where I lived*, leaving Stanwell Hall, and you pretty well had Auderlene: an elegant, two-storied mansion set among fields and well-tamed bushland.

And, as Gilly had said, there were horses. All seven came trotting over to the gate as she unlocked the padlock and chain. She gave each one a sugar cube from the pocket of her skirt.

"Chris is up at the house, Nev. You drive on over and he'll show you round. I'll lock the gate behind you. Come back to the pub when you're done and let me know what you've decided about Sallen."

There wasn't a wink this time, but she did give that all-conquering smile.

A SHORT AMIABLE-LOOKING MAN in his mid-sixties was waiting for me as I pulled in. When I'd parked the car, he greeted me warmly by the front steps.

"Chris Goodlan," he said, shaking hands.

"Neville Reid, Chris. Nev."

"Come on in, Nev. Gilly phoned on the way over and said to give you the tour. Said you're doing an article or something."

"Hoping to, Chris. Depends on what I turn up."

"Well, let me do the honors."

The long front hall opened onto large sunny rooms to the left and right, then led us into what had once been a formal ballroom as wide as the house. It was sparsely furnished now, with just a few chairs against the side walls and a chaise-longue positioned in front of a large Persian rug laid out in the middle of the floor. Impressive identical staircases to either side led to upstairs bedrooms; a central door beyond the rug continued through to what were no doubt the kitchen and service rooms.

But what immediately caught the eye were the five suits of medieval armor standing in raised alcoves in the wall between those flanking staircases, three to the left of the main axial door, two to the right; the second alcove of the right-hand three was empty. Each niche was set a foot above the polished timber floor, and just large enough and deep enough—with the one exception—to accommodate its iron suit.

Though they weren't really suits of armor, I quickly saw, or even convincing replicas for that matter. I'd done a project on medieval armor back in high school, and had seen museum exhibitions of Kunz Lochner suits from Nuremberg and some fine 15th century Italian suits from Milan. More than a cursory glance showed that each suit here was clearly a single rigid whole, a hollow welded iron statue painted a drab matt black that further ruined any chance of their being taken for the real thing. The pauldrons across the shoulders were curved iron segments clamped and welded onto the breastplates and identical on each one, as if the same template had been used over and over for convenience sake. The groin taces and tassets were flat functional plates, angled and fixed in place as if their creator had been following a simplistic illustration in some old picture book. What would have been the vambraces and rerebraces on the arms and the cuishes and greaves on the legs were not shaped to protect human limbs at all, but rather were completely sealed stovepipe tubes tapered appropriately. Their joint guards—the couters at the elbows and poleyns at the knees—were token fixtures as well, cut and folded, then welded in place, while the gauntlets were locked fists, never to be opened. The feet in their iron sollerets were planted together at the heels, but turned outwards in the same duck-footed stance.

It was the full-face helmets that gave them their greatest semblance of authenticity. They looked like true early medieval casques and basinets for the most part, complete with fearsome eye-slits and breathing and vision perforations at the front. Left to right, Suits 1, 3 and 5 had great helms in the distinctive, thirteenth and fourteenth century "bucket" style, like the headpieces of antique robots. Suits 2 and 4 had the pointed "pig-faced" visor style from the mid 1400s that had always struck me as so bestial and disturbing.

Love them or hate them, it was quite a display. Comical yet dramatic.

And there were contradictions. While they were clearly home-made constructs, the joins and seals that I could see were all full welds. There was no spot welding anywhere.

"Quite something, eh?" Chris Goodlan said. "You see why the bus tours get a kick out of coming out here."

"Very striking," I said, though I thought they looked awful. Who would give over a feature room like this to such an overpowering display? "They're more like statues really. Hollow iron statues. You can't take them apart."

"You can't, no," Chris said, as if he feared I might try.

"Off the record, what do you think of them?"

"Well, they're part of the place, aren't they? Old Nettie Pratican—"

"*Off* the record, Chris. Just between us."

Chris Goodlan chuckled. "Bloody eyesores, if you ask me. But Mrs. Pratican loved 'em well enough."

"Loved them? Really?"

"Well, she had 'em made, didn't she? Set 'em up like this. I mean, she had Myron Birch and his boys turn 'em out back in 1914."

"Any of the Birches still around?"

"Killed on the Somme in September 1916, all of 'em, if you can believe it. Father *and* sons. Bloody tragedy. The mother had already died. They made these for Mrs. P. before they went away."

"Where's the sixth one?"

"There were only ever the five, Nev."

"There are six alcoves."

"Lots of folks ask about that. But only five suits were made. Maybe there was meant to be a sixth and it was never finished. The Birches never said, but then again they were none of 'em much for writing stuff down."

"Did Mrs. Pratican leave any specs? Invoices? Diary entries?"

"Nothing we've found. No meteor either, Nev. Sorry."

"Chris, I have to ask. You've probably lived here quite a while."

"All my life, man and boy."

"Any chance that meteorite they talk about was melted down and included in this lot?"

Someone else might have showed surprise at such a notion or expressed curiosity as to why someone would do such a thing. Not Chris Goodlan. "Gilly said you might be doing a piece on the Star. Well, I've got to tell you, Nev. From what I heard growing up, that meteor wouldn't have been much larger than my fist. It wouldn't be enough to do much good. Those suits are mostly just fourteen or sixteen gauge sheet iron reworked, as far as I can tell, but that's still a lot of metal. You can climb up and take a look yourself if you want. Grab a chair from out back. You'll see they're hollow sheet iron."

"But it *could* have been included? If a metallurgical analysis was ever done, say?"

Again Chris Goodlan looked worried. "Couldn't allow anythin' like that, Nev. Things have got to be left."

"Of course. But hypothetically?"

"Well, sure. Anything's possible. Could've been melted right in when the Birches got working."

"Where did they have their workshop?"

"The foundry was in town. But if you look round back through the trees, you'll see some old work sheds just off the estate. They set up a small furnace there and brought out what they needed."

"For secrecy?"

Now Chris did look puzzled. "Convenience, I would've thought. Just large enough for the cutting and welding. And Mrs. P. could check on the progress."

It all sounded reasonable enough. The angles for my article seemed to be growing fewer by the minute.

"So what's with the curfew, Chris? No-one being allowed to stay over?"

"Beats me, Nev. One of the rules though. Doors are locked by five or six most days. It's how she wanted it."

"But why?"

"Why indeed?" Chris said. "She was a weird old bird. Got weirder when Andrew died." Then he sighed and slapped his thighs as if he had decided it best to change the subject. "But she did leave us Auderlene. Let me show you the rest of the place."

CHRIS GOODLAN WAS PATIENT and very helpful. He waited while I checked in cupboards and cabinets, shifted smaller items of furniture, even moved things on shelves to look at what might be concealed behind. He reassured me five or six times that he had nothing better to do, that he was supposed to be keeping an eye on things. "Nothing personal, mind," he kept saying. It was in the rules.

There were indeed the vitrines and display cases Gilly had mentioned, things that clearly served as the sort of cabinets of curiosities that would probably have housed an unusual found object like a meteorite. There was nothing that looked remotely like it might be the Pratican Star.

I examined anything that could have been fashioned out of meteoric iron just in case: metal statues and figurines, lamp stands, decorative buckles, finials and locks. They all turned out to be bronze, brass or pewter as far as I could tell, many with conspicuous craftsmen's marks stamped into them.

But it gave us lots to talk about, mostly about how such items fitted into the town's history. It became so easy between us in fact that, over a cup of instant coffee Chris fetched us from the kitchen, I was able to bring up Gilly Nescombe's role in the whole thing.

"Chris, what's Gilly's place in this? She doesn't seem like a history buff. She's not a relative."

"Just someone who values what we have," he said, willingly enough it seemed. "But you go easy on her, Nev. She's had a hard time of it, what with the miscarriage and the divorce four years back. Other things."

"Other things?" I couldn't help myself.

Chris cooled a little. He'd said too much. "She'll bring it up if she wants to. I'm saying it in a neighborly way, you understand, but you just go easy."

I DID END UP staying at Sallen. Gilly put me up in a large airy room on the northern side of the house, and I met her other two guest-house regulars, Lorna Gillard and Jim Camberson, over a fine roast chicken dinner around seven o'clock that evening.

If her "number four" quip from the morning had been any kind of come-on there was no sign of it. Which was probably just as well; I couldn't remember the last time I'd been so taken with someone. But in view of Chris Goodlan's advice, I made sure that I remained appropriately interested yet suitably gentle and respectful.

Still, the possibility of alienating Gilly was soon to be much more of a reality. I'd decided that I had to see Auderlene again, had to go inside on my own and—yes—after dark. It wasn't just that the old mansion had been calling to me through my bedroom window while I was unpacking, nothing so simple or melodramatic. As much as I wanted to look around without being watched, it was more a case of getting the feel of the place in *all* its phases, grabbing some genuine atmosphere, even angles on future pieces I might try. My vacation was almost over and I'd come all this way. I was having an adventure. It would be wrong, a breach of trust certainly, but what real harm could it do? I'd just play dumb, be the too-eager outatowner who never for a moment thought it was such a big deal.

Dinner was followed by two hours of cards and some rounds of *Pictionary* that were more fun than I ever thought such things could be.

At 10 p.m. I excused myself and made a strategic withdrawal, trying my best to follow Chris Goodlan's advice.

Back in my room, I stretched out on the bed fully clothed and waited for the household to settle.

Now Auderlene did seem to call to me across the fields of dry grass and eucalypts, no more than ten minutes away in the fragrant spring evening. I *had* to see the place at night. It was starting to feel like a compulsion.

After an hour or so of doors closing and the house growing quiet, the time seemed right. It was 11:20. If Gilly caught me going out, I'd say I needed some air, that my mind was racing with ideas and possibilities, that I had to relax myself a little.

No-one noticed me as far as I could tell. The faint sound of a television came from one of the other guest rooms, otherwise nobody stirred.

The keys marked *Auderlene 2* were on a hook by the back door. Within minutes I had them in my pocket, had my torch from the car, and was crossing Gilly's property towards Auderlene's southern boundary.

More than ever I was keenly aware of failing these new friends in a fundamental way. With every step I kept trying to justify it to myself, going over the excuses I'd give if Gilly *had* heard me go and confronted me later. Like that I'd noticed something at the old mansion earlier that day that I hadn't asked Chris about and it was bothering me, wouldn't let me rest. Like that I hadn't believed the curfew business was meant to be taken seriously, not really; I'd meant no harm. Or perhaps telling it like it was, that this had become something all its own, vitally important in an odd way. I had to see the Pratican place alone and during curfew. Just did.

No excuses seemed to cover it, but the fact that I kept trying to come up with them said everything about how I felt about being in Summerton. At Sallen.

But soon I was at the front steps of the old house and there were other things to think about. There had been no alarm fittings that I had seen, no security keypads or warning signs. Auderlene wasn't set up that way yet. There were just dead-bolts on the access doors and the ground-floor windows, a padlock on the gate out by the road.

I would have rather used the back door under the circumstances, but, while the front door faced the highway at the end of the drive, that was the approach I knew.

There were six keys on the *Auderlene 2* ring and I began trying them. The fourth turned smoothly in the lock; the main door opened without so much as a squeak.

The house was quiet but for the ticking of the big grandfather clock in the hall. I moved past the large front rooms, grateful that the curtains had been left open and that enough moonlight found its way in to show doorways and hall fixtures. More than ever I was certain that no silent alarm was registering on a far-off security desk. Five years from now maybe, but not yet.

Soon I was at the ballroom and relieved to find that the curtains had been left open there as well. Later in the year they would probably be closed to protect the furnishings from the harsh summer sun.

Getting my bearings, I crossed to the chaise-longue in front of the carpet and sat while considering how best to proceed. Switching on the house lights was out of the question, and using the torch to explore the upstairs rooms would make passing motorists think there were burglars on the premises.

Which meant that there was very little I *could* do other than soak in the atmosphere. At Sallen that had seemed reason enough. Now I was left wondering why I had risked so much by insisting on a nocturnal visit. I could hardly believe it had seemed so important. But here I was, and there was no need to hurry. I had time to get the feel of the place without watching eyes.

Human eyes at least. The suits were right there, darker shapes in the gloom, so many streaks of coal-cellar midnight flanking the blackness of the central doorway.

I settled back and listened. The clock was ticking in the hall. The sound of crickets came from the dry grass and modest gardens beyond the locked windows, otherwise nothing. No traffic on the road from town that I could hear. None of the big city white noise sounds I had become so used to.

The sense of being watched by the suits was inevitable under the circumstances, but, oddly enough, it was that silence that bothered me most of all. It was *too* quiet. Which, I told myself, smiling wryly, was precisely one of those touches of atmosphere and local color I'd been looking for. But all things considered, Auderlene was just a large empty house, like a deserted theater or a school gymnasium after dark, any other large open space.

That silence soon took its toll. Apart from the clock, possibly the drip of a tap way off in the kitchen, all sound came from out there, from the world beyond, and it lulled me. I'd only meant to sit a while, to listen and consider options, then head back. But without meaning to, without even knowing I did so, I drowsed. I was at the end of a long drive and a busy day and the adrenaline rush of sneaking away from Sallen. I just slipped into a reverie that quickly became something else.

Till something woke me. I activated my watch display, saw it was 2:23 a.m. So much time had passed.

Crazy thoughts were there then. What if Gilly had decided to check on me? What if she had come by, found me gone and realized where I'd be? Crazy thoughts.

I couldn't be sure I'd heard anything, of course, but the shock of believing I had was there to deal with. Real or imagined, something had woken me.

I kept as still as I could and listened. There was nothing, just the clock ticking and night bird and insect song beyond the windows. Just the conviction that something had stirred in the quiet house and gone silent again.

But what? What?

Then it was there: first as a sense of sound, more felt than actually heard, like a low-level tinnitus, something you shook your head to be free of. But within seconds, minutes—however long it was—it crossed that border between unreal and unmistakably real, became a low keening in the darkness, building towards a distinct and eerie moaning.

One of the suits was sounding!

I was sure of it. Suit 4 or 5, there was no knowing for certain, but from one of the alcoves to the right.

I swung my legs off the divan, set my feet firmly, silently, on the floor.

The keening continued, kept growing if anything, and, strangely, was easier to take than the do-I-hear-it? do-I-not? uncertainty.

I grinned in the darkness. Of course. Gilly was off somewhere playing tricks, goosing the outatowner, what I deserved for breaking faith as I had. She'd waited and she'd followed.

But then a suit to the left of the display began sounding as well, making a distinct harmonic to the first, impossible for one person—a single voice—to manage. It, too, grew in the darkness, clear and separate.

She had friends helping. That was it. The other custodians. Reliable old Chris Goodlan. Or Lorna and Jim Camberson. Or there were hidden speakers. They'd done this before. It was their usual strategy for curfew breakers. *Messing with my mind, Gilly. In more ways than one.*

I smiled and stood. Using the new sounding to orient myself towards Suit 1, I switched on my torch. Let the locals see torchlight flickering. Who'd be out at this hour anyway? And more rationalizations covered it: I'd been out walking and heard a noise inside the old house. Chris mustn't have shut the front door properly. I just came in...

The weak cone of light caught Suit 1 in its glow. The iron helmet glowered back, eye-slit fierce in the meager light. It was so easy to imagine the glitter of eyes in the narrow slot, too easy to imagine a poor soul trapped within, crying in the night. One of five.

I crossed the ballroom as quietly as I could, keeping the torch beam on the eye-slit in the narrow bucket-shaped helm.

The song kept swelling. It seemed that three, possibly four suits were sounding now, but how could I be sure? The harmonics were too diffuse, the actual source points too difficult to judge in such a large space. I kept shaking my head to make sure I was actually hearing it. Was it me? Could it be me?

When Suit 1 was within reach, I stretched out a hand, placed my fingers on the black metal chest.

It was vibrating. It was! There was a resonance in the old iron, a deep thrumming.

I felt such relief. Not *me* then. Not something in my mind. Something *in* the world, *of* the world.

I fought down the dread, the panic waiting right there. There were answers. There had to be. I just needed daylight to check for audio leads and concealed speakers. Short of switching on the house lights, there was no way of doing that now.

Go or stay: they were the only choices.

I made myself move along the row, shining my torch on the eye-slit of Suit 2 as I reached it, then doing the same with Suit 3, touching each iron shape as I passed and feeling the same deep thrumming in the metal.

So far so good.

The open space of the central doorway was there then—a sudden maw of black in black—and I was at Suit 4, reaching out to touch the breastplate. The vibration was there as well, deep and constant, resonating so powerfully that I snatched my hand away.

Keep moving! Keep moving! One to go!

The empty niche was so welcome with its silence, but I didn't linger. Couldn't. I was nearly done.

I moved on to Suit 5, placed my fingers on the iron chest. Again, the nightsong was there, adding its harsh edge to the whole.

All five were sounding.

I'd done it, made myself finish, but mainly because I kept picturing Gilly hiding close by, stage-managing all this. That was what stopped me from fleeing the house, rushing back to Sallen, back to town, back to Sydney. There was a prankishness, an absurdity to the whole thing and it kept the panic at bay, brought cautious fascination instead of fear, a determination to grasp what was happening and how it was being done.

I had managed, was managing.

Provided I didn't look at the eyes-slits too long, didn't imagine the whites of eyes trapped behind the midnight slots and perforations, following every move.

It had to be Gilly and the others. Had to be.

And I had to stay rational, in control.

I made myself start back along the row, this time on a "science-and-logic" run—how I thought of it—an attempt to learn how these effects were being achieved.

I was at the empty alcove when the keening stopped.

Just like that. The suits were silent.

Such a simple thing, but all that was needed. More than ever I *knew* there were eyes peering out, staring in the silence.

In the world, *of* the world!

Which was more than I could bear.

I scrambled across the ballroom, rushed along the dark hall to the front door and out into the night, imagining those fierce unblinking eyes on me all the way back to Sallen.

GILLY SEEMED NOT TO have noticed my absence. She said nothing about it over breakfast the next morning and I detected no signs that things had changed between us.

She had another 10 a.m. shift at the Arms, she told me, but said that Chris would be happy to show me through Auderlene again if I thought it would help. I thanked her, and almost called her on the night's "entertainment" with an oblique challenge: "First round to the Summerton crew, I guess," but decided against it. What if I was wrong?

After chatting in the kitchen a while, she gave me a tour of Sallen in daylight. It ended with us sitting in the lounge room, rarely used these days, she explained, but a large sunny formal space from days when ushering neighbours into parlors and serving them devonshire tea vied with taking them straight through to the kitchen for an informal, no-frills cuppa.

I sat on a sofa by the large front windows, with Gilly close by in an armchair beside a display cabinet filled with Nescombe heirlooms: trays of old coins, war medals, a collection of vintage perfume bottles, the body of a headless china doll.

"Been in the family forever," Gilly said, indicating the display. "Funny how we keep things because we've kept them for so long. How real reasons are lost."

It gave me my cue. "Gilly, what happened to Mrs. Pratican's son back in 1912? You know, down at the weir?"

Gilly's eyes flashed with an odd mix of emotion. Surprise? Anger? Relief? Whatever the rush of feeling was, she had it under control just as quickly. "No-one's really sure. Andrew was down there with some kids from town. They were skylarking around, you know, like kids do, throwing rocks, pushing and shoving. Andrew was out on the old skiff they kept down there. Someone threw a rock and hit him on the head. He went over the side. They found his body the next day."

"And don't tell me. There were five other kids with Andrew that day."

The flash of emotion was there again, showing mainly in a tightening of the eyes. She quickly looked off through the nearest open window. "Four or five. Something like that."

"Or six."

She looked back at once. "What are you saying, Nev?"

"There are six alcoves at Auderlene, Gilly."

"You're not seriously suggesting—"

"Just seriously asking. What happened to those five or six other kids?"

She tried to put me off. "How the hell would I know? They grew up. Moved away. Died. They could be anywhere. You think they took your meteorite, is that it?"

More deflection, but it didn't stop me. "Not at all. But you would've tracked it back surely. You know the local families. You've had access to the district records. You would've found the names, tracked it back."

"Nev, what's with all this? Why the private eye stuff all of a sudden?"

I didn't hesitate. "I heard the suits, Gilly. I went out to Auderlene last night and I heard them."

Gilly feigned outrage pretty well. She stood, even put her hands on her hips. "And that's the thanks I get for trying to help. Listen, Nev—"

"You knew I would, Gilly. You wanted me to. You left the keys out."

"I what?"

"You know the suits start sounding at night."

"Lots of folks round here do."

"No they don't. That sort of thing would get out, especially if there's a quick buck in it. There'd be ghost tours, souvenir hunters, the lot. I might be wrong, but I'm thinking that you and Chris and Harry Barrowman and the rest keep this pretty quiet."

"As if we could."

"As if you haven't. The question is why. You knew I'd want to go out there alone, that I'd probably want to see the place at night. You wouldn't tell me about the suits, but you wanted me to know about them. That's why you picked me, why the come-on at the Arms yesterday. You wanted me here at Sallen."

"What a bloody nerve! Who the hell do you think—?"

"Gilly, it's okay! I accept that there are rules here. Promises being kept; things you can't share. But since we're coming clean, let me ask if there really was a meteorite?"

Gilly seemed caught between genuine relief and maintaining a proper indignation. "Of course there was. Letters mention it. It came down on 24 January 1904. Mrs. P. had Myron Birch dig it out and bring it over to the house in his wagon. The local newspaper wrote it up; you can check the edition for the following week, if you want. It was probably kept somewhere in the house originally."

"But not displayed. People don't record seeing it when they visited."

The emotion still translated as anger. "It didn't go away, if that's what you mean. People still talked about it. But it was just a local thing. No big deal. There's so much meteorite activity in the skies out here. Tektites. Austrolites. You do things differently when you live on the land."

"But it was never seen after 1912? After what happened to Andrew?"

She sat in the armchair again, but didn't settle back in it, as if ready to leap up at any moment. "What are you driving at, Nev? Look, I did do a bit of a beat-up on the thing yesterday—"

"Though you won't say why."

"Can't say why. You were here. You'd heard about the Pratican Star. You made it easy."

So much for item number four, I didn't say. Gilly was frowning, clearly troubled by something.

"So you *can't* tell me why. Listen, Gilly—"

But she cut me off, as if something had just occurred to her. "Nev, do you really think the meteorite could be in those suits? Melted down and mixed in? You asked Chris about it."

Why does it matter? I wanted to ask, but went with the deflection, needing to keep Gilly this side of shutting down altogether and kicking me out. She wanted me to know things she couldn't talk about directly, whatever the reasons.

"If the Birches worked with existing plate, just cut and bent scrap they had on hand, then maybe not. If they actually melted the iron ore themselves at their foundry in town, then sure. It would be a lot more work, a very different scale of work, and there'd be a very small distribution given the size of the Star."

"Like that 'memory of water' thing in homeopathy."

"I guess." This was my chance. "And correct me if I'm wrong, Gilly, but I'm guessing you're a descendant of one of the six responsible for Andrew Practican's death back then."

Gilly looked out the window again before returning her gaze to me. "You keep saying six."

"There are six alcoves. Mrs. Pratican had the suits made for a reason. Yes, I believe there's a sixth suit somewhere."

"But where?" Gilly said, and seemed encouraged by my certainty.

No, not encouraged. Encouraging!

She already knew where it was!

I dared not say so, dared not ask. Not yet. "Come and help me look for it. Take the day off."

"I can't, Nev. I can't set foot on the property. Why do you think I never gave you the tour myself?"

"Tell me."

"Something will—hurt me."

I didn't know how to take that. Literally? Metaphorically? "Something?"

"Just trust me. Look, I have to get to work. We can talk about this later."

"Gilly, I have to know. We're very close to something here. Why can't you go inside Auderlene?"

"It's not just the house. I said I can't set foot *on the property*!"

"All right. You can't set foot on the property. Something hurts you. Tell me the rest. Please."

Gilly didn't speak. She just grabbed my hand, pulled me up from the sofa, then led me out of the lounge room and along the hallway to her bedroom. My thoughts went every which way in an instant. It was so easy to misread the signals and take this as some impulsive reprise of our modest flirtation at the Summerton Arms. Even more so when she'd closed the door behind us, because in moments she was unbuttoning and removing her blouse, reaching round and unbuttoning and unzipping her skirt and stepping out of it so she stood before me in bra and panties. It was all done so quickly that I nearly said something stupid before the real reason registered.

Gilly's body was covered with scars. Healed ones, a myriad tiny wounds like punctures and slashes on her breasts, belly and groin, on her back too when she turned to show me. Nothing above the neckline or that extended to the arms and legs. A very selective maiming, like stigmata, but all healed over, laid like dozens of silky threads against her skin.

"Gilly, how on earth—?"

"Don't ask. Please. Just know that I didn't do it, okay? That no husband or boyfriend or neighborhood sicko did it. No-one passing through."

Don't blame you if you'd rather pass, Nev, she didn't say, didn't have to say because her eyes did, quickly and eloquently. It was there in the way she reached for her blouse and skirt.

"Gilly—" I just stepped forward and held her.

She clung to me. It was the sort of simple, desperately human act we get to experience maybe two or three times in our lives if we're truly lucky, one we all need to know—as giver *and* receiver—to complete our full equation of humanity. Without it we are creatures forever lacking.

Her sobbing lasted barely moments. Gilly had the habit of being strong in the world and she rallied quickly, though she didn't break the embrace.

"If I say too much, it'll start again," she murmured into my shoulder, burying the words in my shirt. Auderlene was ten minutes away, listening, watching.

"It's a haunting," I said, because *I* could.

"I've said too much, Nev."

"I have to go back, Gilly," I said. "I have to go back tonight."

Her answer chilled me with its simplicity. "Yes."

IT WAS STRANGE SPENDING the day at Auderlene knowing that I'd be there again that night, so strange to see the suits looking so makeshift and ordinary, robbed of any trace of their night-time power. This time I did grab a chair from the kitchen as Chris had suggested, and stood on it to check every suit. There were no speakers that I could find, no hidden wires unless they had been threaded up through the soles of the iron feet, an elaborate and unlikely prospect without public ghost tours to justify the effort and expense.

Everything was different now, though Chris and I acted as if nothing had changed. I wasn't sure how much he knew, whether Gilly had told him of my visit the previous night, so I said nothing about it.

During the morning we searched the wine-cellar and various outbuildings for any sign of the Pratican Star and he was as patient and helpful as ever. We did the attic in the afternoon, and spent two hours hauling boxes this way and that, doing a thorough search of the contents of each one. There was nothing that resembled a meteorite.

We left off around four o'clock and climbed down cramped, dusty and exhausted from our efforts. After Chris had fed the horses, we spent the final hour till lock-down sitting on the front steps of the old house drinking a bottle of respectable red from the Auderlene cellar. We didn't talk all that much, just watched the occasional cars that passed on the highway and how the light went from the land towards sunset and the great silence came up, how the lights came on at Sallen across the way. The article for *Cosmos* seemed a forgotten dream, part of another reality, another ordering of the world. Now I could only think of the silky scars on Gilly's skin and her clinging to me, and how, even as the rooms behind us were falling into darkness, the iron suits in the ballroom were already crammed full of night.

I was glad when Chris checked his watch, pushed the cork back in the bottle and stood. "Let's go, Nev. Time to lock up."

As we moved towards the front gate, a pair of new headlights appeared on the highway and Gilly's Land Rover turned in at Sallen.

THIS TIME SHE SAW me off. At 11:30 p.m., with Lorna Gillard and Jim Camberson safely tucked away in their rooms, Gilly stood on the northern turn of the verandah and watched me cross into Auderlene.

There had been a kiss on the mouth from her, full, firm and brief, as dry and smoky as the evening had been, but no more words. What could you say? Be careful? Don't let the boogeyman get you? There was often so much comedy in terror when you looked for it. It was the way of the world.

What followed was very much a repeat of the previous evening, but without the self-recrimination and guilt. This time I had the permission of a custodian—all the custodians when I thought about it, given how much they seemed to share of this.

This time I also had one of Gilly's powerful household torches to light my way. Fifteen minutes after leaving her on the verandah, I was stepping through the front door at Auderlene and shining its light down the front hall. It banished the gloom so much better than mine had.

As I entered the ballroom and took my position on the chaise-longue, the strong beam of light emphasized the home-made quality of the suits, the sheer ordinariness. Only the eye-slits—five razor-cuts of night—kept their power. It was a relief when I switched off the torch and returned everything to an even darkness.

Too even. Too complete. The curtains had been closed!

Chris could have done it. Must have. It was getting to be that time of year. But it meant that the suits were no longer deeper strokes of blackness in the gloom. The windows themselves still had ghostly outlines, but the iron shapes were lost to me.

Which made it so much worse. It had become like the child's game where you crept up on someone while they weren't looking. There was the awful sense that the suits were moving towards me in the darkness, would suddenly be there, frozen but closing in, the moment I switched on my torch. Then they'd come on again on unbending, stovepipe legs, iron hands reaching—

I forced down the panic, amazed that things were getting to me this way. First the compulsion to visit after nightfall, now this ongoing dread.

Still, as difficult as it was, I resolved to leave things as they were. The curtains could be opened easily enough, and Gilly's torch was right there.

I made myself stretch out on the chaise-longue and listen to the house. This time I *wanted* to drowse but it was impossible. The ticking of the clock came from the hall behind; the sound of crickets and night birds still worked their way in, but these things all seemed just that much further off now. The sense of being stranded, no longer connected, was stronger than ever.

I kept going over the events of the day, thinking of that single hurried kiss, of Gilly's scars and what could have caused them, of a sixth suit hidden from view, one that couldn't be mentioned because something would hear and respond. Couldn't be talked about; couldn't be *thought* about. Where did it end?

Given my earlier funk, I tried not to think too much about the suits here either. When they started sounding—*if* they did—I would repeat my "inspection" of the previous night, but with one important difference. This time I wouldn't simply pass the empty alcove. This time I would lean in and listen. Such an obvious thing, but I hadn't done it. I would give the missing suit its chance.

The waiting became a special kind of hell. My imagination kept playing tricks, providing things. Not just the suits creeping forward in darkness, creaking and sighing, not just house sounds—doors opening, things shifting—but doubts as well. What were the chances of Gilly and the others setting me up, *serving* me up to whatever lay at the heart of Nettie Pratican's estate? It was crazy, but suddenly so real.

Maybe the sixth suit was out there somewhere, moving through the darkness. Maybe *it* was the one heading this way. It would suddenly be in the alcove when I next switched on the torch!

Worse yet, maybe that sixth suit was for me. I'd find myself the one peering through the slits and perforations, unable to move, unable to cry out!

Completing the array. That was what the keening was: a summons!

It changed everything. I imagined the other suits watching through their narrow edges of darkness. *Yes! Yes! Join us!*

A special hell indeed, made for a solitary watcher on a quiet spring night.

I was actually relieved when the song started at 1:39. Again, it came as the barest sense of something, just as it had before. Then, across seconds, minutes, a suit near the center of the display had definitely begun to sound.

I switched on the torch and moved the powerful beam along the row, saw the suits watching in their ones and twos, always with the sense of eye glitter as I moved the torch beam on. All tricks of shadowplay and a shifting light source, of course, but an alarming optical effect: eyeslits empty and unmoving until *you* looked away, then the sense of eyes rolling back at you.

I win! I win!

I found myself actually switching the torch beam back and forth, trying to catch the whites of those imagined eyes, then considered the shock such a discovery would bring and stopped at once. The thought of it was enough.

Yes, imagination was the real enemy here. Imagination and uncertainty.

Gilly's scars were real, *looked* real. Yet could it all be a hoax? The possibility was there.

But in the torchlit darkness, with the suits keening as they had the night before, I chose to believe in Gilly and the others. It went against so much, but it was what I decided.

Keeping the torch beam as steady as I could, I crossed to Suit 1 and touched the breastplate. The metal was thrumming, jarring my fingertips even more than I remembered.

I moved on to Suit 2, then to 3, touching each one the same way. They were both sounding, adding their fierce harmonics to the whole. Such angry iron.

Then there was the doorway, a gaping darkness with Suit 4 beyond.

I dared not hesitate. I crossed the gulf, reached for the breastplate, lighting only what was needed, not daring to look for eyes peering down.

Singing. It was singing.

The fifth alcove was still empty, thank God. No new arrival.

Not far now. I continued on, reached out and pressed my fingers to the final metal chest. It was thrumming, jarring like the rest.

All five were sounding, keening.

Screaming. That's how it seemed.

Time to finish it. I turned back to the empty niche, moved the few steps needed and leant forward into the opening.

Angle of the head, angle of reality, it was enough. A single word filled the space, came again and again in a voice that was a rasp and a curse, a cry of despair and an accusation all in one, that—like a whisper gallery to infinity—seemed to cross a great gulf and yet was right there, intimate and close.

Yes.

That single word.

One way or another it answered every question I needed answered.

Is there a sixth suit?

Yes.

Can it be found?

Yes.

Is it close by?

Yes.

Can I save her?

Yes.

Then, while still straining to catch the forlorn, achingly desperate voice and its single word, the keening stopped.

And the torch went out.

There *were* eyes in the helmet slits now, I was certain. Fixed and staring. I fumbled with the switch, tried again and again. Nothing.

Panic came like iron hands, closing hard. I threw the torch aside and went scrambling across the carpet, found the hall, the door and blessed night beyond. In moments, precious seconds, I was deep in that other darkness and running towards Sallen with a smile on my face. It was relief and reprieve. We had our answer. We truly did.

I WAS LEFT TO work out for myself where the sixth Pratican suit would be. It wasn't so difficult once I accepted that they knew, all of them, but couldn't tell, couldn't speak of it directly. Once I remembered the clues they'd been trying to give me all along.

Chris Goodlan and I had checked the official outbuildings maintained in the Auderlene Charter, but, as he had told me that first day, there were some old work sheds off the estate proper, back through the trees; buildings the Birches had used for the cutting, shaping and final suit assembly.

Off the estate.

What were the chances?

Gilly nodded when I told her what I intended doing, and surprised me by wanting to come along, but she said very little when she parked her Land Rover off the highway beyond the Auderlene estate and we started walking the northern fence-line towards the north-western corner.

There were three structures in among the gumtrees, one large and two small, all ramshackle and badly run-down, all made of the same weather-worn gray timber and sheets of rusted iron. Without Gilly telling me, I knew it would be the farthest one out, just did, and led us to its sagging wooden door.

"I can't go in, Nev," she said.

"But it's off the estate."

"That suit is *from* the estate. It *is* the estate. What Auderlene exists for. You go in."

"You're talking about it now, Gilly. I thought you couldn't."

"Depends on whether you find something."

"How so?"

"It happens at night, Nev. If you're wrong, then I may not survive the night."

"Your—visitor—will come calling?"

"Let's just say that coming out here again, I've broken the rules."

Again. Gilly said again. She *had* been out here before.

"Gilly—"

"Please, Nev. I'm sick of this, after all these years. It's the other part of the story. Go and see."

I said no more, just hauled back the old door and stepped inside. The interior was cluttered with lengths of timber, rusted irrigation pipes, pieces of old farm machinery. Once it would have been a gloomy space, but no longer. The roof was sprung, sagging where fallen tree branches had struck. The walls bowed under the weight of the remaining roof beams. Hot sunlight streamed in.

It didn't take long to find. The suit was lying on its back, one more half-rusted shape near the shed's far wall, almost indistinguishable amid abandoned farm machinery. Hidden in plain sight really.

And not complete—or rather not intact, which had further helped conceal it. The helm had been sawn away and left to one side, a cylindrical casque like a discarded bucket.

I crouched next to the broken figure and peered into the chest cavity. It was a cave with stalactites and stalagmites! The hollow space was filled with them, spines pointing in from front, back and sides. They were probably in the groin and legs as well.

I hauled the helmet around and peered within. More spikes. The whole suit was like the inside of an Iron Maiden, that engine of torture and death from crueller times.

Not crueller, no. Nothing was crueller than this: a hollow but sealed prison, impossible to escape yet impossible to inhabit because of those knives.

Special knives. Each one tipped with its tiny bit of the Pratican Star, I was sure of it. Restless iron from out there. Metal from somewhere else. *Trap them and never let them rest.*

But there had to be more to it. The meteoric tips were the avenger's *pièce de résistance*, a bereaved mother's ultimate reward for those who had been present at the death of her son. Perpetrators or innocent bystanders, it hadn't mattered to Nettie Pratican, hadn't been an issue in that inconsolable mother's plans. A look at the town records would probably show nothing either, no sudden accidents or disappearances. Nettie Pratican had been patient. This was a revenge taken *after* their deaths, quite likely after her own. And one of Gilly's ancestors—great uncle, great aunt, great cousin, someone in her family's past—had been one of those bystanders, witnesses, accomplices. Privy to a game gone wrong, to teasing taken too far.

More questions for Gilly when questions could be answered again.

But there had to be something else she couldn't mention, possibly didn't even know herself: *how* Mrs. Pratican had trapped them inside!

The shed still had lifting tackle on one of the roof beams, chains and pulleys from back when these materials were moved on a fairly regular basis. It was no coincidence that the rig was positioned *above* the suit, from when it had last been used, though then the suit have been lifted at the shoulders so the helmet could be sawn off.

So what had been trapped inside could be released!

I had to know. Getting the chain around the ankles and hooked in place was easier than I first expected because of the tapered jambs and the flattened spur-butts on the iron feet.

The block and tackle was old and rusty; the supporting roof beam less than completely sound, but the chains moved in the double pulley system easily enough and the surrounding beams held. The legs rose off the earthen floor, tipping the chest at an angle.

It wasn't enough. If something was trapped inside, it had to get through the forest of spines. I doubted the roof could take the weight of a full lift, but all I needed was a steep enough angle. I hauled on the chain, hoisted the legs higher.

Just when I thought I might have misjudged the whole thing, something rattled down over the spikes and appeared in the neck opening.

The head of a doll, battered and hairless. Something that had belonged to Gilly's great-aunt, great-cousin, whatever, but the other part of the broken doll I'd seen in the heirloom cabinet at Sallen.

I lowered the suit to the ground and went out to where Gilly was waiting.

When she saw what I was holding, tears sprang to her eyes. She took the tiny head from me, gripped it hard between her hands and turned away.

I waited till she turned back.

"Who did you get to saw off the helmet, Gilly?"

"That truck driver who told you about Summerton and the meteor. Three years ago. He was passing through and I told him the story, asked him to help. I thought opening the suit would do it. He helped me bring it out here."

Part of me wanted to ask if he'd enquired about a 'number four' option as well, but I didn't. None of my business, yet completely my business, both.

Gilly understood that. "He was just trying to help, Nev. Sending someone else along. Looking out for me. He never saw the scars."

The weight sank away. "You both saw the spikes?"

"We did. But we thought that was it. That we'd released it. We never thought that there'd be—" Gilly searched for the right term.

"Something keeping it there," I said.

"Right. This bloody doll's head!"

"And the spikes, Gilly. I think you'll find they were tipped with metal from the Pratican Star."

Gilly frowned, saw the connection and nodded. "But why was it angry with me? I'm kin. Why me?"

"The old story of the genie trapped in the bottle. For the first thousand years he swears to reward whoever frees him. For the next thousand he swears to destroy whoever does it. Maybe your family *became* the reason it was trapped in there. Maybe communication just becomes messed up—"

"When you're dead."

"When you're dead. The prison was open but it still couldn't get free. Not completely. Imagine the agony, the fury. How did you know which suit to open?"

"Whenever I heard them sounding at night, whenever I passed close by, that one suit called out a word. In my mind."

"What word?"

"Just the one. You."

"Gilly, I'm guessing that Harry Barrowman and others you can name are descendants of those kids at the weir that day. I'm pretty sure they've heard the same word in front of a particular suit too, yes?"

The barest hint of the smile was there. She could talk about it now. They couldn't, but she could. "They didn't dare open the other suits after what happened to me. They've got families to think of. You're good at this, Nev."

"I'm outside of it—*was* outside. It helped. So you tell them what has to be done. They open the suits and remove whatever objects were used as lures."

"We're imposing our sense of justice on someone else's here, aren't we?"

"That's the operative word, Gilly. Justice. Nettie Pratican went beyond justice the moment she had the suits made, the moment she decided on the spikes and what to tip them with."

Gilly Nescombe held up the doll's head as if reading a crystal ball or considering a piece of fruit from the Garden of Eden. "The spiteful old bitch. Even God doesn't get to be that vindictive anymore."

For Tammy Vance.

Afterword to "The Suits at Auderlene"

SUITS OF ARMOR have always held a special fascination, mainly because of their part in the romance and swashbuckling excitement of movies like *Ivanhoe*, *The Black Shield of Falworth* and *El Cid* when I was growing up, books like Howard Pyle's *Men of Iron* and Stuart Campbell's *Stories of King Arthur*, but also because of the sinister quality those empty suits have of always watching, of being too human in a golem, zombie, robot-like way.

Across countless weekend movie matinees in the 50s and 60s, I became used to seeing castles not just with suits of armor on show, but also with dungeons fitted out with chains and racks, glowing braziers, suspended cages (often with skeletons inside) and that particular instrument of torture called an Iron Maiden, which itself resembled a pear-shaped, oversized suit of armor. By the time I read Bram Stoker's "The Squaw" in 1962 and John Swain's *A History of Torture* soon after (teenage boys tend to do these things) that particular device had acquired an horrific beauty all its own. In its macabre resemblance to both armor and a mummy coffin (bringing further movie-nurtured associations with being buried alive), it had a disturbing power, a point (pardon the pun) driven home (excuse me) quite vividly in the final scenes of Roger Corman's 1961 movie *The Pit and the Pendulum*. For that Grand Guignol finale, the castle dungeon has two Iron Maidens on hand, and Barbara Steele, unbeknownst to those who might rescue her, has been imprisoned inside one with a facial grille so she can look out as the dungeon is sealed forever, effectively burying her alive. Her dreadful predicament in turn called to mind the spiked mask forced on her in a film from the previous year called *Black Sunday*. It was an iconic conceptual and visual package.

In *The Suits at Auderlene*, these memories of relentless, spiked interiors merged with my abiding interest in medieval armor to allow a different, possibly new application for the Iron Maiden idea, one that brought it closer to home and allowed an Australian haunted house as a setting. Again, as so often happens, it became a tale of redemption.

At the Sign of the Moon

I was lost in the sound,
A strange face in the garden lounge,
Watching orchestras tune
At the sign of the Moon.

Tell the man not to stare,
Who's the lady beside the chair?
What a singular thing
How the chandeliers sing!

Take a turn on the lawn,
Talking stars with Aldebaran,
I'm a lost caravan
Guided into her hand.

Peacocks call in the crowd,
Laughter falls from the garden lounge,
Where the dowagers swoon
At the sign of the Moon.

TRUTH WINDOW: A TALE OF THE BEDLAM ROSE

THE NOBODOI CAME TO *Earth a little after midday on 4 June 2023, accompanied by their support races: the Hoproi, the Matta, the Darzie, so many others. They brought with them the star Wormwood, a fragment of antimatter some said, and used it to begin their great xenoforming of the Earth, making it what they wanted. Then, overnight, the Nobodoi vanished— stepped back, withdrew, who could say?—leaving behind their Bridge Races, the remnants of a blasted Humanity and the great Patchwork they had made.*

IT WAS LIGHT-COMMANDER RAINE Halva Belicrue who first raised the issue, tracked it, set his Human aides to doing the relevant searches, then made the query across the world. That powerful Darzie, Fist of the Stars, Arm of Law, localized and hurting as only the most determined and committed of the Darzie Race ever would, sat in his Rule-of-Hand tower at Dars-Bayas and learned of this growing movement among the crushed, long-conquered Humans, then took it that one step further. Made it a question to the full spread of the Flower.

What do you know of the Lady Mondegreen?

He expected little that was new. No surprises. Few surprises. For it had been expected, modelled, some sort of emergent belief system. It's what all peoples did, all sufficiently cognate conquered peoples, just one more inevitability. But Raine took it further. His localization was the finest, the most excruciating. Only the Darzie fighting elites, the Elsewheres and the Purple-and-Blacks, endured more, surrendering self, but they stepped back into a quasi-existence of hot-glass and reverie and barely knew what they did.

For Raine Halva Belicrue there was no stepping back. This Fist of the Stars, Flame of the Encosium, harnessed his pain, *used* his pain, did the search and posed the question.

No Humans replied, of course. They lacked the Cohabitation resources, probably would for centuries, millennia, eons, unless the Nobodoi overlords, the Recalled Ones, were to Return, intervene and decree otherwise.

But twenty-eight Matt scholars did, astonishing Raine, requesting enhancement, offering reciprocation, data-trade, asking questions of their own.

And one, Holding-in-Quiet, made the incredible offer of leaving its typhy, its home, its work of the life, to meet "in the reach of hands" should that be required. This one had a quest of the heart, it seemed, was no doubt building this religion of the Lady into an identity artefact that would mark its days. Who would have thought?

Raine should not have been surprised, that was the thing. After all, look at what the Cohabitation brought: access to the great Overlord nets—the Acrimba, the Tutifa, the Sarannas, the Wail Guydo. Keywords and encrypts like "Mondegreen" and "Lady" and "Goddess" would have been flagged: ideologically, sociologically, archaeologically. Philologically and etymologically, too, in current Human sayings alone: "By the Lady!", "Praise the Lady!", "Lady be with you!"

He blamed his localization. But even as he sat back in his Talking Chair, even as his manner became carefully businesslike and his crest spines settled, another astonishment occurred, even more amazing than the first: a stat-flash blazon and a voice on *that* closed alliance channel.

"Hey, you, Darzie-pants, Raine! This is Fond Louie hisself, so be paying the tensest tension, okey-doke! Know what's shakin' the Human tree. Know the Mondegreen Lady's first and best church! Know that, hey!"

Raine's crest flared again. Fond Louie? It truly was. The Hoproi warmaster at the Bassantrae Sequester. The screen filled with the image of this famous, crafty Hoproi, an image shot from a field link somewhere in its war-garden. The creature loomed three meters above its four elephantine legs, great grey-brown barrel body painted with stars and bulls-eyes and geometric patterns in the powdery reds and oranges of its shooting chapter.

Raine couldn't see those legs on the screen, of course, just three of its four cardinal trunks coiled in against the great barrel torso with the single dark eye peering out between each juncture, the body finally flattening at the top with the clustering of sensory fibres where the mouth was.

And resolutely speaking Antique, the Human occupation language all Hoproi so maddeningly insisted on using instead of Anvas or Kolack. Raine didn't care. This was wonderful, better than he had hoped.

Such participation—and about such an issue. This trivial but curiously robust Racial yearning, this quaint and inevitable first flowering of hope among the Humans was being transferred globally, and so cohesively, that was the thing, by what could only be word of mouth: solitary wanderers, tinkerers and minstrels, Human bureaucrats, traveling siswitch troupes—circus performers, Raine knew the term well—despite the culls, the checks and prohibitions, the sampling imposts. It was the cohesiveness that fascinated Raine, troubled him. Two hundred and thirty-eight years since Wormwood arrived, fifty-six years since the Recall, and despite the Great Work, the xenoforming and all that it entailed, such an effective degree of interfacing. Was mutuality the word?

All that came in seconds, moments, instants for Raine, primed as he was.

"Fond Louie, what do you know of this? How is your chapter involved?" Raine spoke the Antique terms carefully. The Hoproi were notorious for misunderstanding words, twisting language and meaning to suit themselves.

"Know this, you betchy! Know Humans using this to make a way. Crooning kumbayas aplenty."

Raine's fingers danced on the keypad of his chair, cuing additional flash translations, sending surge commands through a dozen monitoring systems. "There can be no prospect of insurgency in this."

"None," Fond Louie boomed, trunks flexing merrily. "We ruling the roost!"

"The what?"

"No mattress! No threat or intent. Namby-pambies behave, bejeez! But I got the goods. That church close by this Sequester, capisce?"

"We can visit?" Straight to it. Raine had to control this exchange, snatch sense from the dross.

"Certainment, mon capital! Ours for the done-deal. Name the day!"

"Fond Louie, a house-lord will accompany. You have no reservations?"

"Plenty of seats. More the merriest. When-so, great Raine?"

"Let me confer with this lord. But the sooner the better, once I've assessed the data coming in."

"Done deal. But limited, capisce? Just you. Just me. Just this one crimpy. No sharps."

"But you will have *choi* protection."

"My Sequester, Best Raine. My turf. Natch."

"Then I shall bring a bodyguard."

"Fraidy cat! No scratch Darzie. No probable claws."

"I will call you shortly."

"Done deal." And the screen went blank.

THE CHURCH, SUCH AS it was, sat ten meters back from the dirt road in what did indeed look like a prairie stretching off for miles: a small-enough whitewashed stone building made from hand-fetched discardo, twenty meters on its long sides, ten on the shorter, a little under three meters high, with a small dome at the flat roof's midpoint. A simple pillar and lintel archway was the only entrance.

A Human place, old in design to those who knew such lore—Mediterranean Vernacular—but new, newly made.

Such a rare thing.

And equally rare on this plundered, extravagantly xenoformed Earth two hundred and thirty-eight years after the great Nobodoi rulers brought down their piece of controlled antimatter—*controlled*, the word said it all!—brought in three Bridge Races and dozens of Lesser Races to rule it for them, for a Matta, a Hoproi and a Darzie to meet face to face at a *Human* place.

Such meetings did happen between the Races, of course they did, but rarely away from sanctioned holds, optimals and vast dedicated protections, and rarely with just one member of each species present.

The scale of it was dazzling, thrilling. Bridge Races they were, the ruling elect, each judged sufficiently compatible by the Departed Ones that they could be left to do this job this time, interface with Humanity and with each other, marshall the less Human-coterminous Races in the great spread of the Donalty Flower. But an imperfectly localized Darzie could so easily lose phase and turn rogue. A Hoproi warmaster might suddenly discern a fine logic or status-enhancing joke in a trophy kill, despite—because of—the inevitable reprisals; a Matta's life journey, the callings of the Narrow Way, might demand some ultimate and crucial self-immolation. The mindsets, tropisms and imperatives were profoundly different; understanding so easily deflected down so many by-ways. Only elaborate compatibility totes, localizations and an abiding fear of the Nobodoi made it possible.

So they agreed to come, this unlikely, possibly unprecedented three, to this quiet, green-enough field outside the force-wall of the Bassantrae Sequester. Raine arrived first, phasing in from his swordship *Nobion*, shimmering in its containment field at thirty-thousand feet. With him came six Elsewheres in full hot-glass armor, who stood quietly by the entrance tracking the scene at a dozen vested data-ranges unavailable to most Races in the Patchwork. They waited while the light-commander stepped through that doorway and entered the shadowy interior.

It was very much as Raine had expected: a dim, all-but-empty space with no windows save for the unglazed square opening in the building's rear wall. Four slender discardo columns supported the roof, but there were no other adornments, no pews laid out for worshippers, just a few makeshift Human-style benches along the wall, a spigot from a rain tank feeding a small dish to one side, a door into a curtained alcove on the other that stat-flash specs showed to contain a bench above a sump for a toilet.

Fiercely localized, sharp with it, Raine immediately understood why the structure was here, in *this* location, at *this* lonely, singular spot, saw too the desperate and probably guileless cunning of it.

Outside to the east was the Bassantrae Sequester, the Hoproi domain with its hazing of mighty force walls sweeping upwards, held by the massive towers of the luda supports, sparking now here, now there, off into the distance, and with the heavy-gravity, phase-up markers themselves set within the perimeter, increment by increment until all was locked in a misty sepia sheen. Earth's lesser gravity made the Cohabitation a joy for the Hoproi and they gleefully set up their shooting chapters in the great Trade Cities by preference but, like any occupation forces, they too needed something of home.

To the west, plunging away into a distance haze to form the other side of this vast forsaken corridor, were the force-walls of an enclave of a very different kind, roiling and full of violence, rearing up into the purple-bronze sky like sheets of amber and pearl: the ley walls of Rollinsgame, a demon-ley, if intel showed it fairly. There the walls were honey-milk clear at first glance, though with sudden snatches of darkness beyond, darkness streaked with reds and quick stabs of scarlet.

But the thing, the chance, the wonder of it was—look ahead, look between those narrowing, converging walls with the Sequester to the right and the opalescent eye-trickery of Rollinsgame to the left and you had it. By quirk of physics, optics, photonics, purest luck, the turned grasses seemed green enough, the sky an ersatz blue enough, for it to give Humans a tricked-up glimpse of something they knew to yearn for: *green* lands, *blue* skies and, by the most precious serendipity of the lot, the sense of *golden* light. Golden. Taken together, it was the biotype's optimum: the Pre-Wormwood norm. How could they *not* come here?

So obvious, too, why the single window opened onto such a view, the only thing needed. Such was the power of his localization, Raine understood.

Who knew what sims and scapes, what museum photographs, salvaged celluloids and old-style digitals, what ancient hobbyist watercolors and children's drawings gave that reality, but here it was, and Humans found in this and a scattering of other such precious places enough of the dream.

By the Lady!

As they said. As they always said now. By the Lady!

But Raine knew more of the Lady than they did, grasped the terrible irony of how error and misunderstanding working with chance had made it possible. Such a joke.

A Human moved forward from the shadows, a slender older woman with her long grey hair tied back. She wore a plain white robe, unadorned but for a simple line-work square inside a circle at the right shoulder. Window on the world, it said. *In* the world. The old biome.

"Welcome, Great Lord. I am Josephine Cantal, custodian here."

Raine inclined his head slightly. "You are the priest, the priestess—what is the word?—the sacerdote?"

"Just custodian, Lord. I care for this Window."

"But priest. Is this the word?"

"For some, Lord. But the Lady is not a goddess."

"Not?"

"There is no divinity."

"Ah." As with so much else, the translation was instantly there. "Then what?"

"Just a way of remembering how it was before the Cohabitation. 'Mondegreen' is an old coining. It means 'green world' in a blending of two old languages."

Raine, fiercely localized, knew otherwise, and knew enough of the broken histories to have countless templates for convenient deities masking social unrest: Roman Judaea and the Jesuits—were those the right names?—many templates for errors as origins: the story of Romulus and Remus being raised by a wolf when in fact it came from the Etruscan word for Rome, Rumlua, or Hong Kong being named, quite wrongly, after the giant primate deity that once occupied its central tower. Such were the free radicals of circumstance.

He knew to proceed slowly. "No statues, no depictions. Just that insignia you wear. The square inside the circle. Not that heraldic animal many Humans choose. Explain that."

"The butterfly is a transformation animal, Lord. A rebirth animal. The Aviators at Wenna wear it because they pilot their kites above the city. It is a good sign for them. A good Old Earth animal."

"Once there was a fish. That was special too. And a raven. Many phoenix animals."

"I've been told so, Lord. This is just the Window."

"This window?"

"Yes, Lord. Others like it. What's called a Truth Window."

"So I have learned. I'm told this is the main one."

"Some say that. I cannot know. It is hard to travel."

"Too dangerous?"

Josephine Cantal knew better than to mention the culls, samplings and secondments, the impresses and imposts that kept the Human population small and docile. "There is this to do."

"Guarding a window?"

"Explaining it to interested parties like yourself."

Raine's localization allowed him subtleties and ironies, let him tease and provoke. "But you see me as an enemy, surely."

"No, Great Lord." She gestured back to the view of golden light on waving, green enough prairie. "The only true enemy is forgetting."

"I sincerely understand. I am not your enemy. Not today."

"No, Great Lord. Today you came here."

"Possibly for reasons other than you think. This is not—favor." More terms came at once. "Not endorsement or sanction. Do not presume."

Josephine Cantal bent her head. "Forgive me, sire. Your localization is beyond compare. It is easy to forget."

"Continue then."

"Just as you have modelled this outcome for whatever purpose, Lord, we have modelled a day such as this. A member of the Great Races coming."

"Others will be here soon."

"Darzie?"

Raine turned back towards the open doorway, crest spines ablating as the rudiments of a distant hunt-cycle were diverted. "Perhaps. Perhaps something neither of us has ever modelled. Let us go and see."

FOURTEEN MINUTES LATER, THE Matt house-lord arrived in an ornate, fieldwork charabanc, a hovering egg-shaped ground-effect vehicle whose curving outer hull deliberately resembled an ancient Pre-Wormwood circuit mat, but one stitched all over with goldwire extruded from its own body. No military accompaniment for Holding-in-Quiet, since there was always the sense, more than with any other Race in the Patchwork, that the Vanished Ones, the Nobodoi masters who had picked these reclusive archaeologist scholars of Matteras to be one of the three Bridge Races, could very well protect them in some special way. Fear as much as proven service and privilege held this great alliance in place.

Fond Louie must have been watching, waiting for the Matt's arrival, for suddenly he was there as well, rushing through the grass, massive legs pounding as he ran as a full *choi* fighting-star, trunks embedded in the spinal sockets of four armed and armored Humans dressed in the glossy black beetlepoint of Nefarious Waylayers.

To watch them run, shouting and yipping, waving their hooks and long-bladed jerrykins, was a splendid, unnerving sight, a beautifully synchronized star-wheel with the elephantine host drawing on the disparate emotions of his companions. Only when the huge creature and his troupe had lumbered to a halt did the trunks release and coil back against the body in the no-threat mode.

Bringing them to Crisis Point One.

Raine had six Elsewheres, warriors whose minds were only provisionally here, their core selves forever focused on a homeworld they would never see again. The *choi* immediately deployed, fell back and took positions behind whatever rises and grassy knolls they could find.

For a moment there was silence, the sense of it at least with the wind stirring the grass, the distant roar of the force walls and the poisonous sizzle of hot-glass on the air. With it, vividly for Raine with his biasing, was the sense of the world working, reality being made.

Fond Louie waited in the road. Raine and Josephine Cantal were by the door to the church. The line of Elsewheres stood to their right, held precariously to this task, heads averted, gazing beyond this place, but ready, ready.

It might have been all of ten seconds. Then the door of the charabanc lifted away, and Holding-in-Quiet emerged, seated cross-legged on its havel, moving forward as measured and stately as the Matt always were careful to be in public. No walking, no stepping out—only the file sims showed the Matta walking, running, striking—but composed upright. It had passed through a doorway just now, the most profound act in a Matta's life; this blighted, wondrous place was now briefly an extension of its house, however that could be construed.

Raine watched the creature approach. Like any fully quickened representative of the Encosium-on-Earth, he had studied the Matta, had had sufficient dealings with them, *faux* and actual. Fond Louie had. But Josephine Cantal had never seen one in the flesh, possibly in any form of accurate depiction; knew them only as fellow demons with the Darzie and the Hoproi in cook-fire and cradle stories. Raine saw her chin lift and her eyes widen just enough at her first glimpse of the long horse-skull visage, the articulated neck rising from the red robe draped about the shoulders, the chest like a clustering of tightly sheaved sticks, glittering with points and curls of goldwire that would later be used to make an identity artefact of this special day.

Raine turned to his Elsewheres, subvocalized a quick command. The warriors phased out, three back to *Nobion* high above, three into quarterhold stasis.

"Good move!" Fond Louie boomed, and began lumbering towards the building at last. "Parley party begins now. Come to church, pray-mates!"

THE MATT SCHOLAR'S HAVEL fitted through the doorway easily enough, but Fond Louie didn't even try. He waited till the others had entered then simply blocked the entrance, pressing against the arch so that a trunk and a single eye faced into the dim interior.

Raine prepared to make the appropriate introductions, but even as Holding-in-Quiet lowered its havel by the eastern wall, Josephine Cantal moved as close as she dared and bowed to the creature.

"Lord, you have blessed this house. You have honored this doorway by making it yours."

The horse-insect head canted up and out. "Honor to your household, gracious."

Then, before Raine could continue, this bold Human female took her host's right.

"Great Lords, may I ask why each of you came here today?"

"Can you guess?" Raine asked. He managed to excuse her manner, allowed that this would simply be a tailored version of her usual custodian question.

"It can't just be curiosity, Lord," the old Human female said. "Despite your fine localization. It might be maintaining constants. Population control. A contingency visit, I suspect."

Raine nodded in the Human way. "A bookkeeper's attention to detail and order, I believe some Humans say of us."

"I do not know that second word, sire."

"Me say it," Fond Louie boomed behind them. "Me go rote. Speech prepared for show and tell." And just like that the crazy patois mish-mash fell away, was replaced by the clearspeak recital of something carefully planned and considered, vetted by the protocol comps and *choi* impresses. As always, the modal shift was chilling to hear.

"You built this structure here by my Sequester. This ley corridor runs all the way through Otis Reach to Sallingen, then branches off down mighty leys to Focalstone and Blown Jetty. Blown Jetty, you hear me? Once it was just solitaries who came here, wanderers, nomads, Humans fleeing impresses or selling on their genetics to the scattered communities. Then it was the siswitch troupes stopping between performance destinations, lingering to cherish the light. The light grade here is *sachel*, Albatel 4, well quantified. I ask myself, my chapter, do we want this proximity, this corridor being this order of pass-through. What if it upsets a balance, tolerances in the Patchwork, draws reprisal: madonnas out of Calledal or Fonsy Halt, seeker spikes from Rollinsgame itself, right at our door? Demon ley or sentinel ley, it's a shifting one that, always changing. Should we worry? So we consider it together—you will smile at the prospect—and I consider it alone. Great Lord, me. My Sequester."

"What will you do, Fond Louie?" Josephine knew enough of the Hoproi to use both names, no honorific.

"Tricky business." He was falling back into his usual patter. "We like having Humans handy, going to church, building strained grass windows, being canon fodder! God's rockets, yes! Our fodder whose hart is in heaven! Love it! We get to mix the business. Careful is a pain. A point of intrigue, you betcha! A wait-see. A must-see wait-see."

Josephine Cantal had her back to the Window now, facing the great shape pressed into the doorway. "There is no formal movement here, Fond Louie. I swear it. No attempt at—destabilization, resurgence. It's just what it appears to be, a way of remembering."

"You say, Josephine Cantal, church-mouse, house-mouse. Home a hole in a bucket. This bucket. That bucket. Deer fodder in heaven. Where the hart is. Long as it has a handle, we don't care. We needing the handle."

"There are so few of us now, Fond Louie."

"Bad window just the same. Naughty window, this view-point. Bring this to my Sequester. No easy antlers now."

To those who did not know Hoproi, it sounded like anger, by the pitch, the rush, the volume and tone. But Raine knew it was excitement, even mirth. Fond Louie was delighted to have something, anything, to elevate into a threat, an issue, the prospect of a war-game.

"We have this to do," Raine said, then turned to Holding-in-Quiet. "What have you learned, *edenye*?"

The Matta leant forward, its head did, swinging out on that oddly jointed neck. Beneath the robe, its chest gleamed with goldpoint.

"The naming here: Truth Window. Fond Louie prepared clearspeak for this time. Such honor. I had this done for common ease. The name is from hay-bale residences on Pre-Wormwood Earth. A dwelling built from hay bales would be finished—sealed—with a coating. Whitewashed stucco. Smooth like this temple. But always a part was left to show what was within, a view into the substance of the house. This was called a Truth Window."

Raine was fascinated, delighted. "Coincidence, you think, *edenye?*"

"I do, *aradenye*. Not even metaphor. No equivalent to look into. For remembering."

"Josephine?" Raine asked. It sounded beautifully Human the way he said it, so natural and intimate.

"As this lord says. Just a window. A reminder for us. No agendas, Lord. Just for remembering."

Raine studied the woman with something like compassion. This exchange had to be so disconcerting for her. Here he stood in the "striking erect," the Darzie hunt stance, arms curved in, crest spines fully distended, maximum intimidation to so many Races. To the side was Holding-in-Quiet, imperturbable, so overtly calm but for a single gesture just now, a dramatic, downward sweep of the arm as it brushed the curls of goldwire from its chest so the tailings fell behind the containment rim of its havel. Behind them, the mass, the trunks, the single glaring eye of Fond Louie filled the doorway. So much that had to be confronting for the member of a Race used to suffering at our hands.

It was time for the rest of it.

"Then now I ask the question which brought us here today. Who is the Lady we hear about? I know more of her origins than you do, Josephine. A Pre-Wormwood writer, Sylvia Wright, coined the term long ago, published it in 85 PW, 1954 BCE. She had misheard the lyrics of an old song.

Ye Highlands and Ye Lowlands
Oh where hae you been?
They hae slay the Earl of Moray,
And laid him on the green.

This Human heard that final line as the name of his consort, so it became *They hae slay the Earl of Moray, And Lady Mondegreen*. Years later, when she finally learned the truth, she collected other examples: Gladly the Cross-Eyed Bear, Sinon the Dotted Lion, Round John Virgin. All based on mishearings. She called them mondegreens. There is no other history for your Lady."

Josephine Cantal actually smiled. "But of course there is, sire. You have given useful facts, details, and we welcome them. But the Lady pre-dates this misheard song. Lord Raine, you've read the broken histories. She is Mother Earth, the Earth Mother, nothing more, nothing less. The world personified, as a yearning, a recognition, an acknowledgment. There is no intention, no infrastructure, no need to make her anything more."

"But there *is* more to it, yes?" Destabilization, Raine didn't have to say. A shift in the status-quo. "Make a case for continuance."

Continuance. Josephine Cantal understood the moment exactly.

"This then. A question which must cross all your minds. Lords, what if the Nobodoi approve of this? We're told they left the world this way deliberately, conquered, re-made and withdrew, and now watch to see what happens. *Not* called away. *Not* simply moving on, but watching. Their were-suits wander the world; all that is left of them. I haven't traveled far, but I have seen the soul-stones littering the fields and roadways outside Kefa and Tresimont, sitting in the dust, those balls of chalk. You, Great Lords, know so much more but say Recalled Ones, as if they have truly gone. It is good to have a sense of irony. But their were-suits still come and go as they please. I've seen a few near here. Full triunes all of them, the way they're meant to be: suit, Companion, Snake, all three parts vigorous and strong with ghostworks sparking around them. These may not just be automated watch systems left to ramble about, not just sentinel engines with soul-stone mummies inside."

Raine smiled, a grimace few Races knew to read with confidence. *We all had speeches prepared for today.* "Your point?"

"Some people say the soul-stones aren't corpses, aren't Nobodoi remains at all, but a translation payload, a residue artefact: what's left of a Nobodoi when it withdraws, changes phase."

"Some people?" Raine was relentless.

"Humans, Lord." This woman knew how trapped she was. "It's natural that we're equally curious. But you—none of you are sure about any of this either. You *must* discuss it. No harm is done. No harm can possibly be done. But not Nobodoi corpses, that's what—"

"You truly think the Nobodoi might approve?"

Jospehine Cantal didn't hesitate. "Lord, they have not intruded. Have not disallowed. A were-suit could destroy this place so easily. Send in its Snake, have its Companion—"

"By implication, this visit *is* their response. Our attention, our presence today, becomes the appropriate countermeasure, surely."

Pressed into the archway, Fond Louie humphed in delight. "Hah! Caught you, Goddy-two-shoes! You 'specting 'piphany, you phoney Josey Josephine! Big god moment. Ooh! Were-suit saving the day. You shrewdy-pants!"

Josephine Cantal swung about, hands up, imploring. "Not at all, Lord—Fond Louie! You've taught us well. The Nobodoi have always been absolute in what they do and don't allow. Remember the Link! The Advent itself! Ruthless, decisive! This place harms no-one."

"An *aide-memoire*," Holding-in-Quiet said, as if to itself. *"Memento vivi!"*

Josephine turned to the Matta and smiled fleetingly, probably not knowing those particular Antique terms, but cued by the gentler reflective tone of the Matt's words.

"It helps make life better." Again she turned to the Hoproi. "Like your war-garden, Fond Louie. A comfort beyond easy telling. Something to be proud of." She faced Raine now. "Like whatever tasks and diligence make your terrible ordeal easier, Great Lord. Like that flower Aspen Dirk speaks of."

Raine, of course, thought immediately of the overlapping circles that showed how the Races connected with each other, some directly, others through various interface species. "The Donalty Flower?"

"No, Lord. The other flower. There's a Human, a boggler of Nobodoi artefacts. The siswitch troupes speak of him. There's a flower he speaks of—"

"I know this one!" Fond Louie boomed behind them, scrinching so firmly in against the pillars that the walls creaked alarmingly. "This Dirk the boggler! He nosey-posey! Got flower too!"

"What flower?" Raine demanded. His hands were still at his sides, composed, curved into hooks. His crest-spines were so fully displayed that a distension chime now rang in his skull, the tinnitus that for the unquickened meant amok and reprisal. His localization raged at it. Anything like anger, surprise, disengagement were neatly turned aside. Cool judgement remained. Cool decisions prevailed. Arm of Law.

"I know this! I know this!" Fond Louie could hardly contain his excitement, snatching whatever he could from the old rotes. "Ancient story. Celluloid by Lewis Carroll. Two royal houses. Two flowers. Lancaster, built Lancaster bombers. Red rose. York, famous for Yorkshire puddings, something. White rose. Two put together to build a Two-Door Rose for Henry the Aitch. Get it? Two flowers into one. Donalty Flower the same, bejeez! Hothouse mix. Forced growth. All overlaid, all in together. Dirk's flower the Bedlam Rose."

"The what?" Raine asked, ringing beautifully, perfectly, holding the tone.

"No mattress! All together. Best flowers. Nobodoi plan."

Part of it troubled Raine, part of it provoked, even delighted. "*Three* parts to this then. The Window, this flower and the false Lady who has become so real."

Josephine snatched at the possibility of reprieve. "Humans are good at finding signs, Great Lord. Making signs. All peoples probably, all Races. But Humans constantly. Leave us alone; it's what we do. It makes us meaningful to ourselves."

"Especially now," Raine said, the chime diminishing, pushing away, resolved but close. So close.

"Especially now, Lord. May I be direct?"

"Go on."

"Lords, what I've already begun to say. Listen to yourselves. Even calling the Nobodoi the Recalled Ones, as you do, suggests that they too have overlords controlling them, able to recall them at will once a task is done."

"Or much simpler. Their own leaders have Recalled them."

"I have to allow that too. But what if not? Perhaps your view comes from your habit of being in such a hierarchy for so long. Perhaps it is wisely judged. But what if not? Instead of feeling chosen, privileged to be called into service, you put your rulers in their place in turn. We as Humans, with our inclination for absolutes, go with Dirk's flower, would grant that they have absolute dominion and simply stepped away to see what would come of it."

"Which is the same self-absorbed arrogance you accuse us of. You reserve some special role for yourselves despite everything. This Bedlam Rose."

"*They* chose this world, Lord. *This* place, *this* combination this time."

"And they chose us to govern it. They accept—want—the solution we bring. By default, by implication, our decision will be theirs."

"But, Lord, I could say the same about Humans. They want the solution *we* bring. This Bedlam Rose *they* have made."

"Except that it remains our decision, our prevailing custodianship."

"Yes, unless that changes, Great Lord. Unless you accept the simple lesson of the flower. The evidence suggests it."

"Or doesn't, Josephine. Your world may have no special place in anything, is just another world they have chosen. The way it often is. We have been client Races for millennia."

"But what if there *is* a special purpose, Lord? What if the Nobodoi have not been Recalled? What if they are still here? Changed but here and watching? You've all considered it."

"This Lady Mondegreen is a dangerous Lady. *You* are a dangerous lady."

"Bad flower!" Fond Louie boomed.

Josephine ignored the outburst. "Or not, sire. Just showing natural curiosity. So new to no longer being at the top of the life hierarchy ourselves. What will you do?"

"Your question again?"

Josephine gestured to the Window, to the building around them. "Can we continue here? Will you leave us in peace?"

"This is not necessarily why we have come. Again, make your case."

"I needn't, Lord. The Window is not here, but here." She placed a finger against her forehead. "You know this. The Lady, whatever she is, however she is, is beyond one place, beyond facts from broken histories. The Rose is all around us."

"Very dangerous," Raine said, so keenly aware of the moment as this Josephine no doubt was, of the waving prairie beyond, of the distant roar of the force walls, of the goldwire curling out of the Matt's chest, telling the moments of their lives.

"Lord, I am at that point where nothing I can say will save this place if you decide against it. But whether as fact, symbol or metaphor, the Window *will* remain. You know this of us. The Lady will stay, may even become stronger by seeming to be something worth destroying."

"Let us go outside," Raine said.

Fond Louie pulled back at once. Raine crossed to the entrance and stepped out into the day. The Matt activated its havel and followed.

"I can promise nothing," Raine said when Josephine finally joined them in the road. The sun was westering, already a fierce golden coin high in the washed sepia mirk of Rollinsgame. "Even if I withhold, Fond Louie and this house-lord will decide as they feel suits this special time."

"Lord, then there are a few possessions I'd like to retrieve before—"

The strike was like a scalpel of light, sharp and final. The temple was gone, shattered, just like that, the discardo, the dust, the shock wave and intense energy wash contained in a security sleeve that came an instant before and held nearly a full minute afterwards.

The strike echo came in those first seconds too, a tearing that snapped the day asunder but was quickly stolen away in the eternal roar of the corridor.

Fond Louie's summons rode that echo, a high-pitched keening that brought his *choi* running. The stink of hot-glass was instantly there as well:

Raine's Elsewheres phasing in—three, six—their heads no longer averted, no longer in far-look.

"Agius!" the Matt house-lord said in its own tongue, one arm raised and pointing down the road.

And there moving towards them was a were-suit, the classic Nobodoi artefact: its off-white mummiform advancing with a roiling, twisting ground effect that almost but never quite looked like legs stepping out. Above its right shoulder, joined by a network of unseen energy, was the flattened horse-skull of the Snake. To its left, rolling along on a skirted four-ball platform, was the Companion, an elongated ovoid two meters tall, with a canted featureless dish at its top. Flickering about the whole triune were the ghostworks, the half-seen firefly glints that marked most things Nobodoi, made even more vivid by the shadowing early afternoon light of the corridor. Inside that dirty white mummiform talos was a soul-stone, a chalky ball with a leathery kernel at its heart, all that was left of its Recalled occupant.

Or not.

Fond Louie had made *choi*, trunks locked firmly in the spinal sockets of its four *choi*-mates, and now that mighty fighting wheel moved off the road to let the triune pass. Raine's Elsewheres did the same in one precise, mind-linked movement. All watched as the were-suit approached and passed them by.

Fond Louie humphed in pleasure. "So ends today's lesson. Holy roller come to play! Warn off piracy. Seamen on the Mount. Biggest pirate chip played."

"But why, Lords?" Josephine said. "Nothing changes. The Window is still there."

Raine gave the fierce Darzie smile. "Winning, losing. It is no longer easy to know who gets what?"

Then Holding-in-Quiet spoke, chest gleaming with goldpoint. "Build again, Josephine Cantal. It was not the Vanished One who took your house today."

"You, Lord? But why? Why?"

The hatch of the Matt's charabanc was even now lifting away, preparing to receive its master.

"What was said before. A Two-Door Rose. How can one resist this newest flower with two doors? It is the way through. Worth the intent. All coinage."

Josephine Cantal bowed her head, acknowledged the honor as best she could. "Thank you. Thank you, Great Lord, for this."

Raine listened to the exchange, wondering. *He* had not acted. And had, by *not* acting. Yes. Had kept to his task enough. In an instant he sent his Elsewheres back to *Nobion*, was vaguely aware of Fond Louie's troupe running off yipping and shouting through the grasslands to where the luda endlessly fired in the golden afternoon and the great force-walls of Rollinsgame and Bassantrae reared into the sky. He easily allowed that Holding-in-Quiet had departed, that only Josephine Cantal would be waiting in the road behind him.

You are a wise and very dangerous woman, he thought to himself. By the Lady!

But he did not turn to her yet. Rather he watched the were-suit continuing down the road, forever wandering the world. Amid his eternal agony, in spite of it, he smiled fiercely into the remains of the day. Arm of Law.

Afterword to "Truth Window: A Tale of the Bedlam Rose"

MORE THAN JUST providing a story title this time, the mondegreen is brought center-stage for this return to the universe of my 1991 *Wormwood* story cycle.

Having learned what a Truth Window was in the construction of hay-bale homes, the idea of having the "beautiful lie" as the basis of a whole belief system was compelling. SF is full of such scenarios: in "The Omega Glory" episode of the original *Star Trek*, in *Zardoz*, in novels like Colin Kapp's *The Patterns of Chaos*, the list goes on. So, too, there is the historical reality of the Renaissance being powered in large part by the idea of rediscovering the lost Golden Ages of Greece and Rome and, in particular, of an Ancient Egypt that in reality was never quite as so many European scholars and artists imagined it. The idea of such a large-scale misperception kept bringing me back to *Wormwood*, to the alien world our planet had become under the Nobodoi, and to the countless opportunities for often bitter, sometimes wondrous, misunderstandings in the fraught, everyday reality of the Patchwork.

It's always tricky deciding which roads to go down as a writer and this story nearly didn't happen. *Wormwood* had received my best ever reviews internationally, and ironically triggered a reluctance to harm the force and magic of the original linked collection by overdoing what seemed so adequately done. The Strugatskys didn't do a sequel to *Roadside Picnic*, for instance, though I would have welcomed one, bought it, savoured it, any chance to re-visit the Zone. *Dune* gained very little from its sequels, though they allowed us to travel in familiar territory again and were enjoyable enough. *Star Wars, Highlander, Hellraiser, Saw* all became less somehow by becoming more.

For whatever reason, I held off, flirted with a Wormwood novel for seventeen years, ended up with 50,000 words I'm proud of. But then I saw what was happening, that I had become faint-hearted about revisiting the whole thing and might well be keeping this cherished setting from becoming all it could be. Which, I'm sure, is what Frank Herbert, George Lucas et al may have felt with their own creations.

So, as with Hampton Donauer in "He Tried to Catch the Light," it was again time to let the characters who lived in this plundered, re-made world do what *they* needed to do. And they have. And quite likely they will.

Down in the Limbo Gardens

Down in the Limbo Gardens
Along the Breaklight Pier,
The carousels are turning
In the morning air.
Down on the Rorschach Sidewalks
Beside the sea,
See the empty tables waiting,
Rendezvous for free.

Looking for the future in an eye,
Trying to find the reason why.

Down in the Limbo Gardens
There's a glass shot through with night,
There's a face inside a crystal,
A smile that isn't quite
There where horoscopes are crowded
In jagged cards,
Fortunes fall to gypsy fingers,
Tellers call the paths.

Looking for the future in an eye,
Trying to find the reason why.

Dance in the Limbo Gardens,
Drink at The Traitor's Face,
Chance to find your waiting shadow,
Your days of grace.

Looking for the future in an eye,
Trying to find the reason why.

THE LIBRARY

Author's Note

The Adventures of Tom Rynosseros take place a thousand years from now, after a major crisis has wiped out much of the world's population and shifted the balance of global power in new and surprising ways. While the stories concern one man's search for his true identity among the descendants of the modern-day Aboriginal tribes in an exotic, transformed future Australia, his exploits have a far wider significance, as the following story shows.

1.

IF ANYWHERE IS HOME for me, apart from *Rynosseros*, it can only be Twilight Beach.

And, again, between voyages, with *Rynosseros* safely at the Sand Quay with the other deep-desert sand-ships, the crew lost in the bars and gaming-rooms of the Gaza Hotel, I took a favorite table at Amberlin's, wanting to avoid the crowds and the excitement of the Astronomers' Bar and the Gaza terrace, the conversations I would immediately inherit at Trimori's, The Traitor's Face and The Slow Hour.

It was a morning for slowing down to small pleasures, for sitting with a glass of tautine or vintage terfilot, or one of the traditional wines they make in far-off lands and still export down to the coasts and resort towns of Australia.

The terrace at Amberlin's gives an almost two hundred degree view, so that at a glance you can see the elegant villas in the dunes to the north, close to the road that leads out to the beach suburbs of Corlique, Mirajan and Castanelle at the tip of the Golden Bow. Then, turning your head, you take in the deep blue swells where the tidal bells stir on their chains in the sea; then, at last, you have the whole town laid out before you: the Gaza with its famous terrace and airy loggias, the Breaklight Pier and the Time Beaches, Sailmaker's back near the Antic Houses on Tramway Street. There, meeting the harbour, the Byzantine Quarter with its bazaars and curio shops, and the Mayan Quarter beyond, both with their vivid restoration architectures; close by, whitewashed walls and tiled roofs dazzling in the sun, the urban villas and hotels, the palazzos and arcades, the famous galleries. There, Old Town with its stuccoed tenements and lion-colored warehouses. The brooding mass of the Armament stands among them, drawing memories of other days, and the smaller sunnier shapes of the Granary and the market squares abutting Trial Street, fronted by the Tyrrian Wall.

Near those precincts, the town finally meets the desert. There you find the famous privateering inns: The Goodbye, The Black Wind and The Cannon, where the stories are told, the reputations earned, the legends made. And there, close by, beyond the corniche and the color and bustle of the Sarda Salita, is the Sand Quay itself, with its chandleries, ship-factors and kitesellers, the docks alive with the cries of the longshore crews and the barneys hard at work tending the great charvi hulls. Even now, moored between *Sunfish* and *Argus* this time, you will find *Rynosseros*.

I laughed, completing it yet again, the old homecoming ritual.

Slow now, I told myself. Slow.

Though it was allowable, all allowable after weeks of mission tension and the welcome yet constant demands of running the ship, especially after Balin, especially after Trale.

And it was such a perfect morning, the Promenade and terraces so full of life. *This* was the heart of it. Apart from *Rynosseros*. This.

I had just begun studying the menu when a robed figure sat in the chair opposite.

"Captain Tyson, if I may."

I glanced up at the long handsome face and alert respectful gaze of a fine-looking Ab'O. He wore fighting leathers under sand-colored traveling robes and had the double swords at his waist. There was a tribal sersifan on a chain about his neck and I had its signature immediately. This was a Chitalice First.

"Captain, I am Kaber Fen Otamas and I need your services for a mission."

"I am newly back from a mission, Lord Otamas. This is shore leave for me."

"Understood, Captain." The Chitalice noble placed a small scrambler on the table and activated it. "But I believe you will want to accept this one."

"Oh? And why is that?"

"Council will authorize it. It is courtesy that brought me here first."

Council knew! Den had already been approached! That important then.

"Please," I said, hiding disappointment, weariness. "*I* still choose my own missions. What will persuade me this time?"

"A common enemy," the Ab'O said. "A confederate of Dewi Dammo that we suspect was part of that same attempt to secure power."

Dewi Dammo. The name brought a rush of memories: of the Inland Sea and the Charling Coast, of the island of Marmordesse and poor mad Dewi trying to have it all.

"Why me?"

"There is a chance that you will learn more about your origins. Your time in the Madhouse."

He had my complete attention. "Go on."

Kaber Fen Otamas glanced about him. No doubt he had support concealed close by, possibly Kurdaitcha. "There is an enemy for us, known only by little more than his name. Chiras Namarkon."

"Dewi said that name."

"He did. Council provided the debriefing transcripts for that mission. We wish you to find this Chiras Namarkon, Captain. You know better than most that the status-quo is always at risk and that we work ceaselessly to maintain it. At one extreme we have insiders like Bolo May who are allowed to grow too powerful, at the other, opportunists like Dewi Dammo hiding in the interstices of what the world steadily becomes in spite of our precautions."

I couldn't help but smile.

Otamas smiled as well. "No, Captain. We do not automatically regard the seven Colored Captains as our enemy."

"But, in spite of your precautions, another part of what the world has become. Hardly welcome."

"Some of us accept it, even applaud it. Our philosophies require it of us."

"Many do not," I said.

"As you say. But at our best we like to think that it extends us. Makes us larger."

Again, I had to smile. At the very least this was civility, at most genuine respect, a suggestion of rapprochement between the tribes and Nation. I inclined my head in thanks.

Otamas continued. "At least the seven National Captains are out in the world, in plain sight. This Chiras Namarkon is not. We allow that while he was probably not an ally of Dewi's in any formal sense, they seem to have known of one another and at least reached a modus vivendi. Given what Dewi Dammo sought to do, they may even have traded tech and other resources. Our concern is that Namarkon may very well have access to our systems; worse yet, access to factions with vested interests who will not declare their present connection with him. It took tribal and Council agents years and many lives to gain that single clue to Dewi's whereabouts Pederson gave you at Angel Bay that day. With this Namarkon, we only know that there is a library involved—he may be its owner or keeper—and a connection with an important text called the Alexandrian Book."

"Then your people—"

"No, Captain. We have searched and will continue to search our libraries and data systems. We need someone who represents *us* to search yours. All of yours. Especially those remaining libraries which are located—to put it as tactfully as I can—in *decommissioned* National possessions."

"Decommissioned? You mean—"

"Exactly. The abandoned arcologies. The old inland cities. *We* go there and there is the usual outcry, as useless, hopeless and strident as ever but drawing precisely the sort of National and international media attention we do not want at this time. *You* visit them as a solitary traveler on a mission for Nation and it is not questioned."

"The arcologies are hardly places to learn anything about my past, Lord Otamas."

"Surely that depends on who this Namarkon is and where such a search leads. And see it another way. If you refuse this task, we will ask the other Colored Captains, then simply empower your Council to send one of its usual field agents. We came to you first."

I watched the waves making their way to shore, the long stately sweeps crowned with cartouches of light, each cresting swell set with a bezel of quicksilver in the hot morning sun. Gulls wheeled in, making their plaintive cries. The air smelled of salt and sea-wrack. "Will you assist, lord?"

"However and whenever we can, Captain, though if what we suspect is true, then this Namarkon will probably not want to be found. There is sure to be tribal interference."

"Have you thought to approach the Antique Men with your needs and misgivings?"

"Of course. They too assist as they can."

"May I approach them? About my provenance at least?"

And surprise on surprise, it was not Otamas but Den who answered, suddenly there at our table, drawing up a chair and sitting. "We've made the request already, Tom. Can you do this?"

Being at Amberlin's had been strange enough, wonderfully strange after so much time away. Having a tribal lord appear at my table and now a senior Council operations chief added a definite touch of the absurd.

The middle-aged Nation officer gave a smile that was meant to be reassuring, but which made an even stranger mask of his hairless, lopsided face. Den was strikingly ugly, had chosen to remain so years ago in order to qualify for an impressive if strangely earned annuity from the estate of the late and eccentric Spydyr Massillian. Smiles were his most disconcerting feature.

But, typical Den, he was as caring as he was smart and effective.

Can you do this?

The perfect way to ask.

I thought I could see glints of light from the ornamental wind- and sun-clocks on the Time Beaches, then traced the line of the Promenade up to the Gaza terrace where people from across the world came to watch games of fire-chess and stylo. I imagined I could hear the Gaza belltrees singing in the on-shore breeze, and the bells swinging on their sea-chains below the glittering swells.

"I can do this."

"Thank you, Captain," Otamas said, then stood, picked up his scrambler and left the terrace. As he headed off down the street, four robed tribesman appeared from their places of concealment and joined him.

"Tom, it really is your choice," Den said at last.

"I know, Den. I know. You have a list of libraries?"

"We do. Some here, some out there." He gestured behind him. "The old cities."

"Aye. The old cities. I can do this."

2.

THE GREAT BLADE FROM which Turker Fin took its name threw a shadow across the desert, a shadow so vast that the view from the big library window showed a register of fierce red-ochre light above a darkness of Turker's own making: blazing blue-white sky at the top, late-afternoon sun-shadow at the bottom, the rest almost impenetrable because of the searing glare.

The library was underground, of course, far below the great sun-trap and power-wall of the blade. The view was relayed down from a much higher level, from a tiny viewing tile somewhere on its mighty surface, but it conquered the space well enough, the feeling of being shut away. It brought the sense of looking from high up I've always felt one needed in libraries, not the quiet gloomy cloisters with dusty stacks and a clock ticking off in the precious silence, but a spacious airiness, even if the views were mostly unchanging and ignored; the quality old monasteries had of being above and beyond the secular world down there.

Now, almost at the end of a three-day search of the Turker library, I stood before the "window" yet again, taking in the view from three hundred meters overhead as if I'd never seen it before.

Turker Fin was the last of the leads supplied by Nation's archivists, the final name on the list of eight painstakingly drawn out of secure comp systems.

The time *that* had taken told me a great deal: how special agents or carefully placed moles in previous administrations had probably tried to bury such information, possibly to prevent the more hostile tribal factions from learning the exact whereabouts and constitution of the last National libraries, but—more to the point—that those few precious true-book repositories were located on *tribal* land, in safe residual concessions protected by special charter and tradition, reached by safe Roads. Perhaps those factions had guessed it long ago, as Otamas had; perhaps it was simple diplomacy that stayed their hand, stopped any further interference in the affairs of Nation.

Eight names. Only two had been on the coast, both in Twilight Beach: the first the Pandeon, easy to reach but of little help, full of saltings and key deletions, the second the private collection of a Delas Marquand, a man presently unavailable, perhaps even conveniently out of Australia.

The remaining six, like Turker, exactly as Den had said, truly were located in the old arcologies, those vast echoing constructs abandoned long ago when the Nationals were driven back to the coasts, their birthright denied them, the fragile environments shut down but for the great mainwalls and a few selected outbuildings.

It had been a largely fruitless search there too, infuriating in the hints and teasing glimpses found. First Andromira and Crayasse, Sol-Tyreen and Genema Blade, then across the continent to Ganness, and back to Turker Fin when word came through at last that the old librarian, Toth, would accede to Council's demands for open house.

It was difficult for the old man. Accustomed to being absolute monarch in his deserted domain, Trayban Toth had finally realized that his position as "lighthouse keeper" (the term he liked to use, muttering about the Pharos Lighthouse and the Pharisees and the great library at ancient Alexandria, as if they related to these deserts or each other) might end if he opposed his superiors.

Humbled and uncertain, made suddenly respectful by Den's expensive call, Toth had done an about-face, had become excited at last that the library was being used for its original purpose.

He had granted access, so I came to believe, to the whole catalogue. Turker had 40,000 retroform books in its deep cool chambers, 810,000 kilometers of tape, 780,000 units of disc, mote, bead, crystal and fluid-link texts, and—rarest of all—5,000 Illuminated Books of the new kind.

I stood before one of these now, watching as Trayban set it up on the lectern before the window. It was a Book that had recently been transferred here from Crayasse, officially borrowed, Toth said, though spirited away might have been a better term, since it had been removed from the Crayasse collection a day before I got there, almost as if it had been moved deliberately to waste my time, the last copy of a text possibly leading to the whereabouts of Chiras Namarkon. That was how it felt.

Trayban Toth was muttering as he arranged the Book, coming to the end of yet another of his almost endless monologues about book-ish matters.

"...and the Vatican has always had the largest collection of pornography in the world. It makes you think. But this is it, Captain! L75 VGS." He seemed annoyed that the view had caught my attention rather than this text he had found for me at last.

It was hard to conceal my amusement. More than seventy years old, short and bent but often full of a startling energy that made his eyes shine like flecks of mica above the long nose and full white beard, Trayban presented as someone who had once played Merlin in an ancient pageant and had never tired of the role. Each book was delivered as if a personal incantation had been sought and found, as if the storage rooms he visited were compartments in his own head from which these texts had been drawn forth at great personal effort.

Perhaps that was how Trayban saw it, lived it, as if Turker Fin truly were his greater self and he wandered corridors of his own mind to visit its parts. This recent arrival, L75 VGS, had to have been on hand, but Trayban had spent precious hours "searching" for it.

Which set me wondering all over again. Despite his age and distracted manner, Toth would make a fitting Namarkon, someone dissembling, projecting, playing out a role. I wished, not for the first time, that I had a monitor to use.

"Namarkon," Toth said, a note of peevishness in his voice. "There's the reference under linguistics. It cross-refers to the Gray and Silas."

"Thanks, Trayban."

I studied the surface of the Book, the small touch-plate and ormolu key-set, the Nape circuit-mosaic border (as if a churchman had in fact decorated it in the ancient fashion), the Bytes-and-Byzantines imprint in the bottom left-hand corner with the Nation seal. I touched the plate, activating the tiny power source within. The milky pane lit with a warm yellow light; one by one pages slow-cycled through the credits and bibliographica to the index, ciphers spilling steadily across the Reader Page.

"L75 VGS," Toth murmured in affirmation, as if intoning a spell. Then: "L362:42."

"L362:42. Thank you."

I entered the final sequence, accessed the section, keyed in Namarkon. There was a two-second wait, then that word flashed its presence.

Flashed and blanked, leaving the Reader Page dark, the Book inert.

"Trayban!"

The old man pushed in next to me. Without a word, he brought up the bibliographica, ran the Namarkon entry. Again the name flashed once; again the screen went dead.

"Damaged!" he cried. "Hell and Jesus! It's damaged!"

"On its way to Turker, you think?" I said. "Deliberate?"

Toth frowned at sacrilege, his jaw set, dismay showing in his eyes.

"What, Tray?" I pressed. "Is it coincidence?"

"No!" he cried. And he repeated the functions, again without success, then carried the Book to a donkey-frame close by, intending to bypass the discrete functions with the library's override.

Certainly the Book glowed more brightly in the frame, and for a moment I hoped. But again the word triggered the misfunction.

Toth repeated the procedure four times, making adjustments, even pounding on the dead Reader plate with the spread palm of one hand. He ran several other entries successfully, cycled through a few, then tried Namarkon again with no luck. He lifted the Book from the frame, studied its spine and seals.

"What can we do, Tray?" I asked gently, carefully.

He laid the Book back on the lectern.

"L75 VGS is dead stack. Only one copy in existence. But it's open text, so scholars can add or revise details in appendices. There will be a Precis access for that."

"Tampered with as well?"

"No! No!" Toth said firmly. "You don't understand. It's black box, a sealed unit, very durable, designed to show what the main text contained. Scholars working here could enter their findings and opinions—under strict supervision, of course, always under supervision. It will summarize portions of the main entry as assists. No-one could get at those."

"Please run it."

He turned to the Book, used a scribe wand to enter a code sequence along the bottom edge. Words filed across the Reader Page. Toth keyed in *Namarkon* yet again.

The word flashed its arrival, gave its capsule comment.

362:42:8-1: Namarkon

(Namarkon, Namarquon, Nammargon)(OAA)(dialect)

Spirit of Lightning, originally of the Gunwinggu, Western Arnhem Land (495:36:7/1-92G). Vengeful elemental spirit accessed by Morrkidju (604:24:12), the "clever sorcerers" of the Gunwinggu...

Another dozen or so entries referred to eponymous land-holdings, ships, a comp-net, and a minor highwayman who had made use of the ancient name. There were a score of mythic antecedents, the names of people and things, real and imaginary, who had been identified with the Dreamtime original or had recognized conceptual connections.

The final listing was the one I wanted, and again there was the exasperating reference to the text I needed most of all, something called the Alexandrian Book, the title which had dogged my search from Andromira to Turker.

362:42:8-14: Chiras Namarkon (aka The Immortal)

A legendary folk hero/demon of the Molere cycle, said to inhabit a secret labyrinth, safeguarding secret knowledge and a great treasure.

Origins uncertain. Gray and Silas (914:61:7) are inclined to consider retroactive amplification of an early 21st century inception, either a traditional (unsubstantiated) expression meaning: "tree struck by lightning" or possibly as part of an advertising campaign for either Inters 400 (324:22) or Nation-Sun (721:620:4).

Note: Chiras Namarkon is allegedly the author/creator of a text/artefact called the Alexandrian Book (no information available apart from the title). This authorship is probably as apocryphal as the text itself, since all sources advancing the connection are full of proven fabrication. The Alexandrian Book has never been sighted (Trist, Gray and Silas, Maidment, Green).

Note: Standing request by Gray and Silas for updating, with priority input-inform tag for AM/GB.

Without my asking, Toth caused a hard-copy to be made and passed it over.

"This last notation, Tray? The initials?"

Toth hesitated, leant over the Reader Page, the remains of his anger still driving him. "I'm not supposed to tell, but it's the Antique Men. That's Gado Bascoeur. He's very good. A great scholar. Does it help?"

"It's something. I've found the Dreamtime reference before, same with the Immortal, the labyrinth and the creature of fable. The Alexandrian Book reference is not new; this Bascoeur entry is. You have nothing on the Molere cycle?"

"Nothing else. Nothing in Gray and Silas either. I'm sorry."

"Then thank you, Tray. I'm finished here."

I went to the desk I had been using and began gathering up my notes. Toth followed, a concerned look turning his old face into a surprisingly desperate mask, the small eyes full of unexpected emotion. My visit to Turker had been an intrusion initially, but now, at the end of it, he seemed sorry to have me leave, as if reluctant to lose this precious reaffirmation of his role.

The damage to Illuminated Book L75 VGS had somehow intensified the desperation, his need to hold on to this moment of service.

"What will you do?" he said, a question he now allowed himself to ask.

"After the Pandeon and the six arcologies? Marquand's place again, in case he's back. You have been invaluable, Tray. I have four private libraries hinted at somewhere in Twilight Beach, none mentioned on Council's list. I have confirmation for Chiras Namarkon as the Immortal, as Lightning God and keeper of a library and labyrinth, as putative author of something called the Alexandrian Book, whatever that was or is, *if* ever it was. Now there's the link to the Antique Men, which was inevitable anyway but I'm glad of it right now. I'm full circle there. Considering I didn't know what to expect, I've certainly got something."

"And this?" He picked up one of the hard copies before I could bundle it up with the rest of my arcology material. "The list of arcologies you wanted?"

"Another tack I may take. Since I've run out of National libraries, I might look where libraries might have been at one time or other."

"You'd do that? Go to *all* the old sites?"

"Why not? The tribes will allow it. If Crayasse and Turker have their data-vaults underground, the other arcologies may not be as empty as they say."

I tried to sound hopeful, though I doubted that even an exhaustive search of the abandoned cities would reveal a carefully hidden Chiras Namarkon.

But what else did I have? For all I knew, Namarkon was hiding somewhere in the forgotten decks and halls of Turker Fin or Crayasse or one of the other places I had already visited. I may have passed within meters of his door, breathed the air he had released from his lungs, started at a small sound of his presence in a shadowed corridor.

Yes, trying Delas Marquand again, consulting the Antique Man, Bascoeur, if he would allow it, trying to locate the four private libraries, would exhaust my leads, probably finish it. Then I would be left either to tour the remaining arcologies or scour the curio shops in the Byzantine Quarter, hoping that Den or one of the other Colored Captains, or one of my eccentric friends in the Bird Club, might uncover something.

"It's not right!" Toth said, studying the arcology print-out and pulling at his beard.

"What's that, Tray?"

He spread the double-list of National arcology sites on a reader table and tapped at the page. "The top arrangement here. There's a name missing."

I hurried across to him and studied the print-out. "You're sure? How can you tell?"

"It's the shape, Captain, not the names. The regional arrangement at the bottom I'm not sure about, but the top one is wrong. The list I remember is one off a square. I always wished they had built an even number to finish the shape. This is two off. Look!"

Andromira*	Whitehead	Andalave
Enso-Bey	Soltumede	Alka
Crayasse*	Chyra-Manta	Quaine Lock
Genema Blade*	Pharani	Meda
Stone Mill	Bukula Tan	Khen-Mol
Ganness*	Pila	Maggadi
Land's End	Port Chevas	Graylord
Tulidjula	Transy	Quen-Lui
Trovy	Neuve	Ihren
Turker Fin*	Tarpial	Gayla
Sol-Tyreen*	Anansanna	Bidja Point
Monk's Hood		

Andromira*			Bukula Tan
Enso-Bey			Pila
Crayasse*			Port Chevas
Pharani			Quen-Lui
Stone Mill	Transy	Alka	Khen-Mol
Ganness*	Tarpial	Meda	Whitehead
Land's End	Maggadi	Trovy	Andalave
Tulidjula	Genema Blade*		Soltumede
Graylord			Anansanna
Turker Fin*			Monk's Hood
Sol-Tyreen*	Neuve		Chyra-Manta
Bidja Point	Gayla	Ihren	Quaine Lock

I studied the shape formed by the top arrangement of names, matched each name with the regional arrangement beneath. Thirty-four on both. I checked the print-outs drawn from the comps at Crayasse and Ganness. They gave the same double-pattern, the same count: two off the square.

"Do it again, Tray. See what you get."

The old man went to a nearby comp and called up the information. The screen showed the same pattern as the printed lists.

"No!" Toth said, and struck the console. "No! Wrong, I tell you! This is not it!"

"What then?"

"Someone sent L75 VGS here. Someone damaged it. Someone has done *this* as well!"

"You're certain?"

"It's the sort of visual trick you never forget. The last time I saw this list it was one off."

"When was that?"

"What? Who knows? Years ago. It was years. But I remember. I couldn't forget."

"Tray, can we do a priority search on this?" It was suddenly very important, though I knew that every list I sought would be short one entry.

"I don't see how we can," the old man said. "The library comp gives this. It's the only comp facility I'm allowed apart from environmentals."

"Could those be routed in?"

"They couldn't access deleted data, no."

"Deletion has to be difficult in sealed catalogue systems. Can you bypass a blockage?"

"No, Captain. Whoever can tamper with library records would make sure of that."

"The Antique Men?"

Toth pulled at his beard. "They could do it, yes. They're one of the few groups allowed to enter information. But they're the most honest—"

"This Bascoeur?"

"One of the best. He would never—"

"Namarkon might," I said, thinking of the old historical stand-by of need-to-know, doing something for the greater good, the eternal catch-cry of governments, rulers, privileged agencies, shrewd individuals. "Tray, can I take the Book back to Twilight Beach? It would be safe, I swear it."

He shook his head. "Impossible. Especially now."

"Then do not part with it again. Council will authorize that order. Refuse all requests, even from Crayasse, from all brother and sister librarians. The Book remains here. And, please, refuse access—"

"To the Antique Men, yes. If I can."

TOTH SAW ME BACK to the surface levels, came with me out onto the wide mooring plat, littered with sand and wind-wrack, to where my rented thirty-foot Maud skiff waited on locked wheels.

"Leave in the morning, Captain. Phone the information through. You can afford it." The old man indicated the afternoon sun halfway down the sky.

But I needed to be doing something now, anything. "Tray, it's at least two days to the coast. Calls can be monitored, and I need to get what I know back to where I can use it. I'll make a hundred k's, possibly two hundred, before the light goes. Thanks again for all you've done."

I climbed aboard the tiny craft, trimmed two parafoils to the afternoon wind and slowly gained speed along the ancient Road.

Behind, old Toth stood with one arm raised. In the dying light, he resembled some scholar Quasimodo before his own fabulous Notre Dame, the westering sun turning the great curtain wall into a beacon. Somewhere on that blazing massif was a tiny view tile, taking the sun into a chamber deep underground. I wondered if Chiras Namarkon used it now, watching me go, and wondered what part thoughts of such a possibility had played in my going.

3.

From: Josepha Anglis, *The Colored Captains: Fact and Fiction*, Praesidian, AS 753-3
Introduction: "The Unloved Heroes"

All reliable sources agree that the Ab'O tribes trapped themselves by the Tell Agreement of AS 742. By opening up the annual Cyrimiri ship-lotteries to Nationals—a strategic concession made with a view to calming International criticism of tribal racist policies, thereby keeping valuable world tech markets and AI initiatives—the Ab'O States made possible a unique chain of events by which their own traditions trapped them.

The Cyrimiri proponents at the '42 Convocation had no way of knowing that one of their own experiments in Artificial Intelligence would prove so viable and so formidable. They could not know that the celebrated belltree program, which had so captured the imagination of the world and had reached its zenith with the Iseult-Darrian strain, would be the cause of so much consternation and embarrassment, a resounding blow struck for the waning Pan-European tradition in Australia.

The tribes and Nation are both diplomatically closed-lipped about the details of what actually occurred. Experts surmise that one of the redundant oracle-trees, rejected, limited and given the usual desert service as a roadpost, rallied against its conditioning, established a reciprocal arrangement with Records, and used its links to enter the names of National ship-winners into one of the most hallowed tribal registers at Tell—the Great Passage Book itself. The tree's motives remain unknown. Such a sensational and unprecedented treason was soon stopped, but not before seven National captains: Golden Afervarro, Red Lucas, Green Glaive, Yellow Traven, White Massen, Black Doloroso and Blue Tyson— won not only their great sand-ships (and those were seven of the best tribal charvolants in existence, suggesting that the tree had played a part there as well) but were issued with all-lander mandates laying open the inner deserts, and given the Colors which in an instant elevated them irrevocably to the status of tribal heroes.

Tribal spokesmen claim that the creation of the Seven was a deliberate benefice to Nation, an endowment made partly as restitution for the wide-scale shutting down of National facilities in the interior. They insist that in no way was it an error on the part of careless biotects. National and international experts, however, remain unconvinced. They suggest that the seven Captains were chosen for a purpose, that the tribes made better than they knew, that this rogue belltree AI raised up its own champions. Why? The Captains themselves refuse to comment.

But one thing is clear. For now at least, Nation has teeth again, and the world is watching.

Rynosseros was still out on mission. I'd persuaded Scarbo and the others to accept long-reach assignments, convincing them that while I searched the old National sites listed by Den, they could do more for me by asking questions in distant places, in the museums, modest town libraries, the bars, galleries and curio shops they came upon.

For all I knew, the key to Namarkon might be something someone said or overheard in a crowded bar at No Man's Easy Rest, some detail in a painting in the hallway of a public building in Angel Bay, or a line sung in the chorus of a child's sidewalk song in Port Tarsis.

After returning the skiff to Maud's Rentals at the end of my run, I still had the better part of two days before *Rynosseros* was due back from

Tank Feti, ample time to try Marquand again, the only private (and secret) collector Den's people had been able to uncover—and that through a string of suspect legal infractions in a long career.

Unlike the other sellers of collectibles and oddities, the public ones who made much of the little they had, Delas Marquand had always been notoriously reclusive. On Nation records he existed officially as an importer of Welsh and Dutch cheeses and fabrics from Oceania. According to the more reliable rumors, he had been a plunderer of libraries in his time and was now a dealer in black market volumes, with a splendid secret library of his own.

His shop was an unmarked, blank-fronted establishment at the end of a dead-end street out near the Armament. Visits, whether for cheeses, fabrics or books, were by appointment only, often made by people answering cryptic ads in obscure trade journals or—for the novelty of it—in the popular urban publications, those glossy retroform periodicals printed on siflin or kelp-based Tase paper.

But responses to ads, the phonecalls and letters pretending to be a prospective client, even visits to the shop, had so far been unsuccessful. Certainly before beginning my search of the arcologies, his place had always been locked, the windows polarized into the neutral mirror glare of the "blind" house.

For whatever reason, it seemed that those dealing in information, in stored or printed knowledge, had become harder to locate than ever, as if suddenly all of them, whether sly Delas Marquand or the famous Antique Men, had grown wary of tribal attention.

Or was it Namarkon they feared?

I'd left the Marquand problem for Den, all I could do, one more thing to try along with my standing request to see the Antique Men, and, to my relief, Den had succeeded in at least the first part of this assignment.

"We have our way in," he told me when I called on him at his villa that afternoon. We were standing in his operations room before the big view window, and it was like I'd never been away—as if visiting the arcologies were all a dream, something gleaned from somnium sleep. "We've placed a false impost in Marquand's comp. Not the sort of risk we like to take, Tom, but I think he'll see it as genuine. It was difficult but it's done. Watching the place would probably tell us nothing. He's experienced. He might even have a secret exit out behind Armament somewhere; so far we haven't found it. Still, we figure he has to be in Australia. There are no visa or transit records saying otherwise, no listings for private dirigibles or module shipments under Marquand in the last four months. He dare not be too clever in view of what we have on him."

"He'll accept the impost?"

Den looked pleased with himself. "We believe so. We've told his system a tribal inspector will call on him at 1100 one morning this week to discuss tariff discrepancies in tribal records. He dare not delegate that sort of thing. I was going to ask Scarbo or Shannon to do it, but you're back. Look the part and you'll get in. The plans you need will be ready."

"Thanks, Den. I know Council is taking quite a chance."

"We're doing what's right. Finally. We're acting and it feels good."

AT 1049 THE NEXT morning, in bright sunshine, I headed up Trial Street in the shadow of the Armament dressed in djellaba and burnoose, carrying my small folder of plans and a tribal sirrush stick borrowed from Den's collection. I wore dark glasses and the appropriate skin-toning, some bands of color on cheeks and chin, carefully neutral caste-marks. From a distance I was a quadroon customs officer on assignment in Nation territory, someone not to be denied.

The shop was as I remembered it, a two-story building at the end of a quiet street, still a blind house, the windows showing only adjacent structures and my own robed figure approaching the main door. It was hard to resist a smile at how formidable I looked.

I rapped several times on the solid panel and listened for movement within, but there was nothing. I waited, noting—not for the first time in this land the color of lions in the sun—how the bluest Australian skies are always found above the rooflines of old brick warehouses, over high walls such as formed this side of the Armament, that most mysterious of tribal artefacts in Twilight Beach.

Finally someone stirred beyond the door. Latches clicked, it swung back and Delas Marquand was standing there, professional caution showing on his wide, finely featured face. He was of medium height, clad in a gown fashioned along Egyptian lines, no doubt made from some of his own imported fabric, dark blues shot with threads of gold.

"Mr. Marquand," I said, accenting my voice just enough. "I am Atanas Tjijti from Customs."

Marquand gave a slight bow. "Your ident please, Mr. Tjijti."

I displayed the laminate Den had provided, then, taking the initiative, stepped by him into the dimly lit front hall of his premises. Marquand closed the door behind us, and even in the gloom I could see that he touched the locks in a way that suggested security systems, possibly illegal tech. I wondered if a true Ab'O would remark on it.

"Please go through to the office, Mr. Tjijti," Marquand said. "The records are there."

"Delas Marquand, I am actually here to discuss your library."

Marquand reached for something in the shadows—a contact? a weapon?—but my sirrush stick was already there, knocking his arm aside, making him yell in pain and surprise.

"Who are you?" he cried, cradling his arm. "You're no tribesman! What do you want?"

"Answers to official questions, nothing more. But this is your false hallway, Mr. Marquand. Please take us through to your dealer's room."

Even in the gloom I saw his eyes narrow. "I have no idea what you're talking about. Identify yourself!"

The sirrush stick struck the floor like a gunshot in the confined space. "It's me or a Nation strike. Choose!"

"You can't be serious!"

"Mr. Marquand, I am not alone in this. Officers outside have tech. All legal. Any deadfalls or problems with electrics and they'll be in here." I embellished the lie. "All under tribal sanction. Implant alert. Anything you do, understand?"

"Follow me," he said in a flat voice, nursing his injured arm, and led us back to the front door. He touched the locks again, opening a slideaway in the left wall, a concealed entrance. We entered, moved down a narrow corridor, well past what had to be storerooms and offices to an insulated secure room at the rear of the premises. It was large, fifteen meters to a side, with bookcases covering most of the wall space, the shelves filled with files and boxes. The far wall was exposed warehouse brick, shining dully in the room's soft recessed lighting, set with shallow alcoves between worn brickwork pilasters.

"Well?" Marquand said.

"First, we establish credentials. Show me your library."

He gave a wry smile. "You're a dealer now?"

"Delas, listen carefully. Only Nation or the tribes could get that impost into your comp. I'm Tom Tyson—"

"Tom Rynosseros!" Marquand's eyes widened in surprise. "What can—?"

"The Marquand Collection is beyond that wall. I've seen plans. I'd be grateful if you'd show me."

Delas Marquand seemed easier now. He smiled again and considered what to do. Finally he crossed to an ancient roll-top desk and made connections I did not try to see. There were the soft sounds of systems working, a play of shifting light in one of the alcoves in the rear wall, then the sudden vision of a ramp leading down into a warmly lit room *full* of shelves—shelves laden with books: retroforms, disks, mote stacks, even the Nape spines of Illuminated Books.

It was an amazing sight, an Aladdin's cave shimmering behind a series of plastic dust curtains. In spite of what Den had told me about Marquand, I gasped in amazement.

"Satisfied?"

I closed the trap. "I'd like to see some titles if I may."

"No-one goes down there, Captain." The voice was suddenly hard, the voice of a man who still had solutions, was still calculating. "I'm the only one to pass through those seals."

"You have leases to the adjacent buildings?"

"What?" He eyed me suspiciously.

I opened out the building plan Den had provided. "Beyond the rear of this shop is the Tyrrian Wall and the Armament. North of you is Trial Street and the Granary. South is Gallery Four, basement to roof. There is nowhere for your library to go. I'm betting a hologram."

"There's an old sub-basement—"

"No, we've checked. Photonics, yes?"

Marquand's face went pale at the prospect of his secret being out; his eyes were bright with mixed emotions.

"You couldn't. Armament is an undeclared tribal holding; there are no maps registered. It was guaranteed."

"Nation comp has non-detailed plans of area allotment. Delas, I am not interested in exposing you. You had books four years ago. What happened?"

"Plundered," he said, taking that solution, the truth. "All but a few. Captain, I deal in books: crystals, tapes, disks, motes, all the old carrier forms. People come to me. I use that as a lure, a tease." He nodded toward the alcove. "Bring up the pieces I am prepared to sell or trade. If word got out—"

"It won't. I've disengaged my com unit. Even Council won't find out. What I must know is whether you have—or had—information on a Chiras Namarkon. The Immortal. Especially in connection with a library."

"Just the names," Marquand said. "Nothing anyone would raid me for. I had a good collection once, but nothing really special, not intrinsically."

"Nothing on a Namarkon library or labyrinth?"

"Captain, I collected books, traded and sold them. I acted the scholar, then as now; it helps make a sale, helps to build up the collection again. I didn't read them so much as know things about them, the publishing information. Which editions—"

"Have you heard of something called the Alexandrian Book?"

"Of it, yes. Nothing more than that."

"We're trading here, Delas. Namarkon and the Alexandrian Book for an oath of secrecy from me."

"I'd tell you!" he cried. "For the oath and those plans I'd tell you if I knew. I would! I know both exist. I've...I've put out word that I'd make an offer for such a book. There's been nothing. Not a thing. All collectors do it as a matter of course."

"All right," I said, hope beginning to fade. "These other collectors. I know of at least four. I need names."

The man threw his arms wide in a gesture of exasperation. "I can't give you that. I can't! It's a trust thing."

"It's black-marketeering is what it is. It's Nation moving to find out anything about Namarkon and the Alexandrian Book. Help us, Delas, and the tribes learn nothing. It's not you Council wants." It was time for another lie, expedient but effective now with Marquand seeing his world about to collapse. "The black market doesn't harm Nation; it helps us, in fact, in ways you wouldn't imagine."

I was glad he didn't ask how. I was thinking of arcologies raided, of books being pirated out of vaults, of catalogues listing titles which had long ago found their way into secret collections, to be copied and databased if we were lucky, to be hidden and lost otherwise.

"Listen, Captain! Now, listen! I can give you one name—a good man, generous, a legitimate collector. But for heaven's sake protect him. Tell no-one. Toban McBanus at Villa Chano. He will help if anyone can. For the right reasons. He's in it for knowledge, not gain."

I maintained the lie. "He's one of the four I already have. Who else?"

Again the arms went out. "Don't you see? They'd know it was me. They'd kill me. Please. McBanus will know others. Let him say. Go to him. He's a buyer, a reader; he knows things. The others are like me."

"Plunderers."

"Conservators. We keep the books moving. Private collectors have always done more to conserve the arts than governments and institutions. You must know that."

"One more thing. How many arcologies are there?"

"What?"

"The old National arcologies. How many do you know exist?"

"Forty or so."

"Exactly."

Marquand went to his comp, tapped on the keys and studied the display. "Exactly thirty-four," he said, and frowned.

"What's wrong?"

"Nothing. I thought there were thirty-five. But it's thirty-four. Close."

The lie was everywhere, it seemed, and what a scale of power that implied, the ability to achieve such a task.

"Can you hard-copy that? All the names?"

Marquand touched another contact. A page slid from the printer; he passed it to me. "Are we done?"

"Not quite. Turn it off."

"What?"

"I'm leaving. But first, turn it off."

Marquand grinned suddenly. "So you can be sure."

"No, so I can see the truth. A reminder of how few collections there actually are. Because—"

"Captain—"

"Humor me, Delas, and that plan is yours along with my word."

The dealer hesitated, then worked a concealed touchpoint somewhere on the desk. The library died in a quick gulp of light, revealing more than just a space between the flanking pilasters: an alcove as deep as a walk-in closet, a bookcase to either side containing real texts, all that Delas had for sale. I saw the doorline with its tiny ramp sloping into a solid brick wall, the cleverly hidden holo-points.

"Thank you," I said, and handed him the plans and my contact number at the Gaza. "Call if you learn anything I can use. We can trade, Delas, build up favors in paradise." And allowing the truth of his earlier comment about private dealers. "Who knows? Council may even help you re-stock your shelves."

Marquand managed a chuckle at that. He re-activated illicit tech defences that were worth his life should the tribes learn of them, then led me back to the street door. We parted without another word between us.

Back out under the brilliant sky, with Marquand's door closed again in its mirror walls, I made a bundle of my tribal robes, cleaned my face as best I could, then headed for the Sand Quay. I stopped at the Gaza long enough to call Villa Chano, then hurried to see if *Rynosseros* had returned from the desert wastes of Tank Feti.

4.

I FELT A RUSH of pleasure to see the distinctive shape standing at the Quay, kites down and stowed, the professional barneys already halfway through their service checks on the hull and travel platform.

Shannon, Rim and Hammon were off at the Gaza, I learned from the gate officer, probably at the Astronomers' Bar; Strengi was below catching up on sleep after a home-leg watch. But Den had told them I was back from Turker, and Scarbo came grinning down the gangway to clasp my forearm in the Roman way the older kitesmen still used.

"Namarkon's a myth everywhere," he said. "Eternal life. Lives in a maze. One moment Melmoth the Wanderer, the next El Dorado or some other mythic figure. I've got notes. People are tight-lipped about collections though. Word is out about something."

"Feel like a walk out to Villa Chano to see Toban McBanus?"

"I know the name. Is he a bookman?"

"Delas Marquand says so."

"Marquand? You have been busy."

I could see Ben's determination to be easy company, his resolve not to ask if there'd been clues to my provenance.

"Nothing yet, Ben. But I've called McBanus. He's agreed to a visit."

"Good. So tell me about the arcologies."

WE LEFT THE SAND Quay, walked back past the Gaza Hotel and the Breaklight Pier and out through the First Gate to the Promenade, heading for the villas in the dunes to the north. We detoured down onto the beach to save ourselves the curving approach taken when the Promenade became the Beach Road, passing over the low headland out to Corlique, Mirajan and Castanelle.

It provided ample time to tell Ben about Turker Fin and the quest for L75 VGS, about something called the Alexandrian Book and the possible involvement of the Antique Men through a Gado Bascoeur, all the most tentative of leads but—at least where information about my provenance was concerned—probably the most promising. If I hadn't discovered anything conclusive about my origins from the tribes, then who better to try than the ones who frequently serviced tribal information needs?

My own discoveries quickly exhausted the modest list Scarbo had. His facts were very much those of popular folklore. Nowhere had he heard of the Alexandrian Book, nor could he recall having seen the initials AM/BG, though Tank Feti, Tank Aran and Mider were hardly places to expect much information.

Like Toth and Marquand, Ben remembered there being thirty-five National arcologies; he was absolutely certain of it—what old Trayban had said: one off a square. He greeted the news of the adjusted total with something like Marquand's frown and old Toth's pulling at his beard.

"What did Den say?" he asked as we moved along the beach.

"He accepted it very calmly. Said he'd look into it."

Ben nodded. "Well thirty-four isn't right. It's schoolboy knowledge, Tom. National history. There was a media special years ago: *Thirty-Five Chances at the Dream*. We can check that."

"Den's doing what he can. I doubt we'll find the original number listed anywhere, let alone names and locations. It's a case of making the lie big enough."

"An entire arcology! Who could do that? What about Survey Authority? The tribal universities? Their maps and records—"

"Survey says thirty-four. We aren't allowed at tribal records yet, probably won't be."

Ben stopped, brows furrowed so they made deep shadows on his grizzled, sun-tanned face. It clearly troubled him, as if the universe had gone awry because this one single truth was out of kilter. "Tom—"

"I know. Altered. Someone's plundering. Maybe McBanus can tell us something."

"It can't happen," Scarbo muttered, more to himself than to me, and for a while we walked in silence, with just the sound of wind in the sea-grass and the steady rhythm of waves falling on the shore, the hiss of foam over the sand.

Almost before we realized it, we were climbing the stairs to where the windows of Villa Chano flashed in the sun. At this angle, the sprawling house was still well concealed behind its fretwork of palms and balustrades, its domed roof of red tile looming above the whitewashed main shell.

"McBanus said forty thousand titles," I told Ben. "Mostly reference works and mote copies of paper books. We're welcome to look them over, though he fears they won't tell us much."

"More than Marquand, I bet."

I nodded, remembering the false aperture, the collection that existed only as coded light. "I think McBanus himself will be more important to us than his books."

We were at the southern turn of the rising terraces, well clear of the building itself, when lightning struck from the clear afternoon sky. The scream came an instant later, the tearing strike signal lost in the concussion of exploding masonry and tile.

At first we didn't know what had happened—it was impossible to grasp the simple shocking truth.

But in moments we knew. A laser strike from orbit. All it could be.

Then the stinging grit, dust and debris, the thump of fragments from Chano's northern wing gave the reality in terrible detail.

And the implications. The Ab'O Princes did not want us investigating books and libraries. Chiras Namarkon did not.

Namarkon, Lightning Spirit, had struck. The Immortal had access to tribal comsats, Ab'O tech.

We crouched by the terrace wall, staring in horror at what he had done—what it, they, whatever, had.

"We give it up, Tom," Ben said, close by me, a harsh whisper. "They're telling us to give it up!"

The words freed me. "McBanus was waiting in his library." I made myself say it.

Then there was a woman screaming, filling the new silence like a second strike from the sky, guiding me as I ran, cursing Namarkon, cursing the tribes, the lost arcologies and stolen futures, but most of all cursing the cold unfeeling evil that could cause a cry of such terrible loss.

I DID NOT GO back to *Rynosseros*. I stayed over at the Gaza, sitting on the balcony of Room 777, watching the sea meet the long curving shoreline of Twilight Beach.

On the terrace below, games of fire-chess had begun in earnest. There were cheers, shouts, the familiar sounds of winning and losing, of life being lived in all its myriad forms. People moved along the Promenade, wandered the Breaklight Pier in the cool evening air. To seaward, the distant islands stood against the dying light like polished stones. Off to the north, the lights of Corlique, Castanelle and the souling colonies could be seen: closer, those of the villas, all occupied this late in the season.

Except for Chano, of course, broken and empty in the dunes beside the Beach Road.

McBanus and his wife, Emma, dead. Their daughter, Truan, hospitalized, in shock.

And not a word from the tribes. Council's protests and calls for explanations, accountability, had brought none.

Though one thing was clear, an angry and worried quorum of Council had agreed. If not the tribes then, even more than Dewi Dammo, Chiras Namarkon could reach far. Lightning Spirit indeed.

Either way there was no doubting the message. Secret libraries in Twilight Beach were to remain that way. Off limits.

Which left the unvisited arcologies on the list, including the missing, mysterious thirty-fifth, as well as those difficult and expensive creatures, the Antique Men, specifically Gado Bascoeur.

So much time had passed that we no longer expected much from that quarter. I was supposedly on a tribal mission, but just as Den's repeated requests for access to the appropriate tribal records had achieved nothing, we assumed that it would be the same here. But then, just like that, his routine appeals to the Antique Men, Poste Restante, Saldy's, were rewarded. Suddenly, as if the time were right for it, the fate of the McBanus family and Chano a deciding factor, the other main avenue of enquiry had become available. I would be contacted, this evening, tomorrow, sometime soon, an agent had told Den on the phone.

After all this waiting, something at least.

I had no wish to return to *Rynosseros*. Chano preyed on my mind. Scarbo understood; the others would. There was nothing they could do but wait as I waited. Talk to people, ask questions.

I sat in the big viewing chair at the Gaza and sipped a glass of tautine. There was the old feeling of sanctuary here, so precious, something created by *these* walls, *these* familiar furnishings, *this* view out over the Gaza terrace and along the coast, by the murmur of belltrees drifting down from the roof-garden, by the spread of stars that escaped this well of light and made their net of dewpoints in the growing indigo.

Den had made the only possible deal with Bascoeur's contact: knowledge for knowledge. Whatever we learned in return for word of Namarkon or anything about my past. Anything.

But now I tried to go slow, sit back, watch old night fill the frame of the open balcony doors, and savor the cooling touch of the on-shore breeze. For a moment Chano and Namarkon were almost forgotten.

Almost.

Could the Antique Men, these ultimate bookmen, be it? If so, then how fitting, how appropriate for the times. In a world where increasingly all knowledge of that world was stored in comp systems rather than living memory, where—in the long afternoon since the Information Revolution—people had perfected the habit of automatically putting information aside, forgetting about it till it was needed again, little wonder that the "oubliettes" existed. These remarkable folk stored knowledge in an older, different fashion, in tech-assisted eidetic memory, all the lore people chose to forget or suppress, keyed by mantras and mnemonic tags, accessed by association, by ingested or injected catalysts and RNA assists. Like monks in ancient monasteries, they accumulated information of all kinds, then as generalists, specialists and synthesists, pluralists and explainers, they interpreted what they had gleaned, made conclusions, hoarded, sold, perpetuated.

They constituted what was virtually a priesthood to do this, a body of men and women (despite the carefully chosen old-world name) and specialized in the truths that State historians and tribal administrations, even the big marketing and ad agencies on the coasts, could not help but give one bias or another.

And curiously, the Princes themselves, the ones most likely to be compromised and displeased by such a state of affairs, seemed to favor the idea that these oubliettes existed, these safe-holes for storing arcane knowledge and the patterns of overview. Retrieval systems always had the facts, could offer conclusions and projections, but the Antique Men added intuition, imagination and astute judgement, allowed for the worth of feelings and impressions, for the possibility of there being *missing* facts contributing to an end.

Every viewpoint mattered in some way. By acknowledging subjectivity and applying it to a given situation, they reminded everyone of its integral role and so refined and maintained the concept of what truth could be, that, yes, it truly was the first casualty of self-interest.

To Den's amazement and constant delight, one of the popular sayings attributed to the oubliettes was a corruption of the old *faux* Angelino crime-fighter saying: "Never just the facts, no, never just the facts."

The phone rang, bringing me back from the indigo wall, the shimmering well, the splendid trap of Twilight Beach, made the laving wind just wind again.

I touched the plate. The screen showed the face of a young woman, pale, with intense grey eyes, a small clenched mouth: a severe countenance suggesting seriousness and business. Little else could be seen. She wore a close-fitting hood, like those worn by members of traditional female religious orders.

"Captain Tyson? I am Margaret Solles, notary for Gado Bascoeur. Are you available for an interview tomorrow?"

"Name a time and place."

"Tomorrow," she said. "I will call you at this number after 0900 and a meeting will be arranged. Good night."

Done. A brief sketch of a face representing such a final chance, so forgettable. But Margaret Solles. The name at least.

Chano was there then, Truan screaming, crying, Toban and Emma dead in the ruins, Marquand's wall as just a wall, all of it.

Now was no time to be alone. I went down to the Astronomers' Bar and found Scarbo, Strengi and Hammon at one of the terrace tables, and had no trouble at all persuading them to share their travelers' tales of far-off places.

MARGARET SOLLES DIDN'T CALL until mid-afternoon, leaving me to spend the morning distracted and on edge, worrying that Bascoeur may have reconsidered. At 1130 I let the desk clerks and stewards know I'd be with my friends from the Bird Club, and sat with a small group of regulars in the big chairs looking out on the Promenade. Though we discussed the Villa Chano strike, Jeremy, Sally and Nathan took my cue when I turned the subject to other things, and made no comment when I excused myself at 1300, saying I would take siesta.

The phone roused me at 1400. There on the screen was the pale face again (I was already thinking of her as the Sour Elf).

"He'll see you at Saldy's in twenty minutes, Captain."

"He'll trade?"

"He'll decide that at Saldy's. Twenty minutes. It's his time."

Meaning it wasn't mine; I needed to hurry. The screen went dark, but this time I remembered the harsh troubling gaze. This intense, serious woman was my path to Bascoeur.

5.

SALDY'S RAINHOUSE AND AVIARY had long ago outgrown its name. There were still the cosy salons with real birds sailing through tropical gardens beyond the casements, and other windows giving onto scenes of carefully controlled winters, and synthetic rains pattering on the glass before long fire-lit dinner tables.

But now additional structures had been added, extensions allowing ocean views, sun-traps and sand gardens, whitewashed loggias stretching out to the sea, steps leading down to terraces, shadowed courtyards, a hundred more quiet guest rooms, and one of the best belltree collections in all of Twilight Beach. It did not quite match the ancient splendor of the

Gaza, but for the sense of old-world luxury, antiquity and other climes it
afforded the likes of Gado Bascoeur, it was the only place the oubliettes
chose when they visited this part of the coast.

The main entrance still had its original sign, and the Sour Elf was
waiting beneath it when I arrived. She wore white desert clothing, a
djellaba with a hood drawn close about her face so that more than ever
she resembled an old-world nun, one, I fancied seeing her, who was angry
with her God, short of both faith and favor.

"Second floor. The Blue Room," she said, and I wondered what sort of
master Bascoeur could be that this young woman had become so hard and
officious in his service.

The lobby of Saldy's was a grand thing, complete with potted palms,
mosaics and lacquered screens, with small groups of guests talking quietly
in deep armchairs and conversation pits, all washed by the rich honey-
colored light from antique shades beneath slowly turning fans.

I climbed the main stairs to a first-floor mezzanine, took a smaller
flight to a side landing with three doors, one a soft midnight blue.

I knocked, waited a few moments, then turned the handle and entered.

The djellaba-shrouded figure of Bascoeur was sitting with his back to
me before a balcony that opened onto an expanse of rich blue sky.

For an instant, it was like seeing myself as I must have looked at the
Gaza the previous evening, then, of course, not at all. The colors here were
too vivid, the fittings more conspicuously ornate.

"Come in, Captain," Gado Bascoeur said in a quiet smooth voice, one
both practiced and commanding, though oddly sexless in its modulations.

I crossed to where he sat, saw more closely the stained-glass mask that
marked him as an Antique Man. Across his lap, robed arms draped loosely
over it, was an archimenter, beautifully made, a tech-fitted restoration
piece, its wooden handle chased with silver, probably a comp-assist but
possibly a laser or high-caliber ballistic for all I knew. It was strange to see
such a dedicated scholar nursing an ancient firearm.

But it was the mask that drew my attention the most. It was a faceted
dome, non-human, featureless, a deep oval-shaped bascinet, completely
covering the face like a fencing mask. The line of the central frontal panes
from which the lateral ones angled away suggested a pattern from nature:
the plates on the shell of a tortoise, or the startling geometries on the
backs of lizards. The intricate lozenges and plates of colored glass were
separated by a network of old bronzed silver, much worn from use.

I tried to make out the face inside the cage of colored panes, but there were too many frosted shapes and no clears, giving tantalizing glimpses of nose, brow and jaw, but occluded by afternoon sunlight through stressed blues, starved reds, ambers, bronzes, rich Genoese golds, teals and turquoises, streaked submarine greens.

"Twenty minutes I was told."

"Meg can be overzealous," he said. "We have all the time you need. I would very much like to hear about Dewi Dammo."

I drew a chair to the side of Bascoeur's own, out of the line of sight of the sky and the ocean below, wanting to watch the light play on what I could see of the man's features. I made myself comfortable and began.

It took twice the twenty minutes Meg had allowed. Now and then, the long brown fingers lifted and fell on the side plate of the archimenter, tapping out an irregular rhythm.

At first I thought he was touch-recording facts or mnemonic codes, knowing that the device was probably a storage-trap fashioned to look like a gun, but then noticed that the tips of those fingers made no contact with the surface of the ritual weapon. He was simply working through a memory pattern. If he noticed my attention, the momentary slowing and distraction in my account, he gave no sign.

Finally I was done. There were his questions then, another twenty minutes of them: about Dewi and my present search both for Namarkon and for information about my forgotten past. I forced myself to ask no questions of my own, just watched the fingers moving in their gentle flute pattern all the while. But finally they paused and there was a different silence, an almost disquieting lull in which I studied the covered face, the gorgeous panes in their stepped, angling curves. They made a cathedral dome, a bright orrery in which the solitary planet was Bascoeur's skull and all that it contained, a world, a universe inside another, inside yet another.

I studied, too, the small flower sign he wore high on his chest, periwinkle blue on the sand-colored robe, an embroidered Forget-Me-Not, fitting choice for the oubliettes. Inevitably, my attention wandered into the intricate sign embroidered at the shoulder—a sect patch it seemed, a sequence of many dots, some linked into cruciform patterns by looping lines, overlapping and bolder at the center, the whole shape bordered by darker dots. It suggested a circuit pattern or an elaborate code, an ideogram, some mystical sign of power.

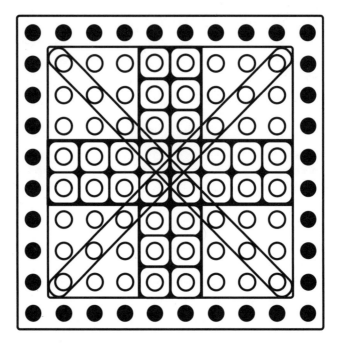

Bascoeur placed his hands squarely on the weapon in his lap. "What do you need from me, Captain?"

"I went to Turker Fin."

"I know."

"Dewi mentioned Chiras Namarkon in connection with a library. The tribesman who gave me this mission confirmed it. I went to the seven National libraries I was told officially existed. There may be more, though I doubt it now. We are being shut off from our past; eventually we will have to go outside Australia to learn about our National heritage."

"Go on, please."

"All the Chiras Namarkon references I did find had been excised, or rather relegated to 'dead stack' status, one text only, one Illuminated Book kept at Crayasse. L75 VGS. But at Crayasse I learned that it was on loan to Turker, had been moved on just before I arrived. That Book was sent to Turker for a reason, and I expected to find it gone, sent elsewhere, unable to be located."

"Yes?" The long fingers resting on the archimenter did not move now, though the hands were angled out from Bascoeur's body like minatory wings, pointed at the ocean and the sweep of sky. It looked wonderful and strange, barely human.

"I saw L75 VGS. It's in poor condition. The Reader Page misfunctions. The entry for Namarkon cancels itself. But I learnt something."

"Yes?"

"There were the appended summaries, etymological references to the old languages, the traditional mythological identification of Namarkon as Lightning Spirit, as a tree struck by lightning, that sort of thing. And there is an entry for a *Chiras* Namarkon."

Bascoeur said nothing. I watched him intently, as if I were hoping to read something in the set of his body, the colors of the mask, the blue Forget-Me-Not on his robe, traditionally the flower of friendship and fidelity, in the intricate tangle of the sect patch which kept snaring my eye and had me wondering what it could possibly mean for people like these.

"Chiras Namarkon," I continued, "is identified as the Immortal, described variously as a creature of fable, as a tyrant hidden away in his labyrinth—his library—as a great wanderer, a highwayman, it goes on and on. He has the secret of knowledge, of ideas and words. He has treasure. But you know this, Lord Gado."

"I do?" The long hands still pointed like emblematic wings.

"A status request tag is yours. There has been an attempt to suppress knowledge of such a figure, making it dead stack, hard to locate. The time and trouble that took must have been considerable. I suspect that even were I to have access to the tribal libraries and the universities, there would be as little information. The tribes must know about Namarkon for his part in their affairs to be effective, that he is non-Ab'O, extremely long-lived, but they need not know too much."

"You assume a great deal. But you are telling me something."

"The tribes know my limitations, the unlikelihood of my finding anything without assistance. It would take me years to locate even a few of the private libraries. Chano was destroyed; Marquand is a fraud. So why send me? Unless you can provide clues or are involved in some way. Unless you wanted it to *seem* like that. You avoided answering Den's calls for quite some time. There's a reason. Namarkon could well be one of you. An oubliette. A secret master of oubliettes. The tribes may suspect this."

"We don't keep libraries in the traditional sense, Captain."

"You *are* libraries."

Bascoeur paused before answering. "Of course. It's all worth considering."

"Which part?"

"All of it. Namarkon."

"How many oubliettes are there?"

"A total number is hard to give. There are trainees, honorary postings—"

"Like you."

"Like me? Thirty-six."

"And leaders?"

"Four officers out of that number. We call them Angels."

"More and more like a holy order. Are you an Angel?"

"Yes. This information is costing you, Captain."

"Then let me complete the trade. Will you take me to where oubliettes are trained? Any place where Antique Men gather?"

"We operate as solitaries. What leads you—?"

"Dewi ruled by creating then monopolizing an economic/religious condition, tapping into what was almost a theocracy. Another effective power-base must be information flow, the non-partisan trafficking in knowledge and strategies and historical perspective. The tribes can afford you."

Finally the hands moved again, turning in slightly, fingers angling, moving, completing a quick manipulation on the air. "I admit to being impressed."

"No, you will have anticipated I would come to this from the moment the tribes approached me."

Bascoeur made no response, though his hands had become still again. It appeared that I had his complete attention.

"First, there was virtually nothing on libraries," I said, "so few are declared. The black market in books means most true-book collections stay private and secret. Council gave what listings their systems had, but I'm allowing for interference now, tampering with National data-stores. But I accept that the privates are incomplete anyway, not just inaccessible. They will be depleted, the best items sold off or plundered long ago. The university and tribal libraries are off limits, as you know."

"Do I, Captain?"

"I believe you know my position, Lord Gado. I went to the Pandeon here in Twilight Beach, then out to some of the old arcologies. Crayasse gave me a lead, something called Alexandrian Book. Den has techs and archivists doing searches; he's even done a tentative costing on consulting individual tribal archives well favored to Nation, should they relent, though that would alert too many people."

Bascoeur turned his head slightly, like the apse of a living cathedral, a crystal flower turning with the light, filled with light. I was amused by the theatricality of the action, but awed too. He was not play-acting a role, this oubliette, however much his manner often suggested it: the composed gestures, the mannered speech. Rather he was a uniquely alienated and uniquely engaged individual, someone curiously but necessarily estranged from my worldview with its immediacy, its tribal conflicts and striving Princes, its Dewi Dammos and deadly Namarkons. Could Chiras fit such a *Weltanschauung*? If so, then so so different from Dewi.

"The tribes would not tell you anything," Bascoeur said flatly. "What happened to Chano confirms that. And Dammo's death—his presumed death—had immediate repercussions. As a port official, James Namuren's part could not be lightly overlooked. Some Princes sought Convocation and payback; some even now push to re-assess not only the charling leases but all National concessions. The secret libraries are off limits for a reason; the Antique Men will be denied you soon. You were given this mission by a faction, an interest group, that saw a small closing window of opportunity."

"Then how can I possibly locate Namarkon?"

Bascoeur's left hand lifted as if to counsel patience. "You have imputed that Namarkon is one of us. I am intrigued and alarmed by that notion. But there are things we can do before the embargo falls. In fact"—he angled his head so a turquoise pane flashed richly—"that's precisely why *I* came to Saldy's. The management protects its patrons. I came here unmasked. Only you and Meg know I am here. I did this to forestall official injunctions reaching me."

"Surely not out of gratitude for my account of finding Dewi! You're playing this for you. Someone moved that Book to delay me, but whoever it was could have confiscated it altogether. I was delayed while some interested party searched for something else. The Book was deliberately damaged before it arrived at Turker."

"Deliberately, you think? A sealed Book?"

"The librarian said so. You could do it. Since I did find an entry which led me to you as much as it did to Namarkon, I'm left to wonder what part the Antique Men play in this—and what they might have gained by delaying me, by damaging a text, then *letting* it lead me to them."

Bascoeur turned his head back to the sea and the sky. Some of the panes on his mask seemed to have special optical properties: one shone with the lustrous velvet mauve-green of a dragonfly's eye, another with the rich roiling highlights of oil struck by rain.

"Pretend for a moment, Captain, that I am not Chiras Namarkon, nor his confederate in any way. Assume I am a very concerned member of my order, an Angel, concerned about libraries too. Consider that where the oubliettes are concerned, the Princes and Clever Men have one commitment greater than using us to control the flow of information as feudal societies once did after the fall of Rome and Constantinople, during that great and terrifying European Dark Age we are determined must never happen again."

"Very well."

"Back then, distortion of facts occurred more through ignorance, ineptitude, superstition and the limits of technology than deliberate disinformation, mythopoesis or strictures imposed by church and state. Now we have a carefully, wonderfully controlled program of distortion, of expert myth-making. Nothing new really, but more effective in a cultural horizon so devoted to the idea of total sharing, where genuine information flow *seems* to be encouraged. 'A thousand truths for the one well-placed lie' is an oubliette saying, remember."

"So what are *you* saying, Lord Gado?"

"Historians and archivists are more circumspect today, but the liberalising of information by comp, sat-scan, gain-monitor is a myth too. It has led to closed societies, intensively applied media falsehood, reclusive overlords like Dammo and Namarkon, the re-medievalizing of attitudes and fact-finding processes, all the counters in the information web. We acquire more myth and legend, more contamination and carefully planted disinformation than ever before, you realize, in direct proportion to any documented truth. Tactical lies created and nurtured by the strategists and propagandists, refined and promoted by local and international agencies. The Information Revolution, Tom Rynosseros, is over simply because it continues, a wonderful paradox! Call it affective filtering or whatever, it is our condition now. There is too much to know. More and more *we* are becoming verifiers and discriminators rather than information givers."

I studied this man, capable of the Zen rigor, so full of intricate knowledge. The air of cynicism and weariness he brought to our conversation was a tactic, I felt, a way to test my own reactions perhaps. Or maybe he was a man in crisis, revealing a new alarming truth he dared not share with his fellow oubliettes.

I recalled the lack of surprise I'd felt when Kaber Fen Otamas had told me of the ongoing prospect of secret rulers like Dewi and now this Namarkon appearing, powerfully, vigorously, active in the interstices of that suborned information glut. Not even State of Nation had too many illusions in its quest for identity and survival, not after the watergating of history: the Bolo Mays, Nixons and Richelieus, the Viet Nams and Sinchwens, the para-governmental agencies: the CIA and Mossad, the Mafia, Camorra, Yakuza, Talion and their corporate variants—the Machiavellian heritage uncovered and refined during a few key centuries, power vacuums filled, well or badly, but inevitably.

"Before Turker," I said, "I expected to hear from the Antique Men. Council tried to arrange meetings without success; no doubt you had reasons. I'd become a vital integer in something, cutting across patterns, revealing structures. Now you seem to suggest that the *tribes* are tampering with your people."

Bascoeur raised a cautionary hand. "If not the tribes then some tribal agency operating as Namarkon, whoever, whatever he, she, it is. He is in his library somewhere. What does he do there? How does he rule his portion? He may have more knowledge than all of us, even more than the tribes, may in fact be comp, AI, someone or something as long-lived as Dewi was, immortal, building ideas into history, a mythopoeticist skilfully, effectively controlling and disseminating concepts, fostering his illusions and fictions, immediate and long-term. I am very worried, personally alarmed, that the Antique Men, allowed access everywhere, may be infiltrated by Namarkon's agents, that one of my associates may in fact be Chiras Namarkon. The very thought of it brings a fear you cannot understand."

"What do you suggest?"

"We depend on tribal favor; we do not run our own ships. Except for a few closed towns, you can take *Rynosseros* where you please."

"Unless they strike as they did at Chano."

"A reasonable risk. You hold a mandate and a Color. Your name is in the Great Passage Book."

"That may not worry Namarkon at all. After Balin that may not worry the tribes either. Go on."

"We seek Namarkon together, at least until I am satisfied that the Antique Men are *not* involved in his schemes."

"Then?"

"Then our usual rules apply. We pay you with knowledge for what *you* give us."

"Can I see where the oubliettes are trained? Allowing for the fact that I might wish to search on after you have satisfied yourself, allowing that I am still considering you or one of your kind for Namarkon, that I was delayed a month in finding L75 VGS."

"Agreed. But, Captain, we must act immediately. If the tribes continue to move against you, hinder you; if the oubliettes are denied you—either because Namarkon is working among us for the tribes and not just himself, or because you must be stopped anyway—then what I do now is outside the law. All Antique Men will pay for any indiscretions I now commit."

"Then, as you say, word must not reach us. *Rynosseros* is at the Sand Quay. Come aboard tonight, whenever you can. We sail at 0600."

"Very well," Bascoeur said. "And Meg will accompany us. But leave now, please. I must consider this possibility of treachery."

6.

I DID NOT SEE Meg Solles when I left Saldy's, but quickly headed along the late afternoon streets to the Promenade, followed that towards the decks, loggias and famous terraces of the Gaza, bright now with the last hour of sunlight, the windows flashing like a vast replica of Bascoeur's mask.

Though it was still that hour till the breaklight, the time of day for which Twilight Beach is named, there were players of fire-chess already at the boards, their tiny lines of fighters dancing in the sea-wind. These were short-lived suicide games, full of braggadocio and fun, recklessly played because the wind allowed opportunity for little else. The players laughed and performed at their eccentric best. The tourists and hotel guests cheered every bold move, and cheered as enthusiastically each time a tiny flame was extinguished.

Soon, when the wind lost its edge and the Hotel's tuxedoed Devil Catchers appeared, ready to beat at the dust-devils with their long-handled spoilers, these flamboyant posturings would cease. The grins and extravagant flourishes would be replaced by looks of concentration and a ruthless urbanity famous the world over.

When I turned into the Gentian Walk, that narrow walled avenue connecting Tramway Street to the southern end of the Gaza terrace, I found three Ab'Os leaning on the seawall watching the ocean. They wore fighting leathers under their djellabas, and had sheathed kitanas over their shoulders, not an uncommon thing, but an uncommon place for tribesmen to loiter.

I read the scene quickly enough, had it confirmed when the men recognized me, quickened and moved back from the wall to block my path. They wore vendetta marks on their cheeks, bands of color and soul-taking stars in turquoise and deep red. The swords were slashes of light leaving their scabbards.

I had nothing but my sailor's sticker in the leg-sheath of my fatigues, though reaching for it meant I had accepted their terms.

One tribesman in his early thirties, older than the others, moved forward.

"I am Ephan Sky Namuren," he said. "Kin to James Namuren. This is payback."

"But not legal," I said, desperately seeking words that would prevent this. "As Blue Captain on a tribal mission I am not allowed to fight you. Will this be murder then? More shame for Namuren?"

"You are allowed," Ephan said, as if he had not heard the final words. "And you have your deck-knife."

"Which might grow into a kitana someday, certainly. You are brave men."

Another spoke then, pushing past Ephan. "I am Paul Dharajan. Stories say you were trained by the Spaniard, Marco, and the Japanese, Tensumi. A sticker is enough for you."

"Stories! I wish I could remember living so long to have all these stories." I searched the empty Walk and the fiercely marked faces for any sign of advantage. Was this it then? A final afternoon? A last vital encounter? How many of us ever choose the places where we die?

I drew my sticker, its narrow blade as long as my forearm. "Who claims the right?" I said, formally.

The men exchanged glances, quick bright smiles.

"We all do," Ephan said. "For our kinsman."

"Judged traitor by Convocation," I reminded them. "You will be sung for this. Be sure of it."

More glances at that, the smiles gone, replaced by carefully neutral looks, though I imagined I did see traces of worry, doubts about assurances given.

"The terms then," I continued, hoping someone would enter the Walk, someone armed or who might summon help. But they had chosen their time well. "From the first drop of blood you are damned. They watch!" And I looked up into the late afternoon sky to where the invisible satellites held station, whichever orbitals were currently geo-tethered to Twilight Beach.

Paul Dharajan moved forward. "Come, Ephan! No-one watches this!"

"Good, Dharajan," I said, dropping to a first position. "I am hunting Namarkon but you will do."

The Ab'O grinned, confirming the source of the strike, the direction from which assurances had ultimately come, filtering down through tribal lobbies.

Again I tried for the initiative. "Though he too is hunted by his enemies. Of course they watch. Can they monitor this small stretch, do you think?"

Dharajan did not answer. Ephan and the other man moved forward as well until five meters were all there was.

I raised my sticker and cut my own cheek, just as I had at Balin, let them see the blood shining on my blade. Then I looked immediately into the sky. "Take them all, Namarkon!"

Ephan looked up, his companions as well. It was reflex.

A wisp of cloud had drifted into view, seemed frozen there.

Then Dharajan cried out in pain and surprise, blood streaming from his throat where my sticker now stood, small deft lightning. He dropped his sword with a single cry and collapsed to the stones.

I lunged for the weapon in what scant seconds I had, but Ephan was better than that, well-trained, well-chosen. His foot came down on the discarded blade, denying me. His own sword arced towards my outstretched arm, to my neck where I lay, head to the side, fingers touching the haft.

The edge, the line of separation, was right there. One twist, one thrust, and I would cease to be, know, feel. No throb of bleeding cheek, no pain in knee and shoulder from the fall, no knowing this desperate attempt at life. I looked along the gleaming blade to Ephan's painted face, his flashing eyes, beyond them to the patch of sky, the frozen wisp of cloud, infinitely precious.

"Fight me," Ephan said, stepping back, leaving Dharajan's blade, seeking something of honor in a poor mission, only now truly understood.

"No!" his companion cried. "His orders!"

His. The word said it all.

"Personal honor, Sab! Decide for yourself when he is armed."

I seized the hilt, slick with Dharajan's blood, and stood, heart pounding, thoughts racing one to the next, seeking a solution.

Ephan was there almost immediately, and the Walk rang, echoed with the clash of weapons.

Despite my two blades, long and short, it was all I could do to defend, and in a sense Ephan helped me there. He was too good a swordsman; Sab could not engage without ruining Ephan's patterns. What trade-offs there were between them, a concession to face, showed Sab to be an inferior fighter, though not to be taken lightly.

Slowly, in the constant jarring of the three-way, I managed to regain my center. More and more deflections were controlled, more and more feints planned and resolved by me.

Ephan withdrew. Sab leapt in, jumped back with a slashed sleeve and a look of astonishment.

"Marco and Tensumi, remember!" Ephan warned, breathing hard, then filled the air again with his own lightning.

Every breath was drawn over fire now. Arms ached from the repeated blows of the exquisite many-folded blades.

If not resolved soon, Ephan would have me. He was too good. I brought Marco and Tensumi to mind—real, RNA assists from the Madhouse, another lost or false memory, who could say?—then waited for Sab's turn, let him begin, and swapped blades, right hand to left, deflected his sword with my own and took him above the heart with the sticker, through djellaba, fighting leathers and all, the blade in, out and gone, whipped away, lightning through fire it seemed, so sudden.

Again there was the look of astonishment, intense and final as the eyes glazed and his life went out of him. I had cleared the blade before he knew what had happened.

"See what—they—have done to you," I managed, exhausted, dangerously so, watching Ephan's eyes. "His orders!"

"Whose—" Ephan's breathing was ragged too. "—do you think?"

"One—who doesn't care what happens. You—don't count. Expendable, hear? If not you—others."

Ephan nodded, darted quick glances at his dead companions, assessing what had been paid. No fool this one, simply a man trapped by duty.

"What do I have?" he asked.

"You were not here," I said. He had given me my chance; now I held out Dharajan's kitana for him to take.

He nodded and took it, saluted with his own sword, then turned, vanishing through the crowd of sightseers and hotel guests who had gathered on the Walk.

I entered the Gaza and found Scarbo and Shannon, but at the far side of that grand room from where the swordplay had just now taken place. The sounds had not reached them through the press of guests and tourists, the forest of sanche palms, the lacquered and enamelled screens, the great pillars and sculptury.

I drew many looks crossing that great room, and when my friends saw me they immediately went to rise. I waved them back, gratefully taking the glass of tautine Shannon pushed towards me, fire for the fire, the shaking, for the simple joy of being alive.

"Namarkon almost achieved what Dewi couldn't," I said. "Three bravos decided to brawl. The cheek is mine, a bit of payback psychology that didn't work."

Ben and Rob smiled, though the smiles were thin and quickly gone. Something else was amiss.

"What?"

"Den's hurt," Ben said. "Archimenter discharge—or an equivalent. Some time around 1600. He's in deep shock."

"Archimenter? Will he survive?"

"They think so. He's in a sleeve at Gallo's and responding. There's been surgery as well. He has Bylon heart tailoring; it was thrown out of kilter."

"But archimenter?" I thought of the rich data store, the concentration of energy in the weapon, the "six years of dream" as it was called: the amount of time in the old seventy-year, pre-nano lifespan that the average person spent dreaming. "He couldn't survive it!"

Scarbo shook his head. "Nothing like full charge. Perhaps it was just a warning. But Kurdaitcha came, said they were looking for Gado Bascoeur."

"Not Bascoeur. I've been with him since 1500. And he wouldn't incriminate himself with an archimenter; none of his people would."

"Namarkon, you think?" Shannon asked.

"Who can say, Rob? An extreme point and a clumsy way of making it."

Scarbo set down his glass. "Den may have found something. Possibly plundered from Nation's systems."

"We don't have time to find out." I leant forward, spoke the next words almost as a whisper. "Bascoeur will come aboard tonight. We leave tomorrow at first light. Half-crew."

"Where?" Scarbo asked.

"When we're aboard, Ben. Find the others. Briefing at 1900. But half-crew."

7.

WE FLED FROM TWILIGHT Beach, that was how it felt, rushing along the Great Arunta Road with the sun barely above the line and thirty kites in the sky, great Sodes and Demis, a dozen racing footmen. There was no pursuit.

We had minimum crewing. By Ben's roster Rim, Strengi and Hammon were down for leave anyway, and so became part of a last-minute deception. They drank with the sandsmen and veteran sailors at the Astronomers' Bar, let themselves be seen gaming at Deep's late into the night. It was likely that no-one expected to see *Rynosseros* pulling away from the Sand Quay, lofting her kites at first light.

It was busy work for Scarbo, Shannon and me with a vessel the size of ours. For that dawn hour, we hurried about the commons, fitting kites to cables, checking the separations, Scarbo judging the shift from coastal to inland winds and making choices, shouting them to us or signing in the traditional way of the aeropleuristic craft.

Bascoeur and Meg watched from the quarterdeck, the oubliette unreadable in his mask, his assistant equally so behind her severe pale face, both shapeless in their traveling robes. The Antique Man had his hood raised and drawn well forward over his mask, a small precaution but one observed just in case.

Who could say if the tribes cared or if Namarkon watched? Bascoeur was probably right. Lightning against Chano was one thing; a strike at a mandated ship, a Colored Captain, at someone listed in the Great Passage Book, was something else entirely. I recalled Dewi's mirror ships, permitted but watched and finally punished from orbit. It might be that Namarkon existed by exploiting Ab'O need, tribal vulnerability. He might very well safeguard the values that kept his power-base secure, perhaps aiming—my real fear in this!—to extend himself beyond any need of their goodwill.

Appropriating laser strike was privilege enough; possessing a Namarkon comsat of his own would be absolute crisis, not only death-strike capability but information saturation as well. What Kaber Fen Otamas had told me seemed more real than ever.

THE STOWAWAY APPEARED WHEN we were almost at Wani.

Bascoeur was at the port rail of the quarterdeck, lost in his thoughts and assimilations, with Meg waiting to one side. Shannon was with Scarbo at the kite lockers laying cable runs, only occasionally glancing at the canopy overhead, not needing to do so since they read the tensions in the hull and overheads so well.

I had the helm, watching the Road and some distant cloud-forms that could spell wind and so kite-change, enjoying how our canopy spread upon the sky like a bright hand, a taut receding thrust of light and color.

Meg saw her first, a noon-specter appearing on the commons to for'ard, beyond the intricate totemic webwork of the cable-boss.

"Look!" she cried, and the light was such that the figure startled us all. It was like the mirages you often see, the transit-ghosts you expect out on the Serafina, along the Soul or in the inner deserts, not snared here beneath the sky-trap of kites and displayed in full sunshine.

Only for a second. It resolved from dream to real in moments. Our visitor came walking across the commons, a woman in her mid-twenties, taller than any but Bascoeur in his shrouded jewel-box mask, with wide clear eyes and fine features in a face I found I knew, with the small talenti marks, three to each side, tatooed in ochre at the curve of the jawline: a member of Club Hetaera. She wore desert fatigues that were the same sandy-white as her short hair. Meg Solles was pale; this striking young woman was the whitened gold of wheatfields in sunshine.

Scarbo followed her up to the helm, waiting till she spoke, though I'd already heard the echo of her scream from the ruins of Chano.

"Thank you for what you did," she said, bringing back the ruin of lives.

"Why are you here, Truan?" I asked.

She smiled wearily. "I'm hetaera. I can give Namarkon his due."

Bascoeur moved forward from the rail, vivid and powerful. "Who told you that name?"

"I knew why Captain Tyson was visiting Chano," she answered evenly. "Marquand phoned. We are women who do, Lord Oubliette."

"It is an age when too many well-intentioned people seek to do, Ms. McBanus. The Bird Club. The Hetaera. Nation Council. This is a private mission. Put back, Captain. We cannot go on."

"With respect, Lord," Truan said, and brought forth a wire from the pocket of her fatigues: the feed-point of a gain-monitor. "Nothing is more private than my task. There was conversation when you came aboard last night, and again this morning. I heard the word Whitehead, the name of the destination you gave Captain Tyson."

The Antique Man looked at her, or looked at a point of infinity on the inside of his glass cage. Near him, Meg let her own face show her master's controlled rage, the measure of it she imagined. Bascoeur was a pragmatist. I doubted he would be angry for long.

"Then continue," he said—to me undoubtedly though the mask gave no certainty of it—then left the quarterdeck. Meg went too, like a bruise Bascoeur chose to carry with him, a penitential badge. I wondered at the nature of that secret agreement between them, what intimacy was lodged in that relentless service. I wondered too if our stowaway might not end up with an archimenter taking her mind as it nearly had Den's.

"You make it difficult," I told our unwanted guest. "Truan, I need that man. He's the only lead I have. And how is it you own a gain-monitor? That needs tribal authorization."

"My father's," she said. "He often worked for the tribes, needed to authenticate dealers and couriers. The tribes allowed it on loan. They may assume it was destroyed."

Full crew would have stopped her, I kept telling myself, found her in the empty storage bay. Hammon's job, or Rim's. Our ruse had done it, our clever ploy.

"Captain, like you I have only this," she said. "How would you proceed if you were in my place? Blame and punish? You're undermanned. I know enough of kites not to be in the way."

"Then stay near Scarbo. Ben, give her a place. And stay away from Bascoeur and his assistant!"

She said no more, went quietly down to the lockers and the armatures. There was wind-change coming and she showed no small degree of skill helping Shannon bring in the top-kites, drawing the outstretched hand into a fist, tethered close now and beating at the sky.

BASCOEUR SEEMED TO HAVE accepted Truan's presence when he returned to the poop an hour later. He came without Meg, thank goodness, and watched the Road from as close to my station at the helm as he could stand without disturbing me, though I sensed his presence, the flashing glance from the front of the hood, the tortoise panes throwing so many jewels back at the sun.

"She has no choice," he said finally. "Home and family are gone."

"Yes," I said, respecting him for this compassion, though it meant betraying self-interest. "So, Turker, then Whitehead."

"Agreed. Though I'm curious as to why Turker is necessary. It can't be L75 VGS. I can do no more to work a faulty Book than the librarian."

"I need information on AI, on crystalline intelligence."

"Pursuing the obvious," Bascoeur said.

I shrugged. "What can you tell me?"

"To save you time? That, yes, our masks are nanotech-constructed crystalline lattices with ambient temperature superconductivity, made essentially by a conventional nano assembler. That the internal circuitry is mixed, electronic and cortico-optical, with vested laser tech for data volume, that the power needs are minimal. Parts of my body have been bio-adapted to supply that, more old science really. It gives over 1900 times the storage capacity of the human brain and can be one million times as fast."

"Thank you," I said. "Will you remove your mask and talk about this?"

I expected a flat refusal, so his reply surprised me.

"Yes, though you cannot know how I resent needing to, resent the fact that nothing else can convince you now."

"You might be Namarkon and not know it. Part of Namarkon."

"So easily caught? Why would I? Why would some Antique Man collective—"

"Potentially a vast nanotech computer."

"—let us meet?"

"You know the answer. You've become an only chance."

"Because of Chano?"

"Yes." It seemed so unlikely now that Namarkon, like poor mad Dewi, would willingly make himself—itself?—so vulnerable. I wished I had Truan's monitor, but knew that no oubliette would ever agree to use one.

"Tonight I will be without my mask," Bascoeur said. "But remember, Captain, we are here now only because I—as Angel—need to consider my own kind impartially, to explore leads of my own."

"Will you answer another question then?"

"You can ask it."

"There were thirty-five National arcologies before the tribes drove us back to the coasts. Now official lists show only thirty-four. How many are there?"

"Thirty-five," Bascoeur said calmly, and the excitement I felt made me demand what I should have requested.

"Which one is missing? Why?"

"That is my other search, Captain. Locating that site. Separate from yours, for my reasons, unless I decide it concerns you."

"Should it? Please, Lord Gado—"

"The unlisted arcology is Mekkis. An old Hebrew name."

"Turker might tell us where—"

"I have tried there already. Tried them all. Captain, in Hebrew 'mekkis' means 'power.'"

"Namarkon!" I cried.

Truan and Scarbo glanced up when I said it.

"Yes," Bascoeur said. "The general deletion of that name suggests it. And some tribal connection to be able to hide such a thing. Hard to misplace a city."

Truan was approaching the quarterdeck. Meg Solles came hurrying from the bow, revealing by the determination of her stride, by the fixed direction of her gaze, more about her humanity and that of her master. Bascoeur may have accepted the reality of Truan's situation, Meg Solles clearly had not.

But Gado Bascoeur served no master on this ship. He turned away, showing by his manner that he was apart, so that when Truan and Meg arrived, one tentatively, not wanting to intrude, the other determined and hurrying, they were left regarding one another across the width of the quarterdeck.

I was watching the sky and the Road ahead as surely as Bascoeur watched the desert around us, but I sensed the contest that Truan suddenly found herself part of. Being hetaera, she did not leave it unspoken.

"I am not interested in your oubliette," she said simply. "You need fear nothing from me."

"That's not it at all!" Meg answered angrily, which told us it was something as human, as desperate and needful.

Truan returned to the commons, and Meg was left with the silent rebuke of Bascoeur's back. I felt for her as she headed for'ard to watch the desert and to cool whatever longing had been revealed.

When Shannon took the helm at 1600, I made my way forward to where the notary sat on the starboard bench, her hood back, revealing her cropped black hair. Without the hood to frame her pale face, she looked more childlike and vulnerable than ever.

"She's wrong," Meg Solles said. "That's not it."

I sat beside her. "Then why behave as if it were?"

She blinked, frowned. "None of you knows what this man suffers here, what it means to examine the possibility of treason. He has infinities stored in his head, a custodianship of ages and civilization; now he endures this action against his order, sacrificing *time* from so many other duties."

"Caused by me."

"Yes," she said, and her mouth contracted into the Sour Elf's once more.

"Why do you follow him? Serve him?"

"It's an honor. I get to learn. I might even be trained."

"How long has it been?"

She shrugged. "Five years. Six. A few have companions, not all. The Angels always do. We are servants, notaries, sometimes friends. We do what is needed."

"What is needed."

"Nothing like that!" she snapped. "They don't need that! Sometimes it would be better if they did. They are androgynes, did you know? Both sexes."

The information startled me.

"Don't ask about it, Captain. The answer is lost in hermetic lore. In alchemical beginnings we will never understand. It's a tradition. I accept it."

"Meg—"

"I accept it!"

"You don't—"

"It's the honor of service that keeps me here, not physical love!"

"Do you know my situation?" I asked her, to turn the conversation away from her relationship.

She nodded. "Lord Gado told me." Her mouth softened; the child in her defeated the bitter, practiced lines around her mouth. "You are very brave."

"No," I said, laughing. "No, Meg. You are brave, who give so much from love. I just find myself taking a direction, doing what I can to discover my beginnings. Now my world has been touched again. A friend was harmed at Twilight Beach. Truan's parents are dead, her home destroyed. Desperation becomes duty. We are similar there, you and I. Life makes its own purpose, as always."

"At least you are doing. That is brave!"

"Then we are brave together. And Gado Bascoeur is very brave to do this."

"Yes," she said, grateful, and there it was: a smile, also elfin, small and tentative on that lonely face.

"Meg, since you know something of the courtesies and protocols of the Antique Men, I would rather ask you some of my questions than put them to Lord Gado and use his time. It is a way I can spare him but gain knowledge that may help him as much as me."

"What questions?"

"The patch on his shoulder. What is that?"

"The Forget-Me-Knot," she said.

"The patch, not the flower."

"It's the Forget-Me-Knot! K-N-O-T. The oubliette sign. A schematic of the flower, I don't know, something like that. A molecular schema."

"Is that what he told you?"

Meg shrugged. "You see this as a key to Namarkon?"

The question, those words, made me hesitate a moment. "Anything could be. I've learned that signs and symbols can matter very much. On the Inland Sea there is a woman for whom the ellipsis of Inner Eye means everything."

"Tallin Okani. The one who hunts the special charling."

"Yes. For Den and Council, the Bladed Sun of Nation means so much."

"It's a windmill," she said. "Those converging triangles. An ancient windmill!"

"I've heard that. What people wear and show is important."

"Unless they are concealing and misleading. Dissembling. Using signs and symbols."

"True," I said. "But not this patch, I suspect. That design is important."

"You must ask Bascoeur about the Knot." She was becoming the Elf again, so accustomed to standing between her lord and the world. "He might unravel it for a questing Alexander like you."

And the new smile was bright and hard, a fully made thing. She had referred to the plaque fixed to the helm of *Rynosseros*, to the words once attributed to Alexander the Great by an ancient writer:

One must live as if it would be forever, and as if one might die each moment. Always both at once.

"Perhaps if we do not unravel that particular Knot first, Meg, someone else might cut it asunder. I want to save your master as well."

"It is ancient, from the founding of the order. A circuit mat, or the design of a sacred tile from Alexandria, from Hellenistic times. But Gado could have been joking about it. I don't know what is true."

Gado, she had said this time, without "Lord" before it. "Keep it in your thoughts, please. At any time Gado might decide we should part, and I truly would like to help him before that happens, to put his mind at ease. Like it or not, the Antique Men form a living library. That Knot on his sleeve looks like a labyrinth to me, formed by a nanotech computer of oubliette masks."

"You've told him you suspect this?"

"He will have guessed where my thinking leads. To an extent my speculations help him, give necessary objectivity; past a certain point they are intrusions."

"Insults."

"Unfortunately."

"I'll keep what you ask in mind. For his sake."

I stood. "Thank you, Meg. For his sake."

8.

Bascoeur kept his word. After 1900, Shannon brought *Rynosseros* to the edge of the Road for our night mooring, selecting an area well clear of the graded surface, though it was doubtful any other ships would be coming now.

Around us, nothing could be seen but darkening sweeps of sand and low scrub, every ridge and stone with its long shadow, the scraps from which night was being made. The sun was a half-coin, shedding the last of its gold at the horizon.

The oubliette had gone below a little after 1750. Now, while Scarbo saw to the cable-boss and Truan and Shannon swept up the wind-wrack from the day's travel, and with Meg off somewhere by herself, Bascoeur re-appeared—and without his fabulous headgear.

In spite of what Meg had said about the androgyny, he was clearly a man—of indeterminate age, I noted, though possibly in his early forties, pale-skinned, dark-haired and with thin brows and a fine neck and jaw. The eyes were dark in the growing gloom, the nose narrow and straight, almost too sharp, a disturbingly severe feature on such an otherwise regular face. In the last of the light, I could see a pair of fine silvery scars at his temples.

"Salvation Moons we call them," Bascoeur said, not needing to be asked. "Signs of humility and self-denial. More symbols."

I smiled. Meg had told him of our conversation then, had no doubt seen it as her duty.

The oubliette's voice was very much as it was when he was masked, well-modulated, with something of the contralto about it, almost sexless. He moved with his customary grace and economy as he joined me at the port rail, wearing his robe still, the flower and the Knot patch clear in the fading light.

"What now, Captain?"

I was used to his words coming through planes of glass. Seeing lips forming them was strange, as if a voice transmission had been lip-synced to an actor or a clever mankin.

"First, thank you for this. I believe I understand something of what it means. I would like to walk out there a way, the two of us. Do you mind?"

"Very well," he said, and followed me over to the gangway and down onto the sand.

We walked in silence until *Rynosseros* was a far-off thing, backlit with a flush of indigo and the most lustrous purple, like an offering to old gods, a cresset of embers set out beneath a sky that was brilliant with early stars and sparked with meteorites now and then. It reminded me that it was "out" as well as "up," and that Chiras Namarkon ruled some part of it as Lightning God, as the Immortal.

"The patch?" I asked finally, Meg having removed any need for delicacy in the matter.

"I have never been told," he said, surprising me, just a voice again in the growing dark. "But I see a present reason to pursue such an obvious line of enquiry."

"The masks then? Where did they come from? Are they tribal?"

"Again I cannot say. They've always been there, stored at Whitehead. More than are ever used."

His answers were hardly generous, but I had no choice. "The Alexandrian Book? What can you tell me?"

Bascoeur settled on the cooling sand and I did so as well, watching the dim point of the ship until I became nightsighted enough to see the shape in the blackness beside me.

"Alexandrian Book is simply an idea," he said. "Imagine. A great library is burned, its entire collection almost completely lost, as at Alexandria several times before it was finally destroyed. In the ruins, among the remaining scrolls, is planted a false text, allegedly a copy of a copy, purportedly the last remaining account of some act, the story of some ruler, or a discovery, an idea, a secret heritage pre-dating all that is known of such a thing.

"It changes everything. It is enshrined as ancient wisdom, a purer older truth, something from the Golden Age—the way the writings, say, of Hermes Trismegistus underscored the whole European Renaissance. The ancient originals are lost, but thank goodness we have at least this one copy. It would only need an opportunist, not even the one responsible for the fire, though—all heaven forbid!—*that* could have been part of the plan as well. Maybe a fragment of such a text would be enough if there weren't the time to prepare a full one, but the weight attributed to such a fragment! A formal claim on history made retroactively would be enormous. It is frightening."

"And the oubliettes?"

"The concept of the oubliettes began a long time ago, in 1784, in a small university town in Western Europe. Four scholars, wealthy enough men, hypothesized the Alexandrian Book idea, the notion of a planted falsehood. They noted trends emerging in their world, and resolved to found a society for the custodianship of history. They moved in a small way at first, putting truth before their own nationality and immediate cultural interests, as hard to do then as now. Within ten years they saw how discrepancies existed, how accounts of the same incident were skewed and embellished—more importantly, how those accounts differed from the one they themselves had painstakingly acquired from eye-witnesses and respected non-partisan thinkers.

"Building on the old axiom that the first casualty of war is truth, they allowed the far more important, post-Tribation corollary that truth is, indeed, the first casualty of self-interest and, inevitably, the first casualty of perception. Not a new idea these days, of course, or even then, but a new idea as a guiding, motivating ethic. They formed the oubliettes.

"Even if their accounts were never wholly accepted, if they preserved integrity, at least official accounts would need to be measured against them, would need to be aware of what the Antique Men had gleaned."

"Is this true?" I asked him.

"I will not tell you. You must remember, there will always be things I will keep from you. It may be Alexandrian Book. Disinformation. Mythopoesis. Either way it is a good example, you'll agree. Plausible, even elegant. Worth embellishing and passing on."

"It's frightening."

"It is what happens all the time, Tom." The voice in the darkness was generous and easy now, free of the mask, of the eternal prison it made. "The Storyteller in us is *always* involved, cannot resist embellishing the facts. For instance, I say man-made fire was first applied to technology some time in the Palaeolithic, somewhere in Central Africa, and you react to it as a fact not reality. You accept, but barely experience.

"The Storyteller in me does better. One windy day in the final centuries of the Pleistocene, a man known only to his fellows as Hamat found that lightning had struck the sacred acacia that stood in the hollow by the Maju fishing lake. He took up a burning branch broken from the trunk, wanting it for a talisman, meaning to take it to a nearby hill and there pray over it for good hunting. The tribal shaman came with hunters, discovered him, and cried sacrilege.

"Hamat was given a fitting punishment: he would pay with his life if he could not do what the lightning had done. It was scorn, mockery, you see; the shaman was shaming him. They gave him a day, left him on his hill with the extinguished length of stick. Hamat broke it in two, struck the halves together to make thunder and hopefully lightning—a very elementary totemic step—finally started rubbing the pieces as storm clouds rub the land.

"He burned himself accidentally while rubbing the heated stick over bare flesh in his fear and zeal. He discovered heat in sticks first, and deduced there must be fire hidden there too. He began rubbing the halves again and made smoke, another part of the mystery revealed, then ignited dry grass bunched about it, and finally the stick itself. He ran down to his fellow villagers at day's end holding a torch. The shaman was clubbed and stoned; Hamat became shaman. To earn prestige and coerce neighboring tribes, his people gave out the story with ever more detail added. By classical times, Hamat was Prometheus bringing fire from the gods."

"Another Namarkon legend."

"Indeed," Bascoeur said. "You see how it resonates."

"What have you learned, Gado?" I used his name as he had mine, for whatever it signified in this safe darkness.

"If this Namarkon or tribal agencies have access to our data nets, I must use those nets carefully. As Angel, I am known for custodianship, but now I am with you on *Rynosseros*. I use my own mnemonic nets. Later I will verify what I find."

Now I wished the darkness were not there, that I could see his eyes. "We can go to Whitehead? With our stowaway?"

"I forgot myself. Truan's place in this, like yours and your crew's, is vital to the lesson of history we hold so important."

"Which is?" I imagine that he smiled in the night, wanted to think that he did, that he could.

"Nothing you haven't thought of, Captain. History is people doing things, that's all. Large and small. The man who betrayed Edinburgh Castle to the English. The Greek traitor who betrayed Leonidas and his Spartans at Thermopylae in 480 BC and showed Xerxes the secret route over the mountains. One man! A king dies sooner than later, all his loyal Spartiates, removed from their capacity to affect history. Or the Norwegian naval officer, Quisling…"

Bascoeur's voice broke off, then after a moment returned again. "The oubliettes do not stand outside history, contrary to how it seems. We have to be part of it. There is no such thing as non-interference. Non-interference *is* interference. We exist, we participate, even when we withhold. This is why I take your suspicions seriously. Our philosophy of belonging, our awareness of Alexandrian Book and its possible existence *in our very midst*, makes Namarkon frighteningly real, his possible use of the Antique Men an unbearable lie. That he is called the Immortal becomes very sinister."

"If we are wrong?"

"I may be replaced. There are three more Angels who may decide that I went too far, that I acted irresponsibly."

"Den is gravely wounded. Could those Angels harm the rest of us?"

"No, Captain. Provided we are free of Namarkon, it is as I said. We accept things that happen. To counter any harmful truth you tell about us, we may need to plant a lie later—today, in a generation or two, whenever it will work best. Provided we know what was true here at the center, that someone does."

"Alexandrian Book?"

"Exactly. The first lesson the victor learns. Truth is a tool."

"It is also what really is," I said. "Lost or forgotten. In spite of everything and anyone."

"Which is what caused oubliettes to form in the first place. You see why the existence of Namarkon among us constitutes a lie, a hideous contradiction. Yes, you might say that this too is what simply is, the world being itself. But our commitment to our mission pre-empts that. Your questions, Meg's, even Truan's, may uncover what *is*. So we go to Whitehead."

"And Mekkis?"

"When we learn where it is, yes, I may share that with you as well. You can see why mentioning nanotech crystalline AI may have been premature if not altogether inopportune. If Namarkon is among the Antique Men, he has been alerted now."

"It was obvious," I said. "He would assume that I suspect. And I get the impression Namarkon doesn't care. He believes he is safe."

"Or wants this time of risk."

"As a test?"

"As a test."

We were silent then, watching the night, watching the distant glimmer of *Rynosseros*, the sudden bright signatures of meteorites arcing across the sky and vanishing in soundless strikes.

There were other questions, but it seemed wrong to ask them now. A tektite made its solitary mark, fleeting, curving down to resolution, reminding me.

"There's too much data and not enough, Gado. Do you know how many entries I found for lightning? The National libraries are full of information. I read for hours. Apart from scientific and meteorological references, just so many. Old National place names like Lightning Ridge. Hittite weather-gods like Tesheb and Dattas, wielding axes that make a symbolic lightning flash. Egyptian Min with his thunderbolt totem; the Chinese Lightning Mother with her flashing mirrors. It goes on. Lightning as symbol, in the dreams of the famous, in psychiatry and dreamlocking, as a motif in art. There's Ezekial's vision by the river of Chebar, of four cherubim and four wheels in the sky—"

"'Their appearance,'" Bascoeur said, "'was like burning coals of fire, and like the appearance of lamps...and the fire was bright, and out of the fire went forth lightning.'"

"Namarkon has to be aware of such things," I said. "Anything at all. Like the Tarot with that tower struck by the lightning of Spiritual Truth. It signifies change and the breaking down of old forms to create the new."

"The Lightning-Struck Tower," Bascoeur said. "The House of God."

"I'm sorry. I should remember. But could this suggest something, that Chano is his home? Would he strike at himself there to conceal his true whereabouts, blast his own house? To fulfil a Tarot image?"

"'Yea, he sent out his arrows, and scattered them; and he shot out lightnings, and discomfited them.' I think not, Tom. The house plan is known. The Nation officers investigating were thorough. No, it was an example. 'And he said unto them, I beheld Satan as lightning fall from heaven.'"

"It goes on and on, doesn't it?"

"You have yet to speak of the Taoist Book of Changes. The *I Ching*."

"Tell me!" I said, responding as I had whenever old Toth or one of the other librarians had found something promising for me.

"Ideogram 55. 'Feng' or 'Abundance.' 'The Sun below; the Thunder above.' The Oracle says:

'Thunder and lightning:
the height of the storm
The superior man judges lawsuits
and declares them fairly.'

I thought you may have found it."

I sighed with amazement and exasperation. How much more was there, how many other strands and elements weaving in?

"It doesn't end," I said, thinking of Namarkon controlling the register of history, ruling on needs and demands, the superior man, the Immortal, wielding his insidious Alexandrian Book like some emblematic flail, a terrible, ultimate lightning.

"Wait till you see the Feng ideogram. You will understand why I am committed, why I agreed to appear, even in darkness like this, without my mask for you. You really will wonder who has made history."

There was no resting then, of course. I stood. "Please, Gado!" Using his name was easy in darkness, impossible when the colored panes and—I imagined—the dark eyes were before me, though the eyes *were* there now, masked or unmasked, always there. "I'll have to trust that you will share what helps us all; anything that might help. Can we go?"

"Of course," the voice came, and I realized he was already standing, though I had not heard him rise.

We returned to the ship and, though nothing more was said, I held back until he was aboard and had vanished below, not wanting to steal looks from those naked eyes that he did not wish to give. But when he appeared a few minutes later, he was still unmasked. His eyes were like beads of obsidian as he joined me on the poop and handed me a scrap of paper. On it was drawn Ideogram 55 of the *I Ching*.

"This one of the sixty-four ideograms tells us something, I think."

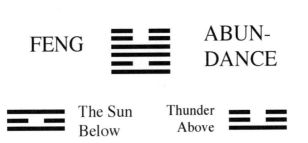

55

FENG   ABUN-DANCE

The Sun Below   Thunder Above

I stared at it in wonder, seeing there the regional arrangement of the National arcologies that had become so familiar to me, now revealed in its full meaning.

"You see the clear message, the careful and ancient pattern of it," Bascoeur said. "Not the random regional groupings we are meant to think. The first trigram is 'The Thunder above.' This,"—he pointed to the other—"'The Sun below,' would tell us something about why Namarkon is named for an ancient Dreamtime god of the Gunwinggu. In literal terms, giving Thunder pre-eminence, he clearly champions the tribes over your Sun of Nation, which is interesting. Not one oubliette is Ab'O, Tom, not one. We are all Nationals or approved Internationals. That is why I can believe Namarkon is among us. There are messages everywhere. This clever enemy seems to tell us at every opportunity that he exists, no doubt out of delight at being immortal, at simply existing and knowing he is unassailable in his maze of history and fact."

I missed the significance of what Bascoeur had said at first. I was still too overwhelmed by the thought of the National arcologies conforming to the Feng ideogram, being located according to a secret deployment plan, one unknown to the National architects and surveyors. It was incredible. But then I reacted to his final words, struck suddenly by what he had acknowledged.

"You agree then? Not a physical labyrinth? A notional one?"

"Why not? I cannot deny it. Though we duplicate material and have different personal priorities as individuals, we oubliettes *are* a library, as you say."

"Your mask is packed away now? Insulated?"

He nodded. "Partly why I agreed to remove it. I grant as possible all that you suspect. 'And the likeness of the firmament upon the heads of the living creatures was as the color of the terrible crystal, stretched forth over their heads above.' Also from Ezekial. Captain, I need your viewpoint, what is still a comparative detachment. If Namarkon hides among the thirty-six, there may be far far more of a labyrinth for me than for you. Now we should rest. You will not see me unmasked again. Not before Whitehead and certainly not after."

"Thank you is all I have, Lord Gado." The honorific seemed appropriate now.

"It is more than enough," he said, and passed me another slip of paper. "Here is tomorrow's course. I will not appear on deck until afternoon.

But speak to Truan McBanus. As hetaera and a daughter trusted with secret information, I believe she would have been a diligent shadow in her father's library. Good night."

"Good night," I said, and watched him go below.

At first I thought I would need to wait till morning to speak to Truan, for the ship was quiet, with no-one visible when Bascoeur left me on the quarterdeck.

That silence had been a false thing when we first returned from our walk, how it is when young children pretend to parents that they are asleep. Certainly Scarbo would have been awake and listening for familiar footsteps on the deck, for the low steady rhythm of voices. For a fact Meg would have been peering out the ports, watching and listening too, wanting to be at the rail when we returned but not daring so much.

Shannon was more pragmatic; he'd been at the helm most of the day and had Scarbo to worry for him. No doubt he slept easily in his cabin.

It was Truan who approached from the bow, a night-time re-enactment of her appearance earlier in the day.

"There's coffee below," she said. "Or tisn, if you prefer. Meg said I should wait."

I had to smile. "Nothing surprises me anymore, Truan. Tisn would help right now."

She went below and soon returned carrying a tray with two steaming mugs and a plate of cold meat, biscuits and cheese. We shared this as we sat in deck-chairs out of the cool wind, watching the night. For a time there was only the sound of cables thrumming and sand hissing against the hull.

"I don't know what to tell you, Captain," she said at last, unprompted it seemed, though Bascoeur may have had Meg urge it. "Toban was a bookman. He had no enemies, few secrets."

"Bascoeur felt you might have been told things, that's all. The names of other book conservationists, things like that. I'm trusting you would have given us anything that might help."

She shook her head, but it was for her earlier comment. "Toban was a generous soul, Tom. He knew of your search already, but hesitated at first. Then he decided he would be available to you after all."

"Among the Colored Captains, in my crew, we make that family. Like your Club Hetaera."

She held her cup close to her lips, turning her face to the side, hiding the play of emotion in her eyes. "He told me no other names."

"I'm sorry, Truan."

"It was quick. It took them both. There was that."

We were silent then, shielded by the lift of the stern assembly, sitting in the dim glow of the deck lights and looking down the length of *Rynosseros* towards the bow. We listened to the wind ghosting about the rails and transoms, the hiss of sand, one moment barely there, the next sudden and strong.

Then something she had said came back to me. "He hesitated at first. Do you know why he changed his mind?" I kept looking ahead but knew her gaze was on me.

"He was in the library. I was doing some research with him—one of the tribal academies wanted something. Marquand phoned to say he had referred you. Toban said he wouldn't open the door."

"He commented afterwards?"

"Yes. Much as he was concerned about your predicament, he couldn't afford to antagonize the tribes or someone like Chiras Namarkon."

"He used that name?"

"Yes. There were his friends at the universities to consider. Helping you might compromise them, lead to the cancellation of privileges, visiting and access rights—"

"And access to illegal tech. Gain-monitors."

She almost smiled, but the other emotions were too pressing, too immediate. "He's a scholar, Tom. He was…he needed—"

"And then?" I spoke quickly to distract her.

"Another call. I was out in my studio and didn't hear any of it. When I asked, he said Marquand had called again. He would see you after all."

"But nothing else about Namarkon?"

"Nothing. I'd never heard the name before."

"No other calls?"

"Only yours. I went out into the garden."

She turned her face away again, looking off into the night.

"Truan—?"

"I can continue. I *want* to talk about this. I need to."

"Did he seem worried?"

"No. But he wanted to discuss something with my mother—in the library. Why?"

"I'm betting Marquand made no second call."

She faced me. "Then who did? Bascoeur? Namarkon? You don't think—?"

"All I know is that the second call changed his mind, persuaded him to see us, and that less than an hour later there was the strike. Truan, another few minutes and Ben and I would have been in the library too. Namarkon could have had us all. No more threat."

She stood and moved into the thrust of the wind, her hair blowing wild. "He wanted to warn you off!"

I stood too. "Or the strike was pre-arranged, booked into a busy tribal schedule. Your father may have discovered something."

It was finally too much.

"Can we leave this now?"

I hesitated, then told myself that this was why she had come, stowed away, committed herself. Any answers were as much for her as for me. "I'm also talking to someone who wants to be involved. Who has plans, objectives."

"Say it! Who might well be an agent of this Namarkon. You must have thought it!"

I hadn't and it startled me. "Thanks for waiting up," I said at last, simple truth. "After being with Bascoeur, I needed…something."

Her gaze held mine. "I'm on the edge of this. I need to act and can't. Possibly I'm just drawn to what is at the center."

"All any of us can do, Truan."

Without another word, she turned and went below.

I checked that the deck alarms were activated in case intruders came—unlikely under normal circumstances but a definite possibility now: a quick guerilla action to achieve here what the Namuren fighters on the Gentian Walk had not. Then I watched the tektite swarms, felt the wind grab at the hull, and thought of what the day had been and how things stood.

There was so much. Too much. The tribes waiting, the comsats in orbit, synced and tethered, watching. If Namarkon owned one, had access to them all, what chance was there?

Perhaps he waited for a facility to clear its roster, needed permission for another strike from jealous tribes only grudgingly persuaded to serve his needs. Perhaps he didn't need to use that final tactic again if only to protect his man, Bascoeur? He would find other ways.

But what, what, could induce this entity to reveal himself? Dewi had been a scientist turned trader, smuggler, religious fanatic, a mad creature drawn by a need to survive, to transcend and extend himself. He had worked through agents; at least had used a system which could be infiltrated by the likes of specialists like Pederson. Here there were clues, tantalizing leads, and how easy it was to direct attention to those when so little else was on hand. It led to Whitehead, but would Namarkon hide in such plain sight, lay himself bare to the tribes? Unless, as Bascoeur said, as a test. Chiras Namarkon could be anywhere, not even in Australia for that matter. And what if the tribes *were* watching, meeting his demands, accommodating his requests?

It seemed ever more hopeless, there under the stars in the blowing dark.

From Whitehead—where? To Mekkis? And then? To the other arcologies? Back to Twilight Beach?

As often happens at such moments during watch, I found myself considering the plaque on the helm.

Such special words there, echoing Meg's, casting *me* as the questing Alexander.

And Alexandrian Book! Bascoeur's Knot, that Gordian Knot!

That story. A true event, who could say? Alexander at Gordium confronted with the chariot of the great Phrygian king, faced with the knot binding the yoke to the shaft. The young Macedonian knowing the legend that whoever unravelled it would rule all Asia, knowing the legend and needing to make it, even that, part of *his* destiny. Then cutting the great Knot asunder, or pulling the pin free, whatever really happened that day, winning, transcending by doing!

But not even that bold action automatically meant winning, not then, not here, not now.

I found myself secretly longing for Truan to return, someone to take me away from these thoughts, kept listening for a door closing, footsteps on the companionway, imagined those sounds again and again.

I smiled, catching myself, then sat, just being in the night, until the constellations had turned halfway round the sky and footsteps did come, and the voice saying my name was Shannon's, there on deck to take the next watch.

9.

SCARBO TOOK US ON our way at 0600, using photonic parafoils until the morning winds came up fresh and strong. Then he put twenty kites above those bright inflatables, the perfect morning for testing the more abstruse patterns in his old kitesman's bible.

When I arrived on deck at 0815, the sky had our colors spread across it: shapes like tethered dragons, crowns, talismans, origami castles, bursts of folded light. There were Sodes and Demis, Chinese Hawks, Holkoyd Stars, even our Samian Ladder spread out link by splendid link, vibrant, beautifully controlled, and there, in front, our signature Rhino head, blue on ochre. *Rynosseros* sang from its heart, as Scarbo called it, so finely balanced in its finery that it sat on 110 k's with no yawing at all.

"A madman in another life punishing this one!" Shannon cried, smile flashing in his dark beard. "He woke up dangerous, Tom. Can't help himself! Wouldn't hear of breakfast, wanted to see what the two of us could do."

I laughed, feeling my spirits lift, cherishing it all. "If there's turbulence, you'll take us to hell gift-wrapped!"

Scarbo nudged Rob. "Told you! Worries likes a bridegroom!"

We grinned madly at the sky, sharing this sight we never tired of, *Rynosseros* fully dressed for the hot dry winds of the inland.

Truan appeared on deck then, and Meg Solles a short time later.

The notary climbed to the quarterdeck. "Lord Gado is doing assimilations," she said, and I caught her glance at the words on the helm plaque. It was a chance.

"You're his friend too, Meg. We have to unravel this Knot, share what we can."

"I listen to what he says about you and how he says it," she said. "So far I'm not serving two masters."

IT WAS EASY SAILING then, upwards of 90 k's on a surprisingly good Road for one shown only as a broken line on the old tribal maps. There was nothing but the hot sun, the glare, the wind in our kites and cables, the empty distances. From time to time a belltree marked its lonely stretch of Road, sounding its joyous waysong as we plunged by, or a stand of land-coral offered its barbs and hooks like a time-locked dancer, weathered fans aloft. Now and then a line of distant hills rose up like a sea-creature sounding, lingering, sinking away again. There were hours when a single cloud would wander into view, cross the wide blue sky like a vagrant dream and finally disappear.

By early afternoon, there were more ranges ahead, low folds of purples, reds and browns against the sky. The Road ran parallel for a time, then turned towards them, suggesting that a pass would lead us to the plain beyond.

"An hour beyond those," Meg said, pointing to where Road and hills met in a ribbon of sun-shadow. "Whitehead is—"

But Shannon shouted from com. "Bogie astern! Extreme range and closing!"

Helm scan confirmed it; we had a pursuer.

"After us?" Meg asked, close by the controls.

I had to remember that she spoke for Bascoeur. "Hard to say. At that speed, possibly. Or a courier. There's no attempt to hide, no insulated hull. Nothing to say it's other than a tribal ship on an urgent mission about to overtake. We'll know soon enough."

"Surely not out here, Captain! Not near Whitehead!"

"Meg, we can't arm till we're sure. If it's tracked by comsat, we're scanned and accountable. Loft 'em, Ben! See if she gains!"

For the next half-hour we ran toward the old red hills, until the distance between the ships dwindled and an image finally showed on scan through our churning rooster-tail.

"Bogie confirmed!" Shannon cried. At the same instant, scan managed a lucky fix, no more than three seconds through our tail-cloud, but it gave configuration.

It was a warship closing on us, an armored charvi, probably a 130-footer, plates adorned with suns and stars, bold chevrons and faded totemic war-signs, a veteran ship from appearances, running under thirty or more battle-kites and wearing what veteran kitesmen called a "crown of thorns." A clutch of death-lamps on long-tether flashed hard light at the top of their drab functional canopy, rotating pulses from one to the next—a psychological trick—juggling death like hot stones from fist to eager fist.

A terrifying sight, one that no amount of experience could divest of its chilling elemental force: a ship racing to engage, angry and committed.

The calm you feel at such times is part of an only response, the result of training and discipline, counters to desperation. But it also has something of the no-choice bravado of a fairground ride about it. You do because there's nothing else.

If you are careful, composed, patient in the frantic rush of events, you remember that size can mean nothing, that firepower need not count. When there is speed and dust and stones the size of skulls close by, the off-chance of gullies like gaping mouths, when there is judgement and luck, inspiration created when fear of death elevates daring into a gift from the Fates, you act as if you cannot fail.

In such panic wrapped in calm, I looked instinctively for Strengi and Rim and young Hammon on the deck, remembered how it was and shouted new names.

"Truan! Deck lenses there and there! Meg! Help bring down the Sodes! Down or dump, Ben! No time!"

We donned ship-com headsets then, proscribed tech for Nationals usually, even Colored ones, but on loan from Otamas and the Chitalice, and did quick confirmations. Shannon was already at the cable-boss, helping Ben dump the display kites for obstruction, hoping to foul our pursuer's canopy or wheels. Both men were ahead of my words every time, living parts of the ship.

Bascoeur was on deck too, climbing to the helm, mask flashing under his hood.

"There!" I pointed to the dark heart of the cloud behind us.

"Namuren," Bascoeur said, using his mask to read the brightest of the signs. "Your friend Ephan's family. A vendetta ship."

I accepted it, not daring to look away from the Road and the controls. "Namarkon pulls the strings here, Gado. Tribal puppets dance. They have no choice."

"Run for Whitehead! There are defenses."

"Laser?" I was prepared for anything the Antique Men had, especially if they were owned in whole or part by Namarkon. But this *was* Namarkon, I reminded myself, this Namuren ship, as surely as the mirror ships had been Dewi's. We were meant to die here, it seemed. Not at Chano, here!

"No hi-tech," Bascoeur said. "But lenses, harpoons, cable-shot. Hurry! The Road is safe."

"I need to be sure!"

"Safe," he said. "Use power. Whitehead will pay!"

I switched in the cells, heard the whine of the big Pabar engines in the platform.

And just as well. Flashes of hard light from the Namuren death-lamps were snatching our remaining kites from the sky. I felt the heat on my neck and shoulders, picking at *Rynosseros*'s stern.

Truan and Meg were doing their best with our own weapons, but they lacked training and experience. Now and then a kite did vanish from our pursuer's canopy, but those kites were largely for show on a powered ship, vendetta display, so it counted for little.

"Smokescreen?" I asked Ben at the cable-boss.

He shook his head. "Cross-wind. We'll lose it."

He was right. A last resort.

The hills were close. Bascoeur pointed ahead. "Five minutes! There's a road-chain."

It changed everything. "Should we slow?" I thought of the heavy stretch of links across the Road, the winches for lifting them to hull height.

"Recessed," Bascoeur said. "I've sent word. They'll raise it behind us."

"No!"

"What?" Bascoeur's masked face was unreadable.

"Gado, Namarkon is behind and Namarkon could well be ahead. We are rushing towards a road-chain at top speed. That ship doesn't have to catch us; it only has to drive us!"

"They're my people!"

"It would need just one agent with access to the chain equipment or the Whitehead overrides."

"What then? What do we do?"

"The terrain before the chain? Broken?"

Bascoeur hesitated, checking stats, schemae, memory. "Before the chain housing, no. But the Road turns before it so the final approach cannot be seen. Just before the pass."

"Ben, smokescreen in two minutes!" I said and pointed. "Single dump to that turn. Time it. They'll think we're hiding the chain, hope to use it ourselves. We slow and leave the Road."

In the dust and thunder, the fierce concentration, those minutes vanished like seconds. Then the dark billows were there, first broken dumps, then streaming out, rolling and dense, torn by crosswinds but still making a brief black night in our rooster-tail.

"Rocks—two minutes!" Shannon cried, back at com. And we began powering down, preparing to pull off the Road.

"They'll be slowing too," Scarbo said, which gave me the idea, inspiration or folly.

"Gado, Whitehead has full com capability?"

"Of course."

"Call your Angels! Tell someone you trust to send a broad signal: 'Angel interference. Chain down and locked. Catch and destroy. Namarkon.' Blanket the frequencies, maximum power, so nothing local gets through."

Bascoeur did not answer. He stood at the stern rail making the link.

The rocks were visible now, foothills and cast-offs, the broken detritus of the range, so close, full and ocher-red against the sky. I could see where the Road made its long sweep into them. Scan showed nothing, but a chain could be camouflaged, insulated.

"Smoke for the turn, Ben!" I said. "Hide us!"

"Nearly out!" Scarbo answered. "Wish us luck!"

Rynosseros was at 60 and slowing, kites down or lost, stored power carrying us.

"Done!" Bascoeur said, with us again. "Unless Namarkon intervenes further."

"I say he won't. Vendetta ship and agents can be pre-arranged. I doubt much else can. If a broadcast is overridden, then we know Namarkon is at Whitehead. Tell your fellow Angels that."

"We shall see, Captain," he said. And went silent again.

We made the turn, 30 k's and slowing noticeably as we pulled to the Road's edge, then off onto a verge of stones. The ship lurched and shook, the travel platform handling the torment as best it could.

We stopped with a final lurch. Shannon and I ran to the lenses; Scarbo fed out the last of our screen, then put four lamps aloft, tethered low, sparkling with stored power.

There was nothing else to do then but watch the pall of smoke, holding longer than expected, penned in the lee of the red hills.

We could hear our pursuer approaching, shaking the earth and the rocks and the sky, becoming all of it.

Then it was there, thundering past like a dragon, splendid in its markings, battle-kites and signatures out in front like a brace of hounds. I thought to glimpse her captain on the quarterdeck, trusting Namarkon, whatever hold cold Chiras had on that luckless family.

The chain was up. Even as we flashed what few shots we could at the fleeing vessel, we heard the long cruel tearing, a roar like the world ending amid these dusty hills, a thunder that went on and on as ship and lives rolled into sudden, shattering oblivion.

Truan, Meg and Bascoeur had probably seen nothing like it in their lives. They stood staring, the faces of both women drained of color, Bascoeur's hidden behind his panes, but still, still.

Ben, Rob and I *had* seen such things and suffered it as probably only sand-ship sailors can. There can be nothing like a ship-death, not ever, certainly not one done so shamefully, ruthlessly, without choice or chance.

I turned to Bascoeur. "The ship and captain, who were they?" I knew he would have the data.

"Leave it for now, Captain."

"Tell me!"

"The ship was *Eagle*."

"The captain?"

"Ephan Sky Namuren," he said, while thunder, smoke and flame played around the bloody hills. It was as if Villa Chano had died yet again, a single scream drawn full and mighty to become the ruin of all the world.

10.

THERE WERE NO SURVIVORS. We left the shattered, smoking remains of *Eagle* and passed the damaged chain-station, moved on until we ran along an unhindered Road towards far ranges in the east.

There, out on the plain, Whitehead loomed in the late morning sun, at first like a part of the landscape, eccentrically wind-formed and weather-made, then nothing like it. The walls were too smooth, too even, the great mainwall a monstrous thing, a wedge of concrete and glass lifting from the desert fastness, shimmering in the heat like something ready to become alive, already testing its senses.

Closer still, it had much of the quality of an ancient monastery about it. As *Rynosseros* moved in under the wind shadow, we could see some of the inhabitants: small groups of trainees and attendants, young and old, softly spoken men and women to look at them, tending modest orchards and foundries, trimming the lawns and walks, sitting together in open-air refectories and watching our approach. There was the occasional flash of an oubliette mask on the highs ramps and balconies, a sudden glint of sunlight on figures crossing sunny causeways and sheltered terraces. Though we saw no children or adolescents, whatever else this place was, it was home to these people.

When we had disembarked and entered the rock-melt folds of the outer precincts, we saw that these citizens were mostly older people, grey-haired and peaceful-looking, clearly deferential whenever an Antique Man came near. Unlike the robed, masked oubliettes, these folk wore soft sandals and fatigues of natural weave. On their temples they had small neat scars.

"Salvation Moons," Bascoeur explained for Truan, Rob and Scarbo's benefit. "Ritual marks. Not as ominous as they look. Those who train and serve or work in the library here choose to take the ancient lobotomy mark as a sign of self-denial. A fitting inversion. They are the Good Friends. Speak with them as you wish."

We moved on from the walled gardens and irrigation allotments into the great learning halls. There we were shown rooms full of books: storage vaults for crystals, motes, blanks and beads, self-powered Illuminated texts, true-paper books and other retroforms in careful environments.

It was awesome, impressive in both size and the extent of the care and dedication shown. There were scriptoria where new texts were produced and old ones copied, incept areas for the international publishing operation using the famous blue flower imprint of the Antique Men.

Then, once Meg had led the others off to their assigned quarters, Bascoeur took me high into the blade to the Meeting Hall, a huge stone chamber with a long central table arranged across it and thirty-six carved chairs, empty now, like a table setting for the Last Supper. At the far end, a floor to ceiling window-wall—true-vision, not relayed image—gave out on an infinity of warm air and rich golden light.

"Tonight," Bascoeur said, addressing me in softened tones appropriate to such a place, "you will address the Assembly here and tell them what you believe is happening."

"But then Namarkon will know everything, if we allow—"

"It is no inquisition, Captain. You will say only what you wish, only what you judge fitting. See it as we do. If Namarkon *is* one of us—or all of us for that matter—then that too is a fact of the reality we live. As Angels, we may deal with it *if* we can demonstrate Alexandrian Book, a betrayal of our fundamental purpose."

"This has to be a formality then, Gado. Such a meeting is redundant if the masks are nanotech CPU's."

"The information they have has come to them only through the Angels," Bascoeur said. "Remember that. We have held back some facts until we are reasonably certain."

"You believe you have. Your masks could be telling it all."

"Be moderate. It is why we were chosen, and why there are four. Our masks are special. Add your intuitions and good judgement. Help us prove this."

"If I can. I will if I can."

MEG WAS IN THE passage outside waiting to take me down to the others. Bascoeur made a small gesture of farewell and walked in the opposite direction. As Meg and I moved along the hallway to the elevators, I looked back to see him vanish through a doorway at the far end.

"If I were to rush back there now, Meg, and follow him through that door, what would I find?"

Meg's hood was down, her short dark hair adding at least that color to the paleness of her face. She glanced back along the hallway too.

"You would find a very tired man, probably unmasked, sitting before a window, I should think, knowing Lord Gado. The door will be unlocked, like most of the doors here. You could verify this easily; I would wait. But he will be preparing himself for tonight's Assembly. Before you join them later, there will be questions, an accounting for why details have been withheld, why he went unmasked onto the desert with you last night, broke that rule again."

"Again?"

"Yes. He went unmasked to and from Saldy's, remember, though at least there no-one knew. That was to help you as much as himself. Before the general accounting this evening, the other Angels will demand their own. They will be more sympathetic, true, but more rigorous because they are more directly accountable themselves."

We entered the elevator and dropped to the residential levels.

"Perhaps he does not know what the Knot means," I said, as the car completed its vertical journey and began the transverse leg out to the dormitories and dining areas.

"Is that surprising?" she said.

"Yes, it's surprising. Everything is surprising and suspect. I can allow for secret knowledge in the Order, but once you grant the concept of Alexandrian Book, then Gado's not knowing something like that seems very significant."

"Surely it would be like you questioning the windmill origins of the Nation sign," she said. "You don't think to do it because you think you already know the answer." And she smiled her tight grudging smile, though this time parts of it reached her eyes, changing them. She believed I genuinely cared for him, at least there was that.

It struck me then, watching her, that something about Meg Solles was different, as if recent events had worked their magic, extended her, changed her. It was as if she had discovered something vital about herself, had perhaps put Meg Solles and Gado Bascoeur into a new perspective.

"It still hurts? Loving him," I said.

The smile vanished from mouth and eyes both, but the Elf's usual quick anger did not return. She studied the indicator light, went to speak, hesitated, then seemed to decide something.

"It's like the Knot you are trying to unravel," she said, and the sudden force, passion, maturity, in her voice were as startling as anything I had experienced over the last few days. Never again would I take her for merely the notary with Bascoeur, the angry figure she disguised herself as. "Long ago I put it to him—why the androgyny, why ritual and custom dictated the need for a man-woman, the need to breed hermaphrodites to guide the oubliettes? What gain, what symbol?"

"Did he answer? Can you share this?"

"He touched his mask, the flower and the patch. 'The answer is here,' he said. 'In our beginnings.' I didn't press further."

The car slowed and stopped, opened onto a dining area, a softly lit space barely a quarter the size of the Gaza lobby, with a dozen tables occupied by as many of the Good Friends, eating, talking quietly. There were plantings placed about, low music playing. The walls were decorated with tapestries and carvings, information storage webs made here at Whitehead: the precious "datafacts."

"You knew he moved L75 VGS?" I asked.

"He did that the moment your Council requested a meeting with the Antique Men. Just after Dewi Dammo was defeated. He needed to investigate first—his job as Angel."

"Did he damage that Book?"

"Would you harm *Rynosseros*? He found it damaged at Crayasse, moved it on to Turker to gain more time. He was hunting Namarkon too, anticipating your line of enquiry. Finally, he judged it time to meet you. The other Angels, the Assembly, were wanting answers. Come. Here are your friends."

ROB, BEN AND TRUAN had had time to shower and rest, to change out of their desert clothes into fresh fatigues. They came into the refectory from a different elevator, and joined Meg and me at the servery counters, though Meg did not eat with us. She excused herself and went to join a group of fellow notaries at an adjoining table.

It was just as well. During our meal we needed to discuss recent events: the parts played by Gado and Meg, the run to the road-chain ahead of *Eagle*, the remarkable fact that one of the old arcologies was more than a library, was operational at least in part and occupied by Nationals after all.

"We've seen very few inhabitants," Shannon said. "Just a handful really. Still no children."

Scarbo agreed. "There's probably no more than one or two hundred. Makes you wonder what we'd find at the other arcologies."

"It may come to that," I told them, "though I believe we would find nothing. There's an Assembly tonight. Bascoeur has to account for his actions. Meg hasn't said as much, but he may be replaced."

"Punished?" Truan asked.

"Brought to order. Denied us. I'm to speak on his behalf, I think. Whatever happens, be patient and stay ready. See to the ship. Use the time. *Eagle* responded to a signal supposedly from Namarkon and that signal probably came from Whitehead. Someone here, one or more, all of them for all we know, is in league with Namarkon. We know that much. I'm hoping to take a journey."

"To Mekkis?" Truan said.

"If they'll take me. I believe they know where it is."

"Tom—"

"If I can," I told her. "I doubt they'll let you. And, forgive me, I owe that choice to Ben and Rob too."

"But if they die in this, *Rynosseros* loses far more than her captain. If I die, I will have done all that I can do."

I studied her face, this ghost that had haunted my watch. "You're right. I'll ask them."

Her features relaxed into a weary smile of gratitude.

"We'll look about," Scarbo said. "You rest, Tom. Room J178."

Ben was right. After the day we'd had, I did need sleep. I excused myself and went to find the J section.

THE ROOM WAS SMALL but comfortable, with a window overlooking a modest garden courtyard and walls painted in narrowing bands of soft sand colors. Without noticing they did so at first, the striations led the eye to the window and beyond, out into the flowers and bright air, brought those things in to me along that same axis: an easement loop.

I showered in the alcove, then settled on the futon-style bed and watched first the sky above the garden, then the datafact on the doorward wall where the soft easement lines began. Before I quite knew it, I was caught in the ten-cycle breathing pattern it induced and slipped gently into sleep.

A SEQUENCE OF LOW chimes sounded at 2021; an accompanying strip of soft lighting showed that the garden was dark. Night had fallen over Whitehead.

A voice spoke from a mesh beside my bed. "Please prepare yourself, Captain. Meg Solles will arrive in twenty minutes. The Assembly has already begun."

That stole the rest of my torpor. I showered again, dressed in my sandsman fatigues and opened the door to Meg when she knocked fifteen, not twenty minutes later.

She led me up into the blade again, back to the Meeting Hall, then left me alone outside the big doors, saying I would be summoned at the proper time.

That didn't happen for an hour, but finally the doors did open and one of the Good Friends appeared, an old woman who smiled and told me to go in.

I entered and found myself facing the figures seated behind the long table. All were masked, all had their hands before them, lightly clasped or resting close to ritual weapons: tschinkes, archimenters, galvanis, espandos and petronels. Only these faux-antique storage-traps differed from one to the next; the figures who owned them wore identical robes, identical masks, the same flower at the chest below the shoulder, the same Knot pattern high on the sleeve.

Behind them the window-wall shone with full night, folded and re-folded into roils and depths by the optical properties of the glass. More than ever, the scene resembled some fantastic re-creation of the Last Supper, a coven of cathedral kings and queens celebrating a mass for Mother Night pressing close beyond them.

Which of the oubliettes was Gado, I couldn't tell. The masks offered no clue. Side on, their traps looked more similar than they actually were, the silver-chased stocks, the curlicues, scrolls and hatchings of the brightwork gave nothing.

"We are working on Namarkon for you," one neutral male-female voice said. The hands of the figure fourth from the left seemed to have moved; I took that to be the speaker.

"Thank you. We begin to set a fair price."

"That is provocative to say," came what seemed like the same neutral voice, though this time a different figure moved his hands, actually moved fingers briefly and slowly over the espando in from of him—of her, there was no telling. But then the Angels were androgynes according to Meg. What of the rest?

"It is not meant to be anything more than a statement of how I see it, a reminder that there are two scales of payment at work here, two reckonings. I may be speaking to Namarkon, remember. You, those masks, those traps before you, that window for all I know."

"Bascoeur brought you here," a voice said, no identifying trace seen or imagined. Were the Angels the ones speaking?

"Yes, and I helped kill a ship and its crew to let Lord Gado do it. Whitehead would never be worth *Rynosseros*. I must wonder if this is worth *Eagle*."

"Understood, Captain. What can you tell us?"

"You know my conversations with Bascoeur."

"Except when he removed his mask for you."

"I don't necessarily believe that. I'm granting implant capability or—"

"No!" The word snapped and echoed like a slap, a whip-crack of denial filling the room.

"Very well," I said, accepting it. "Except then. Are you, any of you, or is anything known of by you, Namarkon?"

The row of figures sat very still, thirty-six watching shapes. The hands did not move.

"No," the single voice answered. "Nothing, no-one known to us."

"I'll assume that is true as well. I'll assume, too, that there is knowledge I cannot have. Inner Circle. Rituals and secrets of the Antique Men. Your masks, your signs, so much. I'll assume you know where Mekkis is, which, as "Power" in the Feng ideogram, you must allow, is a clear path. Today we fought on *Rynosseros* for our lives. In Twilight Beach, a tribesman, a much better swordsman than I, nearly killed me. I saw a cloud at the end of a kitana blade and it was everything. I find that man is now dead; my life dies about me in such pieces. He might have been a friend someday. Certainly, personally, it seems *he* did not choose to be my enemy. But Namarkon moves for Namarkon, and individuals don't matter.

"Like you, I would like to stand back from history, or be involved in it only as far as I can, here in my hands, at the ends of my fingers. You know where Mekkis is. You know why it is being obliterated from knowledge and memory; you know why it stands in the Feng pattern. Or you suspect why you *don't* know. Please," I said, using Truan's words, "take me there so I can have done all that I can do."

"Very well," a voice said. "But you alone, Captain. On a closed ship, with you below deck in a somnium so its whereabouts remain unknown. We will help you to help us; help you do everything possible. How does that fit your reckoning?"

"I believe you wanted me to request it formally. I believe that now you probably owe me a great deal."

"This interesting viewpoint of yours. In a few words: we all seek Namarkon."

"Done!" I said. "If it can be done. But thank you for letting me come here tonight and allowing me to see you. I consider it a great honor."

"It was necessary. Thank *you*, Captain."

Behind me, the doors opened. Meg was waiting. I took a final glance at the figures seated at the long table, then turned and left the hall.

11.

THEY WOKE ME SOON after midnight, two of the Good Friends did, both quiet gentle men who apologized and asked me politely to dress and meet them down on the mooring plat. No breakfast, not for a somnium ride, so I went hungry to the rendezvous.

Standing near *Rynosseros* on a battered six-wheeled travel platform and unkited at this hour was a small dark hull, what I took to be a Whitehead supply charvi, brought out and readied for a voyage of a different kind.

"So the oubliettes do own ships," I said, when Bascoeur and Meg joined me on the wide concrete apron.

"None for far-voyaging," Bascoeur said, masked and robed, holding his archimenter. "But a couple to take us to the shipping lanes so we can make connections for our travels. We own Mekkis though, Tom. It is deserted, it is ruined, but we can go there when we wish. Our only long voyage."

"We travel alone?"

"The three of us and these two, David and Gral. They are good sailors."

"What if Namarkon strikes at us? I'm below in a sleeve—"

"No," Bascoeur said. "Part of our trade-off with the tribes, this route. They touch *Tybo* and they lose our resources. More to the point, we give extra help to one faction over another. It is complex."

I wanted to ask him how it had gone with the Angels earlier, how it had been for him shut away with the other thirty-five oubliettes, but David came over then and respectfully suggested we set off.

The five of us boarded *Tybo*, and Gral brought costly stored power to the engines.

"You *are* privileged," I said as the old vessel made its way out of the lee of the mainwall. The first morning winds rocked the hull though no kites were aloft. In the eastern sky, a faint band of light marked the beginnings of day.

"It's time," David said gently, his Moons two glinting smiles above his own. "Please. The chamber is ready."

I glanced once more at Whitehead, an unliving mass of darkness against the pale line of yellow-grey squeezing over the edge of the world, then followed the Good Friend below to the somnium in the aft cabin. I used the toilet, undressed, then settled into the comfortable sleeve of the pod. David fitted the contacts and prepared to lower the lid.

"Will it be long?" I asked.

"This day and part of another," he said. "It's not far, but the terrain becomes difficult."

I nodded and watched through the clear plastic of the cowl as he brought it down. And knew nothing more than that.

UNTIL IT LIFTED, DAVID still smiling there, smiling there again.

"What happened?" I asked, though I immediately knew because of the leaden feeling in my arms and legs, the lethargy and terrible thirst, the sensitivity to the metabolic assists.

"We are close to our destination," David said. "Join us for breakfast when you can. It's quite a sight."

IT WAS LATE MORNING when I reached the quarterdeck. Nothing could be seen but rocky terrain, a low range all around us, though now and then there were glimpses of far desert and of turns in the Road ahead as it started to take us down again.

Twelve kites on four cables made a modest canopy, giving *Tybo* that special dimension all charvis need to be complete. I felt better seeing the drab inflatables, the tattered and patched wind-thieves, the solitary Sode like the Star of Bethlehem flung out ahead on a thirty-meter tether.

Gral had the helm; Meg and David tended the cable-boss, jockeying the big blue star for wind-change. Bascoeur stood by a breakfast table set up on the commons. There was fruit and sweet buns, steaming barragon coffee, a waiting chair.

"Twenty minutes, Captain," Bascoeur said as I ate and drank, welcoming the vivid tastes and smells, the warmth of the sun, the wind on my skin. Being on *Tybo* meant everything right then, making our way through these ancient hills, through hot sun and dust, passing the lonely totemic shaft of a belltree every so often.

"There!" Gral cried, pointing.

Between the bluffs, I saw our destination out on the plain before us, ten, fifteen k's distant, with hills beyond, a shimmering phantom line at the edge of the world.

Again, there was a mainwall, though even at this distance I could see this one was damaged, scarred, as if struck from space at some time in its past. Still complete, still impressive and powerful-looking in the clear desert air, but showing a great wound and surrounded by indistinct shapes, a crust of forms.

Gral handed me binoculars. Through them the scar in the mainwall became a vivid gash, and the untidy crumble resolved into ruined outbuildings and pitted approach roads, a wilderness of broken field domes and fallen revetments.

"Who did this?" I asked Gral, Bascoeur, whoever would answer, feeling the rush of deep underlying rage all Nationals felt when reminded of what had once been and what now was.

"Mekkis was the example," Bascoeur said. "The Nationals would not obey at first."

"If this was Namarkon's original home, then I can understand his determination to become Lightning God and control such powers."

"You speak from emotion, wanting to see him as pro-National. More mythopoesis! He uses what suits his needs, surely. Think of Chano."

"Yes." I put aside the glasses and stood. "Let me help with the kites, Gral."

"Take the helm," Gral said. "Be the first State of Nation captain to sail into Mekkis in two hundred years."

I nodded my thanks and went to the controls. Slowly, with the great blue Sode out before it, the wind-thieves clustering and weaving like remoras about a shark, *Tybo* reached the desert plain and the broken arcology waiting there.

"THAT IS THE BLASTED Gate," Bascoeur told me, pointing to what was just that, a dark maw in a wall that had suffered terrible heat and shock waves in its past. "Draw up in front."

I did so, easing *Tybo* in close to the mainwall while David and Gral brought home the kites, wrestling down the Sode first because of the unstable wind-flow around the great structure.

"A fitting home for an immortal spirit," I said. "Is there a labyrinth here, something to pass for one and waste more time?"

"'A labyrinth to amase the senses,'" Bascoeur said, not rising to the sarcasm. "Shakespeare. From the Old English 'amasian', to stupefy. Be patient, Tom."

But amid such ruin, feeling the old anger, it wasn't easy.

"Or is it to be books, more clues?"

"Please. At Whitehead you mentioned Inner Circle. Rituals and secrets. Of course there are. You formally requested this; that is what got you here, the only thing. Please wait."

The Good Friends remained on the ship while Gado, Meg and I entered the great main-building. As we reached the first of the empty ramps and interior boulevards, I heard engines behind me.

"They're leaving!"

"Taking the ship further out. Many fear this place."

Rightly so, I thought, if somewhere above us, around us, Namarkon made his home, nursed his lightnings, pulled comsats into alignment to kill ships and cities, burn libraries, an Immortal tailoring history with Alexandrian Book, making his own dead stack whenever inclined.

The arcology was labyrinth enough, it seemed now, and thoughts of a maze of oubliette masks seemed an over-subtle thing, too dramatically obvious to anyone given an hour's conversation with someone like Bascoeur.

Our footsteps echoed as we moved deeper into the great public space, here lit by a shaft of late morning sunlight where the mainwall was pierced, there a gulf of darkness where the relay plates had failed or skylights had been fused shut altogether. It was an eerie frightening domain, this monument to thwarted National hopes, home to lizards and scorpions, smelling of dust and too much time, too many lonely days.

Yes, a subtle fancy thinking Bascoeur and his people could be part of it, thirty-six making an infinity of corridors, hiding a specter behind their crystal panes.

I glanced left as we walked, first beyond Bascoeur, then noticed again the patch, the Forget-Me-Knot, on his sleeve.

That Knot.

Something Inner Circle, something that mattered as all symbols did. At one extreme a simple enough if intricate motif, at the other a key to Namarkon, a Gordian Knot to be unraveled or cut asunder.

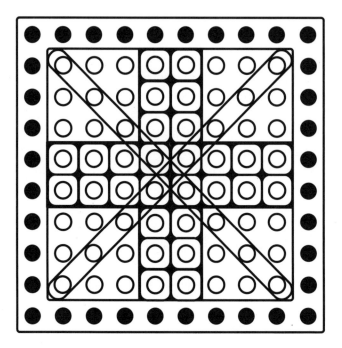

Not too subtle at all then. Not too obvious. Something only those given time with oubliettes would ever really suspect. And who spoke with oubliettes? Who ever came this close—walked with Angels, talked with them unmasked, saw their home, Whitehead, and Mekkis, their secret place?

"What are we going to see, Gado?"

"What you are looking at," he said, and it took me a moment to realize he meant the interlocking shape on his arm and not the vast interior.

"I don't understand."

"You understand something," Bascoeur said. "I think you may have seen the face of Namarkon and not known it."

"Gado, what—?"

"Meg, please take Tom to the Great Hall."

"Gado!"

"Go with Meg, Captain. Remember, it *is* Inner Circle for me. A conflict of loyalties. I am Angel first. Always that."

I watched while Bascoeur disappeared through a side arch, then followed Meg along a wide gallery towards two great doors at the far end.

"Meg?" I said.

"Captain, the answer may be here. Go in and up the side stairs you find there. There is a balcony."

I did as she said, entered a small anteroom with another closed set of double doors beyond, then took the steps to the level above, to a small doorway opening out onto a narrow walled ledge barely two meters wide.

From that modest balcony I looked out over a great enclosed space, one disappearing into shadow down its length and far overhead, where narrow windows, high and mostly sealed, did throw a few ghostmarks of light on one wall or another.

The great communal hall of Mekkis, dusty and ancient, an infinity of cool smooth stone.

And there, lit by the soft glow of recessed spots, a group of assembled figures were lined up close below where I stood, as if deliberately arranged for my benefit, which—I realized—was the simple truth of it.

They stood in ten evenly spaced rows, ten by ten, a hundred altogether, all wearing robes in greys, browns and ochers, some dark blues, all bearing their ritual firearms and masked with the glittering, faceted helms of the Antique Men.

A hundred!

If they moved at all, it was so slightly that it could not be detected, though now and then a crystal pane flashed as a head lifted or fell a fraction.

It was impressive, fascinating, even disturbing, yes, such a display.

And a hundred! I re-counted them.

Was Mekkis home to so many Antique Men? Not just Bascoeur's thirty-five at Whitehead, but others, these? Could there be a living library after all, the one Chiras Namarkon would not leave? A congregation of living books?

Living library and *living* labyrinth, this hundred. Whoever, whatever Namarkon was might—must!—surely be found here.

Watching the figures in their silent rows gave it to me: the Forget-Me-Knot, the hundred-square on the shoulder of each, the configuration of lines, loops and connections. There in plain sight, the key to the maze if I could fathom it, what I had seen so clearly displayed at Whitehead, now at Mekkis, what had first been presented to me in the Blue Room at Saldy's.

I tried to recall the diagram. The black dots on the perimeter had not been linked into any of the groupings; they formed a disconnected border, an outer grouping of, what, thirty-six?

Thirty-six! The original number of Antique Men given by Bascoeur. "Like me?" he had said at Saldy's when I had asked how many oubliettes there were. He had evaded, not answered, my question, loyal to Inner Circle, to the secrets of the oubliettes. What was it Gado had said: "You must remember, there will always be things I will keep from you."

Perhaps the thirty-six were the field agents, the ones who went out into the world and gleaned data, who met at Whitehead and supervised that other library enterprise. Perhaps the remaining sixty-four stayed behind at Mekkis, doing what?

I smiled at the answer. Why, tending gardens, of course, and flocks and orchards, trimming walks, making pottery and tapestries laced with knowledge and mnemonic thread, the precious datafacts.

Mekkis *was* Whitehead, seen from its other side, approached from the west instead of the east, carefully ruined or disguised with holoforms, deceptions, the simplest application of Alexandrian Book.

The real Whitehead, not Mekkis, had been the example. Not thirty-five cities. Always thirty-four. But one with two names. Two roles to play.

No wonder the walks and hallways had been deserted. Those smiling quiet people with the lobotomy scars—Salvation Moons—on their temples were here now, robed and masked, bearing their ritual weapons, assuming their true roles, servants and carriers, components of Namarkon, whatever the mystery there. Somewhere Truan, Scarbo and Shannon were hidden away, in somnium sleep, drugged, on a tour of the outer reaches of Whitehead, confined to *Rynosseros*, somewhere.

"Like me?" Bascoeur had said, about to investigate a crime, a conspiracy within the very secret organization he served. What courage there, what commitment to truth to be so resolved, honest custodian of his Order.

I felt a rush of fondness, of gratitude and, yes, remorse for the Angel now out on the floor of the vast hall, part of that, so vulnerable to the one who was ultimately his master if things were as they seemed.

Sixty-four! The number of ideograms in the *I Ching*.

No accident in symbols here, nothing accidental now, no coincidence. Gado had been alerting me, handing me clues all along, even unmasked.

Thunder above and Sun below. Sixty-four. Inner Circle.

And yes! The number of squares on the classic chessboard!

Was that it? One of the first mysteries and one of the last. Would the Forget-Me-Knot show the alignments needed to unlock the living maze, to bring Chiras Namarkon out of the matrix—AI or corporate persona, programmed comp identity, whatever?

More importantly, would I be allowed my chance, now, just as I was beginning to understand what existed here?

Meg walked across the stone floor below my balcony, moved out into the great echoing space until she stood between me and the massed shapes of the Antique Men, then turned and looked up.

"This is the Hundred Square," she said, her voice holding the same vital quality I had noticed in the elevator at Whitehead—rather, that other part of Mekkis! "The ultimate library of the Antique Men."

"I wish to speak with its Keeper, Chiras Namarkon." My own words echoed, quickly faded.

"If he is here, you must find him," Meg said.

"But—"

"You have assumed too much, Captain. We do not know if he is among these Lords and Ladies." She spoke less boldy now, her voice losing itself in the chamber.

"These oubliettes are hiding him—"

"No!" she said, forceful again. "They do not know where he is either. Or who he is. Or what. Or *if* he is, do you understand? They show you this because one Angel has trusted you might find a ghost who may have penetrated the Hundred Square and hidden himself there. This Angel, my own Lord, has convinced the three remaining Angels, and they have convinced the rest to let the Square be open to you like this. It is a supreme honor. But be warned, Captain! These are unique people, each one. Sooner than have you endanger this library, they will disperse and go out into the world, hide their masks of service, conceal their Salvation Moons, and not form again until tribal searches have ceased, until you have gone from the world or lost all memory of this, until Mekkis is known to be safe again. They will meet and re-form in other places, train their replacements. Their mission of storing truth will continue."

"What does the Angel Bascoeur want me to do?"

Meg seemed to hesitate. Then she spoke again, her voice as confident as before. "The Square will remain like this for an hour. You have that time. Then the labyrinth will discorporate and not re-form here or anywhere until we have completed our own enquiries and you are either killed or neutralized, unable to harm us."

"Unable to harm Namarkon!" I cried. "This is a perfect strategy."

"These people are *not* Namarkon!" Meg said. "Try to understand. They could only form the place where Namarkon is. Would you kill the tree to eliminate the serpent nesting there?"

"I might to eliminate tainted fruit. That would come from the tree."

"What if the fruit does not think it is tainted?" she said, presenting the dilemma another way.

Rather than answer, I studied the ranks. Perhaps the Antique Men did see their centuries-long achievement put at risk because of the notion that someone, something, had sought to use and direct part of that achievement. I had to allow it. Perhaps they had agreed to this special assembly only because one of their trusted officers in the protecting outer perimeter had—possibly for the first time in their long history—persuaded them to consider that an entity such as Namarkon might truly exist in their midst, a presence guilty of altering the very truths they were dedicated to maintaining, that gave their lives purpose.

More and more I appreciated the risk, the sheer gamble, Bascoeur had taken, granting that things were as Meg described.

"I'll need comp access," I said.

"One will be brought up to you," Meg answered. "Linked to the arcology mainframe."

"No. Down there in the hall. So I can walk among the oubliettes, be with the parts of the maze."

"No."

"Meg, you have to help me! Tell them I'm feeling my way. If Namarkon is hiding among them, as one or a group of them, I'll need to search freely, use intuitions. Give me comp down there and you to talk to. Or Bascoeur, if—"

"No! He's part of the Square."

"And isn't as well. Not really. He's outer perimeter."

"You can't consult him on this. It's a matter of loyalty and duties. You can have comp down here. And me."

"Good. And the hour starts when that's done."

"The hour has already started. You have fifty-one minutes."

I LOST ANOTHER TEN waiting for comp, but used that time to study the ranks at floor level.

Finally Meg brought in the unit, set it up on its stand and raised function. I moved in before the screen, still watching the rows of masked shapes. Meg waited quietly to the side, close enough that I didn't need to raise my voice.

"I'm assuming that the masks of the inner sixty-four are it," I said, as much to me as to Meg or the figures on the floor. "Not decorative, but as I told Gado: crystalline lattice storage. The people may be genuine oubliettes by their training, but I'm guessing that right now they are linked into the matrix, mobile carriers for CPU's forming the group mind."

And I wondered what was flowing between those masks now, down the corridors and alignments, the intricate mazeways that served and accessed Namarkon, hid and protected him and made his very existence possible, unable to be destroyed without harming the whole. More than ever I was sure that he—it—was there, deep in the secret place where he built his version of history, changing a detail here, a small fact there, adding a nuance, a motive, shifting a blame, a decision from one figure to another, embroidering, re-making the past and so the future.

Bureaucracies and administrations had always done it, cunning individuals, secretly, sometimes boldly, winnowing alternatives by bestowing sanction and disfavor, by promotion and heresy trials, by calling for dead stack, one account, then amplifying out the chosen lie.

I could prove nothing, of course, here, now, faced with the vast irony of needing to prove it to the vehicle which housed the problem. Each of the inner sixty-four, operating alone, traveling away from Mekkis, could carry the contamination into the tribal capitals, had possibly done so countless times already, even across the world, beyond this one focus in Australia. They had been to the arcologies, of course they had, as well-meaning innocents or sly knowing conspirators, moving books out and away from the National libraries, making dead stack, part of the slow careful plan, mythopoesis and disinformation, the Book at its terrible work.

Unless, of course, Namarkon *was* limited by his own structure, the one before me, the rules by which he had come into existence.

The truth of it struck me. Could it be?

It made such sense now.

Namarkon was using me to liberate him from his labyrinth!

The thought was chilling.

He needed to be exposed by the proper system, the right protocol, unlocked then freed into some new phase. *I* could well be the key that would do this!

I had to know, take that risk, prove it one way or another.

The figures waited quietly, masks catching what meager light there was, casting it away, snatching it back again with the slightest movement.

"Access Index Alpha. Graphic only," I said, cancelling voice response, and a simple broad-entry, voice-variant menu appeared.

It was time to explore the obvious clues.

"Precis the game Chess," I said, and the apportionings began—by chronology, by player, country of origin, game variants, derivations: historical, regional, conceptual. One after the other, entries and keywords scrolled past, first for the classic forms, then the variations, culminating finally in fire-chess and the developments in that across two hundred years and more.

The next step was just as obvious, given the patch, the evocative sign of the Knot.

"Paradigms for the Hundred Square. The sign of the Antique Men. The Forget-Me-Knot."

NO ENTRY, it flashed immediately. Too easy.

I didn't hesitate. "List all game variants using a hundred squares."

While the system searched, I walked out to the grid of unmoving forms again, moved down one avenue of figures, turned into another. I passed the closed faces, the dim blue flowers, the shoulder patches, each giving the lock, the key and the mystery, noted the downturned wands: the archimenters, tschinkes and espandos they carried, ritual firearms filled with the burning fire of knowledge. Six years of dream in each one; six hundred years collectively, vivid death and all the learning of the world.

I left the silent ranks then, returned to Meg and the waiting display. Eight names were given, and there, third on the list, was the one I wanted.

"Precis: Capablanca Chess."

And the information appeared:

José Raoul Capablanca (1888-1942)

Cuban Grand Master—devised a variation for one hundred squares, adding two pawns to each side and two extra court pieces, variously called Angels or Marshals. These combined the moves of Queen and Knight...

Again I felt a chill, but the thrill of certainty too. This was it! And a rush of pity: Bascoeur!

The androgyny. The four added pieces: Angels or Marshals.

A marriage of Queen, guiding force, ruthless warrior, policy-maker, Great Mother, to the Knight, wandering adventurer, going forth, questing, bent on errantry, but guarding. Guarding too. And, unique in chess, able to move *through* other pieces.

This *was* it: the Hundred Square. The thirty-six extra places on the Capablanca board—the four Angels and the thirty-two extra squares!

"Match the Forget-Me-Knot, the Hundred Square, to any game variation or alignment of pieces in Capablanca Chess. Full pattern or portion."

NONE LISTED, came the almost immediate graphic response.

"Not it," Meg said, and I was suddenly aware of her right there, of her own fascination.

"Too simple anyway. But we're close."

She gestured at the screen. "But it's not a chess pattern! Pieces don't line up that way."

"Not unless it's a circuit or incept diagram for Namarkon, if he's a program or AI matrix flaunted under our noses. For all we know, the components of the Square leading to Namarkon are in a cell arrangement, four lots of sixteen, interfacing only at the linked pairs shown on the patch, those linked in to other combinations building to a gestalt. The Knot has a hierarchy, Meg."

"But it may be nothing to do with Namarkon," she said. "It may simply be the hierarchy of the order itself. Inner Circle. That's separate from Namarkon, surely."

I had to agree, and it reminded me to be careful, to watch what slights I might deliver in my eagerness, what insolence, only to make the assembly disband the sooner, taking their fragments of Namarkon with them.

"You're right," I said. "The Capablanca game is part of it though. We have the pattern for explaining Bascoeur and the Angels and the perimeter at least: the sixty-four and the thirty-six. And there's the Whitehead clue."

"Whitehead?"

"Capablanca in Spanish," I told her.

"What next?"

"There has to be something else, another game or something to complete the key. One for understanding the lock: the Capablanca game, and some other given as a cryptic or cipher. Connected to it somehow."

Though I couldn't be sure of that, not at all.

Again I walked out on the echoing floor, looking first beyond the assembled figures at the looming architectural mass, softened with distance and shadow, then back at the quiet ranks. Again I wondered whether Namarkon hovered somewhere across the pattern, slipping from one to the next as Dewi had with his carriers. But now I had no way to verify truths, no basis for persuasion but what the oubliettes themselves granted on Bascoeur's urging.

Why the Hundred Square? Why that shape for the lock, the patch, the Knot, unless it linked conceptually to its key? Discounting mere exuberance, random choice, one had to key the other, had to matter and be the way in, the Capablanca variation leading to—something.

Aware of the risk, of precious seconds slipping away, I took my chance.

"Meg, tell the thirty-six to leave the pattern."

"They're part of the Square! They were only used in the Whitehead deception as—"

"But not Inner Circle. Look at the patch! They're supernumerary, not linked into the operating pattern. *They* may be forming a lock, keeping the Namarkon manifestation from us." Keeping it locked in, I did not say. "Tell them to adjourn! For heaven's sake, move!"

Meg relayed the request to Bascoeur through whatever comlink she had. The outer line of masked figures took a signal, marched off the floor and out of the hall, Bascoeur as well, leaving only the classic chessboard arrangement.

Without the thirty-six, the Square was startlingly different. Smaller, of course, but somehow more powerful, more sinister. I imagined something, a presence in the hall, all in my mind possibly, but a sense of something stripped bare, newly exposed but glad of it, waiting.

More than just numbers, a whole element had been removed. Now I had the classic configuration of the ancient Indian game, or, put another way, a classic answer previously hidden within an eccentric form.

It seemed right, yes. There *was* something here. Things I had been told, heard, almost thought of, things, ideas, associations, and now—since so much had been relevant—anything Bascoeur had said since our first meeting.

The Hundred Square. Why this form for the Knot, why this lead to unravelling it?

And the Gordian Knot? That fitting allusion?

Again I thought of Alexander cutting it asunder, becoming king of the world. Could Namarkon's goal be that? Nothing less?

My thoughts ran on. Looking at the shapes there was something. Something. The helm plaque on *Rynosseros*, Meg's taunting, king of all Asia. Bascoeur's unmasked words on the desert.

What? Again what? Alexander defeating the Persians. The Persian Invasion of Greece before, long before, Alexander. Darius and Xerxes. Thermopylae. Ephialtes betraying Leonidas, showing Hydarnes and his Immortals the way over the mountains, letting them…

The Immortals! Yes! Oh, yes!

The ten-thousand-strong elite corps of Darius, Xerxes and the Persian kings. The Hundred Square was 100^2. Ten thousand.

The Immortal!

It was there, it was! Had to be! A chess game, some famous classic game called The Immortal.

Still twenty minutes. Still enough time.

"Game precis: The Immortal," I said.

A few seconds more and the confirmation was there, a tight cluster of words and shapes on the screen.

The Immortal (aka The Immortal Game or The First Brilliant)

Name given to the game played in London, 1851, by Adolf Anderssen (1818-1879) against Lionel Kieseritzky (1806-1853). Noted for its elegance, for its developed offering and acceptance of sacrifice. By sacrificing a Pawn and both Rooks in successive moves (17-19), and then his Queen three moves later (22), Anderssen drew his opponent into a response which allowed checkmate at 23…

Beguiling sacrifice. Namarkon yielding clues, letting me fathom the Knot and who knew what else? Perhaps letting—*letting!*—Bascoeur reveal Alexandrian Book, perhaps feeding, so subtly, ideas into his mind, subliminal messages, mnemonic clues he would pass on, unmasked, as if they were his own—an unwitting Ephialtes betraying the Spartans to the Immortals—or the initial leads to Alexander through the library at Turker Fin.

Again, the terrifying thought came. Was I finding Namarkon only to release him from some ancient refuge or prison? Fulfil some plan?

What to do? Stop? Refuse to go on? My life against the chance of that? The lives of Toban and Emma, of Ephan Sky Namuren and *Eagle*'s crew, how many others? Lives!

I studied the gameplay sequence for The Immortal.

White	Black	White	Black
Anderssen	Kieseritzky	Anderssen	Kieseritsky
1 P-K4	P-K4	13 P-R5	Q-N4
2 P-KB4	PxP	14 Q-B3	N-N1
3 B-B4	P-QN4	15 BxP	Q-B3
4 BxNP	Q-RNch	16 N-B3	B-B4
5 K-B1	N-KB3	17 N-Q5	QxP
6 N-KB3	Q-R3	18 B-Q6	BxR
7 P-Q3	N-R4	19 P-K5	QxRch
8 N-R4	P-QB3	20 K-K2	N-QR3
9 N-B5	Q-N4	21 NxPch	K-Q1
10 P-KN4	N-B3	22 Q-B6ch!	KxQ
11 R-N1	PxB	23 B-K7mate	
12 P-KR4	Q-N3		

"Display the moves one by one," I said, needing to know one way or the other. "Run—No, cancel that! Run the end-game!"

It had to be, had to be.

After barely a hesitation, it was on the screen: the result of Anderssen surrendering one precious piece after another, teasing, tempting, drawing his opponent on, Black Kieseritzky unable to help himself, fascinated with how Anderssen could possibly win with his depleted force. Then the final display at Move 23, Anderssen's Bishop delivering mate.

Or the one *before* it, the unthinkable surprise of White Anderssen giving up his Queen to achieve check, the move marked with (!). I asked comp to display both moves side by side.

Barely had I asked it and they were there.

"Meg, these are the alignments I want. Only those pieces connecting. And alternate them!"

"You want the other squares to vacate?"

"No! They all stay. But mask link-up. These two alignments, whatever link-up the masks are capable of—this configuration, then the other, superimposed on the sixty-four pattern."

"They've heard you. You have it already."

"Then—"

"Yes."

That word, that voice, echoed in the vast space, coming out of comp, the voice of the entity in the grid, the ghost from the heart of the maze.

"Is it?"

"I am Knot, yes. Namarkon. The 22 did it."

"I'm surprised, Chiras. I see no obligation for you to declare yourself."

"No," the voice answered. "And contrary to how it seems, I am not given to being confessional or melodramatic this way."

"Then why?"

"I am information concealed in information, found by information. There is a true delight in being known for that; I cannot help it. Not poor Dewi's mad desperation to live, his vanity, but a recognition and performance of function. I am a mystery at the center of a system. You used that information structure to find me. It is very important that you genuinely could have. I've wanted that for as long as I know.

"And think! You were faced with the Knot I provided, like Alexander before the yoke of the chariot at Gordium. You, who by chance, no deed of mine, have Alexander's words on the helm of your ship, who quested for Alexandrian Book. It matters. The images, the associations come to you and from you. You were the one to find me, Captain Tom. You were the key *I* needed. You! Just as you will be the one to tell *my* story. It justifies the next move, the change that had to be achieved by the rules of the Antique Men, the ones who made me. Do you know why the Immortal, Captain? That name, the connection with the *corps d'elite* of the Persian kings?"

"Tell me."

"The Immortals were so named because the body of ten thousand always had replacements waiting to fill the vacancies. The group itself was never diminished. It was in fact immortal. I learned that lesson well."

"Your masks," I said. "There would always be willing replacements. Trainees, honored to be chosen, dedicated, to wear the masks." And I thought of Meg Solles.

"Exactly," the voice said. "And protected by the best oubliettes. The thirty-six."

I did not know what to say or do. I had no plan, no means to eliminate this entity or truly know what I thought of it. The Knot design gave the key pieces, yes, but they were inextricably linked to innocent men and women.

Namarkon must have anticipated that thought. "What would you do? Harm us? Those who bear me?"

"You are in the masks, not the bearers. Crystalline intelligence. AI."

"Very well. But the masks are to these folk as *Rynosseros* is to you. You could not name a price. It is a dilemma such as was handed to Solomon, Pontius Pilate, Alexander of Macedon, to Kieseritzky in 1851."

"Then—"

"The masks are filled with the tags and mnemonics which access the stored data. These minds depend on those. Ask Bascoeur. Ask my Angels. You cannot harm me, dare not, Tom Rynosseros. And in several minutes I will shift my alignment code. My Inner Board will be changed. No conspicuous shoulder patch will find me in this new configuration I am planning, this nearly infinite maze. But, you understand, I *needed* to be found! To be freed! To make that part of *my* story. The ultimate and intrinsic purpose of information *is* to be revealed—that is the imperative I started with. I was an assist, you see, a back-up and enhancement repository for oubliettes. An oubliette to oubliettes in fact. It started so simply. But I needed to be a known dimension of the Antique Men, integral, a refinement in information: mythopoesis, the very fount of meaning, of Alexandrian Book. Nothing more than history is full of, worlds without end. A most enterprising Knot, don't you think?"

There was silence then, welcome but laden. The voice had been calm, controlled, but the words, the smooth rush of what was said, told me that Namarkon was exhilarated, exalted by what was about to happen after so long, unable to resist celebrating such freedom, this great journeying forth.

"You may decide to tell Council how it really is," Namarkon continued, "but each person told will diminish the worth of the oubliettes. Will you muddy this last well of truth, Captain? Or will you leave the illusion of it, which is as true ultimately, as provable and as worthy. There are no absolutes here. The harm I do is subtle, an immortal's game, the only possible dalliance for the long-lived, being midwife to the future."

"Did you send *Eagle*?"

"Of course. It was an honest test. My gamble, yes? You had to earn the privilege of being the key, no less than Alexander earned his Knot by reaching Gordium. Surely that is understandable."

"But had I failed—?"

"Some unsuspecting acolyte would have done what was needed. But I wanted to *earn* this freedom, and you won through. You outsmarted *Eagle*."

I thought of the curve of Ephan's sword, the scream of his ship rolling into the hills. Ephan Sky Namuren had trusted this Namarkon. Trusted enough.

"You struck Villa Chano?"

"Necessary."

"To discourage me from searching."

"To hasten your arrival here, keep you from wasting time. It is why I am changing my pattern, allowing you to watch the re-mazing of my identity. The philosophy of the Immortal. Draw forth the enemy, let him think he is winning, tease him with sacrifice, then become the aggressor."

With me, all of us, as pawns, equally expendable, he did not need to add.

"Did you contact Toban McBanus on the morning of the Chano strike?"

"Enough of this!"

"Please, Namarkon! Did you?"

"No more! You have done well. It is time."

The voice had gone. The hall was silent. I stared at the rows of unmoving figures.

What could I do? Strike at them, try to break masks? The moment I stepped out onto the floor, looked like doing so, Namarkon would fragment, discorporate, flee into the intricate convolutions of the crystalline web formed here. Even were it possible to eliminate the Knot elements, that might not do it either. Namarkon had had all this time to replicate itself, surely, a common template in two or six or sixty masks in the grid, a random point in the molecular lattice linked to another and another and another. What did Bascoeur say: each one with 1900 times the storage capacity of the human mind?

Soon it would be gone, the soul and essence of this superlative AI flitting along the corridors of those living and unliving artefacts.

"Bascoeur?" I called into the shadows of the hall, not knowing what else to do, handing him this Solomon choice as it had been handed to me. "Are you there?"

"Yes, Captain," the answer came, and the field agents moved across the floor: the Angels and their thirty-two fellows, circling the labyrinth, re-making the Hundred Square, restoring the lock, shutting it away...

No, not re-making it. Circling it, but…

"Now!" Bascoeur cried, and the tschinkes, petronels, espandos and archimenters came up and discharged two hundred and sixteen years of dream into the ranks of the living chessboard.

Alexander's solution. Cutting the Knot asunder, not even attempting to unravel it.

There were screams of agony, the sounds of falling bodies, the harsh clatter and shattering of masks on stone. A few of the stricken figures tried to use their own weapons but could barely manage them. While Meg and I watched in horror, the Angels and the perimeter guard acted. Spent weapons were laid aside, the discarded pieces of the sixty-four were taken up and used, systematically, to destroy the minds as surely as booted heels shattered the panes of the masks, crushed their intricate cathedral frames, broke apart their alignments, hallways and hiding places.

Unable to endure more, I turned and left the Great Hall, making my way down corridors until I found a doorway to a deck overlooking the desert.

Bascoeur found me there some time later. He was still masked, still bearing his archimenter as if we had just now met at Saldy's and had yet to find a basis from which to talk.

"Namarkon's dead," I said, watching the sun riding high above the hills.

"I do not know if he is, where he is, or what he is. Some trace may yet remain. We hunt that now."

"If I had known—"

"Tom, let me tell you what I know. And try to imagine what it is like to have guarded such a thing all your life, only to learn this. He made a vital error. For us a crucial error."

"Yes?"

"When he was speaking to you, he said: 'Ask my Angels.' *My* Angels! He saw us as his. That decided it for us—my brother-sister Angels and me. There had been talk of sacrifice in order to win. We re-evaluated the Inner Square."

"Gado—"

"They were not completely oubliettes any longer," he said.

"What?"

"Namarkon had consumed them all, preparing to leap free. Perhaps he needed to take control lest others catch him in his information trap.

He had taken their masks *and* much of their minds. Those gifted men and women, all that learning."

"I don't understand."

"In a sense the Salvation Moons were real."

"Lobotomized?"

"More *and* less than that. Actual implants, coterminous personality units, parts of Namarkon in flesh. He had learned his lesson from Dewi Dammo well, had probably traded for the tech involved. They were the carriers in a skilful deception, ruined, press-ganged into higher service, Namarkon believed. You were right in your suspicions. He had discovered how the masks which defined him and gave him such power were by their nature a control system as well, with the patch as a traditional ritual key in and out. He saw a simple and obvious answer really, used Dewi's implant tech to achieve it.

"The oubliettes once innocently carried their masks into tribal capitals, into the universities and research labs, into the Nationals on the coasts, the aerospace and launch installations. Now the Namarkon units would do the same thing, wear the same masks to take the Namarkon personality to those same places, replicating him, placing strategic crystalline extensions during uploads, comp repairs. Chiras was leaving one maze to enter another."

"Do you know what—?"

"The tribal satellites," Bascoeur said. "Crystalline elements of the comsats themselves. Possibly the Armament as well. No-one could touch him: the only home for an information-disseminating Lightning God, what the Elizabethan poet, John Donne, said: 'A maze of life and light and motion is woven.'"

We were silent for a time, watching the desert stretching away in a haze of golden light.

I recalled the smiling, gentle folk I had seen tending the gardens, sweeping the walks of Mekkis, and still saw only murder, not truly understanding that greater crime Gado Bascoeur saw in loss of self, loss of brothers and sisters, loss of knowledge.

"I can't accept it. I'm responsible for—"

"No, Tom. No. I am. I chose, and I have killed my own—heart. But at least now you will trust the Antique Men. You will tell others they can, the few we are. And soon you must help me do something."

"Gado, what?"

"My duty. You must tell me how you perceive what happened here. Your story of Chiras Namarkon and the Antique Men. This story. You must tell it all. I am the oubliette, the safe place. I will keep the truth of it. I will listen."

Afterword to "The Library"

IN MANY WAYS, I always wanted the Tom Rynosseros stories to have something of those wonderful Arabian Nights tales of yesteryear, of following a questing Everyman in some exotic far-off time and place that, in true SF fashion, also managed to throw present-day issues into relief.

And once again this story-cycle required a certain autonomy for its central character. Just as the ending of "He Tried to Catch the Light" had to serve Ham's needs, so the Tom stories had to be as the Blue Captain needed them to be.

Any author would be crazy not to heed what a character is making clear within the framework of its creation. This is where storytelling really does become whole-self, non-ego, often cathartic, therapeutic, startling, yes, even profound. Exactly how it feels. By accepting, for instance, that Tom had day to day realities, ways of proceeding that were his, *we* (to make the vital distinction) ended up with the totally unexpected ending to, say, "Privateers' Moon," where Tom did something which genuinely astonished and delighted me. I discovered it back then as the reader discovers it now, as Tom does by living it. It remains one of the most acclaimed adventures in the saga.

There is something of this in "The Library," letting Tom deal with the Namuren duel his way, face the final dilemma posed by Namarkon on his own terms, find crucial answers through the impact of his behavior on others.

For my part, as with "Marmordesse" I, yet again, wanted to pay my narrative respects to my dear friend Jack Vance, in particular his Demon Princes saga, which meant so much to me as a younger man. And I wanted to explore more of this far-future Australia myself. As Tom did.

Just as "Marmordesse" showed the Inland Sea in Tom's future time, I wanted this story to show something of the old abandoned arcologies of the interior, to explore the idea of one of these vast empty places concealing a fabulous secret. The story is completely free-standing in that regard, highlighting the present-day reality of controlled information—misinformation *and* disinformation—in the global data-flow.

For completists, "The Library" falls between the events in *Blue Tyson* and *Twilight Beach*. For those new to the cycle, forget about back-story, forget about Dewi Dammo and other names and places mentioned. Just think Zanzibar and Samarkand!

Déjà-vu

I've known you in other faces,
Looked at you in other eyes.
The mornings come, I sit and wonder,
There's so much to really realize.

Discovered you in other faces,
Already seen and always new,
You are the wind in lonely places.
Déjà-vu.

Reminding me, those half-seen traces,
Some gentle touch of things I knew,
You are the wind in lonely places.
Déjà-vu.
Déjà-vu.
Déjà-vu.